MW00617369

Émigré

A Novel of the Tri-Cluster Confederation

Mike Watson

COPYRIGHT

Editing by <u>Red Adept</u>. Cover art by <u>Luca Oleastri</u>

Contents

Chapter 1. Arrival

Dundee Orbital, 18 Fourmonth, 3203 FC

Fabien Loche stood at the edge of the ship's passenger lock. He was taller and slimmer than most of his fellow travelers. Millennia of inbreeding, gengineering, and genetic drift had produced height, slimness, and light-colored hair and eyes that said, for those who knew the telltales, that he was spaceborn.

The yellow and black diagonal stripes on the deck marked the edge of the ship's personnel lock, the transition line between the ship's internal gravity and the station's. He stood on that edge, unmoving, not understanding his emotions—homesickness, loneliness, apprehension. A throbbing rose behind his eyes. Loche's sinuses were protesting the change of air pressure and humidity from ship to station. He was in thrall for a moment.

Loche rubbed a small stone in his pocket with forefinger and thumb. It was a gift from Reena, his betrothed. She had picked it up on the shore of Earth's Aegean Sea. He remembered the events of the last year. *Has it been only a year since I was discharged from the System States Marines and survived the riots on Earth? Has it been a year since the mobs on Earth murdered Reena?* He sighed. *Now, I've this new venture far from home. Far from home,* he thought. *It's an exile.*

He had no choice. This liaison position was being forced upon him by EarthGov. They viewed him as a potential impediment to their plans to seize the assets of the Thirty Houses. Nobody sold return tickets to SolSystem, nor would EarthGov welcome him if he ever returned home.

The fast packet *SSMS Leo Tolstoy* had arrived in the Caledonia system earlier today. Unable to sleep, he had been awake when it broached. He hadn't slept well for months.

†††

Loche woke in his dim compartment, panting and drenched in sweat. He swung his legs over the side of his bunk, allowing his heart rate to slow. The glow from the environmental panel and the stateroom's console link provided illumination. By habit, he scanned both—no alarms or alerts called for his attention.

Loche sat on the edge of the bunk, elbows on knees, head bowed and held in his hands. He kneaded his temples as the dreams were fading. In one, he had been standing above a sea cliff. Another was of him dragging Reena from the rioting mob. The latter was a recurring nightmare that left him breathless with a pounding heart and head. However, the pain, the residual ache in his leg, was what had intruded into his dreams and awakened him. Whoever thought a person couldn't feel pain in dreams was wrong.

The pain drew his attention, and Loche vigorously massaged the ache in his thigh, knee, and lower leg. Sometimes that eased the pain. A few minutes later, fingers now aching instead of his leg, he felt ready to proceed with the day. Months before, he would have awakened fresh and alert. Now, he woke in a half state, passing through the transition from sleep to wakefulness more slowly than before his injury. Gone was that instant transition he'd once possessed.

He stripped and stowed his sweat-drenched garments in the laundry compartment. In his 'fresher, Loche checked his water budget and chose a sonic mist, saving the rest of his budget for later in the day. This was his last day onboard. He would take his final water shower just before the ship docked at Dundee Orbital over Inverness, his new home.

The sonic mist wasn't as refreshing as a full shower, but he was used to it. A head-to-toe blast of dry air evaporated any lingering moisture. He swirled a rinse in his mouth to remove its sour taste and spat the residue down the drain. Loche noted the time on the stateroom's console as he stepped from the 'fresher: Early Morning Watch. Broach was still hours away.

This could well be his last interstellar voyage, and he had promised himself he would watch the transition in the lounge this time. He had intentionally cultivated friendships with the crew and the ship's officers because most passengers would not be allowed outside their staterooms during broach. Loche believed they would ignore him.

He donned his skinsuit, rolling it up his legs, body, and arms until it reached his neck. Like all spaceborn, he owned a fitted, skintight vacuum suit with a flexible attached helmet stored the in the suit's collar. The helmet could be pulled over his head and down to his neck to form a vacuum-proof seal with the suit. A pocket on the skinsuit's chest contained thin gloves. In an emergency, he could be vacuum sealed within seconds.

The skinsuit could be worn under conventional clothing. In his present case, that outer clothing was a standard one-piece shipsuit. He dreaded his last act of preparing for the day... inserting his link contacts into his eyes. He had a phobia of anything touching his eyes. Most civilians used nanoimplants to project the output of their links onto their retinas. Few military or military veterans used sensory implants because they provided captors with perfect instruments of torture by overriding one's visual and aural senses. *No, thank you*, he thought. *Not for me.*

††††

<Attention, attention. Broach in thirty minutes. All passengers, please return to your staterooms and strap in. All passengers, please return to your staterooms. Stewards will be available for assistance if needed.>

The announcement ran across screens and sounded aloud in the public areas throughout the ship. The sleeping passengers would be unaware of the emergence from subspace to normal space.

Fabien Loche sat in the small lounge, watching the holoscreen on the bulkhead. Few passengers were present, preferring to remain in their staterooms through broach. He'd spent the last hour secured in a low deck chair in the ship's lounge, dozing, dreaming, and waiting for the announcement.

The *Tolstoy* and her twelve sister ships were SolSystem built. They plied the quantum seas between the System States and the Confederacy, making the 2,500-light-year passage from SolSystem to Caledonia in six months. Their cargo was intersystem mail, data, passengers, and a small number of high-value products such as pharmaceuticals.

The *Tolstoy* and its sisters had been built in the Ceres shipyard in Loche's home station. A SolSystem corporation owned the packets. The ships, however, were crewed by spaceborn. Most of the crew were from Sol's belt and outer stations and, like Loche, members of the Thirty Houses.

The purser passed through the lounge on his way aft. He glanced at Loche sitting alone before the wall monitor, walked over, and said, "Broach in thirty minutes, sir. You should return to your stateroom."

Loche looked up at the purser and pulled down his shipsuit's collar to reveal his skinsuit underneath.

The purser straightened and nodded. "Very well, sir. I'll notify the crew."

"Thank you," Loche said to the departing purser's back.

He had eaten at the purser's table many times during the voyage. He and the crew, being spaceborn, accepted Loche as one of their own. During their dinner discussions, the purser and Loche discovered they were distant cousins. Loche was a member of House DuQuoin. The purser was of House Simmons. A few generations back, the purser's grandfather had married into House Simmons from House DuQuoin. The relationship, distant as it was, was a pleasant surprise.

Loche glanced down at the spot on his suit's left shoulder where his house crest had once resided. The crest had been removed, a simple obfuscation of his origin. He'd worn no outward sign of his membership within the Thirty Houses when he passed through Luna's upper terminal. He was a stationer, one of the spaceborn, but hiding that fact in public from the planetborn and EarthGov officials was wise.

Loche sat, looking at the darkened holo with the time-to-broach counting down in the lower corner. Another ship's officer passed through the lounge, the third officer making his last-minute inspection. He, like the purser, acknowledged Loche with a nod and continued down the passageway.

The countdown continued. Loche was fortunate. Due to his appointments as a Member of House DuQuoin and an Associate of the Seat of the Thirty Houses, the captain granted him visitor access to the ship's interlink network.

The interlink was busy. Loche watched and listened to the captain and the bridge crew for an hour. The monitor showing the bridge captured the image of the captain seated at the center console, with the pilot to his left and navigating officer to his right. The comm and engineering stations were behind the captain, manned by two senior ratings, out of range of the link pickup.

"Captain, bottom is shoaling, now two hundred fathoms," the navigating officer reported.

As the ship approached Caledonia, the mass of the approaching system altered subspace. A ship had to broach at or before the point where subspace shoaled to sixty fathoms or suffer damage. *Tolstoy* was not designed to remain in subspace in shallow areas.

"Caledonia shoals approaching in twenty minutes. Kelton's Reef beacon detected at ninety point thirty-four. The beacon at Barrington Light at two sixty-nine point one twenty-one. Suggest course change as planned in five minutes, Captain."

The Reef was a cluster of planetoids at the edge of Caledonia's outer asteroid belt with sufficient mass to affect subspace. Barrington Light was a subspace beacon built in a swarm of asteroids in a trojan position behind Caledonia's outermost planet. The *Tolstoy*'s course had the packet broaching into normal space just outside the belt, the primary obstacle for this inbound route.

The captain glanced at the ship's chronometer. "On time and on target, Navigator. Well done."

"Thank you, sir."

†††

Loche sat, drifting in near sleep, waiting a while longer. His link murmured as various compartments and stations reported readiness for broach.

<Broach in thirty seconds!>

He roused to full wakefulness and watched the last seconds tick by. At zero, the holoscreen changed from the dappled gray of subspace to a star-filled image. Loche felt… something at the moment of transition to normal space, but it passed before he had time to analyze the sensation.

<Broach completed. All passengers… docking at Dundee Orbital scheduled in eleven hours, zero five thirty hours, second shift, local station time. A reminder: all departing passengers, please gather at the forward lock after docking. Be prepared to pass through Confederation Customs when departing the ship.>

So far from home, Loche thought. A wave of longing swept over him, which surprised him. He'd not always been so sensitive.

The year had not been a good one, and his mind shied from the memories. He shook himself, unfastened his lap belt, rose, and walked aft to his stateroom. The voyage was ending. *Time to move on.*

††††

Other passengers were coming down the passageway behind him, and Loche could no longer hesitate. He stepped forward into the docking bay with his trunk trailing him in follow-me mode.

††††

Donal Harris, Confederation Chief Customs Inspector, used his link to create a window in a corner of his vision to show the passengers disembarking the *Tolstoy*. When his office had received the ship's passenger manifest, Harris decided to greet the new liaison himself.

One by one, the passengers appeared in the ship's lock, walked down the docking bay, and entered the station. There, they chose one of the steadily moving customs lines for inspection.

An agent approached Harris and asked for an opinion on the valuation of some trade representative's product demos. Harris waived the tariff, which would have been low. The goodwill generated by the waiver was more valuable.

There he is, he thought when the tall, slender man walked through the station's lock from the docking bay. Harris looked him over. The passenger matched the image of the man they were expecting, but he hesitated at the lock. *Not too impressive. Not what I expected, from the file we received. He appears younger too… almost too young to have the experience his file claimed.*

Normally, one of Loche's fellow System States liaisons would have been there to greet their new compatriot. However, Dundee Orbital—in synchronous orbit above Inverness, Caledonia's fourth in the system and one of three habitable planets—the station was short a liaison. The previous one's contract had expired, and Loche was his replacement. Another liaison was downbelow on holiday, while the others were on duty elsewhere. The personnel shortage gave Harris the opportunity to observe the newcomer firsthand.

The man noticed Harris watching him and approached. "Excuse me, sir," he said, "could you help me?"

Harris raised an eyebrow. "Indeed, sir. Confederation Chief Customs Inspector Donal Harris. How may I assist you?"

"I am Fabien Loche," the man replied, "the new System States liaison."

No, Harris thought, *not impressive at all.* A kind of hesitancy gave the younger man the appearance of being… lost.

"Welcome to the Tri-Cluster Confederation, Mr. Loche," he said. "We have been expecting you. If you would, please let me check your credentials?" Harris extended his hand.

Loche flashed a quick smile and grasped Harris's in return. Their links exchanged information and confirmed Loche's credentials.

Harris eyed Loche's trunk and led him into a nearby unoccupied office. "Would you please open your trunk?"

"Certainly."

Harris inspected the trunk, noting via his link that he found no contraband and that all the contents appeared to be for personal use. Harris labeled the SSMC combat knife in Loche's trunk as a personal weapon. No tariffs were due. The inspection took only a few minutes.

"The Luna Upper terminal has been lax in the last few months," he mentioned in passing to Loche, "but they didn't let anything slip through with you."

"I checked myself using the latest bulletin. It wouldn't do for a customs liaison to be found carrying contraband."

Harris chuckled. "No, it wouldn't." He instructed his link to record the trunk's contents, noting the identifying numbers of the few manufactured devices. One piece of jewelry caught his eye. From his earlier research, he knew its significance and labeled it as personal property. "I'm done. Your link has been updated with the official customs clearance. Is there anything else?"

"Could you direct me to the local System States office?"

"There is no such office on the station," Harris answered. "Didn't they tell you that you would be working with us?"

"Yes, but I thought there would be separate offices, administrators and the like."

"No, nothing like that. The System States Embassy is on Cameron, but there is no System States customs office here and no administrators, just you and two other liaisons. You'll work out of our office."

Harris continued, "I added directions that will lead you to our station office and a station map into your link. Just follow the path I added to the map. Our office is in Torus Three, Segment C, Deck Two, two decks inward, and I've added the standard visitor- and commercial-information packets to your link."

Loche turned to leave, but Harris stopped him before he could take a step. "Before you go," Harris said while taking a small gold pin from a pocket. He placed it in Loche's hand. "Put this on your tunic. It will keep you out of trouble."

Loche raised an eyebrow, looked puzzled for a moment, shrugged, and attached the pin to his lapel. "What is this for?"

"That gold pin indicates that you are a noncombatant—that you carry no weapons. Those wearing gold pins can't be challenged."

"Thank you for your kindness," Loche said. "I'd forgotten that dueling is legal here. This should help. I don't know what would give offense and what would not."

"Not to worry. Common sense and courtesy are sufficient to avoid most conflicts… most of the time."

Harris escorted him through the customs line to the entrance of the deck's concourse, where a few newsies were waiting. They, too, had noticed Loche's name on the *Tolsoy's* passenger manifest, along with his position as liaison. Most of the passengers were Confederates returning home. Loche was one of the few from the System States.

Harris saw the newsies waiting and shouted, "Privacy!"

Privacy in the Confederation, by Custom and Tradition, was strict, and Harris's declaration blocked their quest to interview Loche. They still could, later, but only by written request and subsequent appointment. That would be Loche's decision, but now he was too new, in Harris's opinion, to be food for a link-journo feeding frenzy.

Loche again turned to go. Harris hesitated, watching him walk toward the torus's inner concourse. "Loche! Wait. I'll walk with you. I'm near the end of my shift."

†††

Loche walked through the crowded station concourse with Harris at his side. Neither spoke.

A steady stream of people passed through the corridors. Shops and offices lined both sides. People entered and departed, some with packages or attended by personal carriers. In many ways, it was no different from his home—former home, he reminded himself—in Ceres station.

As in his home, survival pods and personnel shelters sat at regular intervals, marked with the standard fluorescent-orange cross. He noted the strips from one side of the concourse to the other on the overhead—the ceiling, he reminded himself—marking emergency bulkheads that could drop and seal off sections of the station if necessary. All were standard safety features in case of a hull breach or environmental failure.

I must think as a civilian. I'm not a marine anymore… nor at home.

Weariness fell on him although early by his body clock. He stopped while Harris took a few more steps before noticing Loche was no longer at his side.

"Let's stop for a moment," Loche said.

Perhaps he was feeling a case of traveler's malaise. He had been warned that occurred at times. It may have been caused by the long voyage from SolSystem or, more likely, by being awakened early from his dreams and by the ache in his leg.

One dream seemed to have been occurring more often since his departure from home. He was standing on a cliff above a stormy sea. Low gray clouds scudded across the surface while waves battered the base of the cliff. He could still feel the wind and spray, hear the booming impact of the sea against the cliff, and feel the tremors in the rock under his feet from the hammering waves. Then someone called. Loche turned and… He remembered nothing more. At least that dream wasn't as upsetting as the ones about the mob and riot.

He walked to the side of the concourse, sat on a convenient bench, and watched the stream of people flowing past. Harris followed and sat beside him.

Loche leaned back and rested his head against the cool bulkhead—*No, the wall.* "It is so familiar, just like home," he told Harris, straightening his head as he spoke, "with a few exceptions. We don't see nonhumans often."

Most of the nonhumans were single Coterni. A few furred P'tissa, traveling in pairs, passed as well.

"But something is different." He realized a few moments later what

14

that was—the absence of holos in the air.

At home, holos would be filling the air, extolling wares and services, adverts enticing potential customers to their shops. *Not here.* Loche found it more peaceful without the constant intrusion into his mental privacy.

"No holo-ads," he said.

"We don't like them," Harris replied. "They're an invasion of privacy. They do exist. All you have to do is to activate them via your link. You can then filter what you want to see—or not. The default is no holo-ads."

Loche noticed the wide variety of clothing, styles, and colors. As it rose into his awareness, he realized that he had not noticed before how drab Ceres Station had been in comparison. A man and woman approached, both dressed in clan colors—a short jacket of crisscrossed dark-green, black, bright-yellow, and red lines and stripes. The man's dress included dark trousers and a white ruffled shirt. The woman wore a similar white ruffled blouse and a short dark jacket. Instead of trousers, she wore a long dark skirt reaching her ankles with a tartan sash falling from her right shoulder to her left hip. Both wore identical black boots, holstered pistols, and sheathed knives. *Yes, definitely more colorful, in more ways than one.*

"Is that common?" he asked Harris, indicating the passing couple.

"What?"

"The two with tartans, clan colors," Loche said.

"I suppose so. Most of the station residents are clan members. I would guess they are going to some formal event. We don't dress so for everyday wear. Those two are members of Clan Williams. Their clan is heavily invested in interstellar shipping and freight."

A small boy emerged from the crowd and ran up to Loche. He nodded to Harris and turned to examine Loche. The two exchanged looks. The boy's shipsuit was adorned with ship and clan patches. The boy examined Loche's dark-blue high-collared tunic and trousers. The boy bowed and returned to the stream of people without saying a word.

"A polite boy," Harris said. "His shipsuit said he was of the *Keystone Traveler*, an independent freighter allied with Clan Williams. He has good manners."

A group of people, a family unit with children, appeared from around the curve of the concourse. One man, chasing a child in search of treasure, bumped into two men walking in the opposite direction. One of the jostled men objected. The father apologized and asked forgiveness for his rudeness. Pardon was granted, and the two men continued on their way while the father, child now in tow, returned to his group. Loche noticed that all the adults in that group wore small golden pins identical to the one Harris had given him.

Harris nudged his elbow. "That's why I gave you the pin. Even without one, I don't think anything would have happened. The man chasing the boy was polite. That's all that's needed, most of the time, to prevent conflicts."

The incident was a curiosity. Loche examined other passersby. Many wore some type of uniform, shipsuits sporting ship patches or corporate logos. Most were armed, while those not in a uniform appeared to have bulges under their clothing suggesting they were armed too. The family wearing the golden pins, however, had no suspicious bulges that he could see.

He was aware, reinforced by Harris's warning, that unlike the core worlds of the System States, frontier worlds allowed personal arms to be common. Inverness had a tumultuous history over the millennia since its colonization. Still, he was surprised the custom remained. The Confederacy was as old as the System States. Personal arms, with few exceptions, were not carried nor allowed in the System States.

"I see similarities… between home and here." He watched the family wearing the gold pins walk down the concourse. "Family," Loche said. "I was given a send-off when I left. All my Line Mothers were there, Mother, Grandmother—the Grand Dam of the House—Father, my uncles and aunts too." His eyes misted for a moment as he remembered the rare hugs he received from his mother, grandmother, and great grandmother. They gave him the Blessing of the House in his leave-taking.

Harris looked away as if to avoid seeing Loche's emotional display.

"I apologize, Inspector. It's not seemly to express emotion in public."

"Don't fash yourself. You're a long way from home."

Reena had not been there, at the leave-taking. He shied away from those memories of her. *Too soon.* His own moodiness disturbed him. That was unlike how he had been before.

Harris was with him to help alleviate any cultural conflicts, Loche assumed. Harris was likely familiar with the System States as a whole, but maybe not with the houses.

"What do you know of the Thirty Houses, Inspector?"

"Not all that much, other than the name. They're an association of stations in Sol's asteroid belt and outer stations. I don't know more than that."

"The houses have a history. We, the belt and outer stations, are older than the System States Alliance and EarthGov. We existed long before the formation of EarthGov and the System States, even before the First and Second Protectorates and the Interregnum. The original stations, by necessity, evolved into matriarchies. Men built the stations, mined asteroids for materials, designed, created, and maintained the infrastructure and environments that sheltered them all. The women planned, managed, and worked to ensure everyone's survival. Women, some women, became the Mothers, leaders of the Houses. Men, those selected for specific skills, tasks, and qualifications, were appointed Members of the House. Each house is represented in the Seat, our governing body, but a gathering of the Seat is rare."

He paused in case Harris had questions. When Harris asked none, he continued, "We're still a matriarchy, unlike the Confederacy."

"I suspected that when you spoke of Line Mothers. But calling the

17

Confederacy a patriarchy is a broad statement," Harris replied. "We've over a thousand members of all forms and sizes. Some are unusual. Overall, we tend to be a patriarchy, but some, like your Thirty Houses, are matriarchies. We've a bit of everything—except no slavery. We won't tolerate that."

Loche didn't mention the final ceremony, the Proclamation, where he was proclaimed an Associate of the Seat. Harris had no need to know. Loche's memories of the ceremony were muddled, hazy as it was.

Harris seemed content to let him observe the residents walking by. He must have read Loche's personal history. After all, he would be working, at some level, with the liaisons.

Returning to his thoughts, Loche remembered when he and his Line Mothers returned to their house. His mother was reconciled with his leaving. He would have preferred to return to Earth and extract retribution, but revenge on a mob was pointless. No central person existed who created the riot that murdered Reena. No, not murdered—it had not been deliberate, not like the fate some had planned for Loche. It was indiscriminate. No single individual was identified. It was just a part of the growing xenophobia against those viewed as different, like stationers and the spaceborn, those born in smaller stations and habitats scattered across SolSystem and the System States.

Another wave of homesickness swept through him. *I can never go home again.*

Earth was crowded—perhaps too crowded—and the pressing closeness drove some mad. He was unsure, as were the Line Mothers, whether the rioters were political agitators who viewed the belt's technology and productivity with envy or were a natural consequence of political propaganda. Regardless of the cause, those events had led him to Dundee Orbital.

His link vibrated—incoming messages. One was from his predecessor. Another was a confirmation of a reservation for his new living quarters and numerous commercial messages, including requests for interviews from link journalists. He added some filters to his link to block the commercial and journalist messages and acknowledged the reservation.

Harris nudged his elbow and tilted his head down the concourse.

Time to go.

†††

Dundee's customs office was at the end of a side corridor with thick transparent windows across its width. The windows framed the single entrance to the office. Harris spoke briefly with the agent at the guard desk then continued inside. Loche stepped up to the desk.

The guard, an older man in a uniform similar to the customs agents', looked up, smiled, and said, "Welcome, Mr. Loche."

The guard introduced Loche to another agent, who led him on a quick tour of the office. He was introduced to several agents and inspectors preparing for or ending their work shifts. Loche was gratified to see that all the inspectors, men and women, presented a calm, friendly, and competent manner. The atmosphere about the office exuded a presence that reminded Loche of his service in the System States Marines.

At the end of the tour, they arrived at the office of the station's customs director, Charles Demning. The guide announced Loche through the intercom next to the office door. "Enter" was the response.

Loche walked in to find Demning standing before one wall covered with a large holodisplay. One segment of the holo presented images of the station's interior, sequencing from one location to another. Another segment was a three-dimensional representation of the station. Loche had seen other similar displays for damage control aboard ships.

Demning was a busy man and appeared pale and haggard, as if he'd been stressed for too long with minimal sleep. He turned and nodded to Loche. "Welcome. I'm Charles Demning, the director. Please, take a seat and be comfortable."

Loche stepped forward and sat in one of several chairs before the director's desk. The office was small, the usual for offices on board ships and stations. The wall opposite the monitors was lined with shelves containing memorabilia, awards, and still holos of the director and several other people.

"Do you recognize anyone in the last holo on the right?" the director asked, noticing Loche's gaze.

Loche stood and walked closer to the indicated holo. It contained two men. One was a much younger Demning, and the other… He looked closer. The second man looked so familiar. *No, it couldn't be…*

"Yes," the director said, "that is Emile Loche, House DuQuoin, standing next to me. Your father, I believe."

"Yes… it is. When was this taken? Not recently, obviously."

"3168, Confederation Standard. We were negotiating a trade treaty—staffers—not on the same side, of course."

"I remember him saying once that he attended negotiations, but I never knew the depth of his involvement."

"We became quite friendly. He Introduced me to his house."

The statement surprised Loche. An Introduction to the house was rare.

"We've kept in touch from time to time when we had some mutual interest. I understand he's no longer in government service?"

"No, he's now a Member of our House for Trade. He left System States service ten years ago."

Demning didn't respond, giving the impression that he was aware Loche's father no longer represented the System States. He sat at his desk and waved Loche to resume his seat. "Please send my regards to your father when you next message home."

"I will."

During the subsequent interview, the director confirmed what Loche had expected. "Your duties will be both simple and complex. You will inspect all cargoes leaving the station for System States space. In addition, you and a Confederation inspector will work together, review cargo manifests, perform personal inspections. If you find no exceptions, the cargo containers will be sealed, made ready to be transferred to outbound ships. Lastly, as a liaison, you'll also act as a mediator, a System States representative, if there is some question concerning a personal declaration by System States citizens or cargo in a System States registered ship."

The System States had stricter regulations and prohibitions on imports than did the Confederacy. Occasionally, a difference between the two nations caught travelers with items viewed as contraband. Those cases were often resolved quietly. If the individual was entering with the contraband innocently, the material was seized and no other action taken. However, if it appeared to be a case of intentional smuggling… the process became interesting.

His interview with Director Demning was enlightening. He discovered certain provisions of the treaty were not available to the public.

"Are you aware of paragraphs two twenty-one, two twenty-two, and two twenty-three of the treaty?"

The question was surprising. "No, Director. As I remember, the treaty had only two hundred paragraphs."

"I thought that would be the case," the director said with a sigh. He looked to the side as if something there would help explain the situation. Then he looked back at Loche and continued, "Most of the arriving System States liaisons are ignorant of them." He paused, giving Loche an opportunity to respond.

When Loche asked no questions, the director continued, "Perhaps it is the cultural differences between us. Confederation Customs has jurisdiction for monitoring commerce between member planets and systems. Planetary governments' authority ends at the upper limits of their atmosphere—fifteen hundred kilometers altitude on planets with a habitable biosphere, twelve hundred kilometers for planets requiring enclosed environments, or in the case of System Stations where there is no habitable planet, five thousand kilometers from the station.

"In essence, there's no law in space except for Confederation law, and little of that. Most of our social interaction is governed by Custom and Tradition. The Confederacy has no law-enforcement agency except for the Customs Service, which has jurisdiction over commercial law and, by centuries of evolving Custom and Tradition, civil law in Confederate territory."

"You call your body of law Custom and Tradition?"

"No. The only universal body of law in the Confederacy is our constitution, the Charter of Confederation, and that is mostly a list of 'shall nots.' Some member systems and stations have codified their Customs and Traditions. However, most members have not. What Customs and Traditions are is a recognized standard of cultural and interpersonal behavior. Confederation members have adopted the more common customs and traditions as their own. There are some differences. For example, the Customs and Traditions for Inverness are a little different from those of our neighbor next door, Cameron. Inverness is a clan society. Cameron is not."

Loche nodded. He had reviewed Confederate law and its unusual legal system when he was instructed to apply for the liaison position. His training, however, emphasized the System States side of the treaty with little mention of that of the Confederacy.

"The result," said the director, "is that the Customs Service has assumed the role of law enforcement above the atmosphere and within stations—except for military stations, of course."

Loche considered that. It was unlike what existed in the System States but, on consideration, logical. He was unclear on—or perhaps not understanding—what that meant… to him.

"Consequently, customs officers, now including you, have judicial authority. We enforce station law, keep the peace, and when necessary, give forth judgment for offenses against law or Custom and Tradition."

The statement was a revelation. Loche had not known he would be expected to enforce non–System States law and regulations.

"Director, I know nothing of Confederation law, nor of Custom and Tradition. How can I be expected to perform those duties? Tariffs,

22

contraband, environmental safety, shipping regulations… I expected that. I was trained in those areas before I left the System States—"

The director raised a hand, halting Loche's objection in midsentence. "Please, hold your protests for the moment. You need to read the last twenty-three paragraphs of the treaty. They will answer many of your questions."

"But—"

"Wait," he said. "We will train you. Our law and Customs and Traditions are not all that complex. We will assign you an experienced trainer. You will be trained on the job. Your trainer can explain better than I. You will be probationary until your trainer certifies you. Certification can take months, three or four. Some probationers take longer, some less. We did have one, some time ago, that was unfit, but with your background, I have no doubt you'll be ready in a short time."

He paused a moment to look at his in-desk display. "I believe Donal Harris has volunteered to train you," he said, looking back up. "The only difference between you and Confederate customs officers is that you will be the primary inspector when System States ships, cargoes, or citizens are involved.

"You may have noticed that we have two categories of customs officers, agents and inspectors. Agents perform routine tasks. Inspectors are… well… investigators. They are more than just an agent. Harris will go into that as part of your training."

The director continued, "In those sections of the treaty you've not yet read are some unique provisions. You will be a Confederate employee, not an employee of the System States. We have agreed, in that treaty, to grant you, as a citizen of and a special representative for the System States, unique authority to enforce some, not all, System States law within the Confederacy—under limited and specific conditions."

Demning paused. "This is not publicly known, Fabien. Before this treaty, the System States believed the Confederacy was abetting, through inaction, smuggling into their territory. We were not. After lengthy negotiations, we, the Confederacy and the System States, compromised.

The Confederacy will not enforce System States law inside the Confederacy, but you, as an appointed representative of the System States, will when it is appropriate."

Despite Loche's obvious puzzlement, Demning continued, "You will be a servant of two masters. We, the Customs Service, will be your immediate 'master.' The Systems States is your other and may call on you, from time to time, for special tasks… with our concurrence."

The conversation continued for some time. Loche still had many questions, but those, he was assured, would be answered eventually. Loche's credentials as a new customs liaison were sent to the System States embassy on Cameron. Harris also updated his link with Confederate Custom and Tradition and unique station law. The update also included the complete text of the System States and Confederation Commercial Treaty.

†††

Loche had arrived at the end of Harris's workweek. That gave him two days to get settled, tour the station, and study the material Demning had given him. He was expected to have read the Treaty before joining Harris as a new probationary inspector by the coming Firstday. Harris would accompany him when he was processed and outfitted as a new member of the customs.

Loche's quarters, a small coapt, was in Torus Six, Deck Twelve, Segment B, one of four decks that contained residences for the station's custom agents, inspectors, station patrollers, and their families. His single consolidated apartment was six meters deep and four meters wide.

He waved his link across the panel next to the coapt's entrance and, when it opened, stepped inside. Along the left wall of the coapt was a small desk and chair with a built-in link console. Past the desk was a counter with a built-in autochef. Farther inside the compartment was a small 'fresher with shower, sink, and commode. He had used a sonic 'fresher aboard the ship, but here, with greater access to water and much better recyclers, he had an actual water shower, a small luxury. Opposite the desk and autochef was space for a lounger, side table, and chairs extruded from the floor. Farther to the right was an alcove containing his bunk and a closet.

The sleeping alcove was a refuge. It doubled as a survival shelter with a self-contained environment including communications and an emergency survival suit. In essence, his quarters were a larger version of his shipboard stateroom, self-contained if it ever became necessary in case of a blowout or an interruption of environmental services.

Having nothing else important to do, Loche unpacked his trunk. He had brought little as baggage. His mass allotment was not large, enough for a few personal items, mementos of his past life, a few clothes, toiletries, and his personal skinsuit. Director Demning had told him he would be issued uniforms and skinsuits on his first day of duty.

The trunk emptied, he locked it into the space under the bunk, where it would serve as a secure storage compartment. Fabien stood, at a loss for what to do next. He sat at the desk, activated the coapt's link, and ran down the housekeeping menu. In a few moments, he was registered with the laundry service and with food services, to stock his autochef. He activated his residential financial account and transferred the credit tabs he had brought from home. His last task was to send a message to the System States Embassy on Cameron, confirming his arrival. Those chores completed, he checked the coapt's furnishing list and extruded from the floor a recliner and side table. The time had come to read the trade treaty.

Twenty-some-odd "missing" sections of the treaty took a short time for Loche to read. They explained more. The trade treaty was not just a trade treaty—it was a mutual-assistance treaty. The Harmony of Light, also known as the Hive, was pressing the System States economically and militarily.

The Directorate of Sovereign Corporate States, known in the Confederation as the DeeCees, were doing the same to the Confederation. The Hive and the Directorate were believed to have agreed to a mutual-assistance treaty too. A treaty such as the trade treaty between the System States and the Tri-Cluster Confederation was a counterfoil to the growing alliance between the Hive and the DeeCees.

It dawned upon him that he could be a spy in training. The

question was, for whom and why? Loche reviewed what had happened to him over the last two years. He had been pushed into this place and this position.

His anger flared and subsided. He considered where he would have been had he not accepted this position. His time in the Marines was over because of his service injuries. His medical issue was real with his right leg—thigh, knee, and shin—having been crushed in a training accident. Nanotechnology had repaired the superficial structural, circulatory, and muscular damage. Unrepairable, however, were the crushed and severed nerves… so he had been told.

Those nerves were replaced with artificial substitutes. They worked. However, they also came with a side effect. The artificial nerves occasionally caused pain—not sufficient to be disabling but sufficient to be a constant irritation. The artificial nerves were as effective as the originals. Regardless, his injuries made him unfit for retention in the Marines.

He was not alone. More and more spaceborn were being discharged from the System States military for one reason or another. SolSystem was leading the purge of the spaceborn from its military ranks. The reduction of military effectiveness, as EarthGov said in internal communiques, was deemed to be less than the benefits of ridding the unwanted spaceborn from the Marines and System Defense Forces.

SolSystem was getting too crowded, as was Ceres and the other outer stations. Loche, his family at home, and the spaceborn in general, were being pushed out. EarthGov wanted their assets. What happened to the spaceborn was not their concern. Pogroms were not rare in SolSystem's past. The Seat was preparing in case another occurred, aimed at the Seat.

Loche remembered the message left by his predecessor and opened it with his link. It was a review of his new duties, some notes on specific shipping companies that tried to skirt contraband constraints, and one final passage.

<Forget all you know about the Confederacy. You will find it is

26

different—much different from the System States. Learn the local Customs and Traditions. You won't be able to function without knowledge of them. It will also help your ability to assimilate into this culture. I completed my contract a month ago. If you weren't told, there is an escape clause in the contract—marry and become a Confederate citizen. I could have resigned, but I wanted to finish my contract and leave no strings behind. If you come downbelow, visit us in the Scotia highlands.> His predecessor's contact information was included in the message.

The message continued. *<I advise you to acquire personal weapons—several in fact, as many as you can afford for different situations. You won't be fully accepted until you own and carry personal arms. It is an important aspect of the Confederate culture. Your training officer will ensure you become familiar with weapons. You may, from time to time, need to use them although I've never had to use anything stronger than a shock-stick.>*

<I'm told Donal Harris will be your trainer. Listen to him. He will help you as he has helped me.> The voice chuckled. *<I married his daughter.>*

The message ended. It was sent clear—nothing hidden or clandestine was in its contents that he could detect, and no hidden attachments. The data in the packet included a reference to an arms dealer on the station. *A local System States contact? Probably not. It would be too obvious.* Loche saved the address. He did not erase the message. Something told him he would need to listen to it again… perhaps often.

†††

Harris used his link to make a secure connection. "He arrived," he reported. "He's not what I expected, but he matches the biometrics we were given."

<Are you concerned?> asked the other.

"I don't know enough yet. Let's just say I'm awaiting confirmation. According to his records, if they're not faked, he should do. We'll have to wait and see."

<Very well. Continue as we discussed.>

"Aye," Harris responded and dropped the connection.

†††

Loche sat in the lounger, updating his personal log. He had acquired the habit long before. It helped him set his thoughts in order, a form of self-analysis. He was entering his impressions of Donal Harris when the console link announced two visitors.

<Jacob Swensen and Clifford Tanaki to see Fabien Loche.>

He recognized the names as two of the other resident System States liaisons on Dundee. "Enter."

Loche stood as the two entered the coapt and introduced themselves. Jacob Swensen was of medium height, dark, and a little shorter than Loche. Clifford Tanaki was shorter yet. Both were smaller and heavier built than Loche. Their build implied groundbound birth and heritage. On the average, spaceborn were taller and often massed less than their planet-born brethren.

"Welcome," Loche said. "I was told you were on shift when I arrived."

"We were," said Swensen. "We're partners and just got off shift. Imar Kolskov is the other liaison. He's on Cameron for reassignment. I think he may move to Gateway until his contract expires next year."

"There will be three of us on station?"

Tanaki nodded. "We've been told we may get another agent in addition to you. Maybe. Demning said there aren't many applicants."

Loche was surprised. The employment situation was stagnant in SolSystem and in most of the System States, for that matter.

"Are you from SolSystem?" he asked.

"I'm a Lunie. Jacob is an EllFiver... and you?" Tanaki responded after a quick glance toward his partner.

"I was a marine," he said with a small grin. "Before that, I was a stationer."

28

He immediately noticed a change in the two. Neither made an issue of Loche's ancestry. Nevertheless, he could detect a subtle change in their body language. Those from Luna and EllFive considered themselves aligned with EarthGov instead of with stationers and other spaceborn.

After a few minutes, Swensen said, "Clifford, we need to go. Fabien just arrived, and I'm sure he's fatigued."

Tanaki nodded. "Drop by The Blue Marble when you're off shift," he told Loche. "That's where we usually hang out."

"I'll do that. Thanks for the invitation."

The two departed, almost in a rush. They were a strange pair, Loche thought—Tanaki from one of the Luna city-states, Swensen from Earth's L-5 station. Neither, however, had the genotype of a spaceborn. Perhaps he should have inquired further. He queried his link for their dossiers. According to their data, they were indeed born on Luna and EllFive. After some consideration, he decided to set his questions on their origin aside… for the moment, anyway. His curiosity was pricked, and he resolved to answer that itch. *Just not today.*

†††

The following day, he familiarized himself with the station. The original station had begun as a single torus, a circular ring in geosynchronous orbit over Inverness, divided into ten decks, each deck in four quarters or segments. As time passed, another torus was added, and a spindle connected the rings. Over time, more and more rings were added until Dundee Orbital reached its current size. Depending on where one started measuring, it was either thirty-one kilometers in length or fifty-three kilometers if one included the extended spindle linking the station to the shipyard and the length of the shipyard itself. An outer meteor-and-debris shield transformed the station body into a thirty-one-kilometer cylinder studded with sensor, communication, and defense blisters and maintenance airlocks. The ship and shuttle docks encircled the station opposite the end extending to the shipyard.

The station was divided into four sections, including a residential section, an agricultural section, and an industrial section. Lastly, opposite the shipyard, the end cap contained the docking section with a small military and repair facility, as well as the docking bays and warehouses. The end cap also contained the opening to the internal shuttle bay.

The spindle between the shipyard and the station was ten kilometers long. Shipyard workers could travel to the 'Yard via intrastation trams and transport tubes that moved people and cargo from one end of the station to the other and out to the 'Yard.

The trams aided Loche's self-conducted tour. The station was far too big to explore in a single day. He had no doubt, however, that he would see it all, from end to end, before his contract expired.

†††

Loche was tired. He had walked more than he had in a long time, and his leg ached. Nearing home, he found a bar and grill called Katrine's. It was crowded, but a table became available not long after he arrived. He sat, ordered, and watched the crowd. Everyone was with someone, talking, drinking, eating, and laughing. Some couples danced to soft music from an unseen source. Other groups were families with children.

Several large holomonitors were scattered around the area. Some presented sporting events. Some seemed to be reporting local affairs. On one monitor, a new freighter was creeping out of dock at the shipyard—a two-kilometer, slightly flattened cylinder with an aft end rounded to accommodate the main shunt nodes. The bow narrowed, terminating to a flat face to accommodate the main docking and cargo locks.

The crowd seemed to flow in some Brownian pattern, first here, then over there. Several groups looked his way, many examining him, yet none approached, apparently unwilling to invade his privacy. *How unlike home.*

At home, someone would have approached and inquired of his identity and intentions—not here. He was a newcomer and ignorant of local customs and traditions. He would learn, in time.

Chapter 2. In-Processing

Dundee Orbital, 20 Fourmonth, 3203

Fabien Loche met Donal Harris at the entrance of the customs office. Harris wore a different uniform, a shipsuit—a one-piece coverall with an equipment harness and helmet.

"Let's get inside," Harris said. "We… you, rather, have three tasks today: getting your uniforms and equipment, a medical review, and a weapons proficiency test. If we have time, we'll do a walkabout before shift end."

The two entered the Customs Service complex. Loche followed Harris past uniformed people sitting in cubes, standing in groups talking, or scurrying about carrying folders and packages. People filled the office. They walked through the outer office and down a corridor toward the rear, passing other small offices, another cube farm, and a locker room before entering the quartermaster section. Harris walked over to a small blond woman sitting before a console link and beckoned Loche to join them. The woman looked up and smiled.

"Amilie," Harris said, "this is Fabien Loche. He's joining us and needs to be outfitted. Please issue him the standard inspector's kit." He turned to Loche. "Fabien, this is Amilie Schute. She's our quartermaster and can provide you with all your uniforms and gear. You're fortunate. The System States is paying for your initial issue. We have to pay for ours or have the cost deducted from our pay."

Harris turned back to her. "Amilie, Loche will be my new partner. Let's get him a shipsuit, helmet, and harness first and ship the rest to his quarters."

"Ah, Donal, breaking in a new Essie again?" she replied with a smile. She rose and examined Loche from head to toe. The top of her head did not quite reach Loche's chin.

"Call me Amilie," she told Loche when she had finished her examination. "Everyone does. I don't stand for a lot of formality."

Her response surprised Loche. As his culture was more formal and reserved, he was unused to such familiarity from a woman at an initial introduction. *This woman does not let formality be an issue, not this woman... No, this lady,* he decided. Informal she might be, he thought, but not uncultured. She presented an air of confidence, self-assurance like the women of his house.

He fought his usual reserve and responded in the same manner. "Very well, Amilie, and please call me Fabien," he said, smiling down at her.

The term Essie was a nickname for those from System States. Sometimes, the label was not complimentary.

"Indeed, I will! You've a polite one this time, Donal," she told Harris with an impish expression. "More so than the last."

Harris chuckled. "Thomas will learn. Lillian will make sure of that." He turned to Fabien. "Thomas Leboe was your predecessor. He married my daughter, Lillian."

Returning to her task at hand, Amilie told Loche, "I see you're taller... thinner than our average. We'll do a scan to make sure you're properly fitted." She directed Loche to stand against a wall while she waved a handheld wand over him. "That will take care of your immediate needs. You'll be issued two official uniforms, four shipsuits, helmet, harness, weapons, boots, and two skinsuits." She ticked off the list of issue equipment on her fingers, entered the data into the console link, and turned to Loche. "Let's do a closer scan for your skinsuit."

"I already have a skinsuit, brought from home," Loche replied.

"Is yours standard?" she asked.

"Yes, made in SolSystem."

"Ours are different. Yours uses exchangeable power packs and contains an eight-hour air supply?"

"Yes."

"Ours use embedded microcells throughout the skin to augment the standard airpack for added air capacity—up to twenty-seven hours—and for liquid-waste storage. Every movement provides additional power that extends the life of its power pack. In addition, our communicators are secure. You don't have that on your standard models. I will issue you two. Keep one in your quarters, the other here when you're not wearing it."

Amilie led him to a small compartment. "Go inside, strip, and put all your clothes in the wall compartment," she told him. "Then step inside the circle on the floor with your feet spread to the edges of the circle and your arms extended horizontally. Say when you're ready—I'll hear. Be sure to close your eyes when I tell you until I finish the scan."

In a few moments, Loche was standing naked in the circle with his arms extended. "Ready."

"Close your eyes now," she said.

Loche obeyed and saw, through his eyelids, the scanning laser flash by.

"Finished," she said. "In a moment, your shipsuit, a body suit, helmet, shock-stick, boots, and harness will be ready in the locker next to where you placed your civilian clothes. Put them on and transfer to the shipsuit all you carried in your pockets when you arrived. We'll clean and send your civilian clothes to your quarters."

When the shipsuit arrived, its design was familiar, almost identical to those Loche had worn before. It was light tan with two dark-blue horizontal bars high on each sleeve. All customs and patroller shipsuits were reinforced at the elbows, shoulders, waist, thighs, and knees and included the usual eleven press-seal pockets. It was similar to his marine utility uniform. The material would diffuse a laser strike and would stiffen at the impact of a projectile. A frangible round would powder without penetrating. A solid projectile, however, would pierce the suit. Limited protection was better than none.

A single-piece knit bodysuit that covered him from ankles to neck accompanied the shipsuit. With a pair of socks that reached midcalf, the bodysuit served as neck-to-toe underclothing. The package included an equipment harness and boots that reached midway up his calves. A

Confederation patch was on the left sleeve above the two blue bars, with a System States patch in the same position on the right. Below each patch was a small tag reading Inspector. He sealed the front of the suit and noticed his name, F. Loche, printed on his upper right chest.

Harris and Amilie were talking when he left the compartment, carrying the helmet. "One more thing before we go," Harris told him. "I assume you do not have visual implants?"

"Correct. Just surface contacts."

"Very well. Set your link to communicate through your helmet. The helmet, when you're wearing it, includes a heads-up display. No one will know what you see or hear. You can continue wearing contacts or not. Your choice. We will, you understand, wear helmets whenever we're outside of the office. Try it on."

Loche raised the helmet onto his head. It was like other helmets he had worn, designed to protect his head and neck. It contained a sliding face shield that, when lowered, made his head appear to be a featureless sphere. If needed, the face shield could be made opaque, mirrored, or transparent depending on need or lighting conditions. The helmet also included an optional neck ring to mate it to his skinsuit for long periods in a vacuum.

"Now," Harris told Loche, "that's better. Medical is next."

Loche removed his helmet, tucked it under his arm, and followed Harris.

†††

Loche's medical exam, a review of his medical history, took less time than he had expected. The medical office already had his records from the System States, and the medical officer compared those against the ones in Loche's link. He reconciled two differences and gave a small DNA sample, and it was over.

"I see nothing here to prevent you from starting now, Mr. Loche. Questions?"

He had expected some mention of his genetic differences, but the

34

simple statement from the medic was surprising.

"Uh, how do I stand compared to the Confederate norm?" Loche hoped the bigotry in the System States had not reached the Confederacy.

"Oh? Not much variance at all... Umm, I'd say a couple of sequences. No," he repeated, "not much at all."

"Really? I would have thought there would have been more genetic drift between us and you in the Confederacy."

"There are in some systems, but overall you're not far from our norm. I noticed you have some artificial nerves in your leg. When you have a few days to spare, we'll schedule you for some remedial maintenance, some nanosurgery, and take care of those." The medic spoke as if that were nothing at all. "I'm surprised you haven't had them taken care of before now."

"I-I thought nerves couldn't be regrown," Loche replied.

"That used to be true a century ago, but we can grow new ones in place now."

"I injured my leg a year before I accepted this position. Artificial replacements were the only option they gave me."

"I thought the System States had that capability," he mused. "Well, in any case, I can schedule some nanotube time for you whenever you have a few days free. There's no need to rush for something this minor as long as they are functional—they are functional, are they not?"

"Oh, yes. There's some residual pain, aches at night, but only at a minor level."

"Good. We will leave them for now. Your cost, as a member of the Service, will be covered."

They didn't tell me nerves could be regrown, Loche thought, remembering the session when he had been told his mangled nerves could only be replaced, not repaired. *This new information is another item to consider when I have more time.*

"Now, let's do some stress and mobility testing, and you're

finished."

Loche, with his medical clearance approved, walked into the break room. Harris had pointed it out earlier and told him to wait if he wasn't to be found.

Several dispensers displaying images of food and drink lined the wall. Loche discovered the dispensers recognized his link, and his personal account was usable. Most of the food items had unfamiliar names. Loche picked one based on its image and chose a container of tea. Scattered around the room were tables and chest-high counters. Most of the tables were empty. He chose a table off to one side, sat, and watched people enter and depart while he ate.

He was finishing his sandwich when Amilie Schute entered. She walked to the dispensers, filled a tray with food and a drink, and walked toward Loche's table.

"May I join you?" she asked.

Loche stood and waved her to one of the other chairs at the table. "Of course, Madame Schute." As she sat, he did the same.

"Must I remind you to call me Amilie?"

"No, Ma… Amilie. It is a habit from home. We are… we're more formal except within our family."

"Well, here, you are Donal Harris's protégé. That will become like family, I think, as you will discover. Speaking of Donal, are you abandoned?" she asked, smiling.

"No, he said he would meet me here. I was waiting for him and got hungry. My body clock hasn't yet synchronized with station time. I'm hungry all the time."

She chuckled, taking a bite of food. Her eyes focused on a tall, slim strawberry-blond woman who had just entered the room. "Over here!" Amilie said, waving to the newcomer.

The other woman turned her head, saw Amilie, and walked toward

36

their table. By habit, Loche stood at her approach. Her green eyes seemed to pull him toward her. He blinked to mask his sudden attraction.

Amilie said, "Molly, this is Fabien Loche, your uncle's new trainee." Turning to Loche, she said, "Fabien, this is Molly Quinn, Donal's niece. She's one of our inspectors, too, and I would suggest you treat her as family. In fact, the Customs Service is almost a family trade for her and Clan McLean."

"Just our sept," Molly told Loche. "Many of our clan are spacers or military." She sat facing the two of them.

She appeared to be a few years younger than Loche, but appearances could be deceiving. *Still, if she is Harris's niece,* he thought, *we should be about the same age.*

"I saw you last evening," Molly said to Loche.

"Oh?"

"You were in Katrine's on our home-deck concourse. I noticed you sitting alone. Most of us in the Service live on that level. We know most of the residents. You were new."

"Yes, I was there. I arrived last Fiveday. After six months aboard ship, I had a case of cabin fever and spent the day exploring the station. I didn't notice you there."

"I was with friends," she said. "You were sitting at the only table with one occupant. You seemed deep in thought, so we didn't bother you."

I am somewhat of a loner, he thought as he rubbed his right knee. "I'm not much of a conversationalist… and a newcomer." Something she said sparked a thought. "You said *clan* as if it was significant. I've read that Inverness is ruled by clans. How does that work?"

"Fabien is the new System States liaison, Molly," Amilie interrupted. "He just arrived, and your uncle will be his trainer."

"Ah," Molly said. "Well, Mr. Loche—"

After Amilie's mild scolding, Loche considered whether to accept the formality or to comply with the Confederacy's friendlier and much less formal mores. *Accept it*, he decided. "Amilie said we were all like family. Call me Fabien, please."

"Fabien. Yes," she said with a smile. "Please call me Molly."

"Now, to begin," Molly said. "Inverness was settled by several groups. Most were Scots, Irish, and Canadians from Nova Scotia and the old Canadian Maritime provinces. Some later colonists were from the northeastern and central areas of North America. The concept of clans was part of our culture. During the trip here, colonists grouped themselves by families, kith and kin, as it were. This was in the days when colony ships cruised at less than one thousand lightspeed. During the voyage, it didn't take long before those groups merged into what were de facto clans. When the colonists arrived, they dispersed across the planet in clan groupings. In a few years, the clans became actual political entities over distinct geographical areas. So now, when we speak of clans, it is more than just our immediate families.

"If I was being introduced formally," she continued, "I would be Molly Quinn of Clan McLean, Sept Harris. Harris is my family sept, Clan McLean is my…" She paused, glancing at Amilie as she formulated her answer. "Well, let's say 'nation.' There are differences, but 'nation' is the closest label I can think of at this moment."

"I see… I think. If I understand you, I would introduce myself as Fabien Loche of House DuQuoin, of the Thirty Houses?" he responded.

"Yes, that would be appropriate. A clan denotes many things. Family is one, of course, but it also includes fealty to a group, an organization. Clan McLean in my case. It also signifies my home district on Inverness and the territory of Clan McLean. Our clan's territory is along the Hebridean Peninsula and a string of islands, a rocky archipelago that stretches from the southeastern portion of Scotia, our largest continent, out a thousand kilometers into the Gael Sea. The territory also includes a portion of the adjacent mainland. The land, having something that is ours, gives us a sense of… permanence… of solidarity and commonality… of a communion of land and folk that's difficult to describe to one unfamiliar with the concept."

"So," Loche asked, "everyone in that area is of Clan McLean?"

"No. Most are, but not all. You are born or marry into a clan. My current residence is here, in Dundee Orbital, but I am still of Clan McLean, just as Amilie is of Clan Mieze. I will remain in Clan McLean regardless of where I live… unless I marry out of it. If that happened, I would be of my new clan."

"What of an outsider like me?"

"You have no clan, per se. You, as a liaison, have all the rights and privileges of Confederate citizenship—even though you are not one. On Inverness, by extension, you have all the rights and privileges of a clan member but without clan support and representation." She saw the puzzled expression on Loche's face and explained. "Let me use this example to explain clan support and representation. Suppose I was accused of some crime. I could call on my clan for legal support and representation…"

Harris arrived, interrupting the discussion. "Molly-girl! Good to see you. Back on board now?"

"Yes, Uncle, I came up a few hours ago. Holiday is over."

"I see you've met Fabien?"

"Amilie introduced us. I was just telling him about our clans."

"Good, then I won't have to repeat that." He looked at Loche. "Are you ready? Got your medical approval?"

"Yes, it went faster than I thought it would."

"Let's get you weapons certified." Harris smiled and gave a short nod to Molly and Amilie. "I'll take care of him now, ladies."

Loche rose, said goodbye to the two women, and followed Harris out the door, slipping on his helmet.

††††

Molly watched the two men leave the break room. Amilie was saying something.

"What?" she asked.

39

"I said, Molly, that that was something. What do you think?"

Molly didn't respond. Amilie repeated her question. "What do you think, Molly?"

"Huh? Oh yes, something." Fabien Loche was something. Just what, she didn't know—different, without a doubt.

"With him working with Donal, I'm sure you'll meet him again."

††††

"The armory and range are on Deck Two of this torus," Harris said, his voice clear in Loche's helmet. "After you've qualified, you will be issued a pistol and laser. You're stationborn, so you understand the pistol will be loaded with frangibles. Your laser will be variable, unlike those allowed others on the station. Theirs are fixed-focus, fixed-frequency, and of limited power. You will not have those constraints."

He paused while they followed a down ramp to the next lower deck. "You will also be issued magazines and reloads of nonfrangible ammunition. Those will be solid-cored and armor-piercing. You will only use those to prevent damage to the station—to prevent acts that could cause a hull breach or damage to the station's environmental systems—or when frangibles are useless. You will always carry at least one magazine of nonfrangibles, although it is unlikely you'll ever need them. But… it's regulation."

Loche nodded, understanding the logic. Among station folk and spaceborn in general, endangering the hull or its integrity was the most heinous of crimes. The usual punishment for those crimes was ejection from the nearest lock without a skinsuit.

They took a transfer tube down another deck to Torus Two, Deck Two, near the southern end of the station. The end cap of the station, Torus One, contained the Navy Annex and some docks and warehouses for the Navy. The end cap was Dundee's original docks from the station's early days. At that time, ships docked inside the south end cap of the station. When pseudogravity was added centuries later to the station, they converted the oldest two toruses to house commercial warehouses and large open spaces suitable for storing shipping containers and cargo pods.

The armory and range were located in an area adjacent to the warehouse district. Harris and Loche entered the armory through a pressure hatch that opened into an office complex. Inside were people wearing light-gray uniforms like the customs shipsuits worn by Harris and Loche, in cut and design.

Harris waved a greeting to a few in the gray uniform as they walked past. He answered Loche's unspoken question. "They're station patrollers. That's why their uniforms are gray. They keep the peace and dispense nonjudicial punishment for minor infractions. They don't have full judicial authority like I do—and you will. Patrollers are a component of and subordinate to the Customs Service." Harris led him farther into the complex, weaving around and past more patrollers. "This is their headquarters. We share a forensics lab, the brig, and a few other common facilities like the armory and range."

A few more minutes' walk brought them to the armory.

Harris introduced Loche to one of the armorers. "Loche is a new inspector. He needs weapons and a standard loadout."

The armorer retreated into an inner office and soon returned with a pistol, ammunition, a laser, and its powerpack. He picked up a tablet. "Hold your link here, Inspector Loche," he said, extending the tablet.

Fabien did so, and his personal ID was copied to the armorer's tablet. After a few touches on his tablet, the weapons were added to Loche's issue inventory.

"Stop by when you've been certified, and I'll make it official. Else, you'll have to return them before you leave," he instructed Loche.

The range was next to the armory. It consisted of tables along the left wall as Loche entered. On the right was a waist-high counter divided into individual shooting positions by vertical panels. Each position was large enough for one occupant.

An older station patroller, a senior sergeant, Loche saw, walked into the range through a second door. The sergeant must have been practicing, for an empty pistol and magazine lay in a shooting position down from them. Harris introduced him to Loche.

"Henry, this is Fabien Loche, my new partner. He's also the new Essie liaison. Fabien, this is Henry Hillman. He's the senior patrol sergeant for the station and our hand-to-hand trainer. I'll make an appointment for you with Henry later this week. He will test you, review your physical fitness, and see if you need any remedial training. Since you haven't been out of the System States Marines that long, I doubt you need any, but Henry will certify you."

"Welcome to Dundee Orbital, Inspector Loche." Hillman said, looking Loche over from head to foot. "You look a little skinny. We may have to build you up."

Loche nodded. "That may be true. I was medically discharged for a crushed leg. It's been rebuilt and is functional, but I did lose some muscle tone while in the hospital."

"You pass our physical?" Hillman asked.

"Yes."

"Then you shouldn't have any problems. I may assign you some workout routines. Maybe. We'll see."

Hillman extended his hand and shook Loche's. Hillman was clearly stronger, but Loche maintained the pressure of his grip.

"You'll do," Hillman said with a grin. "I'm open all Fiveday. Pick a time."

With that, Hillman gathered his gear and, with a friendly "Have a good shift," left the two customs inspectors alone.

Harris led Loche to a firing position and laid the weapons on its surface. Tracks ran overhead from the position to the distant wall, allowing targets to be run out various distances. In all, it was a standard range design.

"How far is the wall?" Loche asked.

"One hundred meters," Harris replied, "but today, all you need is to qualify at seven, fifteen, and twenty-five meters."

The range was like ones used by the System States Marines. Harris picked up a target from a stack on a table along the wall and returned to clip it to the overhead track. He ran it out a distance on the track.

"Seven meters," he said.

Harris opened the box containing the pistol and picked it up. He inspected the weapon to ensure the butt contained no magazine or ammunition cassette and racked the slide, locking it open. He laid it on the counter with the muzzle pointed downrange. Next, he opened another box containing loaded magazines and laid one magazine on the counter next to the pistol. "This is our standard-issue pistol. It's a Ballister Model 13 and fires a ten-millimeter caseless round. The magazine holds ten rounds. I'm told it is like your issue marine pistols. You shouldn't have any trouble with it. The safety, magazine release, slide release, and selectable recoil compensator are the same." He pointed at the magazine lying next to the pistol. "These are reusable magazines. When we're in the field, we use cassettes. Some of us prefer magazines over the cassettes."

Next, Harris divided the cartridge boxes into three groups. Starting from the left box, he said, "Standard frangible load. Our frangible rounds have yellow tips." He pointed at the other boxes in turn. "Solid rounds have black tips. Armor-piercing rounds are green. Never mix rounds in the same magazine. Here," he said, handing Loche some small earplugs, "you can use these if you wish instead of wearing your helmet."

"Thank you, but I would still need an eye shield. I'll use my helmet for now."

Harris just nodded, and his lack of further response made Loche wonder.

"That was a test, wasn't it?"

"Yes. You passed. Now, load, make ready, and on command, fire five rounds into the center of the target." He waited until Loche put on his helmet and lowered the face shield. Harris did the same with his own. When both were ready, Harris pushed a button on a nearby column. Above, the overhead lights flashed three times, and an announcement blared from hidden speakers.

The range is hot! The range is hot! The range is hot in thirty seconds… twenty… ten… The range is hot—doors are locked!"

"When you're ready, Fabien."

Fabien picked up the pistol, inserted the magazine, and released the slide. The pistol felt like his old service pistol—more metal… more mass, perhaps. He flicked the recoil compensator off with his thumb, aimed at the target, and squeezed the trigger.

Bam.

It fired before Loche expected, as it should. It wasn't loud at all. He glanced at Harris.

"Built-in suppressor," Harris confirmed. "Adjustable too. Most of us set it at max suppression. Saves civilian's ears."

The trigger had a slight hesitation before it fired. *Just right.*

Bam… Bam… Bam… Bam.

Loche removed the magazine, noting it had four rounds remaining. He racked the slide, and the round in the chamber dropped from the magazine well. Loche caught it in midair and laid it beside the pistol and magazine.

Harris retrieved the target. It contained five holes in the center, none more than an inch from the others—several holes overlapped. "Very good. I noticed you did not use the recoil compensator."

"Old habit. If I can perform—hit my target with recoil—I can hit my target without recoil."

Harris laughed. "Can you do that at fifteen and twenty-five meters?"

"Yes. I was rated Expert when I was in the Marines."

"Show me." Harris ran out two more targets, one at fifteen meters and the other at twenty-five meters. "Do it again, five rounds each."

Loche replaced the used magazine with a full one. He fired at both targets with scores more than acceptable for qualification. He repeated his performance with the laser pistol.

44

"What about PBGs?" Loche asked.

"Particle-beam hand weapons are banned on the station—everywhere in space, except for the Fleet, the Marines, and the station's militia. Too destructive, too bulky. We and the patrollers are considered members of the station's militia. We have some, but they're locked up in the armory."

When Loche finished shooting, Harris had him clean the pistol while he updated Loche's records. Cleaning it did not take him long. The pistol was designed to be broken down and cleaned using just a few materials: a cloth, a brush, and some bore-cleaning fluid.

"You have combat-suit training in the System States Marines?" Harris asked.

"Yes, light, semi, and full-powered."

"Good. We'll run you through a quick familiarization course and get you certified for that too."

Loche looked at Harris. *Is he expecting some response?* "Why are you looking at me that way?"

"I think you'll be surprised when you see the suits."

"Why?" Loche asked, suspicious.

Harris hesitated. "Ah, well. They are the same suits used by the Essie Marines."

"You buy them from the System States?"

"No, 'tother way around. We designed the suits and sold a license to your Marines. Ours are better, though." He grinned at Loche. "We don't license everything."

Harris was right. Loche got suited and ran through the standard tests in standard g, in heavy two-g gravity, and in null gravity. The Confederation suits had improvements lacking in his marine versions. The heads-up display and link integration were a generation or more ahead of the marine suits. They also had several features not present in the System States versions.

"A few more items, and we'll take a short walk along the docks," Harris said after Loche was once more dressed in his customs shipsuit, harness, and weapons.

Harris gave him some tips. "Always carry the Ballister on your strong side. You'll find a built-in holster for the laser on your left leg. The laser is light and shouldn't weigh you down. The Ballister is heavier. Because of that, we carry it in a holster on our harness belt to help distribute the weight. The shock-stick and spare magazines on your other side help to balance the load. It's been our experience that in cases when a weapon is needed, you will be using your pistol with frangible rounds more often than a laser. We practice here each week, and I want you to practice with both with your strong and your weak hand until you achieve equal proficiency."

"I understand," said Loche. "We did the same in the Marines."

"Good. Practice wearing a suit too. We seldom have to combat board a ship, but if or when we do, it's best to be ready."

Loche nodded his understanding.

Harris continued, "Let's take a break. We need to talk."

††††

They left the armory and walked past the docks to an adjacent concourse containing the usual bars, chandlers, and clip-shops found in every station. Most of the people passing through the area were spacers wanting a drink or entertainment. The majority of them wore shipsuits bearing logos of major shipping companies.

The patrol office passed out of sight around the curve of the corridor. Harris walked toward an eatery with a hand-lettered sign over the entrance saying Sen Lee's Chop House. They entered. Loche noted it was well lit and clean compared to some establishments they had passed.

"You drink coffee or tea?" Harris asked.

"Tea… cold if they have it."

"Sen Lee! Two cold teas!" Harris shouted.

46

He led Loche to a corner table and sat with his back to the wall. Loche thought it prudent to do the same, sitting in another chair where he could see the rest of the room. Harris removed his helmet and placed it on a corner of the table, and Loche followed suit.

While they sat waiting for Sen Lee to bring their drinks, Loche examined his surroundings. He noticed the tabletop was scarred from rough usage. *Not unexpected for this area of the station.* The diner had few customers, none nearby.

Their corner was darker than the rest of the room. One light strip overhead was unlit, allowing the two to see while hindering anyone looking at them.

Harris noticed Loche's glance overhead. "Sen Lee hasn't fixed that light strip in all the years I've known him. Before he came here, he was a purser for one of the smaller shipping companies at one time. When he opened this place about… oh, maybe five, six years ago, he helped us with information from time to time.

"That's one reason this corner is darker. It allows us to meet people without drawing too much notice."

Sen Lee appeared with two amber frosted mugs on a tray. He set one mug before each of them and departed.

"He'll bill me at the end of the month," Harris said and took a sip then a larger swallow of the tea. "Ah, I like that."

Loche followed the other's example. The tea was good. Cold and sweet, it quenched a thirst he had not noticed.

Harris leaned back in his chair and gave the room another scan. Apparently satisfied that nothing was worth more of his attention, he turned to Loche. "Have you ever worked with a partner?"

"I… I'm not sure what you mean. I have worked with others in a team, but not with just another person once I was out of basic. Why do you ask?"

Harris's demeanor changed, more distant. "I've read your bio, your resume. You seem to be suited to this job as best as we can determine." He paused, sweeping his gaze around the barroom. "A Confederate customs officer… an inspector, is not the usual run of bureaucrat. We're more… hands-on, you might say." He paused, seeming to gather his thoughts. "We have people who do most of the usual customs work, the paperwork, matching bills of lading with the actual material listed… the grunt work, so to speak. We, the inspectors, become involved when someone finds discrepancies or if there is a history of someone, some ship or shipping company, pushing the limits."

Harris took another sip and continued, "To say we're law enforcement—or treaty enforcement, in your case—is limiting. We're like your System States Central Criminal Bureau." He was quiet for a moment, giving the impression he was about to get to the crux of this meeting.

"In the past eight years, I've had three partners—System States liaisons as partners, I mean. The last, Thomas Leboe, married my daughter at the end of his contract. He resigned from the service, and they moved downbelow. Another of my partners was killed in the line of duty after he arrived. The other quit. I don't know why, nor what happened to him. One day, he was gone, unannounced. We couldn't find any evidence of foul play. He just closed his accounts and took a shuttle downbelow. We lost him there."

"I met Swensen and Tanaki. They said they were partners. Is that normal?"

"No, but they asked to be together, and their performance was acceptable, so we agreed." Harris glanced around the room and took another sip of tea. He looked at Loche as if trying to glean some bit of information, some confirmation of Loche's ability and worth. "This can be a dangerous occupation. That's one reason we look for prior military service, prior law enforcement, or other experience that implies the candidate can protect himself, others, and his partner. In your case, me. I guess what I'm asking is can you guard my back?" Harris said. "Can you do that?"

Harris's manner was almost confrontational. He was looking for assurance, and Loche wasn't sure if he could give that assurance. He returned Harris's stare. "I don't know," he said. "I've never been in such a situation. I would like to believe I could—I've been in some situations where a fight could have occurred. But it's never happened."

Harris mulled the response then nodded as if making a decision. "A truthful answer. It will do for now. I take it you have never been in combat?"

"No, " Loche replied. "I was on a system-defense corvette in the Bernard system during my first enlistment. We boarded several suspected smugglers, but there was never any real opposition. After that, they assigned me to Millersport Naval Supply Base over Durban. I was a new sergeant then, NCOIC of one of the smaller Marines units attached to the naval supply base. The closest I've been to actual combat was a bar fight."

Several more customers had arrived during the discussion. Loche noticed Harris was watching them, but they seemed quiet to Loche's eye.

"Well, truthfully, I didn't expect you to be a combat veteran," Harris said. "The System States has been quiet for a century or more—no significant external threats and few internal ones… that we know of." He waited a moment, giving Loche an opportunity to speak. When he didn't, he continued, "There has been little opportunity for you to see the Elephant."

"Elephant?"

"An old expression." Harris dismissed further explanation.

Loche thought Harris's information on internal threats in the System States was outdated. Trouble was brewing. *I'm glad I'm out of it.*

A group of spacers arrived noisily. They gathered at the bar, shouting drink orders.

Harris waited for the volume to subside before continuing. "Our last major dustup was only sixty years ago. You may have noticed we don't have beanstalks here at Inverness. We did once, but they were vulnerable. DeeCees took them out in a raid—blew the spatial anchors to hell and gone. You can still see the scar whenever the weather downbelow is clear, where one fell. The fail-safes took care of the others, but that one left us a remembrance." Harris took another sip of cold tea. "The DeeCees have been quiet since. So far."

"Are they an imminent danger?"

"No," Harris answered. "They're our local... um, competitors, so to speak. We have border skirmishes on a semiregular basis. Our borders touch in places. It's been nothing too big... ship-to-ship engagements, so far."

More dockworkers were entering—a shift change, Loche guessed.

Harris noticed the increase of patrons too and drained the last of his tea. "Let's get going and see what we can see."

The two stood, set their helmets on their heads, and departed. They walked the circumference of Deck Two. Harris said the walk was 'being seen.'

A thought occurred to Loche since Harris knew of all the provisions of the treaty. "You know how I was recruited?"

"Not the particulars. I assume it wasn't completely voluntary." Harris continued walking, shifting to one side to pass a drunken spacer. "Is that an issue?"

Loche considered his answer. He didn't have a good one, just the truth. "Frankly, I don't know. I'm not feeling particularly happy with the System States at the moment. Some pieces are coming together. We, the stationers and the spaceborn, are being pushed out. It's not just me—it's my entire family, our House, the Seat, eventually most of the SolSystem stationers, the Belters, and the spaceborn we support. We're all considered to be less than human due to the genetic drift of those families who survived the Free-belter plague a thousand years ago. I—we believe there are other, more significant, reasons. Regardless, the result is growing ground-pounder xenophobia."

Harris shrugged. "What can I say? That intolerant attitude is one that drove us out millennia ago."

Loche realized he would receive no sympathy from Harris. "Well, the job appears to be more interesting than I thought, and I don't see any others on the horizon. Before I left SolSystem, I had a discussion with our

House DuQuoin Line Mothers. They see the future too. If—when I finish my contract and the situation in SolSystem continues to deteriorate, they may migrate. There are still unsettled planets and systems in the Confederacy."

"What does that, your completing your contract, have to do with their decision?"

"I suspect if I can fit in, they believe they can too. We're a matriarchal society—yours is patriarchal. There will be issues. We don't know how severe. Hopefully, there will be a place for us if or when we need it."

"Well, I don't see why not. Each Confederate member state is autonomous within the Charter. Some of our members have… unusual customs and traditions."

They arrived at the customs office a few minutes before shift change and logged out. Before Loche left, Harris told him they had received updates from the System States for their contraband lists and Watch and Report notices for various ships. "Review those before tomorrow. Some ships on the list may be in port."

†††

Harris watched Loche depart. When he was out of sight, Harris turned and walked down the hallway, past the open administrative cubes to his office. He didn't spend much time in it, but he had some administrative tasks that needed doing from time to time.

He entered his office, secured the door, sat behind his desk, and activated his office console link. "Memo for Record: Interdiction Office, Colin Schofield. Subject: Fabien Loche," he dictated.

He paused, leaning back in the chair to gather his thoughts. "Completed in-processing, basic issue, medical and weapons qualifications. Nothing worth noting in the medical. He passed weapons qualifications with ease. So far, everything meets our expectations. He handled his weapons with experience. He should, with his training and length of military service. I introduced him to Senior Patrol Sergeant Hillman and scheduled a session with him for Loche. I expect Hillman to

51

certify Loche with little, if any, further training.

"Earlier in the day, he was quiet. He met Quinn this morning with Schute and seemed more open. Agent Schute was able to put him at ease. Afterwards, with me, he was more reserved until we reached the range, where he appeared more confident, unlike when he arrived."

Harris drummed his fingers on the desk, wondering if Loche would be suitable or would be just the functionary he was recruited to be... what the System States expected. He continued, "I had a private interview with Loche after he qualified. He was more alert—observant. I plan to take him through the station this week... an introductory tour."

Harris ended the record. *We shall see. At least Loche appears to be competent.* The other three liaisons were just functionaries, bureaucrats, even his new son-in-law. They did the job but nothing more. Loche, he hoped, would be better... something more.

Chapter 3. Training

Dundee Orbital, 25 Fourmonth, 3203

Harris began Loche's training during their next work shift. The first few days were uneventful. The two spent a half-shift on Deck Eight, an area kept at one-and-a-quarter g to make it more comfortable for Coterni living on or visiting the station. Loche was grateful for the hot whirlpool in the Customs locker room. His legs ached, not enough to be debilitating, but enough to make sleep difficult. The whirlpool helped. He felt vindicated for pampering himself since Harris relaxed in the whirlpool too.

Another day was spent watching passenger inspections from three ships. On Fourday, Harris had Loche spend time undergoing Senior Patrol Sergeant Hillman's unarmed-combat training session. Loche learned a few new moves, as did Hillman, who remarked that Loche was his first student from the System States. The point, however, was Loche passing another of Harris's tests. Most of the time, however, they walked and watched.

The inhabitants of Dundee Orbital were more open and less constrained than Ceres stationers and those of the Thirty Houses. Dundee's main concourses were a hundred meters wide. Bulkheads—*walls*, he reminded himself—in light pastels interrupted with murals of various Confederate scenes decorated the walls. Pedestrians walked without congestion. The overhead—*ceiling*, he reminded himself again—was higher, ten meters on the average. Large, open atriums filled with flowering shrubs appeared every two hundred to three hundred meters and served as commerce, food, and recreation centers. Ceres Station, built inside the planetoid of the same name, seemed small, crowded, and stale in comparison.

Ceres and the other Sol stations had been on starvation rations for organic resources for a long, long time. They had sufficient power, volatile chemical, and metal resources. But biologicals and rare earths came from Earth, and those needs consumed a significant portion of the stations' income. As much as they strove to shield biologicals, radiation played havoc with seed plants and animal DNA.

With cash low, maintenance suffered. Unrepaired wear and tear was obvious to anyone who looked. Dundee, as old as the Ceres and belt stations, was vibrant... healthy. His home station, in contrast, appeared shabby and worn.

Loche witnessed his first duel on Threeday. They were patrolling Deck Six in Torus Four, a portion of the station that contained small merchants who served station residents and visitors, when Harris received a call for mediation. The site was a short walk away, and they were closest. No station patrollers were near. When they arrived, they found two women waiting and arguing. Both appeared to be forty or so standard years old—fit and well dressed. Harris dealt with the two women while Loche watched.

The altercation had arisen from bargaining for an item between a customer and the shop owner. One woman, he was not sure which, insulted the other. That led to a physical response, a slap. The assaulted woman issued a challenge. The other woman could accept the challenge or apologize. She chose to duel.

Harris identified the challenger and the challenged. Another customer, a witness, confirmed the account.

"Do you accept our mediation?" Harris asked.

Both women affirmed they would.

Harris asked the challenged, "Weapons?"

"Knives. Standard blades," she replied.

"When?" he asked the challenger.

"Now."

"Conditions?" he asked them both.

The challenger said, "First blood." The other agreed.

"File your bonds," he ordered. A bond was required whenever mediation services were required. It helped cover costs and the mediator's time.

Harris flicked a glance to Loche. "I don't think there are any dueling courts nearby. Find the nearest empty compartment, one that has at least a hundred square meters of open space."

Loche queried his link and found one not far away. "Compartment 1214 is available—fifty meters down-segment."

While the four walked toward the impromptu dueling court, Harris explained what would happen. "We'll escort the two women inside. You will measure their blades to ensure they are both ten centimeters long. Both should be—that is the standard length for personal knives. When we're inside, you take one to the left side, I'll take the other to the opposite side. I'll say 'Begin,' and then we watch. I'll stop the duel at first blood. If necessary, I'll tell you to call for medical help."

"And if they don't stop on command?" Loche asked.

"We'll use our shock-sticks and write them up for unlawful assault."

They arrived at the compartment. Harris used his link to have the door unlocked. They found the interior empty as expected. The challenger was wearing slacks. She produced her knife from a sheath built into the back of her slacks. It was ten centimeters long. The challenged was wearing a skirt, which she discarded, revealing skintight flesh-colored leggings. Her knife was in a sheath strapped to her thigh. It, too, was ten centimeters long.

Loche escorted one woman to the left wall, pacing off the distance as they walked. Harris took the other one to the opposite wall.

"Ten meters," Loche reported and joined Harris at the entrance. He noticed Harris had instructed his link to record the duel.

"Ready?" Harris asked the two.

"Ready," both confirmed.

"Commence!" Harris said.

The two women crouched. They held their knives, edge inward, thumbs along the flat of the blade. Both appeared to have had training. They circled, sparring, looking for an advantage. The challenger lunged. The other slipped to the outside and drew her knife the length of the other's arm. Blood welled from the cut.

"Halt!" Harris shouted.

The duel was over in seconds. The winner stepped back while the loser stood looking at the blood running down her arm. Harris took a steri-pad from his medkit and wiped the blood from her arm. The nannites in the pad slowed then stopped the flow of blood. He finished, spraying the cut with a sealer. It was not deep and did not require further medical attention.

"You're fortunate," Harris told her. "She could have opened your face."

Later in the shift, Harris explained the duel. "Neither wanted to hurt the other. On the other hand, neither could appear to give in. Price haggling got out of hand before either realized it, and with that witness in the store, neither could back down. Now, the winner can brag about standing up for her honor. The loser can brag she didn't back down from a fight. It was face-saving for both." He walked a few more steps and muttered, "Idiots!"

As dueling was illegal in the System States, Loche had never seen it before. "Does this happen often?"

"Yes and no. Most are like those two women, inconsequential. If they were serious, they would have chosen pistols. Most duels with knives cause only superficial injuries—not all, but most. On occasion, an artery might be cut, and that could be serious. Two women, knives… No, that wasn't a real duel. If I thought it was serious, I would have called for medics to be present before I allowed them to start and increased the amount of their bond." He walked a few more steps and said, "By the way, you get half of our fee."

"Oh?"

"Why not? You were there, and you're an inspector even if you are probationary. You've earned half."

As they walked around the perimeter of the level, a thought occurred to Loche. "Do you have professional duelists? Ones that could be hired to settle grievances?"

"There's no prohibition," Harris admitted. "However, they don't last long. When a pattern develops—when there is a series of duels—duels that seem to be deliberately provoked, a clan or someone will take action. The duelist will disappear. There was a case... oh, maybe twenty years ago. A newcomer from the Hive won a series of duels. He was a trade representative and made a series of challenges against officers of some local trading corporations. He chose pistols and won them all—killed every one of his opponents. One clan—Portee, I think—declared him a professional. His body was found crucified outside Portobella. The local militia received an anonymous call saying where he could be found."

"No one did anything? Wouldn't Clan Portee be guilty of his death?"

"There was no proof other than the declaration. At the time, there was a joke he'd challenged someone who chose nails and lost. There wasn't much effort to follow up on his death. We won't tolerate assassins, and that's what he was."

"But couldn't anyone who won some duels be accused of being a professional?"

"It could happen. If so, he could make a plea in public and give his account, his version of the cause of the duels, to refute any accusation. Sometimes that works. However, if there is an accusation of professionalism or hints that such a declaration may be forthcoming, they pick the gold pin and set aside their weapons."

"Gold pin?"

"Yes, like the one I gave you when you arrived. By taking the gold pin, he could neither make nor accept challenges."

They continued their walk along the concourse. Harris pointed at a group sitting near a food court. "We have groups—sects, some of them—

who have disavowed violence. Many, like those, are of Quaker, Amish, Mennonite heritage. Their culture has culled their aggressive, violent members. Gold-pin wearers aren't problems for us. Newcomers who don't know the rules can be. That's why I gave you the pin, to protect you until you understood the ground rules."

"Thank you. We have a saying at home, 'Ignorance kills.'"

"Very true," Harris agreed.

Loche had continued to wear the pin when off shift. "Hmm, perhaps I should follow up on your son-in-law's suggestion."

"What did he say?"

"He left me a message when I arrived and suggested I buy personal weapons. I haven't done that yet. He left me some addresses of local dealers."

"You can carry your service weapons if you wish. You should buy a civilian holster if you're not wearing shipsuits, and I'd suggest you include a knife."

"I brought one, my service knife, but it's longer than your standard length."

"Wear it with your uniform. I should have mentioned it. We don't issue knives with our basic uniform kits, but most of us add one."

"Do you have a knife?"

Harris drew back the cuff of his left sleeve, revealing a slim knife strapped to his forearm. "I do."

I have some shopping to do. Sheathed, his service knife was about the length of the pocket on his lower leg. Loche would see how well it fit in that pocket. He was used to it and could pick another knife for off-duty use.

†††

When the end of shift was near and they were returning to the customs office, Harris asked, "Did you review your latest Watch and Report list?"

"Yes, on Firstday."

"One ship on that list was here a few weeks ago, before we received the update. I reported it to your embassy on Cameron. Another ship on that list, the *C'seine*, is due tomorrow. She broached this morning. We'll lead the inspection. The agents will be alert for anything on this ship. They will go through the ship's documentation and check the crew's credentials. We will take the cargo. The ship has been suspected of smuggling blueleaf. We'll see what we find. Wear your skinsuit in case we have to go outside."

†††

Loche was seated, testing his issued skinsuit, in the customs office locker room the next day. It was, as Amilie said, different from his personal one. This skinsuit was designed to be used with his service helmet. It had an optional neck ring that matched one that could be added to his helmet. A regular skinsuit included an integral flexible headpiece stored in the suit's collar. This 'suit could be worn under his Customs shipsuit without discomfort.

He was running a pressure test when Harris arrived with Molly Quinn and another man.

"Fabien, I will not be working with you today," Harris said. "Molly, here, will substitute for me. I want to introduce you to this gentleman, Mr. Colin Schofield of the Interdiction Office. He and I have some business today, but I wanted you two to meet."

Loche rose and extended his hand. "Good to meet you, Mr. Schofield."

Schofield returned the shake. "And you, too."

Harris didn't explain Schofield's presence further. They left the locker room, leaving Molly behind.

"You ready?" she asked. Her skinsuit and neck ring were visible above her shipsuit's collar.

"As soon as I finish this last test. I've not worn this skinsuit before, and I needed to run it through the full set of diagnostics before I leave the office." He was holding a small testing module plugged into a socket on the skinsuit's arm, and it beeped as he was speaking. "All done."

"Put it on, and let's be off," she said.

Loche looked around the locker room, seeking a place where he could strip and roll on his skinsuit.

Molly watched him searching for a refuge. "Get moving, Fabien. I've seen naked men before."

Not me, you haven't. He knew no nudity taboo existed in the station, but he hadn't expected her to be there. He turned his back and followed her instructions.

†††

"What is the Interdiction Office?" Loche asked Quinn as they descended to Deck One, where the *C'seine* was docked.

"They are a part of the Customs Service, as we and the station patrollers are. They would be the equivalent of your System States Security Service—counterintelligence, spies sometimes. They fill in the gap for those areas not covered by patrollers and inspectors. I was surprised to see him. Most of the time, Uncle Donal handles that."

"Uncle Donal?"

"Not many know my uncle is the resident Interdiction agent. You need to know because you will work with him." She paused. "I shouldn't have said that. He would have told you when he thought you should know."

Loche considered her answer. "I think I know why he hasn't. I'm still on probation, and I don't think he's accepted me yet."

"He can be reserved. At least he calls you by your first name. He didn't for Thomas his first year. Then one day it was 'Hey, Thomas' instead of 'Hey, Leboe.'"

They arrived at the ship. Customs agents were clustered around the lock, waiting for Loche and Quinn to arrive. One agent, seeing their approach, thumbed a pad next to the ship's lock to signal the crew that the agents were ready to begin the inspection.

The lock opened, and the agents filed inside. One senior agent unfolded a portable desk and linked into the ship's network. The ship's captain presented a liberty schedule and crew list. Some agents began checking the crew members who wanted access to the station. Loche read the crewlist and noted that two crew members did not want liberty.

He held the list before Quinn and raised an eyebrow. "This happen often? When I was in the Marines, we couldn't wait to get off ship. There's nothing to show these two are under punishment."

"Captain," she called. "Why are these two not taking liberty?"

The captain looked at the list. "Oh. Those two were caught with a still they'd hidden in the environmental section. I'm having them rebuild the scrubbers while we're in port."

"Thank you," Molly replied then motioned Loche to follow her toward the cargo bay. "An acceptable story," she said, "but given this ship's history, I'm skeptical of any explanation he'd make. I've made a note for the agents to interview them anyway. Let's head for the cargo section."

The ship, like most freighters, had a dozen cargo bays, some pressurized, some not. Perishable cargos were kept in pressurized bays. According to the ship's manifest, the *C'seine* had, for this trip, four pressurized bays and one unpressurized bay, the latter containing heavy equipment. The unpresssurized bay was sealed. It was just passing through the Confederation on its way to its final destination in the Hive.

Fabien and Molly started in the first bay. The container codes matched the ship's manifest. She chose one cargo container at random. They opened it and made a detailed inspection. All the contents matched the manifest and codes. Loche picked a smaller three-meter container. Its contents also matched the manifest.

They had almost finished three of the four cargo bays by midshift. Something about the third bay troubled Loche, but he couldn't say what. "Molly... anything about this bay seem... unusual?"

"Unusual? How?" she asked, looking up from where she was scanning the ID codes of a container.

"I... I don't know. This bay is standard, right?" All freight was shipped in standard cargo containers. Items larger than a standard container were carried outside the hull in strap-on pods. This ship didn't have any strap-on pods. At least, none were listed.

Molly checked the ship's documents. "Yes, it is a Molean-class freighter—standard bays. It was built right here in Caledonia, in the inner-belt McLean shipyard, as a matter of fact."

Something wasn't right. The bay's deck was covered by three-meter square plates. The plates reduced damage to the ship and cargo during loading and unloading and protected fiber conduits and environmental piping that ran the length of the ship. The cargo bay should have been 150 meters long. The plates should have ended flush with the bulkheads. They didn't. He instructed his link to measure the bay. The answer popped up on his HUD: 148.8 meters. He ran another check of the bay's height. It too was 1.2 meters less than expected.

"Have you ever seen a bay this size?" he asked Molly, sending the data to her link.

"Well, there's some variance..." She looked at the numbers. "But not this much."

Over the customs primary channel, she announced, "This is Inspectors Quinn and Loche. We are declaring a lockdown of the System States freighter *C'seine*. Justification is unreported ship modifications to a cargo bay, requiring a full inspection of ship and cargo."

She and Loche walked back to the lock to await reinforcements. They arrived to find a section of patrollers at the lock with Donal Harris and Colin Schofield.

"What do you have?" Harris asked.

"The interior dimensions of the third cargo bay are smaller than standard. The difference is enough to hide several thousand cubic meters of space," she reported.

Colin Schofield arrived with Donal Harris following a few steps behind. "At last," Schofield said, grinning and rubbing his hands together. "Anyone want to wager we'll find contraband hidden there?"

The ship's captain was complaining behind them. "You have no authority! We're a System States ship!"

Loche turned to face him. "Authority? I have the authority," he said, pointing to the System States patch on his shipsuit. "I declare this ship to be locked down until we complete a bow-to-stern inspection of this ship." That statement quieted the captain.

"How did you find it?" Harris asked Molly.

"I didn't. He did," she answered, pointing at Loche.

"Oh?" Harris asked, looking at Loche.

"Something was wrong," Loche said. "I didn't know what until I noticed some deck plates were smooth and flat. Others looked… bowed, buckled, not what you'd expect of deck plates attached to a ship's frame. I saw something like it when I was in the Marines, when we boarded a suspected smuggler and caught them hiding contraband under the deck plates. They hadn't expected us to act so quick. Anyway… the deck plates here looked like they had been removed and reseated, and I wondered why. That and they didn't end flush with the bulkheads. They should have."

"Good job," Schofield said. "Now, if you don't mind, I'll take over. I've been waiting for this opportunity to run this ship through the mill—a very fine mill at that."

"We're not finished," Loche reminded him. "There are still two cargo bays to be checked. One is unpressurized."

"I'm not suited up," Schofield said. "Check that last pressurized bay and the external hull. There may be some strap-ons not on the manifest. Donal and one of his agents will take that last, unpressurized one."

Molly looked at Harris. He nodded. Schofield didn't have authority to order customs inspectors to do anything. However, rather than make an issue of Schofield's breach of protocol, Harris allowed it to stand.

"We're on it," she said.

†††

The contents of the remaining cargo bays matched the manifest—a dismantled robotic factory to refine various ores. The factory would be assembled in space at its destination. Once it was activated, it would control robotic collectors to gather the raw material. The factory would process metallic asteroids to refine useful and valuable metals and send them to a collection point in the system via a Holmann transfer orbit.

Quinn ordered a small maintenance vehicle, called a clown car, for their external inspection. The clown car was an unpressurized bubble with basic thrusters, navigation systems, communications repeater, and a supplemental air supply for their skinsuits. It also included a pair of remote arms—useful if they found something too big or bulky to manhandle without help.

Strap-on pods came in various sizes and were attached to the hull where reinforced hardpoints were located. That did not mean pods could not be attached elsewhere. In fact, the definition of the term 'strap-on pod' was broad. A strap-on pod was anything attached to the external hull. Most often, that meant cargo pods, but it could be anything. In some areas of the frontier, freighters added weapons pods for more protection.

The *C'seine* was docked via its bow. They started their inspection at the aft shunt nodes and worked their way forward, proceeding in a spiral around the hull. They found a pod at frame eleven.

"I'm seeing an anomaly. Power leakage too," said Quinn.

They slowed the clown car until it hovered over a long bulge on the hull. To Loche's eye, it appeared to be sixty meters long and sixty meters wide, rising ten meters above the hull. It blended into the hull with no sharp corners, unlike a standard cargo pod. It was minuscule compared to the 1500-meter length of the freighter and easy to overlook on a superficial scan. Loche switched to the Customs Service private channel and reported the find to Harris and Schofield.

Harris acknowledged their call. "Mark it and leave a beacon. A pod that size could hold thirty thousand cubic meters or more of contraband. Schofield says he wants to see it opened. He's suiting up now. Finish your inspection, and then join him unless you find more. I've placed the crew in detention. I want to see what we find before we begin interrogation."

†††

Loche and Quinn continued their inspection. Near one of the small maintenance locks, they found another pod. This one was different, a habitat pod used in shipyards to allow workers to recharge their suits, have a pressurized refuge, or provide an emergency shelter. This one was small, suitable for a dozen people.

Molly reported the find to Harris while Loche guided the clown car carefully around the pod. He could detect no power usage, no external signs of actual habitation. The small access hatch on the pod was closed but not secured. The clown car's instruments detected a higher than normal gas density near the access hatch—more than could be accounted for by normal leakage.

Harris came up on their private channel. "Does it appear to be occupied?"

"No," Loche responded. "It appears to be shut down—no power detected. Our onboard instruments indicate the pod hatch has been opened not long ago."

"Check it out and report."

"Aye—" Loche caught himself. He'd fallen into an old reflex. "Will do."

65

He switched to the intercom channel he and Quinn used. "Have you had training for vacuum assault?"

"No."

"I have. I'll go first. Let's switch to solid ammo. Frangibles won't penetrate a skinsuit. I suspect if we find anyone, their skinsuit will diffuse a laser."

"'Kay."

"There may be another hatch. It's doubtful, but watch to make sure we're not flanked. I'll report as I check the pod. Repeat this channel to Harris. One final thing. If there is someone in there, and they get me, leave. Don't rescue me. Don't come in. Stand off, call Harris for reinforcements, and observe. If anyone comes out besides me, keep in shadow, observe, report, and follow."

Old habits were emerging. Quinn was senior, but in this situation, Loche had the training. Unconsciously, he had taken the lead.

†††

Loche hovered above the pod, using his suit thrusters to approach the hatch. The control pad next to the hatch was dark and unresponsive. *If anyone is inside, he must know I'm here.* Sensors would have alerted any inhabitants that they were approaching.

Below the pad was a lever to open the hatch if the pod was unpowered. He secured his suit to two mooring rings and opened the hatch into an airlock. The pad next to the interior hatch was also dark. He slipped inside and opened a plate next to the rear hatch pad. Inside was a test valve. He inserted a probe through the valve. Zero pressure.

"Molly, tell Harris the pod is in vacuum. I'm going in. Keep alert. Whoever was here may still be outside."

After she acknowledged, Loche entered the pod, holding a hand light out to one side, at arm's length. He didn't want to provide an aiming point in case someone was still there. He flashed the light in all directions as he moved forward into the pod. It appeared to be empty. Some remnants, trash, were floating around. He checked the entire pod and found no one, nothing except evidence that someone—several people—had been there. He exited and returned to the clown car. Quinn rose from the hull and entered behind him.

"Inspector Harris," he reported, "the pod is empty. Counting the bunks, it looks like there may have been six people inside. I'm thinking they left the pod as soon as the *C'seine* docked."

"I agree. I'll have our systems people check all the station hatch logs. They had to come in somewhere. We know they didn't enter through the *C'seine*. Schofield is heading your way with some troops. Come back inside when he arrives. It looks like our job here is done... for now."

†††

Molly had had a long and tiring day. She stood before her locker and carefully peeled her skinsuit down her body. She was sore and chafed from the suit's sanitary hookup. *Men have it so easy*. She looked forward to a long, hot shower; maybe some sauna and whirlpool time later; then bed. She placed her skinsuit in the maintenance cubby to be cleaned and recharged and was heading for the shower with only a towel over her shoulder when she received a call through her link.

<Molly, how are you?> her uncle asked.

"Tired and sore, as you should know," she said sharply. "You've spent enough time suited and outside to know that."

<I just wanted to get your impression of Fabien Loche. I didn't have any time to observe him today.>

"He did well, much better than I thought he would. He caught those smuggler hideouts when I didn't notice them."

<How did he act? He's been quiet all week, and I wanted to get your impression.>

"He started out that way this morning. But once we arrived at the *C'seine,* he was more assertive, starting when the *C'seine*'s captain started complaining. Then later, when we found the strap-ons, he knew what to do—his Essie training, I suppose. He took charge. It was like he was another person… No, that's not right. It was as if he… was reverting to an old role, a comfortable one. He wasn't hesitant or indecisive at all."

<That's good to hear. I've been trying to get a feel for him and wanted your impressions.>

"He looks good to me, Uncle Donal."

<Thank you, Molly. It's always best to get additional opinions.>

"I'll have more opportunities tomorrow. I invited him shopping."

<You invited him shopping?> Harris sounded surprised.

"Yes. He needs some things. You should have done it. You know that."

<I've been busy,> Harris protested.

"Well, since you didn't, I did. Oh, don't worry about the *Proprieties*. I'll follow all the social necessities. I'm taking Amilie along."

Harris didn't respond at first. *<Good. That should do>* He sighed. *<I shouldn't have met him on arrival, but we were tight on people.>*

"I know, Uncle Donal. I'm not blaming you, but it has created a situation."

Harris sighed again. *<Yeah. At least Amilie understands. She'll maintain the* Proprieties.*>*

"Yes." Molly snorted. "I expect she will. Or embarrass us all." Molly broke the connection and wondered, as she entered the shower stall, *How did I let myself get into this situation?* Fabien had surprised her. He seemed attracted to her, and she was… interested, intrigued, attracted to him. She wasn't sure what she felt but decided she did want to know more about Fabien Loche, House DuQuoin, of the Thirty Houses.

Chapter 4. Interlude

Dundee Orbital, 1 Fivemonth, 3203

Loche's first week had been busy—revelations had compounded more revelations. Harris and Schofield had been correct—contraband filled the *C'seine*. When the bulkheads and overheads were exposed, over twelve tons of blueleaf were found, along with another ten tons of small arms, ammunition, and ammunition components, plus other military munitions. The external strap-on pods excited Schofield and Harris more. Inside the larger pod were twenty nukes, from subkiloton demolition devices to several multimegaton city/ship killers. The pod also contained an autofac, with spares and components, to produce mobile artillery, missiles and launchers, from manpad fire-and-forget antiaircraft missiles to larger ground-based particle-beam antiship weapons. The personnel pod contained other information sources, including DNA and nannite samples.

Someone was stoking a rebellion or a war. According to the manifest, the *C'seine* was carrying cargo from Perriman in the System States. That origin appeared to be false—at least on first examination. The ship's internal systems had been scrubbed and overlaid with false data. None of the onboard consumables were from the System States. If the *C'seine*'s last port of call had been in the System States, they should have provisioned at their last port, and the ship's provisions should have been produced in the System States.

Schofield was working to determine the freighter's real origin and destination. He doubted it was intended for the Hive. The *C'seine* was a false-flag operation.

The two crewmen working punishment were missing as well. Under interrogation, Schofield determined the two were the actual captain and navigator. The "captain" who'd greeted Quinn and Loche was a fraud. The captain and navigator were added to the search for those in the habitat pod. Forensic techs said six people had been in the pod, at least one female. None of the lock scanners revealed entry by a group. Most of the use was by maintenance teams. The unknowns had separated and entered as pairs to mimic maintenance crews. They would be found. *Sooner rather than later, with Harris overseeing the task.*

†††

Today's exercise was storming a warship. Loche's team was to enter via a personnel lock and move toward the engine room. Loche was in the middle. Three marines had passed through the lock before him. Then it was his turn. He was halfway through when the rising hatch stopped. Loche had one leg through, but something blocked him. He couldn't move forward. The rest of his team was behind, pushing Loche forward. He couldn't move forward and couldn't move back.

The hatch started downward. Try as he might, Loche couldn't move. Down the hatch came. He could hear the armor encasing his leg creak...

Fabien sat up, panting, drenched in sweat. That was a different dream—not of Reena. He checked the time. *Too early.* His meeting with Molly and Amilie was still hours away.

Gah! Loche stood and walked to the small cooler in the kitchen and picked up a bottle of tea. His mouth was dry. Water would not do.

He walked around the room, reluctant to return to bed. Instead, he sat in his recliner, raised the legs, and settled back. He sipped tea from the bottle. A few minutes later, he set the bottle on the side table and settled back to sleep.

†††

Today was Loche's day off, and he was going to acquire some personal items, a pistol, a holster, and a knife. Thomas Leboe had given Loche the address of a weapons dealer on station, and Molly had volunteered to accompany him. He knew weapons. She knew the local prices and the local arms providers.

They met for breakfast at a small family eatery off the main Deck-Twelve concourse in Torus Four. Like many of the small businesses in Dundee Orbital, it was a family affair. A teenage girl greeted him. Her name, according to the tag on her blouse, matched the name of the restaurant. She led him toward the rear of the restaurant, past the bar and the current off-shift crowd, toward an area reserved for families and others sitting for their initial meal of the day. Loche gazed toward the rear of the restaurant. An older couple was serving that alcove, the man cooking and the woman delivering food orders to tables.

Quinn was early and had secured a table off to one side. She was not alone, Loche saw. Amilie Schute was there, too, and was laughing at some remark of Quinn's when he walked up to their table.

"Hello, Molly… Amilie," he said when Quinn asked him to join them. He was still unused to greeting women by their given names. *I must acclimate to this culture, my new home.* Loche sat and scooted his chair closer to the table as a menu appeared on its surface at his touch. "Have you two ordered?"

"No," Quinn said, "we just arrived."

"I didn't expect to see you today, Amilie."

She laughed and pointed at Quinn. "I'm her duenna."

Duenna? He wasn't aware one was needed. *Does the word mean the same as the one I know?* "What do you mean?"

"Ah, you really are from the System States," she declared. "Molly is unmarried, and you haven't been formally introduced—socially introduced to Molly's clan. Work aside, it isn't proper for you two to be seen alone together in public until you've been introduced and acknowledged by her clan—especially a clanless one like yourself. It just isn't done."

Loche had not expected such a custom, but he wasn't surprised. At home, the station line mothers, the matriarchs, resolved such situations— just a dinner invitation with a Line Mother present, and it was done, quietly and efficiently. Most outsiders never realized the purpose of the invitation was to allow the outsider to be vetted. Loche had not expected to find similar traditions on Dundee Orbital. *Perhaps there aren't that many differences between here and home.*

"How is that done… here?" He noticed Quinn appeared to be blushing… or maybe it was just the lighting.

"The usual fashion," Amilie replied, "is for Molly, or perhaps her representative, to introduce you to a senior family member. In her case, here, that would be her uncle, Donal Harris. However, Donal has already been introduced to you as a customs official. He met you on entry. Now, neither Molly nor I can introduce you to him. It'd be a case of the cart going before the horse. If he was here, it would be easy, but he's not. That's why I'm here."

"You are our chaperone?"

Amilie grinned and said nothing.

Loche found he was comfortable with Amilie Schute. Her responses were reminiscent of one of his older cousins, who when she and Loche were together, had developed a habit of exchanging quips, each trying to one-up the other.

He raised an eyebrow toward Amilie, trying to hide his embarrassment while attempting not to laugh. Amilie returned his raised eyebrow. Molly, watching the other two, attempted to raise one of hers... and failed. She could not raise just one eyebrow. Both went up, giving her a surprised appearance. Loche was watching Molly's attempts when he was distracted by snorts. Amilie was trying, unsuccessfully, to control a laugh. She failed and began laughing, louder by the moment. Loche felt one bubbling inside, trying to escape. He controlled himself until he saw the corner of Molly's mouth quiver. She, too, started laughing. With that, Loche lost control, and all three of them were laughing.

Amilie had her head down on the table, shoulders shaking. She would raise her head, wipe her eyes, and look at Molly, who was still laughing. The two would pause, look at one another, and begin laughing once more. Loche wasn't sure how long the action-reaction continued. He was caught up too.

Eventually, the laughter subsided. Molly was wheezing, Loche almost the same. Amilie watched the two, wiping her eyes and blowing her nose into a tissue retrieved from a hidden source.

When Molly regained her composure and could speak, she cleared her throat and told Loche, "Let me explain about the duenna if I can. It's our tradition… No, that's not right. It's our… Let me start over. I didn't think it'd be so hard to say to an outsider."

She blew her nose again, this time with a tissue provided by Amilie, and started once more, "W… when the first colonists… arrived—" She wheezed, recovering. "We colonized by groups that evolved into clans. Each clan selected a specific area, a territory of their own. The landing sites were purposely chosen to be isolated from each other to prevent interclan issues arising from competition for water, mineral, agricultural resources, and all that. It worked for a century until the clans expanded and bumped into each other. Some clans, like the McLeans, selected good, resource-rich sites. The McLeans had the sea for food, water and minerals in the mountains, but not as much land suitable for towns, steadings, and crops. The territory was, however, sufficient to our needs.

"Other clans did not plan well. Several of them were mistaken about the availability or quantity of resources in their territories. When those that had met those who did not, conflicts arose. We call the next few centuries after colonization 'the War Years.' It wasn't constant conflicts. It was more of a jousting for resources, but some clans resorted to conquest. We lost several clans during that period although most were lost through assimilation with the winners.

"That period was when most of our customs and traditions began. Clans created alliances, mutual protection pacts. They guarded their fellows from outsiders." She paused to wipe her eyes once more.

Amilie took over the conversation. "This tradition, among others, still exists. In our case, you are an outsider. It's against Custom and Tradition for her"—she nodded toward Quinn—"to meet socially with an outsider, alone. That is why I am here. Not only is my clan, Clan Mieze, allied with Clan McLean, I am Molly's cousin. Hence, I am here to 'guard her back.' I was joking when I said I was her duenna, but it is close to the truth. We call these traditions, the social ones in particular, the *Proprieties*. Some clans print and teach them as part of their educational curriculum."

That explained several unspoken questions he had. The situation was not all that different from home, he decided as he idly rubbed the ache in his right knee and leg under the table. "Will I always be an outsider? If we have another outing, will there be a *Duenna*?"

Molly answered, "No, the usual circumstance is to introduce you to a senior member of the clan—a formal social introduction. Thereafter, you would be an individual, recognized, vetted so to speak, by the clan. If Uncle Donal hadn't had to work on that freighter, it could have happened today."

Loche was puzzled. "But I've already been introduced to your uncle."

"That was work—business. It is not the same. Custom and Tradition demands that you must be introduced in a social environment, outside work. It is the public acknowledgement of a personal relationship between the individual and the clan… that you are not a stranger. It would have been easy if Uncle Donal were here… but he couldn't be. I invited Amilie along instead."

Loche understood. "I need to get a copy of the *Proprieties*. Are they the same for every clan?"

"For the most part," Amilie replied.

Loche made another mental memo to acquire a copy. His to-do list was growing.

They ordered. Their table was near a portable grill where menu items could be prepared to order. The older man was supervising several younger cooks, more family members, by their appearance. The menu was traditional fare for Inverness: meats, sausages, eggs, hot cereals, cheeses, breads, and muffins with fresh fruit grown in Dundee's hydroponic gardens and farms in the agricultural toruses.

A waiter brought a selection on a portable cart. He lifted the covers, and they pointed at their choices. Perhaps Loche was too used to automated cooking, having meals delivered or produced by an autochef. Seeing food prepared by a human cook and delivered by a live waiter was a welcome change.

They finished their meal quickly. Molly kept silent, mostly. Amilie, however, regaled him with tales of Molly's childhood and events. At home, Amilie would have been acting like a line matriarch. *Is there such here?* It was a question that begged an answer.

†††

The weapons shop was on the third deck of the fifth torus, according to Leboe's message. It was one of several shops near the industrial segment that catered to individuals. This shop, Peatres', had a large selection of weapons from across the three clusters of the Confederacy. The counter held dueling knives, some dirks, and specialty knives. The dueling knives were all of a kind, standard ten-centimeter length with some minor differences in grip and blade quality. Some were doubled-edged, but most were not. He found one with a permanent double edge, made of an alloy resistant to breakage in the cold of vacuum.

Like all System State Marines, he was trained to use a knife in offense and defense. This one included a sheath that could be strapped to his forearm or leg or attached to a belt or harness. The initial price seemed adequate to Loche, but Amilie and Quinn negotiated a discount—a very sizeable discount.

The pistol was next. Loche had intended to buy one similar to his service pistol. Like all current military sidearms, it was basic, lacking optical sights and ballistic circuitry that could be spoofed. Molly disagreed. If that was what Loche wanted, he could carry his service sidearm, she said. However, most Confederates preferred smaller, smarter weapons. She scanned the display case and selected several models. She agreed with one of Loche's requirements—all were ten millimeter and used the same ammunition as his service pistol.

He narrowed the field to one, a Moen Magister made in the Confederation's Montchard Cluster. It was similar to his service pistol but a little smaller, lighter, and easier to carry and featured holographic sights with a threat-assessment computer. The holo aiming dot changed color when the pistol was at the center of the target. It felt right. Potential threats were outlined in the holosight, color coded by priority of the threat.

The proprietor led them to a holographic pistol range in the shop's rear. He programmed a series of random targets. When one appeared, Loche would fire. The range's systems would determine his score and other factors such as the speed of his draw.

"At the beep, draw and fire as appropriate," the man said.

At first, nothing happened. The range beeped, and a target appeared—a child holding some packages. The holosight outlined the child in green. He reholstered his pistol and waited. Another target appeared, a man outlined in red pointing a gun toward Loche. He drew and fired at the target's center of mass. Before he could reholster, another red target appeared to his left, that one holding a long-arm. He fired as soon as he found the center of the target. More targets appeared at random locations. Some, like the first, were children, women, or unarmed men. Most were not. The range beeped again after Loche fired the last round in the magazine.

"Not bad at all," the proprietor said, examining Loche's score. "Your initial draw was slow, but that will change with practice. You should not have reholstered until you were sure there were no threats. Your target discrimination was excellent! How did the pistol feel to you?"

"Good. I'm not used to a pistol that classifies threats automatically," Loche admitted. "What is the rate of false positives? I wouldn't want to shoot an innocent."

"That feature is proprietary to the Moen. There has never been a false positive or negative proven. There have been instances where the target was correctly declared hostile when the user wasn't aware of it being a threat. Moen, in their warranty, includes liability coverage for as long as you own the weapon. There are few used Moens on the market. We have a few customers who don't like the threat-assessment feature. It can be turned off."

"I'm one of them," Loche replied. "I can't conceive of any veteran who would use that option." From the corner of his eye, he saw Quinn nodding.

"Told you so," Quinn said, grinning.

Amilie shook her head, reached into a pocket, and gave Quinn a coin.

The price of the pistol was high, over a hundred Confederate dollars, higher than he had expected. Once again, the two women stepped in, worked their way on the proprietor. Amilie, with more business experience as a Customs Service quartermaster, negotiated a sizable discount and concluded the deal. Loche left the shop wearing the knife strapped to his left forearm, his Moen in a holster hidden under the drape of his shirt, and two loaded magazines in a side pocket. His remaining purchases—more magazines, ammunition, and another holster for his service pistol—would be shipped to his quarters. His financial account was lower, but his purchases were worth the cost.

Outside the shop, Quinn stopped him. "Let's get that pin off you." She took the pin from his shirt and dropped it into his hand. "Keep it as a souvenir. You shouldn't need it again."

A thought occurred to him. "What about a laser? What if I'm ever challenged with a laser?"

"That's rare," she responded. "It's against the *Proprieties* to challenge with a weapon the other doesn't have. Mediators won't allow it. You could, if you wished, carry your service laser in civilian mode, but most of us don't bother. Anyone who challenges us can choose knives or a pistol—and lose."

They continued to stroll through the level. Ahead was a concourse with several drinking establishments. As they approached, he noticed a ship's crew had taken temporary possession of one such establishment—to the consternation of its regulars.

Two station patrollers were already present. "Hello, Quinn," said one. "We don't see you here often."

"What's going on, Sean?"

"Ah, the usual. The crew of the *St. Marie* arrived last shift. They have decided that the Clan and Crown is theirs, exclusively. You know the drill."

"Yes, I've seen it before." She turned to Loche. "It's a favorite of some crews. They will select a pub, throw everyone out, and then dare anyone to enter. A brawl is often the result."

"What will you do? Stop it?"

The patroller laughed and shook his head. "Not as long as there is no damage, no real injuries. I've talked the two parties to a duel of One-Punch."

"What's that?" Loche asked.

"Each group selects a champion. They exchange single punches until one of them is knocked down. The challenged gets the first punch. If the challenger goes down on the first punch, he gets one chance to knock the other down. If he does, they continue to exchange one blow until one goes down—if he can't, it's over."

The two sides chose their champions. The regulars' champion was stocky, almost stubby. Loche suspected he may have been a heavy-worlder. The other, chosen by the *St. Marie's* crewmen was big—very big.

"He's a warehouseman," Sean the patroller said of the shorter man. "I've seen him pick up a one-hundred-kilo crate in each hand and carry them off... I think he's from Clairmont."

"Clairmont is a heavy planet, about one point five gees," added Quinn.

The crewman had the first punch. The patroller had them stand a meter apart. Friends, opponents, and lookers-on surrounded them.

"First blow!" Sean shouted, pointing at the crewman.

The crewman eyed the shorter man for an instant, drew his fist back to his shoulder, and let loose. The punch made the shorter man slip back a step. He shook his head a moment, working his tongue around in his mouth. He spat something into his palm, eyed it, and grinned. "Keep this," he said, handing the tooth to the patroller. "I'll want it back later."

Then it was the challenger's turn. Both stepped forward to stand one meter apart.

Sean nodded to the shorter of the two. "Your turn."

"You ready?" the short man asked. His large opponent nodded.

Loche was watching, and he still missed the punch thrown by the short dockworker. His fist was a blur. The big crewman seemed to stretch and fell backward with a thud felt through the station's deck.

Sean, the patroller, walked over and knelt by the large dueler. "Out, cold… and I think he has a broken jaw," he said. After calling medics, he stood, looking disappointed. The cost of the medics would be charged against the dueling bond, lessening the amount left for the patroller's mediator fee.

Loche watched wagers change hands amongst the audience. He noticed the patroller collecting a few personal winnings too. *Gamblers.* The thought made him curious. "Have you ever been challenged?" he asked Quinn.

She didn't answer at once. "That's a subject we rarely talk about. I've dueled once… when I was younger. I may tell you about it sometime. Amilie, here, has dueled several times."

Amilie? That surprised him. He turned to look at her. She seemed… matronly. His glance caught her grinning.

"Yep. That's me," she said with an impish glint in her eye. "I was much younger and rowdier then. Hot tempered too."

She caught Loche's surprise. "Long story," she said. "I was in a feud—another woman and her family. It was a stupid thing. After a few duels—no one killed, just shot up a bit—they wanted to end it. I didn't. Then one day, I had a visit by my uncle who was our local sept chief. He laid down the law and said if I challenged them one more time, I'd have to take the pin, or the clan would kick me out." She looked thoughtful for a moment. "It was a sobering moment. I'd never thought about it—the duels. Most of them were of stupid things. Others thought so too." She sighed. "I've not challenged anyone since."

"You're still armed?"

"Well, of course. I'm not some old lady who isn't fit to stand up for herself! I didn't say I wouldn't duel anymore, just that I'd not challenge anyone… who didn't need it."

"Has anyone needed it?"

"Not yet," she said, patting a bulge on her hip, "but I'm ready if it happens."

Loche asked Molly, "How often do duels happen? I mean… I've been here a week, and I've already witnessed two. Should I always be prepared?"

"Not all that often. Uncle Donal said the one you saw was for show. There hasn't been a serious duel in… Amilie, you remember?"

"Well," she said, "there was one last year in Hierdahl. That duel ended badly. Both died. I can't think of any since."

"The last one on station that had any real injuries was four months ago, I think. This one doesn't come close to counting. Sean just used a tactic to keep the peace. The losers will relinquish the pub for this shift. Most likely, the two groups will buy each other drinks now that the duel is over. The one I was thinking of was between two ship crews. It started as a bar fight and ended with a challenge. The challenged was unarmed and chose fists. He beat the other so badly he had to be hospitalized."

"Why dueling? What made it… common?"

"It arose, like most of our Customs and Traditions, during the War Years," Molly said. "When more and more interclan contacts occurred, there had to be some way to resolve personal, sometimes business, conflicts without engaging the entire clan in a protective or offensive response and counter-response. Individual dueling was proposed to keep the carnage and the conflict limited and controlled. Once a code duello was proposed, the clans saw that it could serve a purpose, a means to minimize violence that could spill over into a broader conflict. We didn't have a central government then—still don't. We have a Council of Clans that has some functions of a central government—as long as the individual clans agree."

Chalk up another revelation, Loche decided. He could see the logic of the tradition. He could also see where such a tradition could have averted some social stresses at home. That no longer mattered to Loche as he was no longer in the System States.

†††

The morning passed, and the day progressed into afternoon. Trams and transit tubes allowed them to move around Dundee with ease. One area of the residential segment was a large, open park complete with grass for team sports, picnics, and play areas. One part was built up for climbing. Another was modified to duplicate a mountain stream complete with fish. Catch-and-release fishing was available for those so inclined.

The park also contained a swimming area with a UV-lighted beach. Loche was surprised to see nude sunbathing of both genders.

Molly guessed his unspoken question. "No, I don't sunbathe," she said with a grin. "With my complexion, I'd be toast—I don't tan."

"I brought the kids and Andreas here last week. Andreas had the weekend off, and we spent the entire day here," Amilie said

"Andreas is Amilie's husband," Molly explained. "He owns and operates a local freighter—inner worlds to the belt stations—and gets home about every ten days."

"Yes, it was quite a day. Yonnie, my oldest girl, caught a fifty-centimeter striper in the fishing stream," Amilie said, pointing with her chin.

They continued to explore the recreation level. The Dundee Orchestra and Choir were giving a concert in an open area at one edge of the park. "The Choir is famous across the Confederation. They just returned from a tour of the Franklin Republic and the Montchard Cluster," Amilie said. "They are best known for their a cappella pieces."

The concert began. Loche had never seen a live musical performance. The houses were too busy to spend time on… frivolous activities—more so since the beginning of the unofficial embargo of the outstations and colonies. Listening to the concert made him more aware how Spartan life in the SolSystem belt stations had become.

Molly, Fabien, and Amilie left the concert area, their path taking them to a small zoo.

"It is a petting zoo," Molly explained. "Many of the children have never seen any living beings except for people. This zoo lets them have contact with our pets."

"Pets?" Loche asked.

"Yes. All of these animals are owned by individuals who loan them to the zoo."

Amilie walked inside the enclosure. "Willow!" she called.

From the rear shadows, a large tan-striped feline head appeared, followed by the rest of the body. It raced toward Amilie and leaped into her arms, causing her to stagger a few steps.

"That's Willow, a lurcat that lives with Amilie's family."

"What's a lurcat?"

"They are intelligent hybrid felines bred for vermin control and biosphere management on Inverness. The original colonists allowed some rodents loose that created havoc throughout the ecosphere after the first colonization. Geneticists combined DNA from *felis domesticus*, the common house cat, from the Norwegian Forest cat, the Canadian lynx, and the American mountain lion or *felis concolor*, with some human DNA thrown in the mix.

"The result was the lurcat, *felis inverness*, puma size when grown, with the nature and personality of a house cat. Downbelow, they manage the environment from being overrun when a species gets out of balance with the ecosystem. Willow is still young, not in her full growth. Her pride sent her here to observe how humans live in space and in stations."

Willow stood on the ground with her front paws on Amilie's shoulders as she rubbed and finger scratched the tan-striped head. The lurcat's purring was audible from ten meters away. Another tan-and-black lurcat had appeared and was butting its head against Amilie's hip.

"That is Daisy, another lurcat that lives with Amilie. She comes to the petting zoo several times a month. The children like them because they're so playful."

Willow was now rubbing her head against Amilie's cheek while Amilie rubbed and scratched Daisy's head. Molly drew him over to the lurcats. Willow turned her head to watch him approach. She dropped to the ground and sat, waiting for Loche to arrive.

The lurcat was larger than any cat he had ever seen, other than in images. It must have massed at least fifty kilograms and was over two meters from nose to tail.

Reowr, The lurcat said and waved its paws in a pattern.

"Just scratch her ears. She likes that."

Loche complied and was rewarded with a rumble from the cat.

"Lurcats purr. The other large cats, like lions, leopards, and tigers, don't. We have some of them downbelow for a genetic library, but they can't be trusted like lurcats."

"Look at this." Molly picked up one of Willow's front paws and turned it over. She pressed something, and three-centimeter claws emerged.

"Urg! Those can be dangerous," Loche said.

"Yes. Notice that Amilie has blunted them."

Loche looked more closely. All the claws had been rounded, smoothed. They were still intact and could still bruise, maybe tear if necessary, but blunted as they were, they were much less dangerous to people, clothes, and furniture. He also noticed the paw had an opposable thumb.

"Amilie said she got tired of being scratched and having her clothes torn. She uses the same material for her clothes now that is used for our uniforms and shipsuits. Cheaper, she says, in the long term. Did you notice her paws have opposable thumbs?"

"I saw that, but I didn't understand what they were." He mused. "Does that mean…"

"Yes. They are tool users. They understand but can't speak human languages due to the shape of their mouths. However, they can communicate using sign language. It's taught in all schools downbelow. Some lurcats have links too. We consider them to be a sapient species."

"Do any lurcats live with you?" Loche asked.

"Not here," Molly replied.

†††

They returned to Loche's home level and walked toward his quarters. When they reached the final corridor that led to his quarters, Molly and Amilie followed. He was about to ask them why when Mollie laughed at his expression.

"I'm on my home level," she said. "I live here, too, you know."

"Where?"

"A few doors down from you. Didn't you know? All the singles, the unmarried Customs people, live here."

"The thought never occurred to me. This is the first… It isn't 'home' yet, but it's the first permanent residence I've had since, well, before my time in the Marines."

"I think you'll fit in. Stop at the concourse in the evening. We often gather there."

"I'll do that."

†††

Loche stopped at the door to his apartment, watching Molly and Amilie continue down the corridor. He palmed the door pad and entered to discover a man sitting in his lounger.

"Hello, Mr. Loche," Colin Schofield said. "Your grandmother Celeste sends greetings."

He remembered. A post-hypnotic personality overlay implanted by the Seat disappeared when he heard the code phrase. A wind blew through his mind, clearing away a fog that had overlain his memory.

"And please return my greetings for the Grand Dam," he replied to Schofield, providing the correct response.

Loche suddenly had access to portions of his memories that had been... not hidden, just not accessible—memories that could not come to mind without a key. That constraint was gone.

Schofield was not alone. Loche noticed another standing in the dim rear of the compartment.

"Your Great Aunt Eloise sends her greetings as well," Donal Harris said.

Loche nodded. Harris's code phrase didn't require a verbal response. The two different phrases were significant. Harris's phrase indicated he could be trusted. Not so, the one uttered by Schofield. It contained no assurance of trust—it was a warning.

Schofield spoke again. "Welcome, Emissary."

"I'm not the Emissary," Loche replied. "The Emissary won't arrive until and unless it is time. I do not know who that may be nor when he will arrive—tomorrow, next week, or maybe never."

Harris walked forward to stand next to the seated Schofield. "I suppose we'll just have to wait, then."

Chapter 5. Firefight

Dundee Orbital, 2 Sixmonth, 3203

A month passed after Loche's private meeting with Schofield and
Harris in his coapt. Harris never mentioned it when they returned to their
rounds through the station. He continued to search for the intruders from
the *C'seine*. A series of break-ins and thefts throughout the station implied
they'd remained on station. Harris considered a complete, end-to-end
search, but that would require additional manpower. A complete station
scan was out of the question. Large segments of the light-industrial section
of the station were being reconfigured and had no security monitoring
systems.

He considered making a request for a company of marines to
augment his resources. That decision, however, turned out to be
unnecessary.

Loche observed the station's court in action. The Customs Service
charged the crew members from the *C'seine* with several offenses, mostly
minor. The most serious charge was smuggling prohibited munitions.
Demolition nukes, those in the subkiloton range, could be transported
under license, but not the larger ones, the city and ship killers.

Customs Director Demning acted as the justice and Schofield as the
Confederation advocate, with Clifford Tanaki acting as the defense
advocate for the System States crew. Loche, Quinn, and Harris appeared
as witnesses.

The trial was short. The testimonies of the three customs inspectors,
along with the evidence presented and confirmed by additional evidence
from many sources, were enough for conviction. Schofield and Tanaki
called more witnesses, asked more questions, and cross-examined each
witness. The defendants were given the opportunity, through Tanaki, to
present counterevidence, witnesses, or in the case of several of the
crewmen, a plea for clemency.

All were found guilty. No other alternative could be possible, with the overwhelming evidence. To Loche's mind, the sentences were light—various terms of labor at terraforming projects across the Confederacy. In the System States, weapons trafficking carried an automatic death sentence. The Confederate Judiciary would review the sentences, but that review would not halt the execution of any sentences except for death. The sentences were not that severe. Most of the prisoners were on their way to their penal sites within a day. Justice was quick in the Confederacy, he observed—lenient, perhaps, but quick and efficient.

The week following the trial, Loche, Harris, and several station patrollers conducted a sweep through the maintenance passageways of Decks Two and Three of Torus Four. They found plenty of evidence of occupancy. Most of the evidence, however, was months or, in some cases, years old. The break-ins of empty compartments were an ongoing issue with stowaways—stagnants, or Stags as they were commonly called. Stags were the station's social dropouts. Mostly, they were neither violent nor criminals. They performed day labor at the docks and other temporary physical labor in the station. They received enough compensation to meet their basic needs. Together, the Stags formed an underground society and economy that filled a niche within the station—an unwanted niche but a viable one, nonetheless.

They found the first real evidence of the intruders from the *C'seine* on Deck Two. One team swept through a section that, at one time, had been storerooms. Those rooms were sealed, reserved for future purpose. One room had been opened and had been the residence of three Stags. All three were still there, dead. Each Stag had been killed by a bullet to the head. Their meager belongings, food, links, stored water, were missing.

Patrollers did find bodies from time to time. Casualties occurred when Stag fought Stag over limited resources or because of some personal feud. In those cases, cause of death was usually blunt-force injury—beatings by hand and foot. These murders were not just violent theft—they were a warning to other Stags to mind their own business.

The intruders, spies, infiltrators—whichever label applied to them—escaped the sweep. The thefts and break-ins moved up station into the more densely occupied sections. Inevitably, they would be discovered.

They were, three days later.

†††

Loche and Harris were patrolling Deck Four of Torus Three, a segment of the station reserved for light industry and zero-g production, when they received a call.

<Inspectors Harris and Loche. Please investigate unauthorized maintenance access at R-2451, Deck Four. A monitor reported the hatch was opened three minutes ago and remains unsealed. Investigate with caution. The monitors in that area are now off-line. Backup will arrive in ten minutes.>

Harris looked at Loche. "It's them. You ready?"

"As I'll ever be."

The station schematics indicated the hatch opened into several equipment rooms. A passageway branched to the left toward more equipment rooms, a major environmental services control node, and an airshaft that would enable the fugitives to move from one deck to another. The equipment room inside the hatch contained a large pump used to shift water inside the station to maintain structural balance and stabilization. The pumps would provide concealment and cover for anyone hiding inside.

Harris and Loche approached, alert for an ambush. Dundee Central and station security, watching through the surveillance monitors, saw no one in the adjacent public corridors. With the maintenance monitors off-line, nobody could know what was behind the hatch. Harris ordered one of the backup teams to approach via the air shaft from Deck Five. Another team would come through a nearby entryway to flank anyone hiding in the area.

Loche stopped short of the hatch when Harris suggested they armor up first, just in case. They removed their trauma plates from their duty packs and slipped them into pockets in the arms, thighs, chest, and back of their shipsuits, to provide additional protection over vital areas.

Loche extended a fiber-optic lead from his helmet around the corner. Two men were facing a panel next to the hatch. One of the two had opened the maintenance panel and was working on the circuitry within. He shared the image with Harris and passed it to Dundee Central. Something, perhaps a small noise, alerted the two. One man continued to work on the panel while the other turned to keep watch. Loche ducked his head quickly around the corner for another look and was seen. The intruder raised his pistol and fired.

"Shots fired!" Harris reported over his link. "Intruder alert! Case Delta!"

Harris reported a possible network attack in progress. Dundee Central answered one of Harris's questions—the maintenance panel opened to a security module. If the module was compromised, the intruders would have access to the entire deck's security and systems network. Case Delta classified the act as a possible environmental attack. The protocol for Case Delta included lowering isolation barriers throughout the level and the activation of emergency air scrubbers and bulkheads. All the level's environment support systems were sealed from the rest of the station.

While Harris was reporting, the two intruders escaped through the open hatch into the pump room. Loche sealed his helmet and glanced around the corner of the passageway again in time to see the hatch close.

"They've gone back inside," he told Harris, who passed that information along to Dundee Central.

"Can you get a look inside?" he asked Central.

"We're activating an old tertiary system on your level. It won't tell us too much—no audio—but we should have some video from pinhead lenses… Hold on… We have visual inside. We see two… They're attaching something to the pump. The inside corridor to your left is open… No video from the equipment room to the right. It's a sectional power node."

89

"Do you have any chemical sensors working in the pump room? Is that a bomb they're placing on the pump?" Harris asked.

"No, we haven't any other sensors in there, just video… It's possible they're setting up a bomb."

Harris turned to Loche. "We'll have to go in. We can't wait for backup if that is a bomb. It may explode before they arrive. You agree?"

Loche agreed. Nothing good could come if they waited. They had to act immediately. They moved forward to the now-closed hatch. Harris was about to speak, but Loche interrupted.

"I'll go first and to the left toward the corridor. You go right and cover the pumps." He must have seen the surprise on Harris's face. "When was the last time you trained for a tactical entry? Mine was eight months ago—and I'm younger and quicker."

Harris appeared surprised at Loche's assertiveness. He may have been tempted to argue, but Fabien knew he was right. His last training session was some time ago, a year at least. Harris conceded the point. They had no time to argue.

†††

They stood next to the hatch, Harris to the left, Loche to the right, ready to enter. Harris used his link to unlock the hatch and palmed the adjacent panel. The hatch slid open with a soft click and hiss. Loche pushed the hatch open and passed through into the equipment room at a rush. His movement blocked Harris from immediately following him. Before Harris could do so, he heard shots followed by a thud.

Loche was on the deck, facedown, his pistol extended before him. Several meters down the corridor was another body. Harris caught a glimpse of movement at the end of the corridor.

"Man down! Man down in compartment CR-2451." A man-height pump filled the room. Harris slipped behind it, using it for cover. He moved quickly, confirming no one was hiding behind it to catch him in a cross fire. He circled around the pump and peered down the passageway from the side of the room opposite where Loche was lying. Behind him and perpendicular to the passageway was another door leading to a power-distribution room. He heard something from there, maybe machinery or something else.

Harris moved back to cover that door. The change of position blocked his view of the corridor. He knew someone was there. But if he couldn't see them, they couldn't see him either. Plus, he didn't know how badly Loche was injured. Determining if he was breathing was difficult as the trauma plates shielded any chest movements. Some blood was on his shipsuit but not too much.

"Loche is down!" he repeated through his link. "There is at least one active shooter down the passageway to the left. I hear noises in the compartment to the right. I'm out of sight from the corridor—"

"What about the bomb?" came the response.

"I can't reach it from my position without exposing myself. It'll have to wait."

"Roger," the voice from Dundee Central said quietly.

†††

Loche slowly became aware. He had entered the room and was fired upon from down the corridor. A bullet hit his trauma plate. Two shooters were down the corridor. He returned fire, hitting the one in front and saw his frangible round puff on the other's shipsuit—armored. His second shot was aimed for the throat, an area not covered by armor.

He became more aware—movement to his right. Loche rolled his head slowly and saw Harris backing away from the door leading to the power-distribution room. The slight movement hurt. His head pounded. His neck burned, as did his side and hip. The movement caused his vision to gray. He closed his eyes, which helped for a moment.

Harris moved forward to open the door. When the door slipped to the side, someone from within fired two shots. The bullets ricocheted off the pump—solid rounds, not frangibles. The world grayed again. Harris returned fire, unaware of running steps approaching from down the corridor in front of Loche.

Loche opened his eyes again, seeing a silhouette running toward him with a weapon in hand. He raised his pistol, firing low and letting the recoil walk his rounds up the body from crotch to face. The corridor narrowed and faded out.

†††

Harris entered the room low and saw the shooter in the open, moving between two large cabinets. Harris fired and saw the other stumble and fall. He heard shots behind him and took cover. Nobody else moved in this room. From the station schematic, it had no outlet. He slipped from one cabinet to another, circling the room. It was empty except for him and the body of the shooter on the floor. Loche was visible through the open door but wasn't in the same position. He now lay on one side, still facing the corridor. Harris saw two large bloody splotches on his shipsuit.

Once he was satisfied no one else was in the room, Harris moved to the open door. *<We're coming in!>* he heard through his link.

"There are three down," Harris reported. "Loche and two others. He got one, and I got the other."

He stepped into the pump room as three patrollers rushed in through the hatch. "Make that four down," Harris amended when he saw a second body down the corridor and realized Loche must have gotten that one when he was in the other room.

A medic was already attending Loche. Harris looked up to see Charles Demning enter, shipsuited with clamshell armor and a flechette riot gun in hand. Harris tried to holster his pistol, missed the first time, but succeeded on his second attempt. He had to force his fingers open to release the pistol. He took a deep breath and stepped back to lean against the compartment's wall.

The medic removed Loche's helmet and trauma plates.

Demning picked them up, examined them, and handed the damaged plate and helmet to Harris. "They did their job."

Harris looked. The plate was cratered from the impact of a solid round. An armor-piercing bullet would have gone through. Loche's helmet was cracked, having taken a round in the upper quarter. Without the helmet, Loche would have had a portion of his head blown off.

The medic looked up. "He'll live. Two bullet wounds, through and through. One in his left side and one through the hip. He may need a new spleen and kidney. Perhaps a hip rebuild. Was he military?"

"Yes," Harris answered.

"I thought so. He has some nannites that stopped his bleed out. With his spleen and kidney wrecked, he wouldn't have lasted long. Renal artery appears to be severed."

Loche was placed on a gurney and taken out.

"I guess I know the answer," Harris said.

"What answer?" Demning asked.

Harris hadn't realized he'd spoken aloud. "I asked Loche if he could cover my back. He said he'd never been in combat but thought so. He's answered my question. That second shooter down the corridor would have flanked me—would have had me cold. Loche stopped him after he was hit and down."

The forensic team arrived and started their task, recording the scene, the evidence found. Loche's helmet might have been cracked, but all its electronics were intact and functional. They had a complete audio and visual record of the shoot-out. One tech walked up to Harris to take his helmet too.

Harris and Demning moved back and watched. "Do you think they're Hivers?" Demning asked.

Harris focused on the bodies. "Maybe. They fit the usual Hiver genotype. But that matches a lot of people outside the Hive. They might be DeeCees, from the System States, possibly from a Confederate world. Unless we get very lucky, we'll never know."

"I still don't understand why they came here. They were off ship long before we arrived for inspection," Demning said.

"That bothers me too. Schofield said the same and was going to check on that."

"Heard anything from him?"

"No, and that also bothers me. He should have something by now."

"Follow up on that when you're back on duty," Demning said. "We'll process your debrief first and run you through your medical. Then, with the regs satisfied, you can return to duty by the end of tomorrow. I'll waive the mandatory time off for a shooting."

"Thank you. I'll tell Molly too. I think she and Loche were becoming friends."

"That's your sept's business. Just keep me informed if there are any issues."

"I will."

†††

The first thing Loche became aware of… aware that he was aware… was a distant clicking. He drifted a moment… heard some steps and tried to open his eyes. *Are my eyes open?* He wasn't sure, but he thought he saw a glow a few feet away and some outlines of farther objects. But he couldn't quite discern what the objects were. Fabien drifted again and slept.

He awoke and definitely saw light through his closed eyelids, and he sensed someone was close. He heard some distant voices.

"Fabien, wake up."

The voice was familiar. *Who?*

"Fabien," the voice said again. It was Harris.

Loche opened his eyes and closed them. "Bright," he whispered, his throat dry.

"I'll darken the room," Harris replied.

Loche heard him walk a few steps, and the glow through his eyelids dimmed. He opened his eyes and saw Harris return and sit nearby. "Thanks," he whispered.

"No problem. How're you feeling?"

He considered the question. He felt no pain and remembered what had happened. Wiggling his fingers and toes, he found they seemed to move. "All right. I don't hurt anywhere." He raised his head. He was in a bed, covered by a sheet. He wiggled his toes again and saw them move under the sheet.

"You've been under for three days. You gave our medics a scare. Your nannites tried to counter their treatment. Your embassy sent their staff surgeon, and he was able to put them on standby long enough to fix your worst wounds. They're active once again."

"Oh." *That sounded stupid. Surely, I can make a more pertinent response.*

"You're still being treated for some residual issues, but our medic plans on releasing you in a few hours. He said since you were here, he made those remedial repairs you discussed with him."

Loche was surprised at feeling no emotion about that statement and nothing from his leg… nothing more than the sensation of the sheet lying on his skin—no ache, no pain. He didn't remember when he'd last had no minor pain—not since before the accident, at least.

"Are you thinking well enough for a debrief?"

"Yes… did we get them?"

"You got two, I got one. We ran a sweep of the station and found the other five. Three suicided when we cornered them. The rest resisted. None survived."

"Was that all of them?"

"Yes, we believe so. We halted the shuttle flights before the infiltrators could get off the station. With no escape, it was just a matter of time. They had no place to go."

"Not criminals, then."

"No. And… there's another issue." Harris paused. "It's been a long week, and I've not slept much since the shooting. Schofield has been hounding me to find the other intruders." He looked tired. "The medics had to keep you under, in a coma. They used nanosurgery to replace the artificial nerves in your leg and to seat the regen buds for your new kidney and spleen.

"We now believe the intruders… Pack! Let's call them for what they were—saboteurs," Harris said, "spies, were from the System States. We don't believe," he was quick to add, "that they were necessarily under the direction of the System States. We have confirmed they were all members or former members of the System States military."

Loche didn't respond. The news led him down multiple trails of thought.

When he didn't get a response, Harris continued, "You have the same nannites the saboteurs do."

"What?"

"Your staff physician—the one from the System States embassy, said the nannites were a special upgrade for assault and Spec Ops troops."

"Ah." *That explains it.* "I was selected for recon training—had all the prep work finished, including the upgraded nannite package, when I had my accident. I was given a medical discharge and kicked out of the Corps." He had another thought. "Recon and Spec Ops troops don't go rogue."

"We know. Can you think of an explanation?"

He could, but he didn't want to talk about it. He needed to mull the news over for a while. Loche looked at Harris then deliberately looked at the medical panel, the door, the ceiling, and the walls before looking again at Harris. Harris raised his eyebrows, appeared to think for a moment, then shrugged.

96

"Let me think it over a bit," Loche said for the benefit of anyone who may have been listening. "If I'm being released, I'd like to get out of here. Maybe we can continue later."

"Very well, we can do that."

When Harris was about to speak again, a soft knock sounded on the door, and a tall, slender older man entered. He had thick, medium-length hair sprinkled with gray. He walked forward, stopped at the foot of the bed, bowed, and said, "Fabien... Son of the House, how are you?"

"Father! I am well."

"You don't look it, lying there. The initial report I received was... vague," he said. He turned to Harris and bowed again.

Loche spoke quickly. "Donal, please let me introduce you to my father, Emile Loche, a Member of House DuQuoin. Father, please let me introduce you to Customs Chief Inspector Donal Harris of Clan McLean, Sept Harris."

"Honored to meet you, Chief Inspector Harris."

"And I, you, Emissary," Harris replied.

"Yes... we'll speak on that at a better time down on Inverness."

Charles Demning must have been waiting outside Loche's hospital room. He entered and approached Loche's bed. "I see you survived. You scared us for a while."

"So Donal was telling me."

"When you are released in a few hours, you will be on convalescent leave—a full thirty days. I suggest you take the opportunity to go downbelow and tour Inverness. You have some friends there who would like to meet you."

"Thank you, sir."

"I must be getting on. Emile, later?"

"Yes, Charles. We'll have time to reminisce before I have to go to work."

"Yes, there's that." Demning chuckled. Turning to the group, he said, "I'll see you all later."

Chapter 6. Tourist

Dundee Orbital, 20 Sixmonth, 3203

Harris's prediction came true. A few hours later, Loche was released and, with his father, made his way to his quarters. There, he used his console link to order dinner for the two of them. Molly Quinn and Amilie Schute dropped by. Loche made sure they were formally introduced to his father.

"Father, this is Molly Quinn, Clan McLean, Sept Harris. She and I have been partners on occasion. Donal Harris is her uncle."

"Don't forget me!" Amilie interjected.

"And this is Amilie Schute, Clan Mieze, Sept…"

"Lannier," Amilie said.

"Thank you, Amilie. I didn't know your sept."

"Doesn't matter," she said with a wave of her hand.

"Amilie is Molly's cousin and is in charge of our local Customs Service logistics section. They have been helping me get acclimated to the Confederation."

"I must thank you for your aid and assistance," Emile Loche said. "I know from personal experience that differing cultures can be a hurdle. Fabien is fortunate to have friends here that can be depended upon."

"'Tisn't anything," Amilie said. She appeared embarrassed, something Loche could not have imagined happening.

"And I would like to thank you, Molly Quinn."

"You are welcome, sir. And, if no one has yet done so, I would like, on behalf of my clan, to welcome you to Dundee Orbital and the Confederation."

"I thank you. Director Demning has done so, but I appreciate your welcome too."

The two women did not stay long. Amilie brought a bottle of brandy, bottled by her sept, as a welcoming gift. The two Loches stood as the women left then, when the door slid shut, returned to their seats.

"How are you, truly?" Emile Loche asked his son.

"I will be fine, Father. I have been given convalescent leave while my kidney and spleen are regenerating, but otherwise, I'm fit."

"Good. You can accompany me to my discussions with the Confederation."

"Is it the Confederation? Or is it with one of the special-interest groups?"

"I am not sure at this point. Either... both, perhaps. Does it matter, if we get our clearance and terms?"

Fabien Loche sat silent in his quarters. His father was sitting across from him in another lounger extruded from the floor. His father's arrival at Dundee Orbital had been unexpected—it was too soon.

"I am thinking it *may* matter, Father. The Confederation is not as homogeneous as we had thought. There are factions involved. Schofield, of the Interdiction Office, used the 'Grand Dam' introduction. Harris used 'Aunt Eloise.' Harris is also the station's resident Interdiction agent."

His father grunted softly at the unwelcome news. The initial queries from the Seat were to two groups. Both wanted the technology possessed by the Thirty Houses and were willing to use their influence in the Confederation Senate to grant concessions needed by the houses. It was a trade—technology for the Confederation, membership in the Confederation for the Seat... membership and an unused metal-rich system with a habitable planet.

Of the two groups, one was backing Schofield while the other was backing Harris—the McLeans. Loche did not know Clan McLean any better than he did the group represented by Schofield. However, he did know Donal Harris.

The McLean clan wanted the technology for the Confederation. Their space industries would benefit too. Clan McLean was one of the more influential groups in the Confederacy, if not the *most* influential. And they had been the primary source of contact with the Seat.

The other group's motivations weren't clear. They were new points of contact. From the Seat's investigations, Schofield and his associates might have other loyalties.

The Seat knew of the growing division between the System States and the Confederation. The passage of the Trade Treaty used the Seat's last reserve of political leverage within the System States. Emile Loche and others, while staffers of the System States' Foreign Affairs Directorate, worked to get the treaty passed. It resolved some trade issues between the two governments. However, that was not its sole purpose. The treaty was a mechanism that provided the Seat a direct conduit to the Confederation.

Most of the System States liaisons in the Confederation were just functionaries. Others, like Loche, were observers and intermediaries. The Seat knew the growing xenophobia in SolSystem would spread to the rest of the System States. Xenophobia would affect the relationships between the System States and other foreign governments—the Confederation and others too. The recent riots on Earth were just a manifestation of that xenophobia. Reena and Fabien had been attacked by rioters, resulting in Reena's death.

"I'm wondering, Father, if any obligation we may owe in getting our clearance may be, in the long run, as bad as staying in the System States."

Emile Loche didn't answer at first. He took a sip from his brandy snifter. "I don't know, Fabien. We must be diligent and vigilant. We could go out beyond the frontier."

Do I want that? Fabien considered. That was an option, but he'd rather the Seat find a home in the Confederacy. The houses would need allies wherever they settled—true allies. The Seat would not accept being someone's puppet. "When are you going downbelow, Father?"

"Tomorrow, to Kilkenny with Schofield." He paused. "We have invitations from Clan McLean to visit their laird at Dunnsport too. They specifically mentioned you. Is there a reason for that?" he asked, raising one eyebrow.

The question caught Loche by surprise. "Donal Harris is of Clan McLean. He's been my trainer, and I've been partnered with him or his niece since my arrival. Perhaps it is the McLeans whom we should meet. I believe Harris stands high in his clan." He paused and took a breath. "There are... may be cultural issues involved too. A formal meeting, being introduced formally to the clan, is important here. It is a Custom and Tradition and a matter of mutual recognition."

"Ah! It is fortunate that we sent you ahead. You have the best understanding of the Confederates. You will serve us well... My meeting in Kilkenny is with the laird of Clan Monmouth and others in the planetary government."

Loche nodded, decided not to dwell, yet, on the other possibilities of the invitation. "Take note how you are introduced, Father. It is important. You noticed how I introduced Molly and Amilie to you?"

"Yes. Very formal. Is it significant?"

"Very much so. The introduction must include the name of clan and sept plus the individual's position in the clan. To not comply fully is a deliberate snub."

"I'll take note. Thank you for the information."

Changing the subject, Fabien said, "The Confederates fixed my leg."

Emile Loche started. "Really? I was not aware that could be done."

"No, it couldn't, not at home. For the Confederates, it was routine. They noticed the artificial nerves during my initial physical. They said I could get it fixed anytime I had a few days free. When I was under sedation, after being shot, they replaced the artificial nerves as if it were just a routine task."

Loche's father listened and said, "I wonder if the System States could have done the same... if they chose." He did not speak as if asking a question.

Nanotechnology was common. Medical nanotechnology had been in use for a millennium. If the Confederation had that capability, the System States should have had the same capability. That was another facet of the coming rift between the System States and the Seat and the nonaligned stationers. It opened questions about whether the System States, the SolSystem in particular, had the same capability, and whether they just discarded the option of growing new nerves, with its higher cost, over the option of replacing them with cheaper, artificial ones.

"I believe the Confederation is more advanced than the System States," Fabien said. "I've discovered the System States license significant numbers of products from the Confederation."

The conversation ended. "I will leave you now. Please, get some rest. Shall we meet tomorrow in the shuttle bay? Go down together?" Emile Loche asked.

"Yes, Father… Before you go, I have something for you."

"Oh?"

"Yes." Fabien stood and walked to the wall desk and poked through the contents he'd carried in his shipsuit's pockets. "Here," he said, picking up a small object. He walked back to his father. "Please wear this at all times." He bent forward and fastened the small gold pin to his father's lapel.

His father looked down at the pin, puzzled, and back up to his son. "This has significance?"

"Yes, Father, it could save your life. Remember, dueling is legal here, and duels have been used to resolve political issues. Please wear this pin at all times. It marks you as unarmed, a noncombatant."

"Very well. I will remember, Fabien."

Emile Loche rose and stood before his son. He grasped Fabien's arms with both hands. "Be well, Son."

Fabien returned his father's embrace. "And you, too, Father."

†††

Loche sat in his lounger. The bottle, Amilie's gift that he and his father had shared, still rested on the low table between the two chairs. Loche used his link to remove the second lounger as his small quarters did

103

not have an abundance of floor space. He leaned back in his lounger, took a sip from the snifter, and closed his eyes. He placed the snifter back on the table, shifted to get more comfortable, and drifted...

†††

Reena! Come! We can't stay here!"

Fabien, where will we go? The doorways are sealed for blocks around."

There! Across the causeway. If we can get to the harbor, we can escape on a boat."

The causeway linked the city of Hellene to an artificial island in the harbor. Hellene was a new city on the Grecian Island of Poros catering to the wealthy, the influential, and their clients.

Reena and Fabien were on holiday. Reena was of House Tyre, and this trip to represent their respective houses gave them time together. They would be formally betrothed on their return to Ceres.

As members of allied houses, the two were in close company often and had become close. Fabien's enlistment in the Marines had separated them, but this trip for Houses DuQuoin and Tyre to Hellene was a welcome opportunity to renew that relationship again.

Until the riots started.

Zeisskin, one of the original space cartels, owned the resort and casino where they were staying. The Seat had a centuries-long relationship with the cartel, a mutually profitable one that could grow stronger. The negotiations, however, drew attention from some who wanted to break that relationship. A riot was a useful tool to hinder the negotiations and intimidate the Seat, thwarting the plans of Zeisskin and their partner houses.

Reena wanted to shop in the bazaar. She and Fabien were away from the resort when the rioters attacked. Their height and paleness branded them as spaceborn—targets for the rioters. The two escaped for a time... until they were discovered near the harbor.

Although Loche was better suited to Earth's heavier gravity due to his marine training, neither he nor Reena were acclimated to the stronger pull of Earth, and they soon tired.

The mob caught them in the middle of the causeway. A line of patrollers from the EarthGov Constabulary blocked the causeway. Safety lay there… if they could reach it. The mob surged toward them, pelting them with rocks and debris, whatever was close at hand.

Reena, here!"Loche cried.

The mob would reach them before they could find safety.

He ran to the edge of the causeway, swung a leg over the railing, and reached for Reena. Take my hand. We'll swim for it."

I'can't swim!"she yelled.

Like many spaceborn, she feared water of any depth. The Marines had taught Loche to swim, but Reena had no such training.

I"ll support you. All you need is to relax in the water. I'll do the—"

A rock from the mob clipped his head.

Loche regained consciousness in the water as an EarthGov Constabulary launch approached. Reena hadn't followed. The mob had taken her.

†††

He awoke in the lounger. This was the first time the dream reached the end. Most of the time, he woke as the mob was chasing them. Some scenes shifted, but the mob was a constant feature in all the dreams.

At some point, he had knocked over the bottle of brandy. It lay empty on the textured floor. The compartment had cleaned the spillage, but the smell of brandy remained. Loche rose, dropped the bottle and snifter in the disposal, and checked the time. He found that he'd slept through the afternoon and evening. He would have just enough time for a shower and a meal before meeting his father at the shuttle bay.

†††

Loche arrived at the shuttle bay early. He was surprised to find Donal Harris and Molly Quinn waiting for him. He had never seen Harris out of uniform before. He and Molly wore civilian clothes. Harris wore trousers made of the McLean tartan, and Molly was dressed in trousers and a blouse, plus a sash in the same tartan over her shoulder. Loche thought he must appear drab in his more subdued colors.

Harris greeted him. "Schofield took your father down to Kilkenny. A courier arrived from SolSystem. The news isn't good."

"What's happened?" Loche asked.

"We don't know everything. I've not been told it all. What I do know is that the EarthGov annexed the Luna city-states and the EllFive stations. Either they attacked Hellasport on Mars, or the local Mars military forces revolted against the SolSystem government. We're not sure which is the truth… Maybe both. The Deimos Naval Base has been destroyed, along with all the ships of the SolSystem Defense Force that were in port. There were a lot of SDF ships in port, which is, in itself, suspicious. Most of the SDF was crewed by spaceborn, I understand. The reports imply that Deimos is gone, nothing but small rocks and dust. Mars, when the courier left SolSystem, was still in local hands, although damage from the falling Deimos debris was severe. We have no news about the belt, the outer stations, and beyond. There was a packet for your father. It may have more information."

"I'm surprised SolSystem would let that news get out. Was it an official System States courier?"

"We don't think so."

Loche raised an eyebrow. "Whose courier was it?" he asked.

"Well, that's a little strange. The ship appears to be an official System States courier. However, its point of departure was Pallas."

"The Seat owns Pallas… Ceres, Juno, and Vesta too."

"That was our thought too. Would you know how the courier made the passage from SolSystem in only forty-five days?"

"Forty-five days?"

106

"According to the transit log given to us, yes."

"I don't… can't say more at this point."

Harris did not respond. He looked at Loche for a moment then turned to Quinn. "Well, we, at least, can continue as planned."

She nodded.

"Your father," Harris told Loche, "asked that you come with us until he finished his meeting."

"He told me we would go downbelow to Kilkenny together." Loche checked his link for messages and found one from his father dated just minutes before. It confirmed Harris's statement and said he expected to join them later.

"Come, Fabien, let's go downbelow to Dunnsport," Molly urged. "I expect your father will join you there soon."

Loche looked from her back to Harris. "Both of you?"

"Yes. The clan has called us home. We'll ride down with you if you don't mind."

Dunnsport, Clan McLean Territory, 21 Sixmonth, 3203

The shuttle was half full. *Or half empty,* Loche thought, *depending on your perspective.* It was much larger than the ones he had ridden during his time in the Marines. It was far larger than any civilian shuttle in SolSystem too.

Harris explained that with the fall of the beanstalks, the Confederation put more emphasis on shuttles. Beanstalks were cheap, once the initial cost of construction was recovered. However, the passage to and from the surface by beanstalk was slow, a day or more—too slow in an emergency. When the DeeCees blew the beanstalks during their last raid, the Confederation, Inverness, was hard-pressed to move personnel, freight, and munitions to orbit. Given the number and size of existing shuttles, that would never again be an issue.

"Lessons learned," Harris said.

Inverness had shuttle ports scattered all over the planet. Each major clan had at least one. The McLean clan, with their emphasis on space industry and large numbers of clansmen in space, had several. The largest one was at Dunnsport.

Dunnsport was the Clan McLean territorial seat and was midway down the Hebrides Peninsula. It was, at first, a seaport servicing the clan's islands and mariners on the Gael Sea. Over the centuries, it had expanded to serve planetary air and, later, orbital traffic. Like all of Inverness's shuttle ports, it was also a military base. Dunnsport was a secondary shuttle port for the McLean Militia. The clan's primary militia shuttle base was built into an escarpment inland from Dunnsport.

Loche found himself sandwiched between Harris and Quinn. She identified geographic features displayed on a large holomonitor mounted on the forward bulkhead and kept up a running travelogue with Loche. It was a one-sided conversation, with Quinn doing most of the talking. Loche remained quiet, thinking of the news from SolSystem. Harris slept… and snored, Loche discovered.

Quinn seemed to understand Loche's reticence. Rather than allowing Loche to dwell on the news from SolSystem, she continued the commentary on Inverness and the McLean territory.

The shuttle dropped through the overcast hiding Dunnsport, aligned with its long runway, and landed with a double thump and rumble. The shuttle slowed, taking only a portion of the eight-kilometer dual runway. Their links pinged and vibrated as they connected with the planetary network.

Harris woke from his nap, checked his messages, and turned to Loche. "The Laird would like to meet you. He's asked if you would join us as his guest for dinner tonight. It will be a formal affair."

To Loche's mind, that wasn't much of a request—more like an invitation one couldn't refuse. "Yes, I'd welcome meeting him."

"Good. You have a reservation at McLean House. Since you are on convalescent leave, the Customs Service will pick up the tab."

Loche decided he could accept free lodging. His personal account was low. He had chosen to be paid monthly when he joined the Customs Service, and his next deposit was still days away. Besides, he had read that the McLean House, the clan house of Clan McLean, was famous across Inverness, even throughout the three inhabited planets of the Caledonia system.

The shuttle stopped inside a circle of lights on the tarmac. In seconds, the platform, outlined by the lights, descended, lowering the shuttle to the hangar bay belowground. A tug towed the shuttle to a passenger gate where the passengers could disembark.

The three exited the shuttle through its forward port and took an escalator up to the ground-level terminal. Loche had hoped to get a glimpse of the shuttle port but saw no windows in the terminal facing the field nor any holomonitors providing a view.

In the distance, he heard the crackling rumble of a VTOL shuttle climbing to orbit. Dunnsport was very busy.

He was surprised to find no security checkpoints. They picked up their personal baggage at a central carousel and proceeded through the throngs of people to the exterior of the terminal, where a limo parked under a weather shield awaited them. The limo had a human driver, an anachronism with modern traffic systems, dressed in black except for a McLean tartan patch on his shoulder.

Their baggage stowed, Harris, Quinn, and Loche entered the limo to find another tartan-clad man seated inside. "Good morning, Mr. Fabien Loche of House DuQuoin. I am Neil Cooper, Clan McLean, Sept Lillianthal. The clan welcomes you."

"Thank you, Mr. Cooper… On behalf of House DuQuoin, I thank you."

Loche's response appeared to startle Cooper. "You speak for your house?"

"Not all of it… yet. Maybe never."

That was clearly not the response Cooper had expected. If he thought he could claim a political coup by wresting Loche from Schofield's hands, he was mistaken.

As Loche turned back to settle into his seat, he saw Harris's face turning red. *What upset him?* he wondered.

†††

Dunnsport was midway down the southern side of the Hebrides Peninsula, which extended over a thousand kilometers from the Scotia mainland into the Gael Sea. The city of Dunnsport wrapped the original bay and extended up into the dark-green hills surrounding the harbor.

The shuttle port was an extension of the Dunnsport harbor breakwater, enclosing half of the mouth of the bay. McLean builders extended the breakwater as needed, widening and expanding in the shallow waters on the seaward side.

The shuttleport's runways ran the length of the artificial breakwater and covered over a dozen square kilometers. VTOL scramble-launch pits for McLean Militia fighters and surface-to-space defense emplacements lay along both sides of the shuttle runways. The port could support horizontal and vertical takeoff aircraft and shuttles.

The limo left the port in a light rain and drove along the breakwater to the main highway. It ran down the peninsula from the Scotia coast to the hill country at the tip of the peninsula. McLean House, Cooper said, was thirty kilometers north of Dunnsport.

Loche watched the changing scenery through the limo's windows. The sea showed on his right between breaks in the rain and scattered fog. As the highway rose, climbing through coastal hills above the sea, mountains appeared in the distance, farther inland. The seaside changed from beaches to hills to cliffs facing the sea.

Just before the highway turned inland toward the mountains, the limo turned onto a service highway and, after a few kilometers, stopped at a security gate manned by McLean militiamen. Cooper vouched for the passengers, and the limo was allowed to pass. It continued on the private drive until it arrived at a broad paved terrace before McLean House. Their

110

conveyance followed the circled drive and halted before the entrance of the clan house.

The McLean House was built into the base of a kilometer-high escarpment that ended in a huge cliff above the Gael Sea. Molly explained that it had been a fortress during the War Years. Since that time, the clan house had been upgraded and expanded. The "new" exterior face of McLean House was only two centuries old and disguised the outer visage of the fortress that still existed deep inside the escarpment. Loche assumed, although he couldn't see them, that the clan house was encircled by effective modern defenses.

The limo stopped under the covered entrance, and the four stepped out to be welcomed by the house steward. Other clansmen appeared and took their baggage inside. Molly Quinn, Loche noticed, had twice as much baggage as him and Harris combined.

Cooper spoke hurriedly. "I need to report. The steward will show you your rooms and provide anything you may need. We have full, secure communications, Mr. Loche, if you wish to communicate with your father."

Secure from everyone except for Clan McLean, Loche thought.

Before any of the three could respond, Cooper turned and hurried, almost at a run, into the interior of the clan house.

Loche, standing next to Harris, asked, "Am I missing something here?"

Harris looked puzzled and surprised. "I don't know. It seems as if someone has spit into Cooper's morning porridge."

The steward led them inside. "I've assigned each of you a page to lead you to your rooms," he said, "and I sent their contact IDs to your links in case you need anything. Dinner will be at nineteen hundred hours local time—formal attire. We have fabricators available if you need them. We know you have brought little baggage, Mr. Loche. All your expenses are covered as a guest of the clan."

†††

Loche was given a spacious room, a suite with a sitting room, a separate bedroom, and a full 'fresher. The walls were paneled golden wood. One wall contained a small bookcase filled with real, hard-copy books. A few painted seascapes decorated the walls, and a final luxurious touch was the deep-pile carpet in the McLean colors. Loche felt himself sink into the carpet when he entered the room.

Loche's page, Angeal, asked permission to touch Loche's weapons as he unpacked Loche's duffel. "I will clean them, if you wish, sir," he stated.

"No, that isn't necessary. I'll do that myself."

"Very well, sir." He finished hanging Loche's meager supply of civilian clothes in the wardrobe, after which only Loche's formal house regalia remained. "Shall I have this cleaned and pressed, sir? It will be ready well before dinner."

Loche looked at the formal, black nouveau-silk tunic with his house crest on its upper-right shoulder, black nouveau-silk shirt, matching trousers, and polished short, fifteen-centimeter boots. "Yes. Please."

"I'll buff your boots, too, sir."

"Thank you, Angeal."

The page left with Fabien's house uniform in hand. The room had a balcony overlooking the grounds, and Loche walked out and leaned against the rail. The drizzle that had followed them from Dunnsport moved inland. The sky was still overcast, but the clouds were thinning, and a few beams of sunlight danced on the sea. Three floors below and to his right was the paved entrance where they had arrived. The limo was disappearing around the far corner of McLean House. He assumed garages sat around the corner or inside the cliff. Below him was a sloping green grass-covered lawn that continued several hundred meters or more to the abrupt edge of the cliff above the sea. He listened and heard the surf booming and had an intense feeling of *déjà vu*.

†††

The chime from the suite's door interrupted his reverie on the balcony.

"Enter," he responded, turning from the balcony and walking back into the suite.

Harris and Quinn walked in.

"Settled?" Harris asked.

"Oh... uh, yes. I was enjoying the view. I've had few opportunities to look at such a body of water."

"We've brought a gift," Harris said, extending a black tooled pistol belt and a matching sheath containing a knife—no, a dirk. "It's not comely to appear unarmed... even if you aren't. I had this ordered when I was told you would be coming down to meet the laird."

"Thank you." Loche remembered his grandmother's admonition about accepting gifts gracefully. The dirk had a blade thirty centimeters long, a knuckle-duster hand guard, and a roughened staghorn grip. "Real staghorn?"

"Yes, we have stags, elks running through the mountains. It's a tradition they can only be hunted using hand weapons. I killed this one with a bow during my last furlough home."

Loche looked closer. The blade appeared to have been hand forged. The tang was inlaid with copper or some soft metal, and the butt cap was heavy.

"Gold?" he asked.

Harris nodded. "There are nuggets in some streams inland if you know where to look."

Loche was speechless. He noticed a strange look on Harris's face. "I don't know how to thank you. This will be a house treasure."

"Not soon, I hope. Wear it tonight, and when it's appropriate, hand it down to your sons. It's traditional."

The three stood looking at the gift until Quinn broke the sudden silence.

"Perhaps we can tour the grounds before dinner."

"I'd like that."

"Cooper just told me your father won't be able to join us tonight. He is meeting with our Confederate senators and some other clan chiefs in Kilkenny," Harris said. "That will give Robair another excuse for a formal dinner."

"Robair?"

"Robair McLean, Laird McLean," Harris answered.

Loche nodded. "Father said he was meeting with the Laird of Clan Monmouth and some others." *I wonder if my father and I are being purposely separated. The question is, by whom? Schofield? Clan McLean? Both?* He didn't need to ask as long as their task was progressing.

"I'm meeting with the Laird this afternoon," Harris added. "You're free to tour the grounds and the house until dinner. I expect we'll have a long night, if you'd like to catch a nap before dinner."

"It's too early yet, but I'd welcome a tour."

"I'll let Molly handle that. I'll see you both at dinner."

Quinn watched with a puzzled expression as Harris departed.

Loche looked at her and said, "So."

"Yes… so," she replied.

Given the light, Quinn could have been blushing, but it was difficult to tell. Neither said a word for a moment.

"Have we now been formally introduced?" Loche asked.

She hesitated. "I believe that's now true. Apparently." Quinn seemed uncomfortable with the question but appeared to be making the best of an awkward situation. She walked over to the link console. A 3-D holomap of McLean House appeared. Except for the visible exterior, the clan house extended far into the escarpment and deeper underground. Some portions extended out under the sea.

"Those sections in yellow are restricted. Nonclan visitors must have prior permission to enter these areas and be accompanied by an authorized clansman. We'll not go there today. The white areas are administrative, and the Clan Meeting Hall lies here," she said, pointing to a flashing caret in the hologram. "Blue areas are McLean Militia, the clan's military headquarters and an armory. We have three regiments of the militia stationed here. The green is our survival cache. We have enough food, fuel, and power systems to provide shelter for all those assigned to the clan house and their dependents for a hundred years. Most of the cache is for the people in Dunnsport and the surrounding areas in case of an emergency. We also have enough arms and munitions in the armory to defend ourselves and this region of the McLean territory."

She paused and looked at Loche. "Where would you like to begin?"

"Let's go outside. I'd like a closer look at the sea."

She nodded, smiled, and agreed. "Let's."

†††

Donal Harris was tall, muscular, and clean-shaven with short hair, which was a necessity for those who must from time to time don vacuum suits… or Customs Service helmets. Robair Litton McLean, Laird, Clan McLean, Sept McLean, however, was a small, lean man appearing to be in his late forties. McLean was much older than he appeared—an advantage of advanced medical nanotechnology. He had light-brown hair, silverish at the temples, and a short, full beard. The cut of his hair, much longer than was customary among those who spent time in space, and the beard branded him as one who seldom, if ever, left the surface of the planet.

Harris and McLean sat across from one another, separated by a low table that held cups, saucers, and several flasks of hot liquids, plus a small plate of pastries. The two sipped, nibbled, and made small talk. Harris knew McLean's weakness for pastries. McLean paid for his indulgence by running ten kilometers each morning with elements of the clan's militia stationed at the clan house.

The cloudiness of the morning was dissipating. A few beams of sunlight brightened the room through a window at McLean's back.

"What do you know of this delay?" McLean asked.

Harris had just informed him that Emile Loche would not be appearing for dinner. "No more, really, than you. Cooper told me shortly after we arrived."

"Hmm. I suppose I should have expected it. Schofield will take every opportunity to seize any advantage. I expect our senators would like to hear Loche's proposal firsthand. The speed of that courier ship validates at least one of their claims. That drive alone would give us significant strategic advantages over the DeeCees... or anyone else who doesn't have it. If... it is proprietary to the Seat and the System States don't have it either. I suspect the knowledge that those technologies exist may have triggered the troubles in SolSystem. That they annexed Luna and EllFive—"

"They were already in EarthGov's pocket, Laird."

"And attacked Mars," McLean continued, "shows they don't know who developed and has it. If you examine the data carefully, it appears EarthGov panicked. SolSystem isn't monolithic. EarthGov thought they could dictate to the rest of SolSystem. I believe they've found that premise to be false."

McLean grunted and rose to walk about the room. He examined a painting of a sloop-rigged sailing ship on one wall, scuffed the carpet with the toe of his shoe, walked over to the window, and threw back the drapes to reveal not a window but glass double doors giving access to a balcony outside his office.

Harris said nothing as McLean wandered about. He knew the man was thinking about their conversation.

After three circuits around the room, McLean returned to his seat across from Harris. "Could we deal with the Seat alone?"

"Against the Confederation? In competition with the Confederacy?"

McLean shook his head. "No, no, no. Against Monmouth—Schofield and his cabal."

"Oh." Harris leaned back and closed his eyes, thinking for a moment.

Schofield was not a clansman. He was from Littlefield, a system some thirty light-years from Caledonia. Littlefield had been settled during the third wave of colonization… after the formation of the Confederacy. The cabal was a group from those worlds settled during the third—and some from the second—wave who thought themselves shortchanged of the "largess" of the Confederation, such as it was. One of their goals was a stronger confederation—rather, a stronger central government—that could impose its will on member worlds. Their goal was to remake the Confederacy into an organization like that of the System States commonwealth. McLean and Harris supported a stronger Confederacy, but not at the expense of individual members' sovereignty. Inverness was the first step as that planet led the Confederacy. A common slogan was "Where Inverness goes, the Confederacy follows."

"You know our political strength better than I," Harris said. "The cabal and their Consolidation Party affiliates control, what, thirty percent of the Senate? We and our allies control thirty-five to forty percent? Can we get enough nonaligned votes to block them?"

"Perhaps." McLean didn't expand on his reply.

Harris continued, "We can't depend on all the clans to come to our side. Monmouth—possibly Seivers and Kromski too—sides with the cabal. Cooper said all three clans would have representatives meeting Emile Loche tonight in Kilkenny. Monmouth will be there in person, and they will attempt to usurp or split our senators' votes."

"Monmouth would sell his daughters for whores," McLean interjected, "for an advantage over us—if he had any. Seivers and Kromski are another matter… as are our senators."

Harris closed his eyes and rubbed them at the bright sunlight streaming through the windows behind McLean. He leaned forward and sipped from his cup, stalling. McLean deserved a response.

"Seivers wants to underwrite more colonies," Harris said. "That new drive would cut their costs significantly. They'll side with whoever gets them that technology. Kromski... I'm not sure about them. I think they'd like to compete with us and our spaceborne industries. We can deal with Seivers. They need ships, and we can build them cheaper than anyone else, and we can include the new drive if we win instead of Monmouth's cabal."

He gathered his thoughts. "A thought. Our gasdivers and exotic chemworks aren't as profitable as we'd like. Maybe we could make a deal with Kromski. That would give them an entry into space industry."

"It's an idea," McLean replied. "I'll have our people approach Kromski and see if they'll bite."

Harris nodded. Clan McLean owned or controlled most of the space industry in the Caledonia system. Their ships mined the Oort cloud to provide water and oxygen for Caledonia's stations, mines, and shipyards. Clan ships dived into the system's two gas giants for volatiles and exotic, long-line molecular compounds that fueled their chemical works. It was this last industry, he had suggested, that could be sold to the Kromski Clan. Gas diving was profitable, but not as much as Oort and belt mining, nor as much as their heavy industries and shipyards around the system.

"What did you discover about those infiltrators?" McLean asked.

"That is another thing that's worrying me. We thought the ship was a false-flag operation by the DeeCees or perhaps the Hivers, trying to put the blame on the System States. Then we discovered the infiltrators were, or were at one time, System States Marines or Spec Ops. They had the same special nannites as did Fabien Loche. That made us look further."

He reached down and took a sip from his cup. He didn't want to discuss this subject with McLean, but it had to be done. "We, Schofield dissenting, now believe that the ship was from the System States. I'm also convinced that the destination of its hidden cargo was to some group within the Confederacy. To someone on Inverness, perhaps."

McLean sat up, looking stunned. "What!"

"Yes. Someone is importing nukes and weapons."

"That's…"

"Illegal. Yes. It violates the Ban and breaks the Confederation prohibition too."

The Ban had arisen from the War Years. A clan that was now extinct, whose name would never again be spoken, used a nuke during a war with a neighboring clan. The other clans on Inverness united and destroyed that clan, root, trunk, and branch. A universal ban resulted from the incident. No one, no clan could possess nuclear weapons. That war also led to the formation of the Council of Clans on Inverness. The Ban was later extended to all member planets of the Confederation. Only the Confederacy, in the form of the Confederate Navy and Marines, could possess nuclear weapons.

"Monmouth," McLean declared.

"We don't know that."

"I do. I can feel it. You know Clan Monmouth was the instigator of that war. That Clan was just a tool that Monmouth used."

"We can't prove that either—we never could in all the time since. Twelve hundred years and no proof. Don't let your paranoia rule you, Robair."

McLean looked at Harris. Monmouth was a sore point with him… and with several clans. Robair McLean and Lionel Monmouth had been personal enemies for decades. The suspicion against Monmouth remained regardless of the lack of proof.

"Very well," he conceded.

Harris rose and stretched. "I'm as bad as Monmouth."

"How so?"

"I pushed Molly Quinn onto Fabien Loche." He noticed McLean's questioning look. "No, I haven't pushed her to go against the *Proprieties*, but I may have bent them. I don't think she knows that I have. Molly likes him." Harris extended his arms and stretched again. "Truth be told, I do too, but so far, he's kept his distance from her."

"Was that wise? It's your sept's decision. I assume you've discussed it with Lena?"

Lena Harris was Donal's sister, Molly Quinn's mother, and the Chief of the Harris Sept. She was also Robair's deputy. "Not in so many words. I told her I had a new liaison and that Molly seemed to like him. That's all."

McLean sighed. "You shouldn't have pushed her toward Fabien Loche without Lena's approval. You know Molly is her jewel. She's going to skin you."

"Probably," Harris agreed. "I'm getting a headache. I may as well have it out with Lena now while I'm in a foul mood. Lena will get in her licks, and the way I'm feeling, I won't notice all that much." He reached down, took one final sip from his cup, placed it back on its saucer, rose, and said, "By your leave."

McLean nodded, and Harris walked out of the room.

†††

McLean remained seated. He sent a command through his link, and the drapes behind his desk closed, hiding the double doors. If Fabien Loche married into the clan, that would be a coup. But, he remembered, Loche was a Member of House DuQuoin and an Associate of the Seat. With their matriarchal society, Quinn might be joining their house. Either way, it would create an alliance between Clan McLean and House DuQuoin.

If…

†††

Loche and Quinn walked across a paved terrace toward the green landscaped lawn that sloped down to the drop-off into the sea. A wide gravel path some meters wide ran upslope of the edge and parallel to the drop-off. The path followed the cliff until it curved out of sight.

The overcast had dissipated, and Loche could feel the spray from below and hear the surf boom against the base of the cliff. The upflowing breeze ruffled their hair.

120

Molly found a bench next to the gravel track and invited Fabien to sit. "It's not wise to get near the edge, Fabien. Pieces fall off, from time to time, into the sea."

Loche had never seen surf such as this. The only other time he had seen the sea, the Hellenic Sea on Earth, it was placid. This surf was alive like a giant beast beating against the shore. A boom was heard from the direction of Dunnsport. He looked up and saw the contrail of a shuttle coming down for Dunnsport. Hovering in the wind out over the surf was a sea raptor looking for prey. From somewhere out of sight came a *skee!* from its companion.

"Hut! Hut! Hut! Hut!"

A platoon of militia in PT gear jogged down the path in time with the cadence. Loche had a momentary flashback of leading his squad around the track at Millersport Naval Base. He wondered what being a militiaman would be like. The military life had attractions.

He dismissed the thought, letting the past be past, and resumed watching the rollers approach from the distance, aware of Molly's presence at his side. "You said we've now been formally introduced?"

"Yes. It was supposed to be done tonight, with Uncle Donal introducing you to the laird," she said, watching the sea, copying Loche's manner. "He will still, but Cooper spoiled it for him when he introduced himself to you as a representative of the clan. That was sufficient as far as the *Proprieties* are concerned."

"What is the significance? Of the formal introduction, I mean. I don't fully understand."

Quinn said nothing. She sat and looked out toward the sea and the distant horizon.

"Molly?"

She sighed. "It means we're fair game for the matchmakers."

"What? Oh."

121

Loche understood. The clans were the same as home. In his case, it was the Line Mothers who plotted. Reena had been their choice. He and Reena had known each other for a long time. He liked her. The two of them were close friends… but now he preferred to make his own choices, not have them imposed upon him. He realized Molly was in the same situation.

"Am I correct in assuming that you joined your uncle in the Customs Service to escape them?"

"Yes and no. Most of our sept serve or are affiliated with Customs or the Confederation military. Usually, only the men become inspectors, like Uncle Donal. We poor women are agents… except for me. I wasn't satisfied with just being an agent. No, I had to be an inspector to keep out of their clutches.

"Our sept's matchmakers were getting… frustrated. I'd turned down several potential candidates. As my mother's daughter, they kept trying to use me as a pawn in their political games."

"What has your mother to do with it?"

"Didn't Uncle Donal tell you?"

"Tell me what?"

"My mother, Lena Harris, is our Sept Chief. She's also the Laird's deputy. If Laird Robair suddenly died, she'd be the next laird."

"Uh… I can see your situation." *How alike we are,* he thought. *Positions, pressures, but not similar responsibilities.* "I'm in a kindred situation. My grandmother is our house Grand Dam and Holder of the Seat. For us, she is the equivalent to your Confederation Executive. My mother is our House Line Mother. In the clans, she would be our deputy laird…or perhaps a chief. My grandmother, the Grand Dam, would be equivalent to your Laird and is also our house representative to the Seat. Think of your Confederation senators." He looked at her. "My future is as controlled as, it appears, is yours."

122

Silence fell again. Out near the horizon, a ship appeared, heading for Dunnsport. Loche watched seabirds riding on the updraft... so much like Earth, so much like his last dream on the *Tolstoy*.

"Did you meet my father when he arrived?" he asked her.

"Briefly. Uncle Donal and Colin Schofield took him in tow as soon as he identified himself."

"What of your father? You've not mentioned him."

She sighed again. "He's gone. He was a seaman, a hand on a coastal freighter. One day, his ship sailed and never came back. We don't know what happened. No emergency beacons, no wreckage, nothing. His ship sailed over the horizon and disappeared."

Loche didn't respond. All too often, one of the spaceborn departed a station and never returned. He thought of an uncle who, when Loche was younger, departed on a survey of a little-explored sector of the belt and never returned. All that had been discovered, after receiving a short burst from his emergency beacon, was a few pieces of debris—no body, nothing of his one-man survey ship larger than small pieces.

"Da would take me sailing," she continued. "Just around Dunnsport's harbor and bay... down the peninsula... a day trip. He was a partner with some cousins in a small fishing boat. Da wasn't a fisherman, but he'd go out to help from time to time between voyages." She looked at the sea with a wistful expression. "I miss him. He's been gone five years, now."

They sat staring out to sea, neither speaking much.

After some time, Quinn said, "It's getting on toward dinner. I must get ready." She stood as Loche did also. "Why do I feel," she asked him, "like some mare being prepared for show?"

"I'm feeling the same too."

"I suppose it could be worse." She strode up the slope toward the clan house.

Loche watched her for a moment then followed in her wake.

Chapter 7. Guest

McLean House, Clan McLean Territory, 21 Sixmonth, 3203

As promised, Angeal returned Loche's house uniform and boots well before the time came to dress for dinner. Loche suspected, from his prior observations, that he would be drab compared to others at dinner. He dressed, black nouveau-silk trousers tucked into his boots, a shirt, and black waist-length jacket. The jacket displayed his house crest on his upper left shoulder, with a silver pin to show he was a Member of House DuQuoin. The final adornment on his black shirt, at the base of his throat on the short-banded collar, was a platinum emblem encircled with diamonds. The Grand Dam herself had given it to him to signify that Loche was an Associate of the Seat. His last item of apparel was Harris's gift, the holster and belt. It fit snugly around his waist, and his Moen pistol was a perfect fit.

Angeal guided him through the maze of passages until they stepped through an unprepossessing door to a large dining room. Inside the entrance were two large militiamen, wearing the kilts of Clan McLean, guarding the door. Each militiaman had a dirk, a holstered pistol on his weapon harness, and a submachine gun slung across his back. He noted the weapons were well-worn and not ceremonial.

"Customs Inspector Fabien Loche!" one militiaman bellowed. "System States Liaison, Member of House DuQuoin, and Associate of the Seat of the Thirty Houses!"

Well, it's no secret who I am now. Loche hitched up his weapons belt to make it more comfortable and stepped forward.

Harris moved through the other guests to intercept Loche with two others in tow, one a woman. "Fabien, welcome," Harris said. "Please allow me to introduce you to Robair McLean, Laird, Clan McLean and Lena Harris, Clan McLean and Chief of the Harris Sept."

Robair McLean matched images Loche had been shown of the Laird. The woman bore a startling resemblance to Donal Harris. She must have been Molly Quinn's mother and Donal Harris's sister.

He bowed to McLean. "Honored, sir." Then he bowed to Lena Harris. "Honored, Madam."

"I welcome you to the clan," McLean replied.

Lena Harris said nothing except, perhaps, a small snort.

Loche glanced at Donal Harris, who, likewise, said nothing except to give a slight shrug of his shoulders. Lena Harris appeared to have issues with Donal Harris and Laird McLean.

Laird McLean interrupted the sudden silence. "Let's be seated, shall we?" He walked to the table and stood behind the chair at the head of the table. The other guests followed and, finding their name placards, stood behind theirs. Loche's position was to McLean's left, while Lena Harris was to his right, across from Loche. Donal Harris was next to his sister. He heard a rustle as Molly Quinn walked up and stood next to him. She wore a long pale-green nouveau-silk sheath dress that bared her shoulders, with a sash of the McLean tartan over her right shoulder. Other than Loche, she was the only one attending who was not wearing a kilt or, like her mother and the other women, in long skirts of their clan's tartan.

He looked at her and asked, "I assume your suspicions were correct?"

She nodded. Across from them, her mother snorted again.

"Harrumph!" Robair McLean cleared his throat.

The casual conversation down the table faded into silence.

"Gentlemen and Ladies, I would like to introduce, to our clan and our allies, Member of House DuQuoin, Fabien Loche."

Loche bowed to McLean then down the table to the others, standing behind their chairs. *That description lays the tone of this dinner.* McLean sat, followed by the others around the table. McLean introduced each diner at the table, most of whom were Clan McLean sept chiefs. Some were not. The gentleman at the foot of the table stood when it was his turn to be introduced.

"And," McLean said, "Laird Herman Mieze of Clan Mieze, Sept Mieze."

Laird Mieze bowed to Loche and said, "Welcome, Fabien Loche. Clan McLean echoes our sentiments in the discussions to follow."

"Thank you, sir," Loche responded. "My father is the Emissary, not I. However, while I can provide some information, all negotiations must be conducted through him. I would welcome your thoughts on the matters and will be most happy to take them to him. I would ask that you discuss any issues directly with him when he arrives. I can make no commitments."

Mieze nodded and took his seat. The introductions continued up the remaining side of the table. Everyone except Laird Mieze wore the same tartan... except for subtle differences. Distinctive colored threads were woven into the tartan. McLean's tartan had a few distinct gold threads. Donal, Lena Harris, and Molly had bright-blue threads added into their tartan. As Loche looked closer, others down the table wearing the McLean tartan had threads of red, yellow, green, orange, or other hues.

Molly noticed his examination and looked down the table too. "What?" she asked.

"The threads in the tartans. Does each sept have a different color?"

"Oh! Well, uh, yes. Other than the Laird. His will always have gold threads added to his tartan. The usual color for the McLean sept is purple."

"Identification at a glance, then?"

"Yes, at least for clan and sept."

When Molly's turn came to be introduced, McLean said, "And next to our guest is Mary Elizabeth Quinn, Clan McLean, Sept Harris."

"Mary Elizabeth?" Loche asked her.

"Yes. I prefer, however, to be called Molly."

From her tone, Loche understood the issue was not to be discussed.

†††

The dinner progressed. Loche had rarely eaten actual meat from animals. The houses grew protein in vats to supplement vegetables and grains from hydroponic gardens. Everything on the table, he was told, was grown outside, in the open air and dirt. The thought made him uncomfortable. He enjoyed the rack of lamb and slices of prime rib while not thinking of their origins. At first, Molly ate little. He noticed her wineglass was refilled twice, but as the dinner proceeded, she seemed to accept the situation and ate more.

As the second serving, a seafood dish, was being cleared, she told Loche, "I have to eat something, or I'll turn into a drunk before the night is over."

Loche had been sipping his wine. Like many spaceborn, he seldom drank alcohol. He had never acquired a taste for distilled alcohol nor wines. From his experience, he would rather not. It all tasted like vinegar to him. The dessert course was brought out, and with it came several musicians who gathered in a corner and began to play.

McLean leaned over and whispered in Loche's ear, "I like older Celtic music from Earth. This is a renaissance sextet famous for their renditions of nineteenth- and twentieth-century Irish and Scottish classics."

After the dessert and concert, coffee and tea were served, heavily laden with caffeine, Loche suspected. The table was cleared, and the servers, along with the musicians, disappeared. The two guards at the main door locked it and the other exits. McLean placed a small device on the table, and several others, Laird Mieze included, laid more. Loche noticed both Donal and Lena Harris placed several more devices on the table.

McLean stood and spoke to the diners. "I've done my best to ensure we are not disturbed nor eavesdropped upon. Add any additional protection as you wish. Deputy Lena Harris will make a single audio recording of the discussion and will ensure each of you receives a

127

transcript through secure means. Please be aware Fabien Loche is not the Emissary. Therefore, while he has some knowledge of the discussions about to take place, he cannot make nor endorse any proposal. This discussion is for information only—what the Seat desires and a brief description of the items they are willing to trade. After his presentation, each of you will have an opportunity to ask questions. Mr. Loche may not be able or be allowed to answer them all. Please honor his constraints." McLean turned to Loche and asked, "Satisfactory?"

Loche nodded, rose, and told McLean, "It is sufficient, sir." Then he turned to the rest of the diners. "Gentlemen, please let me give you the state of the affairs in the System States as I know them—a bit of history, perhaps—and then I will get to that part you are all interested in."

Loche presented a quick review of the Free Belter War in the Tau Ceti system, the biowar instigated there by the Mining Cartel, which spread to other systems including SolSystem. War propaganda by the Mining Cartel blamed all belters and stationers regardless of their involvement. The houses in SolSystem were not involved in the war on either side, but they were painted as participants and initiators of the biowar.

"The System States government knew the spaceborn of SolSystem—and those in the Tau Ceti system—were blameless, but the Mining Cartel was a large contributor to political campaigns of the SolSystem government and the representatives of EarthGov. SolSystem, led by EarthGov, sided with the Cartel and ignored the protests from the houses and the stations of SolSystem."

"What does that have to do with now?" someone asked from down the table.

After the interruption, Loche continued, "The war was nine centuries ago. Much of the bias and prejudice had dissipated, we thought, until two decades ago."

He paused and took a sip of wine. "EarthGov, for reasons of its own, perhaps to seize the space industries and shipyards in orbit, at the Lagrange points and in the belt, began to feed that long-held bias. At one time, the Seat operated the largest shipyard in the System States. Most of their product was military, capital warships, civilian fast packets, and couriers. Smaller yards at EllFive and in Earth orbit produced ships, too, primarily freighters, smaller warships, and system-defense ships. A decade ago, EarthGov began to shift System States military ship orders from the Seat to orbital yards near Earth. EarthGov has been starving the spaceborn of capital and of the resources that required payment by capital assets. With the recent attacks on Luna, EllFive, and Mars, the centuries-old hatred is coming to a head—civil war, and it is a war the Seat cannot win. That leaves the Seat with one option—immigration… *en masse*.

"What we want is something the Confederacy has in plenty. In the Confederacy's three clusters are many systems that are unused. Many are unclaimed and only marginally surveyed. We are offering a trade—new technology, significant breakthroughs that no other polity, including the System States, has—for a metal-rich system that has at least one habitable planet or a planet that can be easily terraformed."

"The technology we offer is an upgrade of the Hawking Quantum Shunt drive. You've seen proof of that with our courier from SolSystem. A new, faster, and shorter-ranged FTL drive, a new, nonreaction, surface-to-orbit engine, and other technologies that I cannot discuss at the moment—they're recent, and I wasn't briefed on them before my departure from SolSystem."

Loche gazed over his audience, seeing interest and some confusion too. "Rather than continue with more detail, do you have questions? I see some of you may not understand our proposal."

Laird Mieze stood at the far end of the table. "McLean is a spacefaring clan—at least some of their septs are," he said, nodding to Lena Harris. "Would you go further on the significance of these new drives? What function do they perform that our existing drives do not? What advantage do they provide?"

"Thank you for those questions," Loche replied. He knew McLean and Harris knew of the advantages of the new drives as they had seen the original proposal, but apparently, others had not. "Let's start with the first, the improved quantum shunt. Our upgrade allows ships to sail the quantum sea at and below the two-thousand-fathom level."

Mieze rose again to lead with another question. "My clan is mercantile. We have few members in the Fleet, nor are we invested in freight nor shipping. What do you mean by two thousand fathoms?"

Loche nodded to Mieze, acknowledging his question. "When the first FTL drive was developed in the late twenty-first century, the first quantum shunt drive, the initial exploratory ships were crewed by members of Earth's wet navies—specifically, the submarine forces. A quantum shunt operates by altering the quantum state of the ship, diving into the quantum sea—or *subspace*, as those sailors called it. By shifting into different quantum states, a ship in subspace, compared to real-space, can travel faster than light. The deeper a ship dives into the more energetic quantum states, the depths of subspace so to speak, the faster it can travel. However, there are limits. Past a certain energy state, a certain depth in subspace, the stresses on the ship and the power requirements rise until a ship cannot descend farther without being severely damaged or destroyed. That limit is known as the crunch depth. Our new drive extends that crunch depth deeper into the quantum sea.

"In the terminology that has come down since that time, the crunch depth has been twelve hundred fathoms. Most warships, fast packets, and couriers, those built by the Seat, can dive to the one-thousand-fathom line. Freighters and most passenger liners travel at six hundred fathoms.

"Our improved drive dives deeper, to two thousand fathoms, perhaps more, and is, therefore, much faster. When I came to Caledonia from SolSystem, the trip took six months. That was on a fast packet. The Seat's courier, which just arrived, departed SolSystem forty-five days ago."

Mieze blinked. Others around the table appeared to be thinking. Some had predatory grins.

"Think," Loche continued, "of the advantage of moving products to markets faster than your competitors, with only a marginal increase in cost."

Loche could see Mieze seize on that thought, calculating the possibilities.

"The second drive being offered is radically different, and while it is derived from quantum physics, it operates on a different principle. It has advantages and disadvantages, but given the astrographics of the Confederacy, the smaller average distance between stars as compared with the System States, we believe the advantages are significant."

McLean interrupted. "Would you expand on this drive? From the briefing packet we received, I believe it may have some very real possibilities."

"Certainly, sir."

Loche reached down, raised his cup, and took a sip to wet his throat. "The second drive allows for the construction of surface-to-surface interstellar ships."

Lena Harris started, as did several chiefs seated down the table.

"The current shunt drive requires a large ship and a large power plant. One feature of the shunt upgrade is a new power source, a smaller and more powerful shunt engine, and once the startup tooling is completed, a cheaper one. The new FTL drive—we call it a tunnel drive— is small, much smaller than the shunt drive. When activated, it can shift a ship from one point in space to another with no discernable passage of time in transit. Light-years, gentlemen, in a blink of an eye."

He paused to let that statement soak for a moment. "The traditional shunt drive has a lower size limit. Most of the mass of a shunt-drive ship is for the power systems that provide the energy for the dive into the quantum sea. I believe with the new power source, that lower limit for the shunt drive can be lowered. I don't know how much.

"The new drive has an upper mass limit of one hundred eighty thousand tons and, because of the shape of the drive field, requires a spherical hull. When you combine the tunnel drive with the new surface-to-orbit engine, you have a starship that can directly land on the surface of a planet, take on cargo and passengers, take off, and tunnel to a distant system. The tunnel ship can carry cargo from the surface of one planet to the surface of another planet." He paused for a moment. "It eliminates the need for an orbital station or beanstalk."

Loche expected a response. Instead, the room fell silent. Mieze sat at the far end of the table with his mouth open.

Loche went on, "As with all good things, there are disadvantages with the tunnel drive besides its upper-mass limit. A tunnel shift cannot exceed twelve light-years. Another disadvantage is the tunnel drive module must be recharged before it can be used again. The recharge takes approximately a standard week. Attempting a tunnel without a full recharge is dangerous. It will permanently ruin the engine. I'm not sure why that is. It was not in my briefing.

"However," he continued, "with the compactness of the Tri-cluster, the average distance between inhabited systems is three point two light-years. The tunnel drive should make commerce between newly colonized planets much easier and cheaper than regular shunt-drive ships, especially for those newly colonized systems or those who have not yet built orbital stations.

"Our design for tunnel ships include two tunnel drives. If, for instance, you tunnel into a situation that requires an immediate escape, you can fire the second engine and leave. Or use the first drive to travel to a system, take on cargo in a day or two, and use the second drive to proceed to your next destination, all the while recharging the first engine. After that second shift, you will have to recharge the first engine and begin recharging the second, but it allows passages of up to twenty-four light-years in a matter of hours."

"Are there other constraints on the tunnel drive?" one chief asked from the far end of the table.

"It has the same initial constraint as does the shunt drive. It cannot be engaged until the ship has moved out to at least the sixty-fathom line, and it must broach in the new system outside the sixty-fathom line—to avoid the 'rocks and shoals,' as star sailors call them."

The buzz of conversation rose down the table. The possibilities were being realized.

132

"And what of this third drive?" Lena Harris asked, glaring at Loche.

What have I done to anger her? "It's a derivative of pseudogravity. Pseudogravity, for you who are unfamiliar with the mechanics of that technology, is a field that attracts mass. When people first left their home planets, they spun their stations and ships to produce centrifugal force, simulating gravity. Six hundred years ago, pseudogravity was developed. Stations and ships no longer had to be spun, and stations could be built larger without the additional strengthening of the structure to compensate for the stresses created by centrifugal force. This surface-to-orbit drive is an offshoot of pseudogravity. Instead of attracting mass, it repels it. It is not a new sublight normal-space drive like the AQ drive. This one requires nearby mass to function, but it is sufficient to take shuttles to orbit all the way out to your Lagrange points. Your shuttles will not need a reaction engine to reach orbit. The engine has many other uses besides that in a shuttle."

He paused, mentally reviewing the critical points of the presentation. "The Seat has been working on these technologies for some time… many decades. We knew, through our social and political analysis, that EarthGov, using SolSystem, and to a lesser extent, the System States government, planned to take us over or destroy us. We were a competing group that EarthGov could not allow to exist. For that and other reasons, we started the research and development into new technologies. The research on the tunnel drive started nearly a century ago. The development was completed three decades ago. We could have announced it and begun building ships with the new drive."

He cleared his throat, which was getting scratchy. "We did not. Why? It would have ruined the commercial shipyard market owned and operated by EarthGov. We, the Seat and our houses, built large ships— warships and fast packets. EarthGov built smaller SDF ships and merchanters. The new drive can be used only for small ships, and if we built them, we would be in direct competition with EarthGov and their shipyard markets.

"Therefore, we withheld this new drive and other technologies. It gave us time to develop plans, procedures, and methods to preserve our culture—the means for us to immigrate, taking all we have with us."

He continued standing, looking down the table at each diner. "Gentlemen, clansmen, that is our proposal in brief. You may discuss this proposal in depth with my father when he arrives."

†††

The dinner lasted long into the evening. Loche noticed McLean and Mieze, with a few others, sequestering themselves in a corner. Lena Harris caught Loche's eye and pointed toward a corner. Molly Quinn started to come, too, but a glare from her mother froze her in place.

Another glare from Lena Harris quickly cleared the few diners standing nearby. "What I want to know, Fabien Loche, are your intentions."

"To represent my House, madam," Loche replied, implying he misunderstood her question.

"Not that! To Molly!"

"At present, I have no intentions other than those I would have for anyone with whom I work closely."

"Donal Harris has said nothing about her... availability?"

"What availability?" Loche said, again choosing to misunderstand.

"For marriage!"

Donal Harris was the matchmaker, then, not her mother. That explained some of her displeasure with him.

"I'm sorry, madam," he said. "I thought you knew. I'm betrothed."

"What!"

Around the room, several people turned to look, including Donal Harris and McLean.

"Yes, madam, to Reena Elaine Chaim, House Tyre. I must apologize if there has been some misunderstanding."

"No, no. I am the one who must apologize. I misunderstood the situation."

"Others have, too, I believe." Loche saw Donal Harris and Laird McLean approaching with Molly in tow.

"He's already betrothed, Donal," she said when the others gathered around them.

The look of shock and surprise on McLean's and Donal Harris's face was… gratifying—not so for Molly. She had turned white.

He had to explain before the situation got out of hand. "Please let me explain, if you will.

"I was betrothed to Reena Elaine Chaim ten months ago. If all had gone as planned, we would have married last month. Since I am here, not there, it didn't happen. She was killed seven months ago in a riot on Earth."

He saw the revelation was soaking in. "According to our customs and usage, our Custom and Tradition, as it were, I'm still betrothed until a year after her death. Neither I nor my house can make any commitments for another betrothal, nor engage in any preliminaries until that period is over."

"I'm sorry, Fabien," Molly whispered.

"The clan apologizes as well and begs your forgiveness. It was… presumptive of some of our members," McLean added.

Donal Harris looked down, embarrassed. "I'm sorry, lad. I didn't know, and I should have."

"Yes, some of us were presumptive," Lena Harris said, glaring at Donal and McLean. After they were all quiet for a moment, she continued, "That means any such discussions must wait another five months."

Molly looked up as her mother spoke. *Is that a smile on her face? Maybe… there is something for me here.*

✝✝✝

The questions dragged on past the local midnight. At some point, Lena Harris caught Molly's eye. They both rose and left the room. Every sept chief wanted to spend time with Loche. Most of them asked the same questions, phrased differently. Laird John-Paul Portee, Clan Portee, had arrived late but was in time to hear most of Loche's presentation. His clan's primary interest was in heavy industries, and he wanted to hear more about the new surface-to-orbit drive.

Later in the evening, the three lairds retired to Loche's sitting room, where they continued their private discussion. Loche responded when asked direct questions, but most of the time, he listened to the lairds. They were realizing how great the impact would be to the clans—and to the Confederacy—if a deal could be made with the Seat.

Robair McLean sent instructions for an astrographic search for an unused system that would meet the Seat's requirements. The initial response revealed that a complete survey of all the Tri-cluster's systems had never been undertaken. Though many private surveys were performed, none were coordinated, nor was there any centralized depository of stellar information. Somewhere in the Tri-cluster's five hundred thousand star systems must be one that met the criteria of the Seat.

††††

Loche slept late the next morning. His bioclock was not yet in perfect sync with the planet. Dundee used Confederation time, which put the McLean territory several hours behind Loche. He checked his messages. Many were from the participants of the previous evening. None were from his father, which made Loche uneasy. They weren't all that close, but he expected his father to keep him updated on the discussions at Kilkenny.

One note was from Angeal, saying breakfast could be delivered whenever he was ready. The kitchens of McLean House ran around the clock. Loche sent a reply requesting a standard breakfast in half an hour with coffee. He missed coffee. It had been plentiful when he was in the Marines. Tea was the common drink among the stations of Sol. They grew tea shrubs in their hydroponic gardens. Coffee, on the other hand, could not be cultivated. It had to be imported from Earth, but coffee imports stopped with the EarthGov embargo.

A sip of coffee should help him wake. After a quick shower, he would be ready for the day. No messages had come from Molly, Donal Harris, or any of the three lairds, he noted.

Angeal arrived with breakfast as Loche finished dressing. Fresh from the shower, his hair was still damp. Loche habitually did not use the shower's dryers.

"Anything for me on your schedule today?" Angeal asked.

"No… yes! Do you have a map of the clan house—on paper or something I can carry? I think I'll explore a bit, but I don't want to wander into any restricted areas."

"I can load one into your link. It won't have details of the restricted areas, however, just the public ones."

"That will do. Thank you."

Breakfast arrived. He ate, wishing for a breakfast companion, but everyone had duties. After all, he had slept late, almost to noon. He activated the room's link console and let the local news headlines scroll. Nothing caught his interest. The firefight on Dundee Orbital was old news. His visit to the McLean House wasn't mentioned in the commercial media. He noted the Confederation Senate on Cameron had adjourned for a two-week recess, and a new Confederation battlecruiser, the *TCS Tornay Bay*, was being launched from the Dundee Orbital shipyard that day. *What made Tornay Bay significant, I wonder.* The news appeared to be normal that day.

He was about to begin his explorations when Angeal entered again and said, "Sir, the laird would like to speak with you at your convenience."

"Fortunately, it is convenient now," he said. "Lead the way, please."

They followed the same path of the previous evening until they arrived at the lift. Instead of going down to the main level, they ascended. The lift door opened onto a small foyer manned by two militia guards.

137

As Loche stepped forward, Angeal announced, "Mr. Fabien Loche of House DuQuoin for the laird, by request."

Neither guard spoke. One tapped his link, reviewed a holo not visible to Loche, and nodded. He stepped to the door, tapped, opened it, and gestured for Loche to enter. As Loche walked toward the open door, Angeal stepped back and disappeared as the doors of the lift slipped shut.

All three lairds, McLean, Mieze, and Portee, were seated around a low table.

"Join us, please, Fabien," said McLean. "Would you like coffee, tea, or something else?"

"Tea, please. Iced, unsweet, and no lemon."

McLean dropped several cubes of ice from an insulated bucket into a glass and poured tea from another insulated container. "We have more news," he said while pouring. "The scheduled packet from the System States arrived overnight with instructions for you, for all the System States liaisons. You're being recalled. We—the Confederation—received a diplomatic note notifying us that the System States is formally canceling the Trade Treaty as of the first of Sevenmonth. The System States embassy on Cameron is being downgraded to a consulate. The consulate here on Inverness is being closed. They cite changing economic conditions within the System States."

He watched as Loche absorbed the news. "From the timing," McLean said, "the instructions and the note were dispatched well before EarthGov started a civil war in SolSystem. Your compatriots, Jacob Swensen and Clifford Tanaki, have requested asylum. Imar Kolskov has booked passage back to SolSystem."

"I won't be returning," Loche said.

"We didn't think you would, nor could." McLean cleared this throat. "I've made some queries with Charles Demning in your behalf. Donal Harris was about to certify you and sign off on your training. He said you can remain as a customs inspector if you wish. You would be required to renounce your System States citizenship and apply for citizenship in the Confederacy, however. Our three clans are willing to sponsor you."

138

"Would I have to join your clan?"

"No. Not all Inverness citizens belong to clans… just most of them. You needn't apply for Inverness citizenship at all, just Confederate citizenship, to remain in the Customs Service."

Loche didn't want to be rushed into any quick decision. He had intended to seek Confederate citizenship eventually, just not so soon. "Do I need to make an immediate decision?"

"No, you're still on convalescence leave for another three weeks. I would suggest you discuss this issue with your father, but you must decide by the end of your leave."

"Speaking of your father," Mieze interrupted, "have you spoken with him since you shuttled down?"

"Not since leaving Dundee Orbital. I thought he would finish his discussions in Kilkenny today. He hasn't returned my calls, but he wouldn't if he was in a meeting. Is there a problem?"

"We don't know. He hasn't been seen since he met with Monmouth yesterday. We're concerned."

"I echo that concern," said Laird Portee. "I have some… uh… associates at that meeting, and I haven't heard from them either."

†††

Molly Quinn knocked on the door and heard "Enter" a few seconds later. She walked inside and stood before the desk. "Ma'am," she said.

"Please don't, Molly, this isn't an official meeting," replied Lena Harris. "Please sit."

Molly Quinn acknowledged the request and sat in a chair before her mother's desk. "Mother."

The two looked at one another for a moment. Lena, following her habit, took the lead. "I wanted to get your thoughts on all this… this… situation with Fabien Loche. I know the matchmakers are pushing for a joining. It was done without my knowledge."

"I know that now, Mother. You were quite obvious."

"Yes, I suppose I was." She sighed. "What do you want? Your uncle and the laird think a joining would be beneficial to you and the clan. I will fight them if you wish. I promised you I would not let you be a pawn."

"I… I… don't know. I like him, and I think he likes me too. We have different loyalties, of course, and I don't think either of us know what difficulties those differences will create. We are both heirs to positions. How I wish we weren't—it'd be so much easier."

"I know, Molly. Fortunately, we have time, now, to let things simmer."

"Simmer. Yes, that is the situation."

"I don't think you know. He—all the liaisons—have been recalled. Imar Kolskov has already booked passage back to the System States. The other two, Swensen and Tanaki, have asked for asylum and will be staying. Donal and Robair will offer to sponsor Fabien if he wants to stay."

"He'll stay. He can't go back. He's said so more than once."

"I thought he wouldn't go… This whole thing is coming apart."

"What 'whole thing'?"

"The Trade Treaty has been canceled as have the liaison positions… The System States are downgrading their embassies and closing consulates. We think they are imploding. There is civil war in SolSystem, and it's likely to spread. We believe the Seat is just the beginning of a refugee stream."

Neither spoke for a moment. Molly looked out through the window behind her mother's desk. The sky was sunny with a few drifting clouds, she noticed.

"At least the Seat is offering a trade," she said, still looking out the window. "They want to pay their way."

"Yes. I don't expect any others to offer us anything other than personal skills. From what I've been told, there aren't many areas of science and technology where the System States are ahead of us."

"The Seat is offering several new technologies."

"The Seat, Molly, is neither EarthGov, SolSystem, nor the System States. There is a difference. However, we're getting off the subject. What do you want to do about Fabien Loche?"

Molly considered her options—and possibilities. "Let Fabien and I make that decision. When it's time. Or not."

Lena Harris looked at her daughter, her only child. "Very well. Remember my promise, though."

"Yes, Mother, I will."

"Sobeit."

Chapter 8. Castoff

McLean House, Clan McLean Territory, 24 Sixmonth, 3203

Fabien Loche was in a quandary. Donal Harris had returned to Dundee Orbital. He hadn't seen Molly since the dinner the previous evening, and he didn't know if she was still on planet or up at Dundee Orbital with her uncle. Regimental Sergeant Major Salvo Mantini had invited him to tour their facilities and join some of their training sessions. He still had more than two weeks of convalescent leave, and his boredom was growing.

Loche wanted to stretch his legs. Walking was preferable to wrestling with a militiaman, but he was running out of options. On the top of the massif was another shuttle port, a paved, semiprivate one for the McLean Militia, covering several square kilometers. It had started as the clan's primary airport, but centuries before, it had been replaced by the one at Dunnsport. The McLean shuttle port remained an active military base, however, and an alternate landing site when weather was dangerous over Dunnsport. Today, the sky was clear and cloudless and the surface clear except for scattered low structures that housed maintenance equipment, communications arrays, defense blisters, and entry sites for lifts down into the massif, to the clan house.

The top of the escarpment drew him—wide-open spaces, distant mountains, sea, and sky. He did not suffer from agoraphobia, as did many spaceborn, and he liked the nearly constant breeze across the tarmac and the updraft from the edge of the cliff. The faint smell of the sea was like a long-forgotten memory… a sense of *déjà vu* of humanity's home world.

Loche was returning to the lift when he heard horns honking in the distance, warning of an inbound shuttle. He scanned the sky and found the approaching contrail. It was a VTOL shuttle, most likely belonging to the McLean Militia.

The VTOL shuttle settled down just as he reached the lift. It was the first shuttle he had seen landing vertically. It was bulbous, a blunt oval that seemed to dive toward the surface. The shuttle settled on extended landing jacks amid the roar of its reaction engines. As soon as it was stable, the engines shut down, and the entire craft, sitting on its landing pad, was lowered into the depths of the massif.

Loche rode the lift down into the clan house. McLean had scheduled meetings with him and the other lairds. The lift stopped, and Neil Cooper stepped in.

"Mr. Loche," Cooper exclaimed, seizing Loche's hand and jacketed arm. "How are you? I've not seen you since your arrival. Is all going well?"

"Yes, as I expected."

Loche refused to provide any details of the dinner. Some diners had spread a few rumors but no details, but Loche refused to feed the rumor mill.

"Good, good. If you need anything, please send me a message." Cooper stepped out at the next level, and Loche continued down to the laird's level.

The lift's doors opened, and down the hallway before him were the two guards outside McLean's office. When he was a few feet away from the door, one militiaman spoke into his link, nodded to Loche, and gestured for him to enter the office.

†††

After the meeting ended, McLean and Mieze continued their discussions. Laird Portee and Loche left together.

"May I make a suggestion?" Portee asked in the hallway outside McLean's office.

Fabien stopped and looked at Portee while he considered the question. Portee was a large man, almost two meters in height. He was older than McLean and Mieze and sported a short beard sprinkled with gray. During the previous evening, John-Paul Portee told Loche that his clan specialized, among other areas, in corporate security and private investigations—activities that would have been done by global police forces if any existed on Inverness.

"I'll listen," Loche said. "I can't promise more until I hear you."

"That's all I ask," Portee said, motioning for them to continue walking. "Would you accept a… Let's call him a bodyguard until this is all over. Monmouth claims we've kidnapped you. I would hope that, by now, you know that you are a free agent and can leave or go elsewhere whenever you wish. We would hope you would not and would try to argue you out of such a move. Even here, you aren't safe. All clans spy on one another. I have contacts all over Inverness, and so does Mieze. McLean has contacts all over the Confederacy."

"By contacts, you mean representatives, agents… and spies?" Loche asked.

"Well, yes. That. However, that we have… do, doesn't invalidate our concern," Portee said.

They had reached the lift. Its door slipped open, and the two entered. Portee allowed Fabien to pick a destination, and he chose the upper surface of the massif.

Portee continued. "By this time, it's likely Monmouth knows you are here. I believe your father has escaped. We've heard rumors that Demning took him off planet. That will change. Monmouth will know where Demning took your father. If your father arrives at Dundee Orbital, Demning is the authority there, and Monmouth has agents in residence. So have we."

"They are friends and have been a long time," Loche said, referring to the customs director and his father.

"We noticed that," Portee said with a grimace. "We would have preferred Demning work with us, but it appears he has a private agenda."

The lift stopped, and the two exited into a small structure on the surface that housed access to the clan house's transport system. They walked out on the surface into a brisk wind sweeping down from the distant mountain range.

"Monmouth will be driven to act," Portee continued. "If he can't get his hands on your father, you would be an alternative—a tool to be drained of whatever information you may possess. To prevent that, I would like to provide you a bodyguard. McLean and Mieze know I'm making the offer. McLean wanted Donal Harris to do that, but he's occupied up in Dundee."

They strolled across the paved surface. Color-coded lines laced the surface, showing underground systems, taxiways, and other piping and connections common to air and shuttle ports. In the distance, an HTOL shuttle was being serviced.

"I have a person in mind, a former militiaman and security agent in one of my clan's endeavors that I believe would be suitable. He has been trained in personal security and special ops while in our militia. Would you accept him?"

"My first impulse is to say no," Fabien responded. "I've always believed I can take care of myself. I was just in a firefight and stopped two saboteurs."

"And you were wounded as a result," Portee interrupted.

"Yes. I was. There were too many for me alone. Harris took care of another. If we hadn't believed they were about to commit sabotage, we would have waited for backup. But we decided waiting would be too risky."

"And you could not have succeeded alone."

"No, it was a team effort."

"You will need a team again. Even here at McLean House, Monmouth has agents. We know that, just not who they are. Will you accept my offer?"

"Let me meet him. Then I'll decide. I mean no offense, but I need to meet and see him first."

High in the sky, another contrail was coming from the north. He couldn't tell if it was coming here or going to Dunnsport. Fabien took a breath before going back down into the massif. It didn't matter.

Portee nodded. "Let's go back down. His name is Theodore Popelli. He's expecting you to interview him."

†††

Loche followed Portee to the McLean Militia's armory, deep inside the escarpment, where Regimental Sergeant Major Salvo Mantini greeted them.

"Is he here?" Portee asked.

"Aye, he is," Mantini answered, "and having a grand time, he is. He's about to meet Militiaman Chou."

"I have to see this! Chou is the McLean hand-to-hand champion and won a world title in the Games last year."

The two followed Mantini into an open court. Two men were standing in the center within a large circle embedded in the floor. Several hundred, perhaps two or three companies of militiamen, watched, sitting on bleachers surrounding the court. After Portee and Loche were seated, Mantini nodded to the referees.

"Begin!" one referee shouted.

The two combatants were as unlike as any two could be. One was large, fit, and strong but without being muscle-bound. He moved assuredly, watching the other. His opponent was small, lithe, almost too slim. Given that, he did not appear weak. He moved smoothly, gliding to match the opening moves of his opponent.

"Which one is Chou?" Loche asked the sergeant major.

"The boy mountain," he replied with a grin. Mantini leaned over to Portee and said, "Your Popelli will be surprised," he added with glee.

"Let's watch," Portee replied. "Popelli has never competed in formal games. His experience has all been… more on-the-job."

146

Out on the court, the two continued to circle, measuring one another. Chou moved. Popelli danced back. They circled. Popelli moved forward. After an entanglement of limbs, Popelli was flying. He landed with a slap to the floor and rolled into a stance in time to meet Chou's follow-up attack.

This time, with the two grasping, holding, twisting, it was Chou who landed with a thud. Loche imagined he felt the floor quiver with the impact. Popelli continued his attack before Chou could recover. His follow-up failed. Chou broke Popelli's hold and regained his feet.

The two were evenly matched. Popelli had the experience and skill. Chou had youth and strength. In the end, Popelli's experience won the match on points. In the field, either could have won on any given day. As he watched, Loche saw that Popelli did not use some moves that could have won the match—moves Loche had been taught as, he suspected, had Chou. But those moves could be lethal and were not appropriate for a formal match.

"He's skilled, I grant you," Loche told Portee. "Once again, age and experience overcome youth and quickness."

Both men laughed at the old joke.

"Does he have similar skills with weapons and surveillance?" Loche asked.

"Yes. He was my clan's chief of information and data security. That was before he specialized in personal security."

Portee checked the time. "It's getting on toward dinnertime. Let's meet in my suite for dinner, and you and Popelli can get each other's measure."

"Thank you. I'll be there in… say two hours?"

"We'll be ready."

†††

Loche had a few minutes before he needed to leave for the dinner. Molly Quinn had insisted he buy some… semiformal clothing. She said he would need it, and he was glad he had bowed to her insistence. This suit was cut to the same pattern as his house uniform, but it lacked the house crest and was gray instead of black. He checked his appearance one last time. House Member pin in the proper spot, associate emblem at the base of his throat—all correct. Just as he moved toward his suite's door, he experienced a brief wave of nausea and momentary dizziness. He steadied himself against the doorframe, and whatever it was passed as quickly as it had appeared.

Portee's suite was on the same level as his. After a short stroll down the hallway, he was standing before Portee's door. It opened before he touched the admittance plate.

"Come in, Fabien, dinner is on the way," Portee said.

Loche entered and crossed the suite to where Portee and Popelli were sitting. Both rose and shook his hand. He still wasn't comfortable touching others in greeting. He preferred bowing, as was the custom of his house.

"Would you like something to drink before dinner?" Portee asked, to put him at ease.

"Tea, if you please, cold."

His response surprised Portee as if he was expected to ask for something... stronger.

"The Seat seldom consumes alcohol," he told them. "It has so many other uses that it has dropped out of fashion in our houses."

Embarrassed, Portee confessed, "I didn't know that. I know that alcohol fumes can be an issue aboard ships and some stations. I never thought of it as a resource."

Loche chuckled. "We do produce some very good wines in our agricultural stations. We sell most for hard cash, but we keep a few bottles for special occasions. I've just never acquired a taste for wine, beer, or any alcohol."

"You wouldn't have a problem with alcoholism in your stations, would you?"

"No. We cure addictions—sometimes the hard way—and we don't allow recidivism."

Portee nodded. "I can see that tough problems can call for tough solutions."

Dinner arrived. A house steward entered, pushing a serving cart into the room. He placed the buffet along one wall. Hot items were on one end, cold items, fruits, and desserts at the other, with hot and cold flasks for drinks in the center. The steward set the table in the suite with three settings, surveyed the result, and turned to Portee. "Will there be anything else, sir?"

"No, I believe this will be fine. Thank you. We'll call when we're finished."

Loche watched the steward prepare to leave with a growing sense of nausea. He swayed and steadied himself. The room appeared to dim. "Is it getting dark in here?" he asked Popelli. His vision narrowed, and he could feel himself falling.

Popelli caught Loche as he fell. "Steward, call medical!"

Loche heard the steward place the call. He felt as if he were drifting… Sounds, noises became muffled, and soon, those ended too.

†††

The two lairds were sitting in McLean's office, waiting to learn if Loche was recovering. McLean was speaking to Loche's tending physician. The conversation ended, and he cut the link.

"How is he?" Portee asked.

"Better," McLean replied. "The medics say he has a nanoinfection."

"Infection?"

"Well, not quite. The medic said Loche's maintenance nannites detected some foreign ones and reacted like they were fighting an infection, a disease."

"Will he recover?"

"Oh, yes. The problem is that his kidney, the new one, is not yet functional. The invading nannites, when they died, released toxins. Normally, those would be flushed from his system through his kidneys. He would not have known he had been invaded although he might have had a slight rise in temperature. However, with only one working kidney, the toxins built up—just like a disease."

"What caused it?"

"The medics are still running tests, but their initial estimate is that Loche was tagged."

"Tagged? Well, we can guess who's behind that."

"Monmouth," McLean affirmed.

"I think he'll accept Popelli now, but Monmouth knows he's here. He can't stay here now."

"I know." McLean sat back and looked down, thinking. "I think… I'll turn this over to Lena," he said with a grin growing on his face.

"Ah… yes… that could be… helpful."

†††

"It's a place we call Helen's Forge. It's a ways down the coast from Dunnsport. We have sept gatherings there, conferences, elections. It also has some cottages on the grounds for overnight—or longer—guests," Lena Harris explained.

Loche was sitting before Lena Harris's desk, still digesting the idea that someone had unintentionally poisoned him. His options were being whittled away a piece at a time. "How can you be sure you don't have a Monmouth agent there too?"

"I can't guarantee it, but the folks who work and live there have been of Harris Sept for generations. And like all the clan's sept houses, there is a militia unit stationed on or near the premises. Just in case. We learned a long time ago to not concentrate our forces."

"So this is your sept's version of McLean House?"

"Yes, similar to McLean House," she said.

He didn't have a choice. His options were to go back up to Dundee Orbital, stay at McLean House, where there was definitely a Monmouth agent, or… go to Helen's Forge.

"We also have an air and shuttle port nearby," she said. "The sept does a lot of business upabove from there."

"Convenient."

"Yes," Lena Harris replied.

Reluctantly, he said, "I guess one place is as good as another. I wish I knew where Father was." *All in time.* "Very well. Let's go."

Helen's Forge, Clan McLean Territory, 28 Sixmonth, 3203

Helen's Forge came into view. Loche and Popelli were riding in an airbus, a scheduled flight from the McLean House. The bus, while apparently well maintained, was old. The noise of its ducted fans penetrated its interior, making conversation difficult, which made Loche glad. He was not in the mood for conversation, friendly or otherwise. The more he thought of his circumstances, the more angry he became.

According to an informational display on the forward bulkhead, the airbus was at an altitude of three thousand meters, with an effective airspeed of four hundred kilometers per hour. The flight should have taken only twenty minutes. But because of a weather front, the airbus had skirted a storm and was just then, after forty minutes of flight, arriving at Helen's Forge.

Like McLean House, Helen's Forge was on the seacoast. The air and shuttle port, from a distance, was the most visible edifice in the area, a wide splotch of concrete amidst a broad hardwood forest. The Gael Sea was on the left as the airbus approached. Air and shuttlecraft hangars, repair shops, businesses, and warehouses lined the opposite side, fading into the foothills of the spinal mountain range of the peninsula. Brodie's Bay, a small seaport, was only a few more kilometers down the coast.

Popelli nudged Loche's arm. "Ten more minutes. Ground transport will be waiting for us."

Loche grunted and continued to watch the landscape out his side of the airbus. Terraforming had worked well in this part of Inverness. When the Caledonian system was discovered millennia before, the explorers found proteins based on levo amino acids already in place. The subsequent seeding of terrestrial life and plant forms did not have to overcome dextro amino acids. Terrestrial life forms co-opted and assimilated the presiding organic base to accelerate the spread of terrestrial life throughout the planet. Cameron, the next world inward, was not so lucky. Life there was minimal and provided no initial substance for terraforming. It was just now at the stage Inverness had reached at the end of its first century of colonization.

The airbus's fans changed pitch as they swiveled downward. It hovered a moment and dropped to land, without effort, before the air terminal. The engines spun down and cooled, and clicks and pops echoed through the interior as automated fuel and power connections were made. Loche and Popelli remained seated while the other passengers stood to retrieve packages and luggage from storage compartments.

Their links buzzed. Escorts were awaiting them.

††††

The cottage assigned to them was large enough to house a sizable family. It covered several acres and was a distance from the main buildings—near enough, however, for an easy walk to the sept house and central buildings. The outer walls of the cottage appeared to be of cut granite. A bronze plate to one side of the main entrance said it was over nine hundred years old.

The cottage included an outer security wall three meters high, with firing steps and rifle ports, obsolete given current military technology. The grounds had a second, invisible wall farther out—a wall of electronic sensors: motion detectors and geo-sound, seismic, and pressure monitors.

The cottage was used to house VIPs. Popelli had been briefed on the security features and decided Loche had enough on his mental plate. More concerns, along with the reasons for them, would stress Loche with no reasonable profit.

†††

Ruffo Esposito was terrified. Monmouth did not accept bad news well and had a tendency to blame the messenger.

"Where is he?" Lionel Monmouth screamed.

"S-s-sir, at the moment, we don't know."

"Where is he?" Monmouth repeated. Spittle from his mouth sprayed across Esposito's face.

"W-we know he was at McLean House yesterday. Our agent tagged him. Then he disappeared. I expect to hear news later today."

"You let his father get away! Now, you've let the son escape too!"

Esposito was not responsible for allowing either Loche to drop out of sight. But he was the advisor at hand, which meant he was the target of Monmouth's fury. "If he is still at McLean House, we will know when our agent reports. If he isn't, our orbital assets should find him unless he has left the planet or is deep underground."

"You better hope he's found, or your next assignment will be counting seagull eggs on Lippert Island!"

Esposito shuddered. Lippert Island was the northernmost parcel of land in Monmouth territory, an island surrounded by polar ice and isolated for most of the year because of storms. It was also the site of Monmouth's private prison. Few were ever seen again after being sentenced to Lippert Island.

"Y-yes, sir!"

†††

"I think we've found our spy," Alan Spier reported. Spier was the McLean House chief of security. He instructed his link to show a short video on McLean's holomonitor. "Watch Neil Cooper."

153

McLean leaned closer. He saw Cooper stop Loche and, with one hand, grab Loche's while his other hand gripped Loche's arm.

"We still have that jacket of Loche's. We've confirmed it has tracer nannites on the sleeve," Spier continued.

McLean looked down. He didn't want to believe the evidence. He had known Neil Cooper for several years and had never had to question his loyalty. Cooper hadn't been born into the clan, however. He was an outsystem immigrant. He'd passed the initial interviews and background search.

Still looking at the floor, he said, "Search his rooms—discreetly. Keep him under surveillance. Do it quietly. If he is a traitor, we don't want to give him alarm."

"Yes, sir. Quiet and discreet it is."

†††

The cottage had an outlying building on the beach. Loche was feeling restless. Popelli was meeting with the local security forces. *A walk around the premises would be nice.* Out the front door, down the walk, and past the front gate, he walked. If he turned right, he'd head for the central buildings of Helen's Forge. A turn to the left would lead to the beach. He turned left.

The path took him through a grove of trees that had limbs trimmed to create a green tunnel, the branches intertwining overhead. As he walked through the tunnel, he could hear surf up ahead. The path ended on the seaward side of the trees at the edge of the beach.

It wasn't much of a beach. It was covered with small, smooth pebbles instead of sand. The beach was a recent creation, and wind and surf hadn't yet reduced the pebbles to sand.

"Sir, please be careful. There's a satellite overhead."

Loche spun around, searching for the voice.

"Sir! Please!"

In the gloom at the forest's edge, Loche saw movement. A camouflaged militiaman became visible, having turned off his active-chameleon outer covering. Loche stepped back under the overhead coverage. "I didn't see you, militiaman."

"You weren't supposed to, sir. We're outer security. Monmouth is looking for you, and with his satellite overhead, he could see you if you looked upward."

"Of course. I'd forgotten," he said. He'd gotten slack—and careless. He needed to get back to the task on hand with the understanding that he was a target. "Thank you for your diligence."

"You're welcome, sir."

Loche ambled back to the cottage, mindful to keep his head down whenever he was out from under the cover of the trees. His feeling of helplessness and lack of control continued to grow.

†††

Lena called McLean through their secure link. "Monmouth has been rounding up our people and those of our allies and moving them to collection points around and among his militia bases."

"Any official reason?"

"No. Not that we'd expect him to give a reason. It violates Custom and Tradition. Shall we protest to the Council of Clans?"

"Do we have confirmation? Solid confirmation?"

"Yes."

"I'll take care of the protest. I want to coordinate it with our allies. Their people may be in jeopardy too."

"What about Monmouth and his allied clan members in our territory?"

"Reciprocate, but ship them back to their home clans. We'll not take hostages as Monmouth appears to be doing. I'll call Mieze, Portee,

Williams, and the others. Issue a recall to all clan members. The clan will cover transportation costs… and alert the militia."

"The militia is already on alert. I issued it in your name."

"Good." McLean paused then added, "Activate Plan Brandon."

Lena Harris gasped. "You think he'll go that far?"

"Monmouth isn't sane. I, and others, suspect the nukes found on the *C'seine* were for Monmouth. We can't take the chance."

Plan Brandon alerted the entire clan and sept agencies within clan territory to expect an imminent attack. While nukes could not be ruled out, suborbital chemical and kinetic strikes could do a lot of damage.

"Acknowledged, Laird McLean. I'll activate Plan Brandon."

The clan was preparing for war.

Chapter 9. Third Party

Shiloh, Cameron, 29 Sixmonth, 3203

Charles Demning stood up from the table and walked over to the broad windows lining one wall of the conference room. He stretched and twisted from side to side. Even in Cameron's lighter gravity, .92 g compared to Inverness's 1.2 g and the .98 g standard for Dundee Orbital, sitting for hours at a time was fatiguing… and a pain. He paced back and forth, relieving kinks and cramped muscles, before the floor-to-ceiling windows facing the Circular Sea. This resort hosting the conference was built into the sea's ringwall, a geographic formation created early in the planet's terraforming by the impact of an ice asteroid towed from the system's Oort ring. The distant sides of the ringwall had a hint of greenness—lichen most likely, still working to convert Cameron to an earthlike planet. Cumulus clouds were forming over the sea. A storm would develop later in the day, without doubt.

"It looks to be a hot day, Emile," Demning said when he returned to the conference table.

Emile Loche looked up as Demning spoke and glanced out the window. The others around the table were on a pause, a break in the discussions. However, Loche was making notes on his link and did not respond to Demning's observation. The draft of a proposal was almost ready to be initialed. The last of the minor language corrections had been made. The overall agreement had been settled for some time, and they were just quibbling over grammar.

At least it was a basis for an agreement. Work still needed to be done and an alliance to be forged.

††††

The past seventy-five hours had been interesting for Loche. Colin Schofield had escorted him down to Kilkenny, where Lionel Monmouth, Laird of Clan Monmouth, and others were waiting to meet him. He expected to be given a chance to present the Seat's proposal in a meeting with several participating clans. Instead, it was a private session with just Monmouth and a couple of his deputies. What followed was more an interrogation than a negotiation.

Monmouth didn't seem interested in what the Seat wanted. He concentrated instead on what the Seat was offering and what Clan McLean was proposing. The longer the meeting lasted, the more alarmed Loche became.

He was rescued by a private message from Charles Demning. Loche's link had been blocked when he arrived at Monmouth's office. That didn't surprise him as it was a common practice for private meetings. During a break, he had wandered outside, where his link could connect to the global net. Demning's message was encrypted with their old code. It read, briefly, *Need rescue? Come down to the main level. You'll see me next to the lift.* Emile Loche followed the instructions.

When they met, Demning told him that his baggage had been intercepted and was waiting in a limo outside. The two entered the ground car, and another of Demning's associates drove it away. Through a series of subterfuges, Demning and Loche escaped the planet to rendezvous at Cameron's Shiloh Resort with others interested in the Seat's proposal.

Demning walked back to the conference table and sat next to Loche. "Monmouth is still looking for you on Inverness. He believes McLean kidnapped you, but he can't discover how. They found the limo but lost track of you from there. Makes me glad the Council of Clans prohibited public surveillance... not that that means much in Monmouth Territory."

"I wish I could tell Fabien where I am, that I'm well."

"I can tell him without letting Monmouth know where you are."

"Please, do so. I think we're about finished here. We can initial the drafts. Will you speak for your associates?"

"Yes, they've deputized me. They will still need to review the final agreement, but if it is along the lines we've proposed, they should not object. It's a short trip, via courier, to Rajput. Once they see and agree, we can to take the draft to McLean, Mieze, and their allies for the next stage."

"Good. Let's get this done. We're short on time," Emile Loche said. "The hybrid is coming."

Helen's Forge, Clan McLean Territory, 29 Sixmonth, 3203

Fabien Loche had been walking along the forested paths that encircled Helen's Forge. He had spoken with Molly Quinn earlier that morning. She had, as he suspected, gone back to Dundee Orbital. Her call had been routed through McLean House and from there, via a secure, direct connection, to Helen's Forge—a roundabout connection, but it would misdirect Monmouth's spies.

"Do you have a new partner?" he asked.

"No, I'm following some items we discovered on the *C'seine.* It's been interesting. I have a partner assigned, but he isn't on board yet."

"Oh. Well, you are being wasted doing grunt work. You should be patrolling and inspecting."

"Ordinarily, I would partner with Uncle Donal, but he's filling in for Director Demning."

"Where's Demning?"

"No one seems to know. He left a message for Uncle Donal and delegated him as acting director. He said he was taking his accumulated leave. He must have quite a lot. I've never known him to take any."

The conversation ended. Molly had duties to attend. Loche had boredom to fend off.

His walk ended, and he was mounting the steps of the cottage when he received a text message from Charles Demning. It was short. *<Your father is well and with me. Will see you soon.>*

Demning's message eased his fears. Laird Mieze had discovered that the scheduled meeting in Kilkenny never occurred. His father had been taken, instead, to meet Monmouth and his cronies alone. However, he had disappeared in the middle of the meeting. Mieze told him Monmouth had

159

started a worldwide search and was accusing McLean and Mieze of kidnapping his father. That his father was with Demning spoke volumes to Fabien as did his father's abrupt departure from Kilkenny.

Fabien hurried back to the cottage and used its secure connection to call Laird McLean. McLean appeared immediately.

"I've—"

"We've—" said McLean.

"Please continue, sir." Loche was satisfied to let McLean speak first.

"We've heard from your father. He is with Director Demning, and he's well. They are meeting with a third group."

"I just received a similar short message but not mentioning any third party—just that they will see me soon."

McLean was standing before his desk, conversing with a group of people, some of whom Loche had met at the dinner. Mieze and Portee were there along with Lena Harris and a couple of other McLean sept chiefs. The holomonitor followed McLean as he walked around the room. A low table between the chairs and the desk was littered with cups and remnants of pastries. Loche's stomach growled, reminding him he hadn't eaten in some time.

"Have you heard when they, Father and Director Demning, are coming?"

"Not yet. There is some question whether they will come here or meet us in Dundee Orbital. We would be in Confederation space at Dundee. On the other hand, security would be better here. Do you know why Demning is involved?"

"He and Father are old friends, going back to the negotiation of the Trade Treaty."

"I didn't know that. I wonder why Donal Harris didn't mention it."

"He may not have known. My impression from my initial meeting with Director Demning is that he never spoke about his earlier posts and achievements."

"Donal never mentioned Demning's connection with Emile Loche to me either," Lena Harris added.

"I've not known Donal Harris as long as you, but from my short association, I think he would have said something if he'd known," Loche replied. As Harris was his partner, he didn't care to hear negative speculations about the man with no supporting proof. "Why don't you ask him?"

"Yes, why don't you?" Lena Harris repeated the question to McLean.

"I will," McLean responded, peeved. "I don't care to be blindsided."

"Make sure of your facts before making any inferences about Donal Harris. You've known him all your life. You practically grew up together." Lena Harris didn't hesitate to speak her mind. She was Donal Harris's sister and sept chief, and loyalty flowed in both directions.

Lena and McLean glared at one another.

Then McLean shrugged and turned to other business. "Obviously, I would prefer they come here."

"As would I," Mieze affirmed. "But I can see advantages meeting in Dundee Orbital. I suggest we support Demning's plan to take Emile Loche there. He's the customs director and can safeguard his and Loche's safety. Donal Harris is already there and can make any needed preparations.

"We'll send some of our militia fighters and a shuttle to the naval defense annex in Dundee Orbital to pick them up there, out of sight of the rest of the station, and bring them back. We can have other militia shuttles standing by as an escort. I'll add some of my own," Mieze said.

"I'll provide some Portee Militia fighters too," Laird Portee added.

"Do you really think someone, Monmouth or one of his allies, would interfere?" Loche asked.

McLean looked at Mieze and Portee then back at Fabien.

"Oh, yes," all three affirmed.

"Then make it so," Loche declared.

The others at McLean House returned to their discussion, while McLean and Lena Harris remained in the holo's visual field.

"We think it's time you returned to McLean House. If Monmouth attacks, as we believe he will, no place will be safe, but McLean House is safer, better protected than Helen's Forge," McLean said.

"Very well. I'm slowly going crazy here, with nothing to do. I can't even walk outside without remaining under cover."

"Thank you," McLean replied. "It would be unwise to travel by air from this point on. Take the maglev back here. It's slower, but I doubt, if you're cautious, that Monmouth would attack it."

Lena Harris leaned forward, closer into the visual field. She looked older and tired. "I wish I could guarantee your safety there, Fabien, but I cannot. We'll see you tomorrow."

Dundee Orbital, 10 Sevenmonth, 3203

"Dundee Control, Shuttle 405 ready for departure to Dunnsport."

"Shuttle 405, you are cleared for departure to Dunnsport on Exit Corridor Twelve West. Please observe inbound traffic on your outer reciprocal."

"Roger. Shuttle 405 disengaging."

"Shuttle 405 on clearance, shift to Weyland Control on one-five-zero-five-point-three megahertz. Squawk one-zero-two."

"Roger. One-five-zero-five-point-three. One-zero-two. Shuttle 405 out."

The shuttle released its docking clamps, and a brief burst from its thrusters sent the shuttle backing out of the docking bay. Three hundred meters from the station, the shuttle spun on its axis and prepared to engage its engines. Once oriented for its deorbit path, the shuttle waited to start its descent, which would, in time, take the craft to Dunnsport.

"Weyland Control, Shuttle 405, squawking one-zero-two."

"Roger, 405. We have you. Corridor Twelve West is clear. Engage main engines in ninety seconds."

"Shuttle 405, roger. Ninety seconds."

The pilot entered the data into the craft's autopilot. The rest of the flight would be hands-off.

Ten minutes later, the main engines stopped. The autopilot of Shuttle 405 made some minute adjustments. One brief burst of the thrusters was sufficient. The descent corridor would circle Inverness one and a half times before touchdown.

Monmouth territory appeared on the horizon.

Weyland Naval Fleetbase, 10 Sevenmonth, 3203

The admiral commanding Weyland Fleetbase Traffic Control was aware of the tensions downbelow. The officers and sailors of the fleetbase, on the admiral's orders, increased their monitoring of the opposing clans, ready to intervene if they took their dispute above the one-thousand-kilometer low-orbit line. The Confederation didn't interfere when the clans lofted more weather, communications, and surveillance satellites. Some of those were suspiciously overpowered but were allowed to remain in orbit. Suspicion was insufficient to remove them out of hand.

However, the Confederation was prepared to remove any satellites that were armed—providing they could prove it. Armed satellites were banned by the Confederation charter.

Naval Traffic Controller Isen Bruck was following Shuttle 405 and a number of others. Four-oh-five was about to pass over Monmouth territory when Bruck's console lit up with a number of alerts. Radar-lidar sites inside Monmouth began to paint Shuttle 405—fire-control radars and lidars.

Bruck slapped his alarm, opening an internal channel, and announced, "Alert! Monmouth has weapons lock on Shuttle 405. Four-oh-five is a scheduled McLean commercial shuttle en route from Dundee Orbital to Dunnsport."

In another location within the twenty-kilometer base, weapons—missiles, particle beams, and kinetic cannons—were brought online. If Monmouth fired on the shuttle, the naval base would attempt to defend it while it was in Confederation space. That defense could include strikes against Monmouth's planetary weapon sites.

McLean Commercial Shuttle 405, 10 Sevenmonth, 3203

While not strictly legal, all McLean shuttles, commercial and military, carried full defensive ECM suites. The shuttle could, but did not at present, carry offensive weaponry. The ECM side panel lit up and automatically engaged the Monmouth fire-control systems.

Within the passenger module, the lighting shifted to red, and an alarm blared. Passengers were not allowed movement during transit, and when the alarm sounded, each passenger and crew seat enveloped its passenger, creating an armored survival pod. If the shuttle lost pressure, the pods ensured the safety of each passenger. The three stewards raced to their landing positions and were encapsulated like the passengers.

"Jink!" the pilot instructed through his embedded link.

The shuttle began evasive maneuvers to foil any missile or kinetic strikes from the planet. Particle beams were much faster, near light-speed. The shuttle slipped aside just as a particle beam flashed, scorching the outer hull.

The hull remained intact although weakened. Particle beams and kinetic weapons from Weyland Fleetbase responded, destroying the attacking weapons emplacement. At the same moment, a number of Monmouth satellites came alive with radar, lidar, ECM, ECCM, and other sensors sweeping near- and low-orbit space. Following standing orders for the situation, weapons from Weyland Fleetbase commenced destroying Monmouth satellites, one by one.

Monmouth ground-to-space weapon sites shifted from the shuttle to the Confederation fleet base. During the following exchange, Shuttle 405 passed around the edge of the planet, out of the line of sight from Monmouth territory. Behind them, Confederation forces continued the attrition of Monmouth ground-to-space weaponry. Weyland Fleetbase did not escape unscathed and was haloed by escaping atmosphere, water, and metallic debris.

McLean Militia Command, Clan McLean Territory, 10 Sevenmonth, 3203

Most of Inverness believed the McLean military command was collocated within McLean House. It was not, although an alternate HQ was located deep under McLean House. The clan house was the site for local civilian leadership, the laird and any sept chiefs who might be present. The primary military HQ was buried deep under the spinal mountain range of the Hebridean Peninsula.

McLean Militia command monitored the exchange between Monmouth and Weyland Fleetbase. Monmouth had made a strategic error attacking the shuttle in Confederation space, and the subsequent attack on Weymouth Fleetbase compounded that error.

"How many surveillance drones are up?" asked the militia watch commander.

"Twenty. We are randomizing them to confuse snoopers."

"Good. Get more ready. I think we'll need them."

"Aye, sir."

Unlike Monmouth's satellites, McLean surveillance drones drifted near the top of the atmosphere but well within planetary space. They were stealthy, invisible to the eye and most sensors. They were little more than a helium bag with flight controls, an electronics suite, and a small station-keeping motor. Each drone would go active for a few seconds, shut down, and move while another drone would scan then do the same. The drones funneled their data to another drone and from that, via a laser thread, to the McLean headquarters. The information stream gave a complete view of clan territory and much of the surrounding areas, out to the horizon.

"Distress signal from the Mieze freighter *MMS Calliope*. She's been attacked and damaged. SASR has been dispatched."

"Anything from Mieze?"

"Just an acknowledge—no, they are asking our help. They've nothing in range of the *Calliope*."

"Acknowledge their request. What attacked the *Calliope*?"

"We had a drone in sight. It appears the attack was from a Saki submersible."

"A Monmouth ally," the watch commander muttered. "What do we have available to take it out?"

"Nothing nearby, but there is a Williams hunter-killer flight in that area. They can be on site within minutes."

The watch commander flicked his link, searching through the maze of interclan alliances. "Williams is allied to Portee, us... and Mieze! Good. Pass all the data to Clan Williams and ask their help to take out the Saki sub."

"Roger, sir."

The watch continued. Clan Williams acknowledged the request, and moments later, reported they had sunk the sub. They would continue to provide cover while the SASR repair and rescue worked to save the *Calliope* and its crew.

The watch crew was eventually relieved. Monmouth ended its attack on the Weyland Fleetbase—most likely to conserve its remaining surface-to-space weaponry. Around the planet, attacks by Monmouth and its allies dwindled.

"Drone Twenty-two is down. Drones Two and Fourteen report a flash at Twenty-two's location... Drone Eight is not responding."

"Increase the shift frequency. Launch replacements. How long until the new ones reach altitude?" asked the watch commander.

"Three hours, sir."

166

The watch commander increased the alert status. "We've lost two… no, four drones, probably to particle-beam attacks. Suspect an attack is imminent."

"Sir, Mieze and Portee are reporting suborbital kinetic strikes on their militia bases."

The watch commander didn't comment. Everything on his systems were echoed to the McLean House HQ and also to the individual sept militia sites.

On the surface of the escarpment above McLean House, particle-beam cannons rose to the surface, accompanied by the activation of smaller rail-gun point-defense emplacements. Missile silos opened, and sensors watched the horizon for targets.

"Bandits at two-seven-zero degrees, six hundred kilometers. Fifty Miller-class assault boats."

Above McLean House, a volley of missiles rippled from their silos, rose, and curved over the horizon. Azure streaks touched most of the missiles, turning them to balls of plasma. However, some missiles survived and disappeared beyond the horizon. Impact flashes lit the distant sky.

"Inbound suborbital missiles," someone reported over the militia interlink. "Point defense active."

Point-defense radars scanned the incoming missiles. Some of the missiles were pathfinders with active ECM suites to hide the other missiles. McLean point defenses knocked down most of the incoming missiles—but not all.

"Missile sites forty-four, sixty-five, fifty-six, and eighty-two offline. PD sites eleven, fourteen, and twenty-six damaged and inoperative. Runways ten and nineteen cratered."

Another volley of McLean missiles launched, following the first. Again, azure lines touched and destroyed missiles. This time, more missiles survived to continue their interception of Monmouth assault

167

boats. Airborne flashes revealed the attacking assault boats' point defenses remained at work.

"Splash twenty bandits. Second inbound kinetic strike detected!"

The McLean House militia base was also one of the McLean Planetary Defense Centers. Heavy particle-beam cannons, some with one-meter bores, tracked the suborbital strike and fired. Balls of plasma appeared across the sky, one per kinetic warhead. The last one flashed into plasma five hundred meters above the escarpment's upper surface. The beams vaporized that warhead, but the resulting plasma-ball seared half a square kilometer of the surface clean of unarmored sensors and facilities.

The remaining thirty assault boats dropped to treetop levels. One was damaged by a near miss and rose abruptly, where a strike by a McLean missile turned it into an expanding ball of debris. One by one, the remaining assault boats were destroyed—some by missiles, some by particle beams, some by McLean airborne interceptors. The entire attack lasted less than a half hour. At the end, half of the McLean defensive sites had been destroyed or were off-line.

Other strikes against McLean septs and clan allies were unsuccessful, although all took some degree of damage, except for Clan Williams. Several Monmouth suborbital kinetic weapons struck and destroyed Hollowell, the Davies sept house. The underground militia headquarters in the adjacent mountain survived, but the nearby town of Tipley, population twenty thousand, did not.

McLean and its allies struck back. Monmouth's point defenses had been reduced after their attack on Weyland Fleetbase. However, Monmouth had surrounded his military bases with the hostages he had seized. The counterstrikes caused some collateral damage but much less than was suffered at Tipley.

"Sir, I'm picking up radiation emissions from those assault shuttles. They carried nukes!"

"Notify the laird and the Confederation. The laird will want Confederation inspectors if that report is true."

McLean House, Clan McLean Territory, 20 Sevenmonth, 3203

"...can now confirm the nuclear weapons aboard the *C'seine* were destined for Clan Monmouth. We recovered portions of the ship's system logs, including their navigation data. That, plus cooperation from some crewmen, led us to this scenario. On departing Dundee Orbital, the *C'seine* would declare a minor engineering casualty and take orbit around Brigit. A Monmouth shuttle would rendezvous, offload the contraband and return directly to Port St. Regis. Some demolition charges recovered from the Monmouth assault boats are the same model as those removed from the *C'seine*."

Confederation Navy Admiral Honecker finished his report. It was damning proof of violations of the Ban and of the Confederation Charter.

Robair McLean sat at the head of the conference table, and McLean sept chiefs filled the remaining seats. Lairds Mieze, Williams, and Portee, along with lairds from all the clans of the planetary council—minus representatives from Clan Monmouth and a few of its closest allies—attended via hololink. The president of the planetary Council of Clans did the same, as did Admiral Honecker, who joined from Weyland Fleetbase. Fabien Loche was present as an observer.

McLean spoke, his voice low and raspy but firm. "Thank you, Admiral. I would like to thank you for your quick investigation and for allowing us the use of this secure communications network." He coughed lightly and scanned the list of attending clans. Over ninety percent of the Inverness clans were represented, maybe ninety-five percent. All the McLean allies, neutrals, and even a few of Monmouth's allies were present.

"The Confederation has confirmed our suspicions. There were a number of nuclear demolition charges in the Monmouth assault boats. Their fail-safes worked. We were very lucky none detonated. We recovered a few survivors. None of them were officers. The few officers who survived suicided before we arrived. The survivors confirmed the demolition charges were loaded under Laird Monmouth's personal

169

direction. The nukes had yields in the five-to-ten-kiloton range. Monmouth's orders were to invade McLean House, plant the charges, and escape. They were told the charges contained only conventional explosives. We discovered all the timers to be faulty. They would detonate within minutes when set. That would ensure no Monmouth troops would escape to tell their tale. I suspect Monmouth planned to claim McLean had the nukes and they were set off when our clan house was invaded."

He looked at the attendees. Many of the lairds, who had been briefed, nodded. The Council of Clans president's face was white. He knew what was coming.

"I'm calling for Vendetta. The Ban has been broken, and it gives us no option." He looked at the attending lairds and their holo counterparts. "Do any disagree?"

No one spoke.

"Will each clan vote for approval of Vendetta, now?" McLean asked.

Several clans dropped from the conference without voting. However, the remaining clans were sufficient for a quorum, and the votes appeared. Two Monmouth allies and several neutrals abstained. Surprisingly, the remaining Monmouth allies, former allies now, voted for approval.

Fleet Admiral Honecker was an Inverness native. He, like the clansmen, knew the history leading to the Ban and why it existed. If it was invoked, he would not intervene except in defense of Confederation assets. He could not intervene as it was a planetary issue. The lairds were unusually quiet after the vote. All those voting in the affirmative were now duty bound to enforce the Ban.

"Do you request a waiver of Article Three?" Honecker asked.

With nukes already involved, he was required to make the query. The waiver would allow the Inverness Council of Clans the use of nuclear weapons against Monmouth and his remaining allies.

McLean looked toward the council president and shook his head.

On cue, the President of the Council of Clans said, "No."

No one wanted to spread further destruction to the planet.

"Sobeit," McLean pronounced.

"Sobeit," echoed the attending lairds and those who remained via link.

"Sobeit," replied the admiral, who then dropped from the conference link.

Monmouth and his allies' fate was a local issue. The Confederacy would observe but would not intervene.

†††

The conference was over, and the Council of Clans would take the lead. The issue was out of McLean's hands. The Council president appointed Clan Williams the lead and their militia commander as the Council military commander.

Loche and McLean were alone. Events had supplanted them.

"Why?" Loche asked.

"Why?" McLean replied, surprised.

"Why did Monmouth start this? What did he hope to gain? All of Inverness and the entire Confederacy would gain from our proposal. I just don't understand. It's as if he was targeting you and your clan. Our proposal was simply an excuse."

McLean thought for a moment. "I've known Monmouth for nearly thirty years. We attended Scotia College in Kilkenny at the same time. It probably is personal… him and me."

Loche sat up and looked at McLean. "Personal?"

"Yes. We dueled once," McLean said, clearly reluctant to discuss the issue. "It was in our last year. He had a reputation, one for using women. I was seeing… no, courting, Elena Strom, Clan Garrett. Monmouth wanted her, mostly because she refused him. He raped her. She had no brothers, and her father was dead. So I challenged Monmouth."

He stopped speaking. Loche sat patiently. McLean would continue when he was ready.

"Monmouth was spoiled. He was the eldest son of the laird and, following their custom and traditions, next in line to be laird. Most clans have a hereditary tradition for choosing the next laird. But most clans, like us, require approval from the clan's sept council to be laird. Not so with Monmouth."

"He thought he was protected, being the Clan Monmouth heir apparent. Monmouth knew I had won regional sword and knife tournaments. He accepted my challenge—specified pistols, two rounds, solid ammunition—*the stupid ass,* thinking if I was good with a knife, I wasn't with a pistol."

"We agreed upon Herman Mieze as referee and standard rules. We would stand apart at a distance of fifteen meters. When Mieze signaled—a whistle, if I remember correctly—we would draw and fire until empty. Two rounds."

McLean looked at his office window, now shuttered by thick, sandwiched armor. For a moment, Loche thought McLean would rise and open the window.

"He lost. Badly. I wish I had killed him. I was overconfident. He was a better shot. I was faster. I hit him twice before he leveled his pistol at me. My first shot hit him in the groin… shattered his pelvis. The second shot hit squarely in his shoulder, destroying the ball socket in his right arm. The groin hit made him impotent. Ordinarily, medical nannites would have fixed the problem, but Monmouth was one of a few who couldn't tolerate nannites. I should have practiced more. I was… nervous and hurried my shot."

That was motivation, Loche thought. *But… this much? Starting a war?*

"Monmouth was bad before. Unstable. He was worse after the duel. His younger brother died some years later, and that ended the Monmouth dynasty."

"A bad end," Loche said.

172

"Yes. I think his plan was to block the Seat's proposal or to redirect the partnership to his clan—any way to block me... us. When your father disappeared, he switched to Plan B. Regardless of his plan and intentions, it's not yet over."

"What happens now—with the Vendetta?"

"We'll provide troops and support to the Council—to Williams. The last of Monmouth's allies have disavowed him. They claim neutrality. They say they knew nothing about the nukes. I don't doubt them. The Council will give Monmouth clan members fifty hours to renounce their clan or leave. After that, any resistance will be eliminated—completely eliminated. Monmouth will cease to exist. Any Monmouth clan members who didn't renounce their clan but don't actively resist will be exiled off Inverness, likely to a terraforming world."

"What of their territory?"

"That's up to the Council. When That Clan was eliminated, their territory was divided among their neighbors. I don't know this time."

Loche thought, *There is an opportunity here. The Seat wanted a world to build anew, but this could give us leverage in the heart of the Confederacy.* "What if the Seat—or one of our houses—took their territory? I would think the clans would have stiff resistance from any leftover Monmouth diehards. We would be outsiders. The former Monmouth clan members may assimilate easier with us than with another clan taking control."

McLean froze for a moment and looked at Loche. "That... is a possibility. Will your father agree?"

"I need to discuss it with him."

"Then it's time for you to go back to Dundee. I believe your father will be there shortly."

Chapter 10. Vendetta

Dundee Orbital, 23 Sevenmonth, 3203

Loche arrived at Dundee Orbital wearing his customs inspector uniform. He had called the customs medical officer to regain his clearance for duty, and the medic hinted that wearing his uniform would speed his arrival. The Confederacy was taking great pains to ensure the war downbelow stayed downbelow.

Upon arrival, he noticed changes. Confederation marines guarding the shuttle bays were wearing combat armor. Station patrollers wore clamshell armor over their shipsuits and carried 10mm submachine guns. Lines of people arriving from downbelow crowded the shuttle terminal. Each person was being vetted and their baggage examined. The Confederacy was determined to block combatants coming into the station—and to prevent any Monmouth clan members from escaping Inverness.

Loche's link vibrated. The message was from Donal Harris. Loche was to report as soon as possible. He sent his baggage to his coapt and headed for the customs office.

Harris was in Demning's office. "Sit," he said.

Loche sat. Harris had changed nothing in Demning's office. He was taking the "acting" portion of his title literally—the customs director was expected to return.

"I want you to get your medical clearance first thing. I have filed your certification. You are now a full inspector. I'm stuck here, so I can't be your partner. You'll be working with Molly. She will fill you in on the recent changes."

"I thought she had a new partner."

"She does—you."

"Oh!" *That explains some things.* It was a pleasant and welcome surprise.

"No, I'm not pushing you two into a joining. She's the only one available. You're on the third shift. That should give you time for the clearance and signing some paperwork. I believe you said you would apply for Confederation citizenship?"

"Yes."

"Good. That will make you compliant with regulations."

"Have you heard from my father?"

"Not much. I know he is with Demning. They should be back in a few days. They've been outsystem."

"Outsystem? I didn't know that."

"Few did, apparently. There were three parties interested in your Seat's proposal. Your father's old friend, Director Demning, was representing a third party unknown to us and Monmouth."

"You knew the director was friends with my father?"

"No, not until Robair called and asked."

The news from Harris put Loche's proposal about Monmouth territory in a new light.

"Something came up when I was downbelow that may produce still another option, but I must speak with my father before he makes any final commitments."

Harris looked back at Loche, nodded, and said, "I'll pass that along as soon as we link to him. You had better get moving. You've a lot to do."

"Yes, sir."

†††

Harris watched Loche leave. *He's changed.* When Loche had first arrived, he appeared confused, meek, not at all what he'd expected. At some point, another personality arose, a strong, confident man in charge of his actions instead of reacting. The old Loche was gone. *And for the better. Molly should not let this one get away.*

†††

Port St. Regis, the largest air, sea, and shuttle port on Inverness, occupied most of St. Regis Island. It was also the primary sea, air, and shuttle port for Monmouth territory. A multispan causeway connected the mainland to the island, located a few miles off the northern Scotia coast. The port, lying just beyond the curve of Inverness, could not be seen from Dundee Orbital.

The fifty hours of grace for Monmouth clan members expired. Many clan members living near the territory's border, fearing retribution from Monmouth diehards, fled the territory. Those unable to flee and not wanting to be included in the Vendetta, followed convention and flew Clan Council flags on the fronts of their homes. A few flew Monmouth flags upside down if no Council flag was available or, following the millennia-old tradition, white flags.

The refugees were premature in their flight. No acts of retribution were carried out. Large numbers of Monmouth militiamen shed their uniforms and went home to their septs, kith, and kin. Monmouth septs, one after another, renounced their laird. A few sept chiefs were removed, violently and permanently, from office during that process. The septs' primary purpose remained—survival of each sept.

Monmouth loyalists, following their leaders, retreated to St. Regis Island. The port was still active, and Monmouth allowed refugees to depart by air, sea, and shuttle craft. Much of the clan's liquid capital was being shipped outsystem to preplanned depositories. The clan loyalists hoped to regroup in exile. No one expected Clan Monmouth to win against a unified planet.

The terminator passed over Port St. Regis. The seaport was empty as was the airport. Newly arrived refugees were turned back at the mainland side of the causeway. Several last-minute shuttles took off—some to Cameron and some to Skye, the fifth planet from Old Cal and the third inhabitable planet in the Caledonia system. Most of the shuttles, however, headed for Dundee Orbital, where the passengers hoped to seize ships and leave the system.

Dundee Orbital, along with Weyland Fleetbase, kept close watch on Monmouth's last planetary bastion. Both stations saw a flash from Port St. Regis and a glowing ball rising over the island.

NUDET! The alert flashed from Weyland and Dundee to the clans below and across Caledonia system. Military resources on Weyland Fleet base estimated a fifty-megaton fusion device had detonated at Port St. Regis. Most of the island was gone. The surface detonation created a five-kilometer crater, which was rapidly being filled by the sea flowing into the vaporized air, space, and seaport.

Across Inverness, messages were sent to news and media sources blaming Clan McLean for the incident. Many believed the accusation at first, but someone had acted prematurely. Some messages were sent *before* the detonation. At least one message, it was determined later, was sent a full hour early, lodged in an unmonitored mail account.

Monmouth's last suicidal act of defiance failed. The radioactive plume of that last act drifted seaward, sparing the mainland.

†††

Loche was with Molly Quinn. Confederate Marines were guarding the shuttle bay, assisted by a few patrollers. The rest of the patrollers and customs agents were walking beats around the station, as usual. Loche and Molly were on the residential eighth level, watching for any partisan activities.

Braaap! Braaap! Braaap!

"Set Condition T for Thomas, T for Thomas. All residents, return to your quarters. Transients take shelter in the closest survival module."

Like the crying of a baby, the alert could not be ignored. Even the few P'tissa and Coterni stopped, listened, and heeded the warning. Loche's and Molly's links pinged with orders for them to report to the station's armory. Condition T for Thomas meant battle stations. Dundee Orbital had not been in Condition T since the DeeCee raid sixty years before.

With the alarm, internal environmental and segment pressure barriers dropped, isolating the station into smaller, less vulnerable, and controllable segments. At selected barriers, hatches guarded by station patrollers were opened to allow residents to return to their quarters. The station was locking down.

Particle-beam point-defense emplacements rose along the length and circumference of the station's hull. The station had few offensive weapons, and those were placed to protect the shipyard. The remaining weapons, large particle-beam cannons and missile tubes built into the station, were manned and operated by the Marines and naval garrison.

Under battle stations, the intratorus trams halted. A few guarded transfer tubes remained in operation to allow the movement of security teams, patrollers, and customs officials like Molly and Loche.

An hour later, after a trek that usually took only minutes, they reached the armory. Along the way, they received continuous updates. Port St. Regis's destruction had triggered the alert. Several dozen Monmouth shuttles had lifted from the port just prior to the detonation and were headed toward Dundee Orbital. The shuttles ignored calls from Weyland Fleet base and orbital traffic control. No one knew what those shuttles contained—refugees, Monmouth loyalists attempting to escape, or troops.

Loche and Molly were met at the armory by a senior patroller who directed them to another queue, a line containing customs inspectors, agents, and station patrollers.

Molly stretched to look over the people in front of her, turned, and told Loche, "They're issuing powered armor."

"Definitely expecting trouble," Loche replied. "Have you been trained in armor?"

"Yes," Molly said, still looking ahead. "Six years in the militia, reserve captain."

"Ah. When you said you had no vacuum assault training, I assumed you had no military training."

"Not so. All clan members receive training, and all serve at least three years active duty. Some receive more training than others. We have a regiment that trains with Confederate marines and go through all the usual marine training schools."

The line moved forward. Station militiamen were queued in another line. They would receive semipowered armor. Many brought personal weapons, 14mm mag-rifles that could penetrate powered armor.

Finally, Loche's and Molly's turns came. She stepped into an arch, was measured, and received a chit for her armor. Loche soon followed. In the suiting room, their chits were scanned and the armor delivered.

Confederation armor was almost identical to the System States armor that Loche had trained in. The differences were minor. In minutes, they stood in an assembly area. More inspectors, agents, and patrollers joined them in a steady stream.

That stream soon trickled to an end. An alert pinged, and Dundee Central Control made an announcement via their link: <*Attention. We have an incursion by eight hundred to nine hundred troops. The station's marine garrison will guard the shuttle bays. We will guard the rest of the station. We have already received reports of disturbances throughout the station. Most of the permanent residents are locking themselves down. There are reports of looting. Reserve patrollers will be detailed to handle these situations. You will receive orders through your links with your assignments. Do your duty. We will keep you informed of the overall situation as we can.*>

Molly and Loche received their assignments over a private channel from Dundee Central.

<*We have discovered two groups of infiltrators, about one hundred in each group. One group has gathered in the warehouse district. They've overpowered the on-site patrollers and are breaking into some shipping containers. We are receiving no life signs from the patrollers. The infiltrators have disabled the primary and secondary monitors. The tertiary system is still up. They are donning clamshell armor and possess long-arms. Some appear to have individual particle-beam weapons.*

The other group has seized the safety barriers on Deck Four, Torus Three. They killed the four patrollers stationed there. We have sealed all

179

internal barriers. You can still pass using your links. A number of nearby patrollers and residents are keeping that group of infiltrators busy. We don't want that group to reach the docks, nor do we want the two groups to merge. You can monitor the situations via channels fourteen and fifteen. Those are reserved for your use.>

Loche had a thought and sent a query to Harris. *<Can you intercept the communications of the infiltrators?>*

<Yes, but they're encrypted and appear to be using Essie codes. We've been able to determine the codes are the same used by the Essie military.>

Loche had a solution for that. *<I'm sending you a data block. Donner House is the one who licensed the encryption systems for most of the System States. They're one of the Thirty Houses. You may be able to break the encryption with these keys.>*

<Send it. We'll try them out.>

Loche identified the data block stored in his link and sent it to Harris. If they could break the encryption, Harris could listen to all the infiltrators' communications.

†††

Molly and Loche would lead two teams of forty patrollers. Their orders were clear: capture or eliminate Monmouth infiltrators on the warehouse level and prevent others from commandeering a docked ship. Those Monmouth supporters that had seized the internal barriers leading to the docks were to be neutralized.

"They're one deck up and to starboard of us, " Molly said to Loche. "I'll take the warehouse. You take the docks."

"Aye, aye."

His heads-up display labeled Molly a major and him a captain. "I see I'm subordinate to you," he said on a private channel.

"Is that a problem?" she said with a snap in her voice.

"No, not at all. Just clarifying."

"All inspectors have commissions in cases like these. So do some senior agents and patrollers, especially those with military training."

"Any special instructions?"

"No. Take your team and follow your orders… and don't get killed."

"I'll try to not do that."

†††

Loche gathered his patrollers. "All Team Able, on me." The remaining patrollers separated into their respective groups.

"Sergeant Nelson, I believe you are senior," Loche said on the team channel. A subwindow appeared on Loche's heads-up display with the caption "Able 5-6."

"Here, sir."

"You should know the patrollers better than I. Organize them into subteams. You take half, go up to Deck Four, and come down to the docks. Check the barriers along the way to see if they are manned and locked per orders. If you find any open, lock them. If you can't lock them, weld them shut. I want to make sure the infiltrators don't escape upstation. I'll take the remaining half and come up to the docks from here. Check each docked ship and lock it down. If a ship is crewed, make sure the crew members are the ones who should be there. Once that's done, have the ship sealed. Put a team on the transport tubes and report status as needed or every thirty minutes."

"Aye, aye, sir."

"Go." Loche would take his remaining troops and capture or eliminate the group attempting to seal off a section of the docks and access to those ships docked there.

†††

Molly Quinn took her team to the warehouse levels. "Central, status report, please?"

181

<The primary surveillance system is down as is half of the secondary system. The tertiary system is up but with poor resolution. IR scans reveal people near the primary access port and at most of the usual entry points. There have been spotty flares on the barriers. We suspect they have welded some hatches closed.>

"Roger, thank you. Rules of engagement?"

<Your discretion.>

"Aye." She switched to the common team channel so that Loche and his team would hear too. *<Listen up! Rules of engagement: Use sonic shockers wherever possible. If they resist, use frangibles. If they are armored, you may use solid, armor-piercing ammunition and mag-rifles or rail guns as necessary. They may have particle-beam weapons too. If so, those will be your primary targets. You may reply kind with kind. Keep an eye out for noncombatants. Quinn, out.>*

†††

That was that, Loche thought as he listened to Quinn's orders. "Sergeant Nelson!"

<Sir!>

"Pass the word. Everyone to acknowledge to you. Inform me when finished."

<Aye, aye, sir.>

With that task finished, Nelson led his team to make their flanking approach on the docks. Loche and the rest of Able Team proceeded directly to the warehouse and docking levels. He used his access to the station monitors to check for any obvious infiltrators, but too many people were still on the dock level. All surveillance systems were operative. SOP required all ships to seal their locks. Loche's task and that of his team was to find the one or ones that hadn't complied with the station's orders.

†††

Molly Quinn's team arrived at one of the larger access ports to the warehouse district. This portal was large enough to allow shipping containers to be moved to waiting freighters. Her lead NCO checked the closed barrier and found it locked. The monitors on the other side were also out of service, which was not unexpected, given their briefing.

Molly turned to her team sergeant standing alongside. "Sergeant, isn't there a maintenance bypass nearby?"

The warehouse district was the sergeant's usual patrol area. He looked around then raised his eyes toward the catwalks overhead. "If I remember correctly, ma'am, there should be one up there," he said, pointing to the catwalk in the gloom overhead.

"Send someone up to check it."

"Aye, ma'am."

Molly switched to the command channel to Dundee Central. *<This is Quinn. We're on site. Do you see anyone on the other side?>*

<Ah, Zebra-6, IR has six hot spots opposite that main hatch.>

<Roger.>

"Hear that, Sergeant?"

"Aye, ma'am. Swensen says there is a hatch up there, but it'll be a tight fit, us being in armor 'n all."

"If we can get through, we'll do it. Lead the way, Sergeant."

The catwalk was fifteen meters above the warehouse deck. The hatch was barely large enough for an armored patroller to pass. It was normally used only by unarmored techs. Someone's foresight had made the hatch larger. It was sealed mechanically, with no remote operation. The infiltrators were likely unaware of it. None appeared to be nearby or watching.

The sergeant picked a volunteer to pass through and reconnoiter the other side. He was unobserved. One by one, the troops passed through and spread out along the catwalk that extended into the warehouse district. Four troopers slowly descended to the deck below and crept behind the six intruders guarding the main hatch. Each wore clamshell armor, but their necks and extremities were exposed. At Quinn's command, the troopers fired their shockers. Four guards collapsed. The remaining two spun and attempted to find cover. To do that, they had to cross five meters of open space. None succeeded.

"Open the main hatch, Sergeant. Slap a twenty-four-hour sleep patch on the prisoners and secure them on the other side. Tell Central they can take responsibility for them. We'll secure this side and wait for you to finish."

Quinn's remaining troops spread out down a series of aisles created by stacked shipping containers. She assigned a team to go back up to the catwalk to provide top cover. The next group of hot spots was 150 meters spinward, apparently attempting to break into another shipping container.

"Ready to go, ma'am."

"'Kay, Sergeant. Send out some scouts and assign flankers. I've ordered a team to cover us from the catwalk overhead."

The sergeant glanced overhead. "They're exposed up there."

"Yes, but if we need them, we'll need them. They'll have a better view up there than we will down here. I would hope they'll spot trouble before we do."

The sergeant sighed. "Aye, ma'am."

†††

Loche's Alpha Team arrived at the docks to find all the internal barriers down and locked. Dundee Central reported two groups of Monmouth infiltrators. One group was attempting to break through the locked portal to the docks. Patrollers and militiamen, aided by station militia, residents, and business owners, were harassing them.

The infiltrators had broken out soft armor in Monmouth colors. That proclaimed them members of the Monmouth Militia. The Confederation chose, after Monmouth's attack against Weyland Fleetbase, to adopt Inverness's Rules of Engagement by Dundee's defenders. Dundee Central was sending more soft armor to fit out the civilians helping the patrollers and the station militiamen unable to reach their rally points.

184

The second, larger group had already been in the docks before the attack on Dundee Station. They were in the passenger segment of the docks where fast packets from around the Confederacy were located. Fortunately, or perhaps because of their poor planning, no large packets from the System States, nor from any external polity, was present.

One group was attacking the barrier to Bay 23. That bay contained two docked packets from the Harrison Cluster. The two packets could carry one hundred passengers each—too little for all the families and people waiting on the Monmouth shuttles. That was why the other group was attempting to open Bays 31 and 32. Those bays held five docked packet ships from Caledonia's home Jefferson Cluster and from Montchard Cluster. Altogether, the seven packets could barely carry the refugees into exile.

"Sergeant Nelson, let's hit Bay 32 first and work our way down," Loche said. "The patrollers appear to have their people well in hand. We'll take the rest."

"Aye, sir."

†††

Bay 32 held five docked ships. Rarely was a bay full. Central preferred to distribute ships along the docks to maintain the station's positional stability. Sergeant Nelson's scouts reported thirty people working on Bay 32's security barrier. In normal times, the barrier would be raised to allow passage through the bay locks. Lowered, the barriers isolated the bay from the rest of the station.

Loche monitored the Monmouth infiltrators. Most were working on the barrier, but they had posted pickets to provide warning and to block anyone, such as Loche's team, from interrupting the work.

He added Sergeant Nelson to his channel and said, "Notice anything about these people, Sergeant?"

Nelson examined the group in more detail. "Nothing other than they're wearing militia fatigues."

185

"Exactly. No ship suits, nor, apparently, any skinsuits. I think they are all planetborn."

"Sir?" Evidently, Nelson was unfamiliar with the term.

"They're not space trained. What do you think would happen if we turned off the pseudograv?"

Nelson understood. "I think they'd have a big surprise and a bit of difficulty, sir," he said with a growing grin.

"Let's see what we can to do help that along."

<Central, this is Alpha Team. We're at Bay 32. Please turn off the pseudograv for the bay.>

<Hold a moment, Alpha Team.>

Loche and Nelson waited patiently. The delay was only a few seconds.

<Affirmative. Would you like a countdown?>

<Please.>

Nelson notified the rest of Alpha team over their private channel. "Stand by for zero-g. Stand by for zero-g."

<On zero. Five… four… three… two… one… zero.>

Alpha team was ready for the transition to zero-g. The invading militiamen were not. Loche had positioned his team to encircle the guarding pickets. At his command, they were hit with shockers, and most of the guards went limp. Monmouth NCOs did not. They had soft armor under their uniforms. Nelson ordered a three-man team to take them out using long-arms.

The confusion was just as effective with the team working on the barrier, who were soon out of action. Loche used his suit's rail gun on the probable leader in semipowered armor. Casualties among the Monmouth Militia was heavy. Loche had only three injuries among his team, and they were minor.

Nelson muttered, "Nobody invades my station and gets away with it."

Loche ordered sleep patches for the survivors. Medics would tend them later, if they still survived, after the other militiamen were neutralized. Stationers had no sympathy for anyone attacking the station's integrity. Any survivors could expect a high dive out an airlock.

†††

Molly Quinn overheard Loche's request to shut down the pseudograv in the docking bays. It was a good tactic, one she planned to use herself in a few minutes. Unfortunately, the militia had broadcast losing gravity over their communications links, so surprise was lost for Zebra team. However, the members of Zebra team were stationers, and all were zero-g certified. She suspected the Monmouth men cracking the shipping containers were not.

The leader of the warehouse infiltrators alerted his men and ordered them into defensive positions. Only two continued working on the shipping container. Quinn idly wondered what was so important about that container. *I'll find out later*.

On her command, Central shut off the pseudograv in her sector of the warehouse. A few Monmouth men had failed to secure themselves. They were taken out of the fight by shockers and projectiles. The infiltrators responded. Quinn was concealed behind a thin bulkhead where sensors and environmental controls were mounted. A portion of the bulkhead disappeared in an azure flash and crack created by the impact of a large PB weapon. She remembered Harris's teachings about the difference between concealment and cover.

She heard her senior NCO order a flanking attack and slipped around an anchored container while the invader's attention was elsewhere. Two patrollers, designated by her sergeant, followed her. They, like her, wore full armor and copied her movements. They dropped parallel to the deck and slipped, unobserved, past shipping containers.

Her new position was behind a load-bearing pillar. That gave her a better view of the Monmouth men. Like those found by Loche, they had donned, or had painted their armor with, Monmouth colors. More militiamen, she decided. They moved confidently in zero-g. *But not as good as us.*

The firefight was gaining in intensity. Solid and armor-piercing slugs were ricocheting throughout the warehouse. In a few moments, she identified and tagged militia leaders in her link. After a few quick commands to her NCO, railgun slugs from her team put the leaders out of the fight.

Somewhere along the way, Quinn was identified as the Zebra Team leader. Her helmet was splattered with molten droplets from close PB strikes, and her armor was scarred from projectile hits—none from magrifles, she realized gratefully. The Monmouth militia had started the fight outnumbering Quinn, but her team was more experienced in zero-g and knew the station's interior much better than the militiamen.

Monmouth militiamen held their own until Zebra Team removed their leaders. After that point, the invading militia's cohesiveness was lost and, with it, the fight. They knew the consequences of endangering the station and saw no point in surrendering. When it was all over, Quinn had fifteen dead. None of the remaining Monmouth militiamen survived. They went down hard. Molly was one of only a few in her team without at least minor injuries.

She listened on her common channel with Loche. He was mopping up the few remaining survivors cornered by patrollers and the civilian posse. Loche had to hurry to prevent the residents from tossing Monmouth survivors out the nearest lock.

<Dundee Central, this is Zebra. We're done here. Send the medics. I've casualties. Send the bailiffs too. We have a few prisoners.>

<How many prisoners, Zebra?>

She checked the count and found one had died since her last check. *<Eleven. Fewer if you take too long.>*

<Shall we hurry?>

<Yes, dammit! We didn't work this hard just to see them all croak because you're lax!>

Her team and Loche's had done their jobs. Next, Central needed to get off their collective asses and finish it.

†††

The battle outside the station ended. Dundee's point and close-in defenses had been substantially upgraded since the DeeCee raid decades earlier, and PB emplacements covered every portion of the station. They could be integrated with planetary defenses and with the Confederation's Weyland Fleetbase.

When the Monmouth troop shuttles launched assault sleds, few had survived their passage through the PB defense net. Other shuttles launched missiles and attacked with PB cannons. They were destroyed too. Some troops survived to reach the outer hull of Dundee Orbital, only to find the station's meteor shield to be much thicker and stronger than the public specifications indicated—Confederate misinformation aimed at the DeeCees. Dundee's marine garrison eliminated those Monmouth troops with little damage to the station.

Personnel shuttles, loaded with the Monmouth hierarchy and their families, waited for the attack to end. Navy fighters from Weyland secured them. The Monmouth partisans thought they could escape the Vendetta on Inverness. They were wrong. The shuttle survivors were sent back downbelow, where clans with Vendetta on their minds awaited them.

†††

Loche met Quinn outside the armory. Her armor was scarred with impacts from projectiles and splashes of molten metal from close particle-beam impacts. He was momentarily at a loss for words.

His relief at seeing her unharmed was clear in his voice. "Are you all right?"

She didn't reply at once. His armor was covered with scars and PB splashes too.

"Yes. I see you are too."

Both of them had their faceplates up. After wearing a suit for a few hours, nothing could eliminate the sour smell of sweat and adrenaline. Loche reached up, popped the latches of his helmet, and lifted it off.

"I'm just glad it's over. Shall we rid ourselves of these suits?" he asked, nodding toward the armory. "I could do with a sauna, a shower, and something to eat. Care to join me?"

She looked at him, not answering as she reached up and opened her helmet's latches to remove it. Once her helmet was off, she said, "Yes."

The barricade before the armory was still down. The hatch allowing access to the armory was open. Quinn passed through first, and Loche followed. The hatch was not tall enough for him to step through without bending. He was straightening, after passing through the hatch, when a flash of pain tore through him.

Molly! he tried to shout, but the world darkened, and he toppled.

"Medic!"

†††

Molly stooped to check Loche's vital signs. His blood pressure was dropping. The suit injected medication to halt that drop as Loche's medical nannites took control. A medical alert had been automatically sent to Dundee Central before her call. Help arrived in less than a minute.

Chapter 11. Options

Mumbai Station, Mandorva/Rajput II, 28 Sevenmonth, 3203

"That is our offer, sir. Mandoré and Nanak become the thirty-first and thirty-second houses, and we cede the system to the Seat. That gives you automatic membership into the Confederation and a home. We gain your industry, asteroidal technology, and bootstrap financing to finish terraforming Mandorva," said Amit Singh, Second Secretary for External Affairs for the Rajput System.

The discussions had been intense. Emile Loche and Charles Demning had arrived two days earlier on a commercial courier. Rajput was only a day's travel, via subspace, from Caledonia, and it had very good potential. The system contained seven planets, two of them gas giants, an extended Oort cloud, two asteroid belts rich with heavy metals, and one Earth-type planet undergoing terraforming in the middle of the habitability range for the system's G0V sun. On arrival, Emile Loche immediately entered negotiations with the system government on Mumbai Station, the system's administrative center and largest station.

"Why?" Emile Loche asked bluntly.

"Why?" asked Amit Singh. He sighed before replying. "We erred. We are a third-generation colony and we're underfunded. That…" He looked Loche in the face. "We're losing. We cannot meet our interest payments on our loans—don't have the technology or the money to expand our orbital agricultural stations. Nor do we have the orbital industry to do so. We're on the road toward starvation. If we don't get an infusion of cash, technology, and population, we will lose our claim to the system. If the Confederation allows that, we'll end up clients to others— indentured clients, for all practical matters.

"We believe a merger with the Thirty Houses will solve our immediate problems and give us the means to complete terraforming Mandorva or…" He sighed again. "Whatever name you give it."

Emile realized that last concession was significant. Mandorva had a historical link to the Rajput culture, one of the old Rajasthan city-states on Earth.

"If we accept your offer, we can discuss the naming issue. I still have other pending offers that I must evaluate."

†††

Charles Demning had been observing the negotiations. His job was done. Amit Singh, with several aides, had made an impressive presentation. The plan gave the system to the Thirty Houses in return for the merger of the Rajputs and Sikhs into the Thirty—Thirty-two Houses of the Seat, if the merger occurred.

The conversation was ending. With a soft knock, one of Amit Singh's aides stepped inside the room, scanned its occupants, and seeing Demning, walked toward him with an envelope in hand.

"This just arrived for you, sir," he whispered.

"Thank you," Demning replied, examining the envelope. The aide departed as quietly as he had entered.

Emile Loche and Amit Singh were initialing the proposals. Demning opened the envelope and found the secured letter inside. He pressed his thumb on the square in the upper-left corner marked Recipient. If the proper person did not verify receipt within thirty seconds upon the opening of the letter, it would disintegrate into dust. The same would happen if the wrong person attempted to verify receipt. Once he had verified receipt, the letter would remain readable for a longer time, a time that varied, until the letter disposed of itself.

The note was a Confederation alert addressed personally to him. Someone in the government knew Demning's location. The news was surprising but also not surprising. Monmouth had attacked McLean—that was no surprise. Anyone with eyes and wits to watch the events on Inverness knew it was coming. Monmouth's attempt to nuke McLean House and the subsequent destruction of Port St. Regis was unexpected, given the centuries-old Council of Clan's ban on nuclear weapons.

Monmouth partisans had attempted to escape. They invaded Dundee Orbital but failed with little damage to the station and with great loss to Monmouth's troops and followers. Dundee Orbital's close-in defenses destroyed most of the attacking troop shuttles. The eight hundred infiltrators who attempted to hijack docked ships at the station were eliminated too.

Emile Loche approached, his business finished.

Demning handed the note to him and said, "It's time for us to leave. There is unfinished business back in Caledonia. You have lost a potential business partner."

Loche read the note and read it again. "Explain these terms and issues. What is this Ban, and what does a Vendetta mean?"

"For one, Vendetta means that the Monmouth Clan no longer exists. It is gone—root, trunk, branch, and leaf. The Ban is a prohibition against the ownership and use of nuclear weapons by any clan. Proof of either rallies the other clans against the instigator. The last time it happened was centuries ago. When the Vendetta was over, only a few members of the offending clan survived. They were exiled and their clan name erased from all planetary history, written and recorded. Only a few selected scholars today know the name of That Clan, and they know only to ensure it remains erased if it is ever rediscovered."

"Monmouth wasn't alone. He had offworld partners, Consolidationists, I believe they were called. Are they affected by the Vendetta as well?" Loche asked.

"No… as long as they weren't active participants in any hostilities— not technically, anyway. There will be a strong bias against them, depending on their other activities—such as the search for you when I got you away from Monmouth."

"I see… I think."

"I believe we have the basis of an offer here. It's time we return to Caledonia and have you meet with McLean and their allies."

Dundee Orbital, 30 Sevenmonth, 3203

Regaining awareness was a struggle. It was not the sudden transition Fabien Loche had experienced after the saboteurs wounded him. Nor was it similar to waking after the nannite attack at McLean House. He attempted to contact his link and failed. His link didn't seem inactive as he could always feel the ping of its presence, rather it seemed to not exist. He tried to open his eyes and failed.

"I have mental activity," said someone in a voice he didn't recognize.

"Good. Inspector Loche, please be assured you are recovering," said someone else.

Loche attempted to ask, "Link?"

"What did he say?" one person asked the other.

"I believe he said, 'Link.'"

"Your link has been disabled, Inspector Loche. It is intact. You just do not have a means of communicating with it. At the moment. You will later."

Loche again attempted to speak. His mouth was dry, tacky. He licked his lips—at least he thought he did, feeling them to be chapped and dry.

"Give him some ice to suck on. That should help."

Loche felt someone slip a sliver of ice between his lips. The coldness felt exhilarating for a reason he could not determine. It melted quickly, lessening the dryness of his mouth.

"More," he said, more distinctly that time, and he felt another piece of ice slip into his mouth.

He heard someone approaching with lighter steps.

"Inspector Loche?" a new person asked.

"Yes?" he was able to answer.

"I'm Glennis Pollina. I'm the chief of hospital for Dundee's medical center. You gave us a scare."

Loche tried again to open his eyes and succeeded. A woman was standing next to him while two men watched data screens behind her.

"You are in the Dundee Medical Center. You collapsed four days ago after the fighting. Your regrown kidney and spleen ruptured. You nearly died. It was close, but now you are recovering. You will be with us a while yet, but the worst is over. Do you understand?"

"Yes," Loche whispered. His voice was getting stronger.

"You have someone waiting for you with more information. Will you speak with him?"

"Who?"

"Inspector Harris."

Loche cleared his throat. "Yes."

The woman disappeared from his view. He tried to raise his head but didn't have the strength. Donal Harris stepped into view.

Harris looked at the two technicians watching the monitors and motioned with his head toward the door. They followed the woman. Harris placed a device on a roll-about table and pulled it next to Loche's bed.

"Better safe than sorry," he said.

Harris looked strained. He had been in charge of the station during the attack in Demning's absence. His face had more and deeper lines than Loche remembered and shadows under his eyes. "I don't know if any Monmouth infiltrators are left, but I'm not taking any chances. How do you feel, Fabien?"

Loche noticed Harris's use of his first name. "Tired," he said.

"I'm not surprised. You almost bled out, and then we—sickbay—couldn't get your blood pressure up."

"How—why?"

"Your Essie nannites again. It appears they decided your new kidney and spleen were foreign bodies and did their level best to kill them." He fell silent for a moment. "Or it was another assassination attempt. Some of our techs believe your nannites received orders to terminate you. There have been similar incidents with other liaisons, now that we've gone back and looked at the details of those deaths."

Perhaps because he was more aware of the trends within SolSystem, Loche didn't find the information surprising.

"The medics flushed all your nannites," Harris continued. "They mentioned you asked about your link. It's still there and, as far as we can determine, intact and unaffected. You just can't connect to it without nannites. We'll fix that. Since you are a customs inspector and have registered to become a Confederation citizen, we're giving you a new set of nannites. Special ones."

"Special?"

"Well... let us say they are comparable to your marine recon nannites and more. Nannites we provide our operatives... and to members of the Interdiction Office. That is an offer, by the way—it's by invitation only."

Loche was silent for a moment, mulling over the new revelations. "Why?"

"Well, you've become a target. In addition, you are in a unique position—a prospective Confederation citizen and a representative, an Associate of the Seat—a quasi-governmental body. It is probable, if you stay with us, you will rise higher in the Confederation. It is an offer, but you can refuse. In either case, you will keep the new nannites. You just won't receive any updates if you turn down the job as an interdiction agent."

A new thought entered Loche's mind. "I may be involved with the negotiations between the Confederation and the Seat. I need to speak with Laird McLean and the others."

"Hmm, how soon? You will be here for a few days more."

"Can McLean come up?"

Harris laughed. "No. Robair has a problem. He's a space-phobe. He gets sick—no tolerance for zero-g."

"How, with pseudograv?"

"It's psychological. A shuttle won't be out of the atmosphere before he's using a bag… even while under acceleration."

Loche sighed. "Let me tell you my idea, and you tell me what you think."

Harris nodded. "Go ahead."

"Here's my idea. Clan Monmouth is gone as a political entity."

Harris nodded.

"But many former members remain, left behind and under amnesty, I believe?"

"Yes, those who renounced their allegiance to their clan."

"In the past, with that other clan, surviving clan members were exiled, true?"

Harris nodded again.

"This time, there are too many to exile. There are millions who remain in the old Monmouth territory with no protection, no protecting clan, and surrounded by former enemies. They believe their neighbors are planning to divide the Monmouth territory as the neighboring clans did in the past."

"Correct. However, those neighbors don't want the former Monmouth clansmen, just the land and resources. It is a problem. In addition, the Monmouth territory was one of the largest on the planet—as are some of their neighbors. If those neighbors gain more territory, it would unbalance the power across the entire planet," Harris said.

"That was my thought too. Here is my idea. What if House DuQuoin is ceded the former Monmouth territory? The old clansmen need not fear retaliation from their neighbors. They could stay in their homes and swear allegiance to the new clan, us. We, our house, number a little less than a hundred thousand. Other houses are much larger, a few smaller, but not many. The Monmouth territory can absorb us even with the existing former clansmen remaining."

Harris was silent, thinking. "It is an idea, and it eliminates a problem. What do we, the clans, gain?"

"First, a peaceful and productive territory, once things stabilize. House DuQuoin—Clan DuQuoin—would still be a member of the Seat if we can have some concessions from the Council. That gives Inverness, as a whole, first rights to any new development by the Seat and also provides the clans a conduit to invest in the Seat. If an agreement can be properly written, McLean can keep his 'right of first refusal' privileges not allowed to others. From an investment perspective, it could be significant."

Loche's voice gave out. He needed more recovery time.

"I will take this… development to McLean and the others. Do you need anything more?"

"Not that I can think of at the moment." Loche's eyelids were getting heavy.

Harris started to move forward, extending his hand, but stopped. "I pulled rank to get in here. Molly is outside, but they won't let her in—at least for now. I'll write up this… proposition and let you review it. I'm stuck on station until Demning gets back from wherever he has been. I'll use a courier to take this to McLean, probably Molly."

"Or Amilie?"

"Well… maybe. She's not Clan McLean, but she is of Mieze. She'll want to deliver the proposal to her laird instead of McLean… at least first."

"Would that be all bad? At the dinner, some hinted that I was too closely identified with the McLean clan. The proposal may be better received by the Council if presented by Mieze instead of McLean."

"It's a thought. I'll check with both and let them decide."

"Good, and include Portee and Williams as well…" he said, drifting off to sleep.

†††

Harris emerged from Loche's hospital room and walked down the corridor to the waiting area, where Molly Quinn and others were sitting. Amilie Schute was sitting next to Molly and sporting a black eye with a cut above her eyebrow.

"What happened to you?" Harris asked her.

"I ran into some Monmouth clansmen on my way to the armory. They delayed me."

Harris noticed her hands and knuckles were cut and bruised too. Her eye was bloodshot, and her cheek below it was a dark purple.

"How is he? His team is worried," asked Sergeant Nelson. He was the first of several voices that asked the same.

"He'll be okay. He's sleeping now, but they have to regen his kidney and spleen again. The ones regrown from his firefight last month didn't take. He can't have visitors yet. Maybe tomorrow."

"I'll tell the team," Sergeant Nelson said, rising.

The others rose with him and followed Nelson down the passageway to the exit. Molly and Amilie remained behind.

"Really?" Molly asked her uncle.

"Yes. His kidney and spleen ruptured. The medics aren't sure if they did not grow correctly or if it was another nannite attack. They are leaning toward the latter, so they flushed all his nannites. At the moment, he is as clean as a newborn baby, and that will slow his recovery until we can provide a new set of Confederation nannites."

Amilie frowned and looked thoughtful. "Which set of nannites?"

Harris hesitated.

"I know about your extra duties," Amilie said. "Your position as the Dundee interdiction agent isn't a secret."

199

"Sets. Delta, Epsilon, and Gamma."

The Delta nannites comprised the basic nannites available to everyone. Some Confederation citizens chose not to have them, living without nannite enhancement. The Epsilon nannites were different. They were given only to members of the military, Confederate and planetary. The last set, Gamma, was for those performing special duty—Naval Intelligence, Marine Special Operations... and interdiction agents.

"Oh," Quinn said. "I didn't expect that."

"Me neither," echoed Amilie.

"He was extended an invitation. I don't know if he will accept. Regardless, the Interdiction Office has approved giving him both sets. They are comparable with what he had. Since he lost his Essie nannites in defense of the station, it's only appropriate."

The three walked toward the exit, following the path of the others.

"Molly," Harris said, "I'll see you tomorrow. Amilie, would you come with me? I've something to discuss."

†††

Molly Quinn watched the two continue down the passageway. She looked back toward the room where Loche lay on a pad of sensors and surrounded by monitors. She hesitated, standing in the middle of the passageway, then turned and walked toward the exit. "I'll see him tomorrow, and no one will stop me," she muttered.

†††

Harris and Amilie Schute returned to Customs and settled in Harris's office. He sat behind his desk with Amilie across from him. He opened a panel in the desk's footwell and flipped some switches. "We'll have some privacy now."

"What's going on?" Amilie asked.

"I would like your thoughts on something Loche discussed with me when I visited him. I know you're more than just logistics and supply."

200

Amilie raised one eyebrow and tilted her head. "So? You've known that a long time."

"Suspected, not known. You are Herman Mieze's representative on station?"

"So?" Amilie said again, leaning back into her chair and crossing her legs.

"So this. Loche has made a proposal, a proposal about Monmouth territory. You're aware what's going on downbelow?"

"Yes, it has been discussed, and it is a concern—to more than just us and, I suspect, McLean."

"True." Harris took a breath and continued. "Loche has proposed that the former Monmouth territory be ceded to House DuQuoin, replacing the former clan—House DuQuoin to become Clan DuQuoin."

"He wants us to give the territory to the Seat?"

"No, just to House DuQuoin. He expects his house to keep its position as a member of the Seat. He says we, the Council of Clans, would have first access to DuQuoin's products, perhaps including, I assume, marketing, distribution, and investment access with the Seat."

"What do you have for me… us… Mieze?"

"I'm going to spend the night writing out what I think is Loche's proposal. Tomorrow, I will review it with him, make any changes he wants, and get his signature. I can't leave the station to take it downbelow. He thought you would be an acceptable courier."

"You want me to take it to McLean?" she said, her voice rising in surprise.

"Not at first. Take it to Herman first. Get his opinion. Maybe that of John-Paul Portee too. Loche thinks his links to McLean may not sit well with the Council."

"I can see that. You want Herman and John-Paul to see it first and then, if they think it's a good idea, to present it to the Council?"

201

"Not yet. I... Fabien and I just want opinions. Once they have had a chance to read it and consider the proposal, take it to McLean. Fabien is not Emile Loche. He's not the emissary. He wants to present it to his father, with our support, before any decisions are made. I know Demning took Emile to a group that wants to make a deal with the Seat. But I don't know what they are offering."

Amilie sat silent, thinking. She pursed her lips and nodded. "Very well. I'll do it. Call me when it's ready."

†††

Fabien Loche had Harris rewrite the proposal three times before he finally approved the document. He signed it on behalf of House DuQuoin, pending confirmation by his father, the Seat's Emissary. Donal Harris, Amilie Schute, and Sergeant Elias Nelson, who had stopped by to visit, were witnesses after agreeing to confidentiality. Each signed below Loche's name. The original and one copy were treated to ensure they could not be altered. Amilie took one and left quickly. She had just enough time to make the second-shift shuttle down to Loralie, a Mieze shuttleport. Loche kept the other.

Harris departed next, leaving Sergeant Nelson alone with Loche.

"That was interesting," the sergeant commented. "Do you think it will work?"

"I think so. I would like to see our house remain in Caledonia. Our line of business is more into research and development. The other houses lean more toward industry, manufacturing, shipping, and distribution. They would compete with the existing economy if the Seat stays in Caledonia. We won't."

"Do you—House DuQuoin—have a militia?"

"No, not as such. We have proctors, a group that performs the functions of local police, like Dundee's patrollers, but not an actual military. The Seat has naval and marine forces, but they are small compared to the System States or even EarthGov... Why do you ask?"

"Are you aware of my clan?"

Loche thought quickly. Sergeant Nelson had been assigned to his team, but they had never been introduced in the Inverness style.

"No, and I remember we've never been properly introduced. I am Fabien Loche, Member of House DuQuoin and an Associate of the Seat of the Thirty Houses."

"Welcome. I am Elias Nelson… formerly Clan Monmouth, Sept Clement, Sergeant, Dundee Orbital Station Patrol. I don't know in what form my sept still exists, if it does."

Nelson paused, waiting for Loche to speak. At Loche's nod, he continued, "I had the thought, if your proposal was accepted, that House DuQuoin would need someone like me… for a patroller or as a militiaman. My tour here is about over, and I was supposed to rotate downbelow in a couple of months. There are a few more patrollers like me, orphans, who are looking for homes. None of us liked the laird. It's one reason we were Confederate employees—out of sight, out of mind, so to speak."

"My initial thought," Loche replied, "was to keep people in their former occupations as much as we could."

"That would work for most, but not the old Monmouth patrollers… nor much of the militia, for that manner. You really would not want them, sir. The laird has… had corrupted them. You will have a lot of weeding to do, or you'll risk corruption and insurrection."

"I don't think the Clan Council would tolerate another uprising. It could ruin everything. I think some remaining clans would see any uprising as an opportunity to, uh, cleanse any remaining Monmouth members from the planet. It could ruin and fragment the council. I want to strengthen the council, not destroy it."

"My point, sir."

"Yes, and a good one. What are you proposing, Sergeant Nelson?"

"Fealty, sir. With House DuQuoin—for the lot of us on Dundee Orbital and downbelow."

Loche tilted his head upward and looked Nelson in the eyes. "I understand. You are, however, somewhat premature. I am not the Emissary. I need concurrence from my father, our house, and from the Council of Clans. Let us hold this conversation in abeyance for the moment. I am agreeable with your proposal, pending future confirmation. Is that acceptable?"

Nelson grinned, stood, came to attention, and saluted. "Completely, sir."

Loche returned Nelson's salute as best he could, given the spiderweb of sensors covering his body. "Until then, Sergeant."

"Until then, sir. By your leave?"

Loche nodded and watched Nelson leave the room. Nelson had offered a solution to a potential problem—gaining the voluntary cooperation of the former Monmouth clansmen still living in the former Monmouth territory. Again, he longed to speak with his father. Events were rushing forward, almost out of control.

Confederation Courier CNS Ariel. Rajput System, 4 Eightmonth, 3203

"How long?" Emile Loche asked.

"Four hours to the sixty-fathom line, then fifteen hours to Cameron. A few hours less to Dundee or Inverness," Demning replied.

"Have you any further information?"

"Just that it's over. Monmouth lost. The survivors of the attack on Dundee Orbital are awaiting trial and probable execution, exile for the rest to scattered planets being terraformed, where they can find redemption."

Emile Loche stared at the holomonitor on the courier's bulkhead. A stream of text scrolled across the holo, status updates of ship systems. A countdown timer appeared in one corner, counting down to submergence. He queried his link to verify the date. *It will be close.* He wanted to be back in Caledonia before the hybrid arrived.

"How many Confederate systems," he asked, "are there within… ten light-years of Caledonia?"

Demning thought a moment, mentally tallying the names. "Twenty-five, maybe thirty, if you include the new colonies and terraforming projects like Rajput."

"This transit delay is irritating. Could the Seat interest the Confederation in the purchase of some courier-tunnel ships? Dual-engined ships smaller than this one but with the same passenger and cargo capacity?"

"Oh, yes. Definitely."

"Please arrange an appointment for me, with the appropriate office, when this is all over. It would be a good introduction of the Seat's capabilities to the Confederation." He turned back to the monitor and the slow countdown of the clock. *Twenty-three hours. Are you well, Fabien? Were you involved in the fighting? Were any of your friends injured… or killed?* He thought of the young girl, Molly Quinn, Fabien's partner. *If I read her correctly, she would have been in the middle of it all if she was on station.* He wished he had spent more time with her and her uncle. Demning said they hadn't found Monmouth yet, and Loche wondered if he'd been on a destroyed shuttle or was in hiding. No one knew.

"I was thinking," Loche told Demning, "that we could have made this return in seven to eight hours instead of twenty-three if this had been a tunnel ship."

"I hadn't thought of that. That would have a major impact on the economy—faster delivery, faster communications. Eliminating or reducing the financial lag-time between systems."

"And if you have enough couriers, you could expand that ten-light-year coverage to twenty light-years if a return ship was in the destination system, ready and charged."

"The thought also occurred to me that if Monmouth had one, he could have escaped using a tunnel ship and been beyond our immediate reach within hours," Demning observed.

"Hmm, that's true too. Every new technology is always accompanied by some unintended consequence."

Chapter 12. Convergence

Dundee Station, 30 Sevenmonth, 3203

"We're sending you downbelow, Inspector Loche," said Dr. Glennis Pollina. "We have replaced your nannites, adding the upgrades provided by Inspector Harris. The buds for your kidney and spleen look good. They will require monitoring, but your nannite package can do most of that."

"Where may I go? Downbelow, I mean," Fabien Loche asked.

He was sitting on his hospital bed, still wearing a hospital sensor suit, listening to Dr. Pollina when the door to his room opened. Molly Quinn slipped inside as the doctor spoke.

"You have several choices. A number of clans are willing to sponsor you for Confederate citizenship. Clans McLean, Mieze, and my own, Clan Williams, lead the list."

"Will he require constant attention?" Molly asked, startling the doctor, who was unaware of her entry.

"Oh! I didn't hear you come in," the doctor said. "Yes and no. He will need someone close by in case he has a relapse or if we didn't get all of his Essie nannites flushed and they cause problems. He will be wearing a monitor that will alert medical services through GlobalNet if a problem arises. In most circumstances, all he would need is a monitor, but… given his history, the assassination attempt, and the rejection of his kidney and spleen… I lean toward a more prudent approach. He should have a companion."

Molly turned toward Loche and announced, "It's settled. You will come with me."

"I will?"

Her statement and proprietary attitude reminded Loche of the view of the other clans that he was too close to the McLeans.

"Yes. You will. The Customs Service is granting us a month's leave. I have a place in the Hebridean Mountains. It is quiet, and there are emergency and medical services close by. And," she said matter-of-factly, "Mother approves."

Before Loche could reply, Dr. Pollina said, "Well! That's done. We'll get him all prepped, and you can take him in charge this afternoon."

Molly nodded to the doctor, who returned the nod then walked out, leaving Molly with Loche. "Don't think about objecting," she told Loche. "We've a five-hour trip ahead of us. It's an hour flight once we're on the ground at Dunnsport."

"I'm not allowed any opinions, am I?"

"No. In addition, you have visitors coming tomorrow: Mother, Robair, Mieze, Portee, Williams, and Amat Diehl, the chief of the Council of Clans. Your proposal received quick attention."

"Favorable?"

"I don't know. I'm unaware of any real objections… but then I may not be in that loop."

Loche looked at her. She seemed different, more assertive. He remembered the dinner and their talk above the bluffs before McLean House. He was surprised to note that he hadn't thought of Reena for some time. That particular nightmare had not occurred for over a month, a record. In fact, without his link, he was having difficulty remembering Reena's face. It was… indistinct.

"Do you know when they will return my link?"

"I thought they had." She walked over to the closet and rummaged through the drawers inside. Loche noticed a clean civilian shipsuit hanging in the closet, one of his from home.

"Here it is," she said. "You have an external link, correct?"

"Yes."

She returned and handed him the small metallic chip. Loche slipped it into the skin pocket inside his right wrist.

208

"Why don't you have an implant?" she asked.

"I couldn't while in the Marines. They can be manipulated if you're captured. That is also why I don't have retinal nor aural implants. Enemies can turn implants into torture devices."

"They told me that was not possible."

"They?" Loche shrugged. "It's possible. When I was selected for recon, they gave me a demonstration—part of my acceptance training." He shuddered. "It was horrible."

"I hadn't considered that. I suppose that sometimes older is better."

Loche became aware of his link connecting to the station's linknet. He ran it through a few tests, and it seemed to be working with his new nannite package. He decided he might get an upgraded link at some point, but for the time being, that one suited him.

"If I understand the schedule, Molly, I'll not have much time to pack. Would you do that for me? It needn't be much—clothes, toiletries. You may know best what I should take."

Molly laughed. "If you're willing for me to pack for you, you must not have anything that would embarrass me."

"I hadn't thought about that… but… no, nothing like that… except for some things Reena gave me."

Loche was about to say more but stopped. The pain of loss was still there.

"I'll be back at fourteen hundred hours," she said. "We can catch the sixteen-ten shuttle to Dunnsport.

Herrin's Falls, Hebrides Mountains, 1 Eightmonth, 3203

Fabien Loche and Molly Quinn arrived at the small town of Benning's Bridge, via an airbus flight from Dunnsport, just before the local midnight. Loche was exhausted. Most likely, he thought, that was due to weakness from his injuries.

Their shuttle landed at Dunnsport just as the sun was falling behind the western mountains, the spinal range of the Hebridean Peninsula. They boarded a tram that took them to the air terminal on the other side of the shuttleport. An airbus flight took them to another air terminal outside Benning's Bridge, where Molly rented a ground car for the last portion of their trip. Her steading, Herrin's Falls, was sixty kilometers farther into the mountains.

Loche drifted in and out of sleep while Molly drove through the darkness. The road meandered through several valleys, following a river that must have started somewhere farther inland in the higher mountains. They met a few vehicles traveling in the opposite direction, but as they drove farther, that traffic disappeared.

When they arrived at Molly's steading, they were greeted by a sudden activation of lights surrounding the three-story wooden house.

"We're here. My link turned on the lights," she told him.

They stepped out of the ground car and gathered their baggage. Loche saw they were on a gravel drive that continued around the house, leading to the other buildings.

The night was quiet. As he listened, he became aware of small sounds in the darkness… insects and some larger animals howling in the distance. A quick check on his link told him this region of the planet was in late summer. A breeze came up. Loche could hear it rustling through trees around the compound. *Compound?* He thought for a moment and decided the term fit, from what he could see and sense of his surroundings.

Loche followed Molly across the gravel drive, up a series of stone steps, across a porch, and through a thick wooden doorway that opened noiselessly.

"I see Cousin Marcus has been on the job," she said. "He keeps it up and ready for me, along with several other pieces of sept property in this area."

Inside the entrance was a large foyer. Opposite the entrance was a hallway leading to the rear of the house, with rooms to the left and right. Molly stepped to the wall next to the door and tapped instructions into a panel hidden behind a section of the wall.

"That activates the security systems and informs the local services and the Harris Sept at Helen's Forge that we're here. My room is up those stairs, the first on the left. You can choose any room on the right."

Loche had not noticed the stairs farther down the hall leading upward. Molly picked up her bags and carried them up to her room. Loche followed her up the stairs and picked the room opposite hers.

She stood in her bedroom doorway and, as he fumbled with the door, hands still full, said, "Set your alarm for oh eight hundred. I'll have breakfast ready, and we can talk some more. The lairds will arrive tomorrow afternoon around fourteen hundred. That should give you an opportunity to explore the grounds or rest before they arrive." She grinned at him, shook her head a moment, and stepped into her room. "See you in the morning," she said as her door closed.

Loche figured out how to open the door at last. The latch was different. It had no palm panel. The door did not slide to one side—it opened into the room. The latch was a loop of metal with a thumb lever, and when he pressed the lever, it retracted an internal bolt. Then the door could be opened on metal hinges.

It was primitive but effective. He saw that the door was several inches thick, and a wooden bar, leaning against the wall behind the door, could be fitted into slots in the doorsills to provide extra security.

The bed was an antique, with hand-carved head- and footboards. It also included two large pillows and a thick quilted comforter. All the room's contents appeared to be handmade. The bed was very appealing after the trip and his growing fatigue. *I'll unpack in the morning*, he thought as he placed his baggage, two duffle bags, on a settee in the room. A few moments later, he was undressed and sliding into bed.

†††

Today's exercise was storming a warship. Loche's team was to enter via a personnel lock and move toward the engine room. Loche was in the middle. Three marines had passed through the lock before him. Then it was his turn. He was halfway through when the rising hatch stopped. Loche had one leg through, but something blocked him. He couldn't move forward. The rest of his team was behind, pushing Loche forward. He couldn't move forward and couldn't move back.

The sliding hatch started downward. Try as he could, Loche couldn't move. Down the hatch came. He could hear the armor encasing his leg creak. Loche called for help. In his 360-degree view in his helmet, he saw the two marines behind him pushing him forward: a boot against his back and, higher up, a hand pushing him into the dropping hatch.

"Fabien!" Molly was hammering on his door.

"Just a moment!" he shouted.

He hadn't had a dream about Reena for some time. This one, however, hadn't faded.

He stood, wearing only a body sock, and crossed his room to open the door. "It's unlocked. You didn't have to beat it down."

"I-I-I'm sorry. You were shouting—almost screaming. I thought—"

"It was a dream… a bad one. The accident that crushed my leg." He walked back and sat on the edge of the bed. "I remembered something. I hadn't remembered… they tried to kill me, even back then. Why?"

"You wait there. I'll be right back," Molly said from the doorway. She left the doorway and thumped down the stairs. In a few moments, she returned, with a small glass filled with an amber liquid. "Drink up!" she ordered, handing him the glass.

Obediently, he did so. "What is this!" Loche's throat was afire, and his sinuses began running.

"Twelve-year-old bourbon. It's made here. A local product."

"Remind me to never drink anything you give me," Loche said with some heat.

"Uncle Donal says it's a remedy for stress, and you were in stress."

Loche shook his head. Well, Harris was right about one thing. He didn't feel stressed anymore.

"What did you mean, they tried to kill you?"

"I just remembered—the accident—it wasn't one. I remembered feeling a boot and a hand pushing me. If they'd pushed me forward more, the hatch would have cut me in two instead of crushing my leg." Loche looked up to Molly. "I didn't think they hated us so."

†††

A beam of light entered through his bedroom window, splashing across his face and waking him. Fabien sat up on the edge of the bed, eyes closed, as a headache pounded behind his eyes because of pressure in his sinuses, which also made breathing through his nose difficult. A quick check of his medical status indicated he was having a slight allergic reaction to the foliage around the house. The reaction hadn't reached a level that would trigger a nannite response. He engaged them anyway, and in a few moments, they were working. Very quickly, he could breathe better, and his headache was fading.

Fifteen minutes later, showered, dressed, and hungry, he went downstairs looking for Molly. She was in the kitchen, feeding wood to an ancient iron stove. After she tossed another piece of split wood into the stove, she looked up and smiled at him. "You're on time. Coffee is in the thermos. Condiments, sweeteners are on the table. Cups and mugs are in the cupboard over there," she said, pointing at cabinets over the counter on the opposite wall.

"Thank you. I've grown accustomed to coffee."

Molly laughed and continued to gather this and that from the kitchen's cooler and pantry. "I favor a traditional breakfast—bacon, sausage, eggs, biscuits and gravy. Will that do?"

"It seems so much! But yes, I think so. I'm hungry."

"That's because of your growing kidney and spleen. They will take all your available energy."

Loche wagged his head in agreement. "Anything I can do? Help you?"

"No. Two cooks won't work in this kitchen. There's a larger one down the hall, but I like this one. I can whip it all together as soon as the stove is ready."

"I've never seen a stove like that… wood fired. Come to think of it, I don't remember ever seeing a stove before. It never crossed my mind."

"This one," Molly replied, "came with the house. It's original."

"It looks ancient."

"Centuries, maybe a millennium old, from the time of the first settlers in this area. The original house was built, let's see," she said, searching her memory, "eight hundred years ago, I think. It's been updated and rebuilt several times since then."

"It looks…" He searched for an appropriate description for the house. "Rustic."

"That is for appearances. Harris Sept has replaced its original wooden frame with steel, and the exterior walls are armored. The outer wooden exterior has been nannite treated to be fire- and rotproof—interior walls and furnishings too. There is a spring under the house with an underground turbine for emergency power and a sat-link in the attic. In the basement is a small arsenal plus emergency tunnels to the outbuildings. The sept stores more arms in the outbuildings and in caches in the forest."

"That sounds more like a fortress than a home."

"At times, it has been. Our relations with our neighboring clans have not always been peaceful. In time of war, this could be a militia rally point if Benning's Bridge is taken or destroyed."

She moved around the kitchen, retrieving several eggs and a slab of… bacon, according to his link, and butter from the cooler. In a few minutes, the eggs were cooking in a large black skillet with bacon frying in another next to the eggs. The smell made his stomach growl.

"Has your family lived here that long?"

"No," she said. "This steading is known as Herrin's Falls. Herrin was a branch of the Harris Sept that died out a few years ago. The property reverted to the sept, and I had a chance to buy it. *Buying* it, that is. I've several more years to pay off the note."

"Why the name Herrin's Falls?"

"For the falls, of course. I'll show you later if you like."

"I'd like to see them."

"We'll do it. Change into some hiking clothes after breakfast. It is a bit of a walk, all uphill from here."

An hour later, breakfast was over. The used plates, pots, pans, dishes, and utensils were washed and put away. Molly changed into rougher clothes, a woolen shirt, shorts, and hiking boots. She found boots that fit Loche in a storage area. His shipboard boots weren't the best choice for the terrain. Instead of the clothing Molly found in his size, he chose to wear his shipsuit with its environment control. He strapped his gun belt around his waist, having discovered, after months of wearing a weapon, that he was not comfortable without it.

"Anything around that would require weapons?" he asked.

"I doubt it. There are Dragonback grizzlies in higher elevations, but according to the house monitors and our local lurcat pride, none have been around here for years. There are some large ungulates, descendants of wapiti, elk, and deer, but they are herbivores and unlikely to bother us. This is a protected area."

Loche wondered what she meant by *protected*, but before he could ask, she was walking toward the tree line and the start of the trail. He hastened to catch up, following Molly along a path that led farther into the hills. She carried a small pack containing their lunch and other items for a picnic.

At first, the path was paved with large flat stones—fieldstones, Molly called them. The paving stopped within a kilometer. The path changed to gravel and continued alongside a narrow, deep stream. A few more kilometers on, they passed a brass sign that said Herrin's Falls, 1 km, with an arrow pointing farther up the trail.

Molly noticed him reading the sign. "We allow locals and tourists access to the falls when no one is in residence. No one had lived here for decades until I bought it. I still don't get here often, so visitors come to the falls. They call ahead for permission."

The two had been walking for some time before reaching the sign.

"Is all this yours?" he asked. "How much land do you own here?"

"About twenty-four thousand hectares."

Loche did a quick mental calculation. "That's a hundred square kilometers!"

"Yes, that's about right. Most of it, however, is vertical, hills and mountains. The rest is forested. I only have a few square kilometers that is arable, and I'm allowing that to go fallow. It's not needed, and no one has asked to lease any of it for farming. I won't allow any logging other than removing scrub brush to reduce fire hazards."

"How can you afford all…" Loche could not calculate the cost.

"Prize money. I was lucky a few years ago when I first started in customs. Uncle Donal too."

"I don't understand."

"Customs inspectors and agents get a percentage of any contraband we recover. That includes the ship carrying contraband if it is seized too. My first year, we found four large hidden shipments that the captain and owners didn't declare. The ship owners thought they could slip past customs. When the cargo and ships are sold at auction by the Admiralty Court, we each get a nice bundle. A few more seizures in the following years, and I had enough to put a significant down payment on this parcel. It's almost paid for. The prize money from the *C'seine* should be enough to pay it off. Uncle Donal bought Isle St. Marie, down the coast from Helen's Forge. It's a small island, about forty square kilometers with a good harbor, tillable land, and excellent fishing grounds nearby."

"I didn't know we received prize money."

"Have you checked your account?"

"Uh, no." Loche instructed his link to retrieve his account balances. "Three million Confederate dollars!"

"Yes. It's more than the usual. The navy bought the *C'seine* for a Q-ship. She'd been upgraded and armed before we seized it. You were in the hospital when the final disposition was announced. I thought you knew about the prize money."

"No, no one ever mentioned it."

"Perhaps because you were an Essie liaison. I would guess if you hadn't declared your intention for citizenship, you'd have received nothing."

Molly continued along the path, and Loche followed while trying to convert Confederate dollars into System State sovereigns. He couldn't believe the results.

The path continued to climb into the mountains. At one point, Loche was able to look back down the trail. The roofs of the house and outbuildings of Herrin's Falls were visible in the distance. When they rounded another curve of the trail, the falls rumbled up ahead

Loche was glad he was wearing his shipsuit. When they left the farmhouse, the temperature had been cool—not chill, but a hint of coolness that promised to change as the day progressed. Molly had started the hike wearing a light jacket. That jacket was now in her backpack. Loche had turned his shipsuit's climate control on when they left the house. It wasn't needed now.

The stream next to the trail broadened. Its current, instead of the rush it had been, was now slower, almost sluggish. After another turn of the path, they arrived at the falls. Loche felt droplets hit his face moments before he saw the actual falls. At first, he didn't see it hidden in mist. He looked upward and saw white sheets of water tumbling down a series of terraces. The path ended at the edge of a large pool formed and fed by the falls. Next to the pool was an enclosed stone shelter that appeared to be as old as Molly's house.

"The sept requires me to maintain that shelter for the tourists and visitors. It has an emergency comm, medical kits, and a small supply of food in case someone is caught here by bad weather."

Loche walked toward the falls. He closed his eyes and lifted his face. The mist was warm, not cold as he had expected. He said so to Molly.

"There is a thermal power plant about fifty kilometers upstream," she said. "There are also several thermal pools along the way here. This pool never freezes. Not even in depths of winter does the water temperature go below thirty degrees centigrade."

She walked forward to the pool, stopping for a moment to lay her backpack aside and to remove her boots, shirt, shorts, and socks. Loche's last sight was of her nude body diving into the pool.

Reena! Loche froze into immobility. Molly's nudity came as a complete surprise. He was stuck in a cultural deadlock. For a moment, he was transported back to his last visit to Earth with Reena.

†††

Molly rose to the surface and took a few strokes farther into the pool before turning to see Loche standing on the shore. "Fabien?"

He didn't answer. Instead, he looked around, not directly at her, saw a stone bench nearby, walked over to it, and sat with his head down.

"Fabien?" she called again. Receiving no answer, she swam to the edge of the pool and climbed out on steps carved into the side of the pool. She noticed him averting his eyes while she rummaged in the pack and wrapped herself in a blanket intended for use as a picnic tablecloth.

"May I sit?" she asked, standing before him.

He nodded but shifted slightly away from her.

"What's wrong?"

He started to speak but had to clear his voice first. "You surprised me. You see…" He paused. "Things are different in Thirty House stations."

She was beginning to understand. "I didn't know. I didn't… We… I always…" She stopped speaking. They sat in silence for a few moments. Molly stood and went back to pick up the pack and her clothes and carried them inside the shelter. She had brought several towels, anticipating a swim with Loche.

She dried quickly, dressed, and returned to Loche's side. "Are you angry with me? Have I offended you?"

"No! It's… I had thought I was acclimating with your culture. I… was wrong. I can still be startled. We—our customs—are different. Nudity, outside of families, isn't done."

"Outside families?"

"Some houses allow it. Not mine, but some do… not when outsiders are present. We don't swim. There are no pools on stations… too wasteful of water."

"You've never been swimming?"

"I have. The Marines taught me to swim as part of my training. Reena and I… We… uh, she didn't swim. We had planned to wade in the sea on Earth, but the riot occurred, and she never had the chance… She couldn't swim… couldn't… She couldn't follow me! Seeing you… it all came back."

They both sat silent on the bench. Tears were streaming down Loche's face.

"May I?" she asked. When he didn't respond, she pulled a tissue from her pocket and wiped his face and closed eyes. "I'm sorry. I knew the houses were different, but I didn't think it was all that much, and you had applied for citizenship… I should have asked before we came out here."

Loche appeared to be recovering from his flashback. "It's not being from a matriarchy. Well, some, I suppose, but we are more… formal within the family. It was more the surprise." He glanced at her with a small smile on his face. "I did like what I saw."

"I didn't mean to…"

Loche saw her tears. He slid closer and put his arm around her. "It was just the surprise. I'm not offended."

She leaned into his shoulder, crying. "I made a mess of things. I had hoped…"

He squeezed her shoulder. "There's time—they wear bathing suits on Earth. I'd like to come here again."

Molly looked at him and nodded. The wind had picked up, and she shivered. "Let's go inside. It was a long walk, and I'm getting hungry."

†††

Loche and Molly watched the Clan Council VTOL land on the pad a few hundred meters from the house. The other lairds were already inside as their airbus had arrived an hour earlier and moved off the pad into one of the outbuildings. The lairds' airbus was a standard ducted-fan design. The Chief of the Council's VTOL was larger and space capable, the largest craft the Herrin's Falls landing pad could accommodate. Molly and Loche wore earplugs to reduce engine noise and provide communication with the VTOL.

"Shutting down," the VTOL's pilot reported.

"I'm glad I had that pad paved. It was gravel before, and whenever anyone used it, we had to guard against flying rock. A small stone hit Mother once—laid her out cold."

Loche nodded. The engine noise was still too loud for easy conversation until it wound down. A hatch at the waist of the VTOL opened, and Chief Diehl of the Council of Clans emerged with two aides.

After Loche and Molly stepped forward, she spoke first, making introductions. "Chief Diehl, may I introduce Fabien Loche, Member of House DuQuoin and an Associate of the Seat of the Thirty Houses.

Fabien, may I introduce you to Amat Diehl, Chief of the Inverness Council of Clans, Clan Quebec, Sept Allain."

"Pleased to meet you, Member and Associate Loche."

"And I, you, Chief Diehl."

"I would like to introduce my two aids, M'Tolo Anabe, Clan Muule, Sept Obo and Piotr Anachoff, Clan Feitz, Sept Anachoff."

Molly looked up, up at Anabe. He was very large, very tall—taller than Loche—and very black. He towered at least a quarter meter above her. His clan was small, descendants from the second wave, and consisted of refugees from several nation-groups in Africa, fleeing religious terrorism.

"Security, I presume?" she asked.

Anabe smiled. "Yes, among other things. Piotr is the chief's personal secretary."

The other aide also smiled and said, "Among other things."

"Welcome, all of you," she said. "Let's get up to the house. The others are already there."

"Thank you," Diehl said. "M'Tolo?"

"Sir." Anabe strode ahead of them toward the house, leaving Anachoff to carry a small bag the VTOL pilot had deposited on the pad while the introductions were being made.

"And how are you, Member Loche? I understand you were injured during the, uh, intrusion in Dundee?"

"Recovering, sir… and please, no titles for me. My father is the Emissary. I'm just proposing another option. It will still have to be presented to Father."

"So I understand. Shall we proceed? I believe we shall have an interesting afternoon."

†††

221

Quinn conscripted her cousin Marcus and his family to help with the meeting. They proceeded to set up the living room for the meeting. Marcus's son installed a large holomonitor in addition to more security devices to ensure their privacy. His wife and their oldest daughter were busy in the bigger kitchen, ensuring food and drink would be ready when needed.

The house had been used for meetings numerous times before Quinn acquired the property. Each visitor chose a bedroom on the second floor, preparing for days-long sessions.

†††

"…that is the proposal," Loche said. He had formalized, to an extent, his proposal.

Molly had helped, checking for omissions and making suggestions based on her better knowledge of the clans and Customs and Traditions of Inverness.

"To summarize, the Monmouth Territory will be ceded to House DuQuoin, which would, in turn, become Clan DuQuoin. The former Monmouth septs, those that still exist, would, after swearing fealty to the new clan, become septs of Clan DuQuoin. Else, the septs will be disbanded and their property added to the new clan and sept. The members of the disbanded septs would be given the opportunity to move elsewhere, outside of Caledonia, or join their brethren terraforming new worlds."

"Except for Sept Monmouth," Robair McLean added.

"Yes, except for Sept Monmouth," Loche agreed. "House DuQuoin remains a House of the Seat. If the Seat accepts this action, DuQuoin will be the clans' liaison to the Seat. And the last, the Council of Clans will support the Seat's request for membership in the Confederation," Loche recited from notes from his link.

"What about the Seat and the other houses?" Laird Portee asked.

"I believe my father, with Charles Demning, has been working on a proposal for the Seat. My proposal is solely for House DuQuoin."

"What do you put on the table? I see several advantages for your house. Why should that interest us?" McLean asked.

"For one, our house, being R-and-D specialists, is working on a number of lines of research that have great potential. We aren't in competition with many of the existing industries in Caledonia."

"So?" said Amat Deihl. "We'll get access to those lines through the Seat."

"True, but what you won't get is hands-on training and education in these new areas of research. Our house has been limited in several areas of research, lacking space and personnel. We will need to hire help," Loche replied.

"We will bring in our own clan members—just as you would in our place. On the other hand, we can and will allocate spaces, positions, to bring in qualified individuals from other houses—uh, strike that—clans. Individuals who could rotate employment between us and their parent clan. Think of them as 'seeds' to upgrade your own research programs."

"Okay, I'll grant you that has some long-term advantage to the clans, but that can't be the only advantage," Diehl said.

"There're more immediate advantages to my proposal. Who governs Monmouth now?" Loche asked.

The lairds looked at one another.

Mieze spoke. "For the moment, we do—as agents of the Council."

"And who is covering the cost? I understood the Council has limited funds, not enough to pay for garrisons."

Amat Diehl said, "True. The Council is underfunded by design. No clan wants a strong central government. Too dangerous."

"So the clans are paying… for their own troops, I assume."

"Yes," McLean confirmed.

"And it's expensive, I expect."

"Again, yes."

"Then let us consider. If my proposal is turned down, what happens to the Monmouth territory? Will its neighbors divide the territory? I understand that has precedence."

"Precedence, yes," Diehl agreed, "but it could be dangerous. It would unbalance the Council. The neighbors would gain more territory, resources, population, and political power with their expansion."

"And I understand that the population, the former Monmouth clansmen, would be very unhappy to fall under the control of another clan, no?"

"Yes," Diehl admitted. "Some have already left or applied for membership with other clans rather than joining McLean, Portee, Williams, or Mieze. The rest…?" He shrugged.

"When I was in the hospital in Dundee Orbital, I drafted a proposal and was reviewing it when I had a visit from my former senior sergeant, Elias Nelson, my lead NCO during the Dundee intrusion. He was still there when we finalized the message to you and the others and was one who signed the proposal as a witness."

"When the other visitors left, he stayed behind. It turned out that he was a Monmouth clansman, as were several patrollers and customs agents who defended the station against the invasion. Nelson was supposed to return to Inverness, but now he had nowhere to go. He was from Port St. Regis. He and other Monmouth clansmen in Dundee Orbital were orphans.

"Elias Nelson had a proposal," Loche continued. "He and other former Monmouth clansmen were prepared to swear fealty to Clan DuQuoin—if that came to be, or to House DuQuoin. We agreed to hold that event in abeyance. If our proposal was acceptable to the clans, we would negotiate what would be best for both sides, for Clan DuQuoin and for the orphans, as the core for DuQuoin's militia, perhaps. He made the point that the remaining Monmouth—former Monmouth—clansmen would react better to them than other clansmen."

Diehl looked at the other members of the meeting.

Lena Harris spoke for the first time. "He has a point."

Portee and Mieze agreed. McLean remained silent.

Loche noticed his silence. "Laird McLean?"

"I agree that something must be done about the territory and those remaining there." McLean refused to speak the name of Monmouth, revealing that hatred flowed in both directions. "What of our deal?"

"Your proposal was with the Seat. That has not changed. This proposal is only about House DuQuoin."

†††

Robair McLean was not happy. He could see his deal vanishing. Emile Loche was still elsewhere with Demning, whom he didn't trust. Demning was no clansman, and his loyalties were with others. With Monmouth gone, Clan McLean was the most powerful clan—politically, economically, and militarily—on the planet. His alliance with Portee and Mieze was solid as they were almost kin. His relationship with Williams was less than that with Mieze and Portee but still strong. The question was how much of an impact the new Seat technology would cause.

McLean shipyards would take an immediate economic hit because of the need to retool and redesign. Those shipyards would face a period of drawback, and he could expect current orders to be impacted. His customers would want the new engines and power systems if the cost was reasonable. The clan would take years, perhaps a decade, to recover the costs of upgrading their orbital infrastructure and the 'yards. The Seat wanted a home system. They would not be setting up shop here in Caledonia. That was still true. McLean continued to debate with himself the pros and cons of this proposal from the Seat.

During a break, McLean caught Lena's eye as they walked outside on the verandah. "I don't like this," he complained.

"Robair, what you don't like is not being in control," she replied.

He eyed her. She was right, but he wasn't going to admit it. He had planned for a sweet deal for the clan, a deal that would have given him—the clan—political and economic control of Inverness and, most likely, of all Caledonia. He looked at her again and shrugged.

"This is a good deal," she said. "The clans will benefit. We all will benefit. Yes, there'll be costs. The tool-up alone will be expensive, but after that, no one will be able to match us."

"Except the Seat."

"They won't be here. They want a system of their own. And they will have a lot of their own infrastructure to build."

"I still don't like it."

"Don't get greedy, Robair. You could screw this for everyone. Support Loche. Give Monmouth's territory to House DuQuoin. Let them pay the costs of conversion and reconstruction. The remnants of Port St. Regis can't be left fallow. The casualties around it were horrendous, and there's the issue of the survivors." Lena Harris walked over to a swing on the porch and sat.

Robair McLean paced to the far edge of the porch and back.

Lena continued, "The Monmouth patrollers—"

"Don't say that name!" McLean said, his voice harsh with hatred.

Lena continued without pause. "—have accepted Fabien Loche and have offered him fealty. They won't do that for us nor any other clan. We cannot allow a rebellion to erupt in that territory. It would harm us all."

McLean knew she was right. Lena Harris had won again. That was why the clan's septs chose her as his deputy.

"All right," he said. "Let's go back inside."

✝✝✝

McLean and Lena were the last to return. Portee and Diehl were huddled in a corner. Mieze was talking to Loche about his family structure, finding many parallels between Inverness's clans and the Houses of the Seat. McLean returned to his chair at the table, and the others soon followed suit.

McLean started the conversation. "While I am not objecting to this proposal, there are issues that must be examined and discussed."

226

The conversation waxed and waned. Each laird contributed to the discussion as did Chief Diehl. McLean could see the politics shift. Loche was going to get his deal. The time had come to turn the discussion to negotiating concessions.

But not tonight. The session had continued well into the evening. Tomorrow would do.

McLean stood and addressed the others. "It's late. We've all come a long way. I suggest we adjourn and see how this looks in the morning." He turned to Lena Harris. "Lena, we need to review some items. We still have some work to do before we sleep."

The two stood and went up the stairs, McLean leading, Lena following close behind.

†††

Loche watched the two McLeans, laird and deputy, leave. He expected neither one would get much sleep.

He was tired. Molly's Cousin Marcus and his wife were clearing the dining room of the debris from dinner and drinks sipped during the discussions. Diehl and the remaining lairds followed McLean a few minutes later.

Molly walked over to where Loche was sitting. She had been sitting in a corner, ignored by most in the room. "I think there will be a lot of talk among them during the night. How are you?" she asked, looking down at him.

"Tired. Inverness may be only point-zero-three g more than Dundee, but I feel heavier."

"You seemed so… much like normal, I'd forgotten you are still recovering."

"Perhaps. I would like to return there, to the falls, again… just sit in the sun… relax."

Molly extended her hand. Loche grasped it and allowed himself to be pulled out of the chair.

"Perhaps. You still need a month of recovery. I'm sure there will be time after these meetings." She linked her arm with his and followed the others up the stairs.

Before Molly entered her bedroom, Loche said, "I'd like to bring Father here, Mother and Grand Dam, too, when they arrive."

Quinn smiled. "I'd like that too."

†††

The negotiations lasted another day and evening. The final document, initialed by all participants, met Loche's conditions. Some changes on the economic side granted the clans, through the Council of Clans, certain marketing and development rights. Strict conditions restrained those rights and were, in essence, rights of first refusal. Diehl and the lairds were gone by noon. Lena Harris remained behind, closeted with her daughter for some hours until she, too, departed, leaving Molly and Loche alone except for Cousin Marcus and his family.

Loche was sitting in a canvas lounger on the veranda along the side of the house, dozing and listening to Marcus's wife and daughter sing in the kitchen. Molly called the veranda a covered porch.

The singing in the kitchen continued, a lilting song. He heard the words "Caledonia" and "carry me home." The rest of the words were indistinct. Another voice joined them—Molly, Loche decided. A memory of their visit to the falls returned, along with the glimpse of her diving into the pool. He still felt… He couldn't decide what he felt. Some initial shock and embarrassment remained.

Why should I be embarrassed? House prohibitions do not exist here. It was my reaction that embarrassed me… and Molly too. Nor should we import those prohibitions to Inverness if my deal is accepted by all parties. I must talk with Father.

The day promised to be sunny with moderate temperatures. Loche had an appointment in Benning's Bridge later in the day. The local medical facility had called, and the data from his monitors indicated he needed some adjustments to expedite the growth of his new kidney and spleen. A breeze flowed over his face, bringing the scent of the forest. Birds called in the distance while he drifted, not asleep but not quite awake either.

The wooden steps leading up to the veranda from the drive creaked, and something thumped on the veranda's deck. Loche's eyes remained closed as he assumed it was Marcus, returning from chores around the homestead. Something nudged his shoulder, and he felt a warm breath in his ear. After another shove, Loche opened an eye to see a lurcat, the largest he had yet seen, staring him in the face. This solid-black lurcat was half again larger than the ones living with Amilie Schute on Dundee.

Molly chose that time to emerge from the house. "I see Lillith likes you."

Loche had drawn back from the lurcat. He could hear her rumbling deep in her chest. "Lillith?"

"Yes. She and several others guard the place from… predators."

"Uh, how many others?" he asked.

Lillith butted his shoulder again with her head.

"The numbers vary. Some 'cats are shy, unlike Lillith, but I think the current count is a dozen or so."

Every time Loche drew back from Lillith, she moved closer, her eyes only a couple of centimeters from his.

"She's getting to know you. Her pride has guarded the grounds around here for generations."

Loche was recovering from his initial surprise. Lillith closed her eyes, butted him again, and dropped to the floor next to his lounger.

"Run your fingers through her fur. She likes that."

Loche reached down and complied. Lillith's rumblings grew louder.

"She's learning who you are. You have been here with me, and they have been watching. They are deciding if you are a friend or a potential enemy. Lillith has decided you are a friend. If you walk alone in the woods, they will follow and protect you."

"You said they were sapient?"

"Yes, with some differences. Look. You'll see that she… all of them have an opposable digit on their front paws. She can grasp tools if needed."

"Like." The word came from his link.

"I do, too, Lillith," Molly replied.

"She has a link!"

"Yes. They can't speak human languages because of the structure of the mouths. They use sign language to communicate with each other and with us. A few, the pride leaders, have and use links. The 'cats are genetically engineered hybrids. They have very good problem-solving skills but little… what we would call drive or ambition. Most can read and write standard text. They have a large vocabulary. Lillith has left messages from time to time, scratched in the dirt or floor. It was easier to give her a link. They have a verbal language—not Standard, one of their own with around a thousand words. A few people, like Marcus and Ellen Louise, understand it, and they understand us when we talk with them."

"Ellen Louise?"

"Marcus's daughter. You met her yesterday."

"Oh. Yes."

Another lurcat, a tawny one, emerged from the nearby woods and approached the house.

"That's Max. He's another pride leader and has a link too."

Max jumped onto the veranda with a loud thump. Molly was seated in another lounger. Max walked over, sat next to her, and laid his head in her lap.

She stroked his head as she continued, "The lurcats are one reason this site is so secure. Any stranger, anyone not recognized by the pride, who tries to approach the house, won't be allowed to come close. We told them about the lairds, Diehl, and his aides. They already knew Cousin Marcus, his family, Mother, and Robair."

Max chose that time to yawn, revealing five-centimeter teeth. With the yawn, he stretched, and long claws appeared on his… paws.

While Molly and Loche were speaking, other lurcats emerged and approached the house. They were of a variety. Some were black or tawny, like Lillith and Max. Other lurcats were striped or spotted, reminding Loche of images of tigers and leopards, almost extinct on Earth. A few kittens rode on the backs of adults. He noticed many of the adults, Lillith and Max included, wore harnesses with pouches and weapons.

"Is Max carrying a pistol?"

"Yes. They have some small arms, too, modified to meet their physical requirements. And before you ask, they're affiliated with Clan McLean too. Note I said affiliated. Their loyalty is to people, individuals, not some abstract concept like a clan."

So Clan McLean had nonhuman members.

Why am I not surprised? I was told when I first arrived that some clans had nonhuman members. But I thought they were individuals, not an entire species. How many lurcats are there? "How many prides are up in the mountains, Lillith?"

Ten… More tens."

"She… Lurcats have difficulty with numbers," Molly said from her lounger. "The last sept census counted a dozen prides in the region, three of them around Herrin's Falls. The total population is around two hundred in a one-hundred-kilometer circle. A pride is a family group of a dozen or more lurcats."

"Then other clans have lurcats too?"

"Yes, Mieze and Williams do. Several other clans, too, I think. The lurcats are a stabilizing influence. They won't fight one another. In some ways, they're more sane than humans."

Lillith copied Max and laid her head in Loche's lap to be stroked.

"I think she likes you, Fabien."

Loche stroked her head, scratching under her jaw then snapping his fingers to rid them of loose fur. "She's shedding."

"They do that," Molly said with a laugh.

Marcus's daughter, Ellen Louise, walked out of the house. "Lunch is ready."

Molly checked her link. "And right on time. Come, Fabien. Lunch and then a drive into town."

Loche tried to move Lillith. She did not cooperate.

"Move, 'cat," he said.

She opened an eye to look at him, snorted, and closed her eye again.

"Lillith!" Molly said sharply.

The lurcat sighed. Loche could almost hear her complain about having her comfort interrupted. With another sigh, she rose to all fours and slipped past Molly into the house.

Chapter 13. The Prodigal

Herrin's Falls, Hebrides Mountains, 6 Eightmonth, 3203

Loche developed a routine at Herrin's Falls: breakfast, nap in the sun—when the lurcats allowed it—lunch, followed by a walk around the property. The day before, he and Molly had returned to the falls, and that time, she brought swimming suits. Hers was much smaller than expected, just two pieces of cloth. *Two very small pieces*. He felt a smile growing on his face as he remembered.

Today, he and Marcus were prepping the range. The local militia company was scheduled for some small-arms training, and their range was at Herrin's Falls. Marcus was one of their senior sergeants. The previous day, the local militia had sent a truck loaded with several pallets of ammunition that had been stored in their armory. Now, they were about to check the target systems and ensure they were ready.

Loche's link pinged with an incoming call.

<Fabien, this is Donal Harris. Would you call me back on a secure connection from the house?>

"It'll be a few minutes. I'm not in the house."

"That will be fine. It's not that urgent."

Harris broke the connection.

Loche turned to Marcus, who was running diagnostics on the targeting and scoring systems. "Marcus, I have to make a call from the house."

"Donal called, huh?"

"How'd you know?"

"He always uses the secure link. I think it's a habit with him."

Loche walked back to the house, a distance of several hundred meters.

Molly was waiting for him on the porch. "I have the secure link up. Uncle Donal's waiting."

She led him to another room, deep inside the house, which he'd had not been in before. He noticed the door, unlike others in the house, was metal.

"Shielded?" he asked. "The whole room?"

"Yes. Let me know when you've finished, and I'll shut down the connection."

She stood aside and closed the door after he was inside. He heard bolts snick shut, sealing the room. Before him was a holomonitor showing the Dundee Orbital logo.

He sat and said, "Loche here."

The logo disappeared, and the image of Donal Harris took its place. *<You're alone?>*

"Yes. Quinn's outside. She sealed the room as I entered."

<Good. We still don't want to make your location public until everything is settled... which may be soon. Your father and Demning are back. Their courier broached an hour ago.>

"Where have they been?"

<I don't know. We sent them an update on events. Your father wants to meet you. I told him you were downbelow, recuperating.>

"Very well, I have a message for him. Can you forward it to him?"

<Yes, but only with Confederation codes.>

"That will be fine. Your code can wrap ours." Loche searched the surface of the console and saw the link interface. He laid his wrist on the interface and sent the message. "How long will it take to reach him?" he asked.

<They broached right on the sixty-fathom line, about six light-hours out, in their case. But the message will reach them in a few seconds via subspace repeaters.>

"Good."

<They should dock here late tomorrow,> Harris added.

"Did he leave me a message?"

<Yes. Are you ready to receive?>

Loche put his wrist back on the interface. "Send it."

The message was larger than expected, several gigabytes of data. "Got it. Anything else?"

<Demning and your father want you to come up to Dundee Orbital. I told them that was not a good idea, with your kidney and spleen still in the bud stage,> Harris said after the message was received.

"Convince them to come here. If Herrin's Falls is good enough for several lairds and the Chief of the Council of Clans, it should be good enough for them."

<I'll convince them. If Demning returns to work, I'll come down too.>

"I'm sure Quinn will welcome you."

Harris paused. *<The last we spoke, you called her Molly. Has something changed?>*

"She's here. For the next several months, it's Quinn and Loche."

<I'm not sure what you mean, but that is your business.>

"Yes, it is."

Harris blinked. *<A problem?>*

"No, just some culture clash."

Harris sighed and nodded. *<I should have known better. But, >* he said, looking Loche in the eye, *<what is done is done.>*

"Did Father leave any other message? A public one?"

<Just that the hybrid, whatever that is, is due at any time. Do you know what that is?>

"It's a demonstrator of some of our new technologies. It will appear near the sixty-fathom line. We'd appreciate it if you would alert the navy. It will be unusual, and the ship will be armed. They need not be alarmed, however."

<Unusual? How?>

Loche smiled. "Oh, I think you and the navy will know. You have deep-space picket arrays on watch. The characteristics of the demonstrator will not be standard."

<Very well, I'll tell them. A heads-up is always good.>

"Anything else?" Loche asked.

<That's it for now. We can set up a secure link with the courier when it's closer, not through the relays. Tomorrow perhaps, if it's needed.>

"I doubt it. Father would have said so if one was needed."

<That's all from me. I'll let you know their itinerary.> Harris reached out of sight, said, *<Clear,>* and dropped the link.

†††

Molly took Fabien into Benning's Bridge in the afternoon and dropped him off at the medical center. He would be in their hands for an hour or more.

She made a few stops and arranged for deliveries of staples and perishables. With no one living full time at Herrin's Falls, Marcus didn't keep the larder filled.

With that task completed, she addressed the next on her list—check in with the local militia. Her house had alerted the local militia when she and Loche arrived. Her visit today was more of a courtesy call than an official one. Being in residence for a month, she would be the ranking McLean Militia officer in the district. In normal times, that would not be an issue, but Plan Brandon was still in effect and likely to continue until the final disposition of the Monmouth territory.

The Militia HQ was an underground bunker, the entrance guarded by a squad of militiamen in full armor.

She pulled up to the guard post, extended her hand, and placed it on the militiaman's scanner while identifying herself. "McLean Militia Major Molly Quinn. Is your Senior available?"

The militiaman confirmed her identity and said, "Yes, ma'am. Major. Senior Sergeant Barnabas is on duty. Shall I announce you?"

"Yes, please."

The militiaman touched the surface of his scanner and said, "Done, Major. You may proceed."

Quinn drove into the fenced-in yard, parking next to the bunker's entrance. When she emerged from her vehicle, Sergeant Barnabas was standing at the entrance, waiting for her.

"Greetings, Major."

"And to you, Sergeant. I just wanted to drop by and get a status check. I'll be in residence at Herrin's Falls for a few weeks."

"Come inside and take a chair, ma'am. I received a new briefing this morning and was just about to review it."

Barnabas's office was four levels down in the bunker, which doubled as a regional armory and arms cache.

When he and Quinn were seated, he asked, "How up to date are you?"

"My last update was a week ago, after the Dundee Orbital intrusion."

"Well, to summarize, the Monmouth territory is quiet. For now. The people there are still in a state of shock. They're just hunkering down, waiting to see what happens. Food delivery, water, power, and sewage services are back up, so that's one situation that should not cause problems. Port St. Regis's destruction was a major shock. Several surviving Monmouth leaders who remained behind were strung up by mobs. Most of them were Sept Monmouth. As best as we can determine, it was Sept Monmouth who attempted to escape, leaving the rest of the clan's septs to fend for themselves."

"Has Lionel Monmouth been found?" she asked.

"No. According to reports, no one has seen him since the escape attempt. Some believe he stayed behind and died at Port St. Regis. Others think he is in hiding."

"He wasn't seen at Dundee Orbital. We destroyed a lot of shuttles, but we haven't found him in any of the wreckage. The navy is still clearing the orbital flight paths, sweeping for bodies and wreckage," Quinn added.

"The 'cats report small groups of strangers in the mountains. Some, we know, are ours, border scouts and such. Portee and Mieze have notified us they are patrolling our common borders too. Some of them will cross over while patrolling, but they've always told us first. That leaves several groups out there who are unknown. We have a small common border with Monmouth. They could have air-dropped troops back there or sent them in by ground."

"If they were smart, they would call in and surrender."

"Yeah, well, they haven't. The laird has said to treat them like bandits if we find them and they resist. If we had more 'cat prides back there, it wouldn't be a problem."

"You know as well as I, you can't order 'cats around."

"Yeah, but we can ask. You have two prides around Herrin's Falls. Could you ask them to be alert for strangers?"

"Of course, and they will pass the word to the other prides."

The senior sergeant changed subjects. "I prepared a list of discussion topics when I heard you were coming. We're scheduled for arms training up at your place. Will you still permit that?"

"I don't see why not. I need to get current, too, and Marcus is already checking the range systems."

"Good. We're scheduled to arrive tomorrow afternoon and run some exercises overnight, with range work the following day."

"I'll tell our local pride so they won't bother you."

Barnabas laughed. "Ask Marcus what happened to Lieutenant Kline last year. He didn't think it was necessary to let the 'cats know his team was coming."

"What happened?"

Barnabas laughed again. "Marcus was there. He can tell it better than I. Let's just say it was a great training experience—for the lieutenant."

Quinn had an idea what could happen, but she would ask Marcus. He had a way of telling stories.

She continued the briefing with the sergeant until the time came to retrieve Loche. "By the way, I've a friend recuperating at my place. He's a former System States Marine."

"Is that Fabien Loche?"

"Yes."

"We received orders to assist you and Loche upon request—orders from your mother."

"I didn't know that. He was commissioned a captain in the station militia during the intrusion in Dundee Orbital. He did well."

"I heard he has been in a couple of fights."

"Wounded too. That's why he's recuperating at my place… and to keep him out of sight."

"We won't say anything, but the whole town knows about the big meeting up at your place and who was there."

"I'd hoped that wouldn't get out."

"The people know, but they won't spread it around. Your mother had meetings there too. The town knows to keep quiet about the goings-on at Herrin's Falls."

††††

Leyland Kirby was disgusted at being in his situation. But, he mused, he had been stupid, which could have gotten him killed. If he'd been smart, he would have deserted. *Now, it's too late. I'm packed.*

He was one of a company of the Monmouth Militia hiding in McLean Territory mountains. Kirby, like the others, were all Sept Monmouth. They, with a handful of other units, now destroyed, were Lionel Monmouth's personal troops, the Bully Boys. Laird Monmouth used them to preserve his power and position—a beating here, a 'disappearance' there. They were the ones who would not be allowed exile if their exploits were known. Their records had been vaporized at Port St. Regis.

"Comm check in one minute," said his team leader.

The team had gathered inside a hidden assault carrier. Dusk had arrived, and the sun was slipping behind the mountains darkening the campsite. The Monmouth militiamen were vague shadows as they stepped into the carrier. Within, a few instruments and monitors glowed in the darkness. The carrier was on minimal power to escape McLean and Confederation surveillance satellites.

As they waited, the others appeared to be as nervous as Kirby. They had been part of the assault upon McLean House. While en route, they had received a coded order to separate from the group, set down in the highlands of McLean Territory, and wait for more orders. Two days later, they received an update ordering them to camouflage the assault carrier. The message also provided them with a communications schedule.

A week before, their spy in McLean House arrived at the assault carrier. He carried no orders but was just following instructions.

Neil Cooper is a sniveling piece of packing crud who betrayed his own clan. And for what? Kirby didn't know and didn't care. Anyone who was a traitor once could be a traitor again. The team leader had ordered Kirby to kill Cooper at his first suspicious act. Cooper's usefulness was over.

On time, the small comm activated. Instead of the standby code, they heard one word, *<Peacock.>*

The team leader grunted at the message telling them to expect a visitor. "He's coming. Be ready."

"Who?" someone asked.

"The laird."

That surprised everyone. The unspoken consensus had been that Monmouth was dead—killed either at Port St. Regis or in the assault against Dundee Orbital.

"What's our mission?" that same soldier asked.

The team leader didn't answer. He glared at the questioner and walked outside the carrier. If he knew, he wasn't enlightening anyone yet.

Kirby noticed Neil Cooper sweating. At this altitude, he shouldn't have been. Kirby wondered if Cooper knew something and whether it was worth applying some pressure to get Cooper to talk. Kirby glanced at the departing company commander and decided that whatever he knew, they all would know, sooner or later. No need to make Cooper or the team leader suspicious—not at this time.

Kirby followed the commander outside. To the left, in the shadow under a rocky overhang, was the survival bubble tent. It, like their uniforms, was made of chameleon cloth that blended into the background and blocked IR to enhance concealment.

The commander headed right, downslope toward the forested valley and the river at the bottom. According to their maps, a thermal power plant was a few kilometers upstream. Kirby had assumed that power plant was their target although it was a minor one. However, if the laird was coming, he wouldn't be coming for a minor power plant in McLean's mountains. No, he decided, the laird was coming for a more important target.

I'm packed, he repeated to himself.

††††

The sun rose, illuminating the mountains behind Herrin's Falls. The militia company had arrived the previous afternoon and made camp in a nearby open field that had grown wild. Loche grinned to himself, hearing the distant complaints as a detail of militiamen cleared the area of briars and thick underbrush. The far edge of the field sloped down to meet the river fed by the falls upstream. In a few hours, camouflaged shelters appeared, scattered across the open space.

The day's schedule included range time for one platoon and field exercises for the rest. Each of the three platoons would cycle through the range for weapons qualifications for the year. Marcus was in charge of the range. He qualified first with the militia's standard shoulder weapon, a 5mm magrifle. Magrifles, like PBGs, were illegal aboard stations except for armored patrollers, marines, and the station militia. A 5mm round traveling at six kilometers per second had too much penetration for normal ship and station use. The militia magrifle was light, weighing three and a half kilos, including power pack and hundred-round ammunition cassette.

Loche was familiar with the weapon and had qualified with a similar one while in the Marines, but he hadn't used one outside of training. His usual weapon, for shipboard use, had been a 10mm recoilless rifle.

"Would you like to run through the magrifle qualification course, Fabien?" Marcus asked.

"Why not, Marcus? I was pretty good when in the Marines. Let's see if I can meet your standards."

"Okay. Let's start with stationary targets."

Loche's score for the first round was acceptable. That score improved in the second as he grew more familiar with the weapon.

"You passed, Fabien. Now for some moving and pop-up targets."

Loche's score was again high enough to pass the militia requirements. Senior Sergeant Barnabas gave him a qualification ribbon and certificate. The award was not truly meaningful since Loche was not a McLean militiaman, but the achievement would be documented in his Customs file.

††††

As evening approached, Leyland Kirby listened to his team leader.

242

"He'll arrive tonight in about four hours. Kirby, set out some infrared beacons. Don't turn them on until I say so."

Kirby nodded. The ground around the outcropping was loose rock, from boulder sized down to that of gravel. With the assault boat down and camouflaged, they had no room for another to land.

"Where do you want them?" Kirby asked. "There's no room here. Out in the rocks?"

"I don't care. Find a place." The team leader wasn't happy. He wasn't handling the stress of the circumstances well.

"'Kay." *Yeah, I'll find a place. Maybe Monmouth will trip and break his neck. Give me a chance to slip off.* "Stanislaus, come with me. We'll get done faster with the two of us." Kirby was sure Stanislaus had the same doubts as Kirby did. Two were more likely to survive in the mountains than one.

"Get on with it," the team leader said.

Kirby headed for the assault boat with Stanislaus following. The beacons were stored under the floor plates in the troop compartment. With the gratings moved aside, Kirby handed three beacons to Stanislaus and kept two for himself. Five would suffice—four to establish a perimeter and one to designate the center of the landing pad.

The sun was long gone behind the mountains, but the western sky behind them still provided a small measure of light. The two militiamen scrambled down the slope. At the bottom of the slope, near the river and the tree line, Kirby found the only place where an assault boat could land.

Darkness had fallen by the time the beacons were tested and laid out. Kirby pointed an IR flashlight up toward the rocky shelf and the other militiamen. With two quick flashes, he signaled the beacon placement was done. When he saw the answering flash, Kirby and Stanislaus retreated to the trees, found cover, and settled down to await their laird.

††††

The lurcat watched the two Monmouth militiamen set the beacons. The 'cat was aware the trespassers were enemies, but his duty was to

243

observe and report. He wasn't an elder, so he had no link. When the militiamen settled down, the 'cat slipped off into the night. He had a distance to cover before dawn to report his observations. He knew two were there, but he didn't know how many were farther up the mountain. Many. That would have to do for his report.

†††

The dining room was crowded. Loche sat to the right of Molly Quinn, who was at the head of the table. Marcus Quinn and his wife sat on her left. The McLean militia officers filled the rest of the table. Marcus's older daughter served.

The after-dinner conversation revolved around the marksmanship scores recorded during the day, those who'd qualified, like Fabien, Marcus, and Molly, and the very few who had not. Those not yet qualified would repeat testing the next day early in the morning. After that, the militia troops would trek into the higher forest for some tactical exercises.

Dusk arrived, and Herrin's Falls fell into darkness. The dinner, "Dining in" as Marcus called it, was over. The last of the diners were toying with their last glasses of the evening when Loche's link vibrated with an encrypted message.

He leaned over to Molly and whispered, "I've a message. I'll be back." He excused himself to the table and headed for his room.

Inside, with the door locked and barred, he examined the message. It was from his father, encrypted and wrapped inside another Customs encryption. The message header showed it had been relayed by Director Demning. He stripped away both layers of encryption to discover a third level known only to Fabien and his father. With that last layer removed, the text message contained a single word, *Acceptable*.

Loche received another text message from Demning, one with only Customs encryption: *Will arrive with your father tomorrow. Others notified and coming too. Same as previous meeting.*

Loche's father had approved of his proposal. The meeting the next day would ratify it, the first hurdle toward Clan DuQuoin.

Loche returned to the dining room. At his relaxed tread and the smile on his face, Molly tried to raise an eyebrow, a nonverbal question, and failed—again.

He pulled out his chair and sat as the rest of the table continued an argument over tactics. Marcus Quinn noted Loche's return and the change in his expression.

Loche smiled and said, "Acceptable."

Molly gasped. Marcus's smile grew wider. Both Quinns were of the small group who knew what that word signified.

"They *all* will arrive tomorrow. I'm afraid the militia's plans will have to be changed."

"That was our message too," Sergeant Barnabas added.

Marcus's eldest daughter appeared, walked over to Loche, and whispered into his ear, "You have a visitor. On the front steps."

Molly was close enough to overhear the message. "Who would come visiting at this time of night?"

"Only one way to find out."

Loche excused himself and left the table, following the girl to the front veranda. There, under the watchful eye of a local militiaman, was a familiar face.

"Good evening, Sergeant Nelson."

"Good evening, sir."

"And what brings you here?"

"My rotation on Dundee Orbital has expired, and I've been released. I had the thought I'd be more useful here, sir. You need a bodyguard."

The McLean militiaman listened to the exchange. "He identified himself as a member of House DuQuoin, sir," the militiaman added.

"Did you, now, Elias?" Loche asked his former platoon sergeant.

"Well… yes. I have no clan now, and I thought…"

"Yes, I know, Elias. Your timing is excellent. I've received a reply on the proposal from my father."

"And, sir?"

"He said, 'Acceptable,' Elias. Now, come inside, and we'll find you some place where you can lay your head."

Loche turned Elias Nelson over to Marcus's daughter and returned to the dining room. Molly nodded to him as he rejoined the table.

"That was Sergeant Nelson," he told her. "Remember him?"

"Yes. He did well."

"His rotation on Dundee Orbital has expired, and he was at loose ends, so he came here. He identified himself to your militia as being of House DuQuoin."

"Isn't that premature?"

"Maybe, maybe not."

Fabien and Molly turned their attention back to the discussion at the table.

†††

Where is he? Kirby was getting impatient. The time was well after local midnight, and the laird still hadn't appeared. Stanislaus was farther back in the trees, sleeping. Kirby was on watch, and nothing was happening other than the chirp of insects and the distant sounds of night-flying birds.

Kirby shifted his position, trying to find a more comfortable position. *Click.* The notification through their helmets woke Stanislaus, who crawled up next to Kirby.

"One click?" the man asked.

"Yes," Kirby replied. "Start looking for them."

Click-click.

Kirby activated his link and turned on the infrared beacons. He heard nothing. The wind was coming from down the mountain. If the laird came in from the valley below, they might not hear the assault boat until just before it arrived.

A wash of air passed over the two militiamen. *A packin' recon boat!* Any hope of reinforcements vanished. The air recon boat only held two, the pilot and the systems operator.

The recon boat touched down long enough for a single person to exit before the boat took off and disappeared into the night. Kirby and Stanislaus rose and approached the figure.

"Laird?" Kirby asked.

The figure spun around. Seeing the two, he demanded, "Where are the others?"

"Upslope. Camouflaged on a small rock shelf. There wasn't room for the recon boat to land."

Lionel Monmouth simply issued another order. "Take me up there."

†††

The company commander and the former Laird of Clan Monmouth cloistered themselves inside the assault boat after chasing out the other militiamen. The laird wanted privacy.

Sitting at the weapons console, Monmouth began speaking. "They will all be there tomorrow. I received an update on the way here. It's perfect. Both Loches will be there and so will McLean, Mieze, Portee, Amat Diehl, and some others. We can get them all at the same time."

"What's the name of that place where they're meeting?" the commander asked.

"Herrin's Falls. It's a Harris sept house. They think no one knows the meeting will be there." Monmouth was ecstatic. "We'll get them all," he said.

The commander found the site with his link. He transferred the data to his mapboard. In combat, all links would be powered off. The mapboard was isolated and would produce no detectable emissions.

"When can we be there?" the laird asked.

"Dawn is only two hours away. We can use the assault boat to move us there, but we'll be detected by Doppler if we move too fast, so it's low and slow to... here." He pointed on the mapboard. "It will take us about two hours to get there and set down, fifteen kilometers from the sept house. From there, we can infiltrate through the forest to the house in... four hours. Once in place, we signal the assault boat to attack while we move in on the ground. It's all up to us from there."

"What defenses are there?" Monmouth asked.

"All sept houses are small fortresses. It will be a hard nut to crack. The assault boat will do that. Then we'll move in. How many defenders? I don't think many. The lairds and Amat Diehl will have some personal security people. Add the caretakers... maybe a dozen and a half, two dozen in all, plus their principals."

"Good. Remember, when we go in, no prisoners."

The commander nodded. He didn't expect to survive the attack. None of his troops did. But Monmouth was their laird. When he ordered, they would obey.

Chapter 14. Confrontation

Herrin's Falls, Hebridean Mountains, 7 Eightmonth, 3203

The remaining members of the Council of Clans, Amat Diehl, and Lairds McLean, Mieze, and Portee waited for Charles Demning and Emile Loche to arrive. Demning had been able to persuade the navy to provide a VTOL assault shuttle to ferry Emissary Loche to the meeting.

The landing pad at Herrin Falls had been upgraded to allow landing of a VTOL shuttle. The navy shuttle was bigger and heavier than Diehl's, but the pad was designed to handle the larger craft. A seldom-used bunker was available next to the pad and was large enough to shelter all the dignitaries and their security people from the VTOL's exhaust.

"Weyland Fleet base has passed control of the shuttle to Dunnsport Control." The announcement came from a speaker inside the bunker. "Touchdown expected in ten minutes." The speaker fell silent.

"Not long, now," Fabien told Molly as they stood outside the bunker in the light morning breeze flowing down from the mountains.

"Do you know where he's been?" she asked.

"No," Loche answered, "but I think he's found a home for the Seat. I doubt he would have returned this soon if he had not."

"Robair isn't happy. He thinks his deal with your father has been broken."

"There was no deal, just expectations on McLean's part. They aren't the same."

"You know that. I know that. Robair does too. He just won't admit it." She paused then continued, "Mother has him under control."

Loche looked at her when she said that last sentence. *Just like home. The women are in control.* That wasn't necessarily a bad situation. It had worked for the houses for centuries.

<Air defenses are active!> his link announced.

Two local militia companies, the one present for training and another from the district, had been conscripted for additional security. Their responsibility was air and perimeter defense. Monmouth partisans were still scattered across Scotia, and no one had yet identified the intruders in the mountains to the west of Herrin's Falls.

Amat Diehl had wanted to bring some air and space PB cannons, but Molly had stopped that. This was her home, her land, and no one was going to tear up *her* countryside for the armored bunkers and power systems that such weapons required.

The VTOL shuttle should have been visible in the east at any moment. Until then, it had been hidden against the morning sun.

"There it is," one laird said.

Loche, squinting, saw a speck separate itself from the sun. "We better get inside the bunker," he suggested.

Minutes later, after everyone was safely inside the bunker, the shuttle became visible on the monitors. The VTOL descended rapidly with extended landing jacks. Down it came until it hovered a moment above the landing pad, its exhaust cleansing the landing pad of any debris. The VTOL dropped slowly and touched down, and its engine shut off as it settled on its landing jacks.

Around the pad's perimeter, nozzles arose from the ground and sprayed water over the heated pad and the lower half of the VTOL. Steam rose from the pad, and the hull pinged and popped as it cooled and contracted. The craft sat silent, waiting until the temperature was low enough for the crew and passengers to depart.

The militia's air defenses were automated railguns surrounding the landing pad, the house, and property. As one, they suddenly whipped around to the west just as the VTOL's hatch opened and a ladder slid down to the ground.

†††

"Intruder Alert!" Fabien and Molly had just entered the tunnel from the landing-pad bunker to the house when the alarm rang.

"In here," Molly said, leading Fabien to a side chamber. She activated a holomonitor and logged in to the militia's linknet.

The alarm echoed across the steading and rolled across the forested hills. Demning and Emile Loche had just reached the ground when the alert sounded.

"Go! Go! Go! I'm taking off!" the pilot shouted through the closing hatch.

Demning and Loche ran toward the armored bunker and its open hatch, with Marcus Quinn urging them on.

"Elder Loche and Demning are coming into the bunker," he reported over the militia net.

"Incoming!" a voice shouted.

The boat rose from the clearing and moved forward, flying nap-of-the-earth toward the sept house. At five kilometers, it fired a salvo of missiles that were quickly detected by the militia's automated air defenses.

"Assault boat firing missiles."

Molly looked at Fabien and shrugged. They could do nothing but watch the attack. Aboveground, air-defense railguns opened fire. The intruder was identified as a Monmouth assault boat. Extended sensors indicated it had dropped troops in a distant clearing, and they were approaching the steading.

The target of the missiles was the sept house. When they rose above the horizon, the railguns began knocking them down one after another. The Navy VTOL shuttle lifted and climbed for orbit. One missile detected the shuttle's launch and changed its flight to intercept it.

The Navy assault shuttle was armed. It continued to climb. The missile followed until one of the shuttle's particle-beam cannons fired. A bright azure beam flicked from the shuttle to the missile, which disappeared in a ball of plasma.

Monmouth's assault boat was in trouble. The unexpected air defenses had knocked down all its missiles, so not one reached their target. Now those air defenses were firing at the assault boat and taking a toll. The troop compartment was a sieve. The boat's engines and critical systems were armored, but the rest of the troop carrier was not.

A railgun slug plowed through the front of the assault boat and passed through to the rear and out the back. In its passage, it destroyed the pilot's control console and passed through the pilot, dividing him in two. The assault boat, without human control, nosed over and plowed into a ridge well short of the sept house.

†††

Emile Loche and Demning reached the bunker as a ball of fire erupted from the ridge to the west.

"Down here!" Marcus Quinn ordered, pointing to stairs that led to a deeper shelter. "The others are there."

Demning led Loche down the stairs while Marcus Quinn sealed the hatch and the upper shelter. He followed the two down, activating more armor and defenses in the stairwell as they descended.

The three joined Molly, Fabien, and the lairds in the lower level of the bunker. Laird McLean had taken control of the situation. The other lairds continued through a connecting tunnel to the armory, their security people escorting them. If it became necessary, Molly Quinn could lead them to safety in the forest though concealed escape tunnels.

The bunker had an underground communications link to the Benning's Bridge militia base and to McLean Military HQ at McLean House.

"We have forty hot spots to the west of Herrin's Falls," Robair McLean was told over the link. "Our militia outnumbers them four to one. If you just stay in place, you should be safe."

McLean turned to find Demning and Emile Loche watching and listening. "It's my—McLean territory. I hate not being in control."

252

Emile Loche smiled. "I can understand that. Many times have I been in situations when I haven't been in control and could do nothing except wait."

"Since there is nothing more we can do here," Demning said, "shall we follow the others? I believe we have a meeting to convene."

†††

Lillith and Max watched the Monmouth militiamen move through the woods toward the sept house.

Enemies, she signed.

The other lurcat agreed. Behind the two 'cats and scattered across a line parallel to and in front of the Monmouth troops were other lurcats.

The McLean clan's estimate of the lurcat population was wrong. Three prides of lurcats did indeed live around Herrin's Falls. However, those prides were larger, much larger than the clan had estimated. Instead of a dozen members, each pride had over a hundred members. A sizeable portion of each pride was comprised of kits, mothers, and elderly 'cats too old to be fighters for the Pride. A few 'cats were specialists, the equivalent of teachers and medics, but one hundred fifty 'cats from the three prides were waiting for the Monmouth Militia.

Enemies.

†††

Senior Sergeant Barnabas deployed his troops in the tree line around the sept house. Major Molly Quinn was the senior militia officer, but she had wisely delegated field command to Barnabas. She said he knew his troops better than she and was more qualified to act. Laird McLean agreed, and Barnabas suddenly found himself brevetted to captain and in command of three companies, his two line companies and the heavy-weapons company manning the air defenses.

Barnabas watched the Monmouth troops approach on his mapboard. Once the clan and navy knew hostile troops were in the area, several naval and clan surveillance platforms were shifted for his use.

253

The Monmouth troops approached the lurcat line. Barnabas had trouble believing the numbers of 'cats that had appeared. One of the local cats had arrived after the air attack to tell the McLean defenders that the 'cats would take care of the *enemies.*

Lurcats were quiet killers. Barnabas wondered how they would do against trained troops. On the mapboard, the lurcats appeared as green icons, the Monmouth militiamen as blue.

A message arrived on the McLean command link from the pride leader: *Engaging.*

†††

Fabien Loche, Charles Demning, and Molly Quinn watched the fight between Monmouth militiamen and the lurcats on a large holomonitor in the armory. Loche was relieved to learn that Quinn had delegated command authority to Sergeant... no, brevet Captain Barnabas. For all her rank and shipboard experience, she was not an experienced infantry officer. Barnabas was.

"They're moving," Demning whispered. The atmosphere in the bunker was somber. McLean and Quinn expected to win. The others were not so confident.

The green icons shifted. They were firing. Blue icons disappeared. So, too, did some green ones. One of the Monmouth militiamen had a heavy magrifle and was sawing through trees to find hidden 'cats.

"Damn them!" Molly muttered. She was standing behind a chair watching the holomonitor, her clenched knuckles white as she gripped it.

Loche checked the time. The fight was only fifteen minutes old. Half the militiamen were gone, only twenty left. He knew some 'cats had been killed, but their numbers were still strong. He briefly wondered about Lillith and Max. They would be in the fight.

†††

Leyland Kirby was moving through the forest ground cover as quickly as he could while not drawing attention to himself. When the 'cats'

254

ambush was triggered, he immediately realized the militia were outnumbered.

The first thing Kirby did was to turn off all his electronics—helmet, battery pack, magrifle, any item that was powered, even his link. He may be visible via infrared but not by scanners.

How did he know to follow me? When Kirby moved away from the ambush, Cooper the traitor and the Laird followed. He wondered if they knew what Kirby intended. *As soon as I can, I'm moving on. The laird and his spy can fend for themselves.*

Thock! A magrifle slug impacted the tree sheltering Kirby from the distant ambush.

Pack! They followed me! Maybe I can use the laird as a decoy.

"Laird, Cooper," Kirby whispered. "One of them followed us. There's three of us against one of them. We need to flank him while the rest of us keep him occupied. Do you or Cooper want to flank him, or me? Your choice."

Monmouth didn't speak. To Kirby, he seemed in shock. Cooper was using his hands to dig a trench in the soft forest loam behind a large tree root. Monmouth opened his mouth but didn't speak. Finally, he pointed at Kirby then back to where the shooter was hiding.

Kirby nodded. *Good, just what I wanted.*

He no longer had a magrifle, but he still had his backups, a small submachine gun and a 10mm pistol. Monmouth and Cooper had 10mm rifles. Kirby noticed that Monmouth had ditched his helmet too. He must have watched Kirby and done the same.

Kirby pointed back into the forest. "He's around there, Laird. You and Cooper lay some covering fire. Small burst and single shots. I'll flank him around the left—remember that, the left. You don't want to shoot me by mistake. You'd be all alone out here if you did."

Monmouth surely knew, like Kirby did, that Cooper didn't count.

Maybe with that warning, he thought, *Monmouth will stay put long enough for me to get away.*

Monmouth stared at him with eyes wide. Kirby nodded and pointed in the direction from where the magrifle slug had come. Monmouth took cover behind a tree, pointed his rifle in the general direction that Kirby had indicated and ripped off an entire magazine.

Cooper dug deeper.

"Bursts, Laird, bursts, or you'll run out of ammo!"

Monmouth nodded, changed magazines, and switched his rifle from auto to bursts. He settled down again behind the tree and fired a series of three-round bursts.

Kirby slipped off, moving deeper into the forest and away from Monmouth and Cooper—from other prying eyes, too, he hoped.

††††

Loche watched the holomonitor. Few blue icons were left. *Probably the wounded,* he thought. As he watched, one by one, the blue icons disappeared.

Puzzled, he turned to Molly. "Those icons…"

She grimaced. "'Cats don't take prisoners. They don't understand the difference between *enemy* and *prisoner*. There are only *enemies* and those who are *no longer enemies*."

A message from Captain Barnabas scrolled across the bottom of the monitor. *<Body count: thirty-eight Monmouth bodies, two missing. 'Cat casualties—six dead, eleven wounded. Most are expected to survive.>*

Laird McLean had joined them during the ambush. "I pity those two who think they got away."

"Why?" Loche asked.

"They've killed some 'cats. Every pride in the mountains will hunt them. No one kills a 'cat and lives to tell about it."

††††

256

The trench Neil Cooper had dug was deep enough for him to lie in and remain concealed behind a tree root. He had listened to the conversation between Kirby and Monmouth. Kirby, in Cooper's opinion, was taking a runner. Cooper knew he didn't have the skills to hide in the deep woods. The 'cats would find him, and that would be that.

Monmouth was firing steadily, single shots and short bursts. Cooper checked his ammunition—four magazines in pouches around his waist and four more in the small backpack he'd been given when he joined the Monmouth militiamen in the mountains.

Monmouth emptied another magazine and was fumbling with a fresh one from his left ammo pouch. He looked over at Cooper and shouted, "Shoot, damn you!"

Cooper wasn't about to waste his ammunition. He'd wait until he had something to shoot at. He crawled forward, eased upward and looked over the tree root.

Nothing moved. The forest was silent… except… a leaf drifted down from up above.

'Cats in the trees! The branches overhead were interlaced. A nimble 'cat could move from one tree to another without touching the ground.

"In the trees, Laird! They're above us!"

Monmouth looked up in time to see a 'cat dropping with all twenty three-centimeter claws extended.

†††

Kirby heard the screams and the thrashing in the trees behind him. He stopped behind a large tree, his chameleon-cloth uniform blending into the bark. He was invisible as long as he hadn't been seen and didn't move.

One distant scream cut short. *Cooper, I think. Voice too high-pitched for the laird.*

Another scream rang out, lower pitched, almost a bellow. *That's the laird. Lasted longer than I expected.*

Kirby had a grenade on his belt. He would not be taken alive. He had heard what happened when you crossed 'cats.

The forest fell silent again. Kirby remained motionless, blending into the tree. Minutes passed. Then he heard leaves rustling in the direction where Kirby had left Monmouth and Cooper. He caught a flicker of movement in distant trees then nothing.

More minutes passed. *If nothing moves in half an hour, I think I can—*

A vibroknife flashed in front of him. He felt a stinging in this throat, and suddenly the forest floor rose up and hit him in the face.

†††

The battle was over. It hadn't lasted long. Fabien was silently watching the monitor. *How would the Systems State Marines do against 'cats? If equally armed, I think the marines would lose.*

"That was the last one," Molly said. "Has anyone asked the 'cats to ID the bodies? We must check them against the list of known Monmouth stay-behinds," she asked over the militia link.

<On it,> Captain Barnabas said via link.

Robair McLean hadn't stayed to watch the forest fight. He had left earlier to join the other lairds, Emile Loche, Charles Demning, and Amat Diehl.

"Shall we join the others?" Quinn asked Fabien Loche.

She didn't give him time to respond. Instead, she took his hand and led him through a series of tunnels until they climbed stairs into the sub-basement of Herrin's Falls, followed by two more staircases that led to the ground floor. Marcus, his wife, and Ellen Louise were in the kitchen when Quinn and Loche walked up the steps from the basement.

"Fight over?" Marcus asked Quinn, his wife and daughter joining him to hear her answer.

"Yes. The 'cats are IDing the bodies now."

"Our side?" Marcus knew and was friends with most of the lurcats in the region. "Max? Lilith?"

"There are 'cat casualties, but I don't know who. We lost six."

Marcus's daughter turned white.

Fabien noticed the girl's change. "Are you all right, Ellen Louise?"

"Ellen Louise had grown up with the local 'cats and kits," Molly said. "Lillith's pride allowed her to attend classes in lurcat schools alongside her 'cat friends. She, like Marcus, understands the 'cat spoken language and is equally proficient in the 'cat's sign language."

"Excuse me," Ellen Louise said, leaving the kitchen in tears.

"She's afraid some of her friends are hurt," Marcus explained to Loche, "or dead. When she was younger, she spent more time with them than I did. They adopted her into their pride. She wanted to go with them—"

"I wouldn't let her," Marcus's wife added, looking at her departing daughter. "She hasn't had any militia training yet—too young. Next year."

Listening to the exchange, Loche discovered another cultural difference, and he wasn't sure how he felt about it. Marcus and his wife had refused to allow their daughter to join the 'cats against the Monmouth militiamen because she hadn't yet received any military training.

In the houses, women did not engage in combat. Some were allowed to join ships as crews on freighters but not on warships—not that the Seat admitted to having any. For the Seat and the Thirty Houses, the military was strictly a male domain.

I don't think the Seat knows how much assimilation will be needed by them in the Confederacy. I will mention this to Father.

†††

Loche left the kitchen and wandered through the house, looking for his father and the others. When he couldn't find them inside, he walked out the front door and found his father and the lairds sitting around a table on the veranda. They stopped talking when he approached.

"It's all over," Fabien said. "All Monmouth militiamen are down. The 'cats are IDing them now."

McLean grunted something that sounded like "Good."

The others nodded in acknowledgement.

"Sit, Fabien. I've been reading your proposal," Emile Loche said.

A place was vacant next to his father at the table. Fabien carried a chair over from a line of chairs along the wall. Laird John-Paul Portee scooted aside to give him more room.

When Fabien was seated and the others had finished shifting their positions around the table, his father continued, "An interesting proposal. I believe our House DuQuoin Line Mothers will be interested. But what about the Seat? What is in this for them?"

"Us," Fabien replied. "The Seat won't be bringing many freighters. They can't go to markets. The markets will have to come to them. We can do that. We'd still be members of the Seat and could be a direct portal from Inverness and Confederate markets. The former Clan Monmouth territory is one of the largest on the planet. But the territory has made little progress in the last century with Sept Monmouth in control."

Fabien extended three fingers. "First, the Seat gains a direct market with Clan DuQuoin." He dropped a finger. "Second, we'll need Seat members to help us rebuild and update the territory's infrastructure and get paid with biomass, which is still the Seat's highest need, not so?" Fabien asked his father, dropping another finger.

"Yes."

"And Clan DuQuoin will help the Seat assimilate into Confederate culture—it won't be easy." He dropped his last finger.

Emile Loche looked at his son then glanced briefly at the others around the table. They, too, were interested.

Fabien Loche described his observation of Marcus, his wife, and his daughter's distress upon hearing of lurcat losses. "She was distraught because her lurcat friends went into danger and she wasn't with them. Her parents—most clan families, I believe—would have responded the same. Marcus's daughter couldn't join her friends because she hadn't yet—*yet*—received military training. Not because she was female, not because she was too young, but because she was untrained."

McLean and the other lairds nodded in agreement.

"How would our Line Mothers react in the same situation?"

Emile Loche opened his mouth to speak… and stopped.

"You see?" Fabien said. "They would be horrified. It would be unthinkable. Women must be preserved—they hold the houses together. To allow a woman to go into peril—"

"Wouldn't be allowed," Emile answered. He sighed and lowered his head for a moment before lifting it and asking, "Is it too much? For the houses?"

"No, I don't believe so, or I wouldn't have made the proposal. The houses can adapt, but it will take time—and our House—Clan DuQuoin will be ready to help all the Houses of the Seat to adapt."

"And we will have a home system, too, to ease the way," the elder Loche murmured.

Laird Herman Mieze looked at Lairds McLean and Portee. When he caught their attention, he nodded. Jean-Paul Portee spoke first. "It will be a change for both sides, Emile. It won't be any easier for House DuQuoin."

The arguments continued. Would it be better for the Seat to occupy a complete system—such as his father's proposal for Rajput—to help finish the terraforming of Mandorva? Or was the option to settle in the belts of Caledonia the better choice, having the houses compete with the system's existing culture and economic system?

While the lairds argued, Molly and Fabien slipped out.

†††

Molly and Fabien reached the falls at midmorning. This was, if she remembered correctly, their tenth trek to the falls. During the previous visits, they'd taken a short swim in the warm water of the falls, followed by discussions of their individual histories, viewpoints, and concerns. This time, Molly had other plans.

She was wearing a light long-sleeved woolen shirt, shorts, hiking boots, and a backpack with jackets, towels, and blankets, plus food and drink for a picnic—not unlike previous visits. Fabien was dressed the same, with his white arms and legs exposed to the light of Old Cal. He thought he could already see a hint of sunburn and instructed his nannites to compensate for the higher level of ultraviolet radiation.

Molly dropped her backpack inside the shelter and waited while Fabien did the same. When he came out, Molly was waiting, hands on her hips.

"Fabien. Assimilation starts now," she stated.

She raised her hands and opened the closures of her shirt one at a time. Next, she threw her shirt aside and stood for a moment with only a bandeau around her chest. It followed her shirt, leaving her bare breasted before Fabien. She bent, lifted a leg, and removed a hiking shoe and sock. The other shoe and sock soon thumped to the ground beside the first.

Loche felt a flash of heat. This time, he would not let his cultural reflexes control him.

Molly was now bare breasted and shoeless. Her hand undid the closure at the waistband of her shorts and slid them down her hips to be kicked aside, leaving her naked before Fabien. "Your turn," she said. "You decide. Either this works and we have a future, or we don't."

Loche stood a moment, taking her in and noticing she was evenly tanned from head to foot. He reached up and, like Molly, opened the closures of his shirt one by one. A minute later, he stood before her, as unclothed as she.

"Is that a hint of sunburn I see?" she asked.

Fabien, from the neck down, was white with no hint of a tan, unlike his face and hands, which had been exposed to the ultraviolet rays of

Caledonia and the interior of Dundee Orbital. Their previous swimming trips to the falls hadn't given him any tan.

Molly dropped her eyes to Fabien's waist and grinned. His reaction to her nudity was evident.

"Let's swim." She took Fabien's hand and led him to the pool at the base of the falls. "I promise the water's still warm this time of the year, just like the last times."

†††

Lena Harris looked through the kitchen window and watched her daughter and Fabien Loche walk down the trail from the falls. Something had changed. She kept watching as they walked into and out of patches of sunlight on the late-afternoon trail. It struck her—one difference. They were holding hands, and Molly was walking… She couldn't describe it. Something was different.

She looked over her shoulder at her brother. "They're back, Donal. Come. Take a look."

Donal Harris rose from the kitchen table, leaving his mug of cooling coffee behind, to look out the window. "Hmm. Does that mean something, I wonder?"

Molly and Fabien disappeared around the rear corner of the house.

Lena left her brother and walked into the conference room where Emile Loche was conversing with the other lairds and Confederation negotiators. "They're back, Emile. I think you should come."

The senior Loche looked up from the display his link was projecting on the tabletop. He flicked a finger, and the display vanished. "Please excuse me," he told the others. "Coming, Lena."

Donal Harris returned to his chair in the kitchen and rejoined his sister. They heard footsteps approaching from the rear of the house. Molly walked past the kitchen door and climbed the stairs to the second level. Lena Harris rose and followed her daughter. Fabien entered the hallway and was about to climb the stairs when his father spoke to him in a language Harris didn't know.

The two Loches conversed in the hallway for a moment. When they finished, Fabien climbed the stairs and turned right at the top to disappear into his room. Emile watched his son walk upstairs then joined Harris when his son was out of sight.

Harris could hear Molly entering the upper floor's 'fresher and the water from its shower rushing as Loche entered the kitchen. "Coffee?" Harris asked.

"Oh! Ah, no. Thank you, though." He seemed preoccupied.

"What language was that you spoke to Fabien?"

"Our house language. It's a derivative of French. We use it *en famille*. I forgot you and Lena were here."

"That's all right. It was impertinent of me asking about a private conversation."

"No need to apologize."

†††

Lena Harris followed her daughter upstairs when Molly returned from the falls. She caught the closing door to Molly's bedroom, entered, and latched the door behind her. "Want to tell me?" she asked Molly.

Molly was partially undressed, preparing for her shower. Her boots had been kicked aside, and she was sitting on her bed, removing her socks, when her mother entered. She had opened her shirt, and Lena noticed the bandeau that Molly had been wearing earlier was missing.

"I think… We practiced assimilation, Mother."

Lena raised an eyebrow.

"You remember I told you of his reaction the first time we went to the falls?"

"Yes," Lena answered slowly.

"He's over that now. We swam, talked, and… assimilated. I understand some of his cultural issues now, and I made him familiar with some of ours."

"The *Proprieties*—"

"Are unbroken, Mother. We've been twice formally introduced."

Lena Harris had nothing more to say. She suspected what would come next.

In the early stages of terraforming Inverness, when the population was low and some airborne toxins remained, fertility was an issue for colonists. Infertility, compounded by nonviable births and miscarriages, created a tradition—one that called for proof of fertility and the ability to deliver live births. The tradition hadn't been followed regularly for centuries. However, it still existed, and some clans, who closely followed tradition, encouraged it. Clan McLean didn't... At least, most of the clan didn't.

"I've turned off my contraception, Mother."

Lena sat on the bed next to her daughter. "Are you sure you want to do that? What did—you *did* ask Fabien?"

"Yes. I've discovered I'm more of a Traditionalist than I thought, Mother. There is a possibility of issues on his side too. The houses have been exposed to higher levels of radiation for a very long time, and there have been mutations, minor ones."

"Enough to prevent conception, even today?"

"It's a possibility, Mother. That aside, I have more than enough leave accrued to take time off for a baby."

"And Fabien?"

"He understands. It seems the houses have a similar tradition... although for different reasons."

"And the banns?"

"We'll pay homage to the Church afterward."

Lena wiped her eyes and hugged her daughter. She had been waiting for this moment, when her daughter married. *Why am I hurt?* Then she realized the cause. Molly would leave her clan and sept, joining either Clan DuQuoin or, alternately, House DuQuoin.

"Take your shower," she said gruffly. "You stink." With that, Lena stood and strode out of Molly's bedroom, closing the door behind her.

Lena Harris walked down the stairs and joined the two men in the kitchen.

"Well?" Harris asked his sister.

Lena walked over to the cupboard, retrieved a mug, and filled it with coffee from the thermal urn. When the mug was full, she turned and faced the men. "It is going to be okay, I think. They've resolved some important issues. Now it's up to them, and we should leave them be."

"Very well," Donal said. "I'm going back to Dundee Orbital if Demning is staying here. Someone needs to run the show."

†††

Emile Loche had been closeted with Robair McLean, John-Paul Portee, and Herman Mieze. McLean's opposition to Fabien's proposal was threatening the agreement between Clan McLean and the Seat.

"…unless, Emile, there is more than a political joining of the Thirty Houses with the Confederacy," McLean said.

"What do you mean?"

McLean had asked Loche and Lairds Portee and Mieze to join him on the front veranda for breakfast and "discussions." Emile was willing. Listening did no harm.

Instead of sitting with the others after Mieze and Portee joined them, McLean paced. "The Seat has been isolated for decades, maybe a century or more. You've become culturally inbred. You now have that opportunity to alter that situation," McLean stated.

John-Paul Portee nodded. "The Seat and houses need cultural intermarriage. The pressures and drivers of the past must be reduced, if not eliminated. The first step is the Seat migrating from SolSystem to the Confederacy. Assimilation can and must work both ways."

266

The meeting was interrupted by the arrival of the militia's Captain Ellis Barnabas in a small ground car. He pulled up to the front of the house and stepped out, carrying a bag.

"Welcome, Captain," Robair McLean called. "Pull up a chair."

"Thank you, Laird," Barnabas said, stepping up to the veranda. "I have something you all need to see. It isn't pretty." On the table before McLean, he laid the sack, which rolled a little.

McLean reached for the sack, opened it, looked inside, and recoiled. "Pack!"

"What is it?" Mieze stepped next to McLean and looked inside. His face whitened.

Laird Portee also looked inside. He nodded. "Well, that's that." He looked at the others. "You know we'll have to bring in the newsies. No one will believe us without corroboration."

"Yes. I know," McLean said to the group around the table. "Lena can do it. I'm known for my feelings about him."

McLean walked inside the house, leaving the others on the veranda.

"Would someone tell me what's going on?" Emile Loche asked.

Mieze closed the sack. "It's confirmation the war is over, Emile."

"What confirmation?"

"This sack holds Lionel Monmouth's head."

†††

From the front veranda of Herrin's Falls, Lena Harris watched the last of the newsies leave. She had agreed to allow two of them to be present while DNA testing confirmed the head really was Monmouth's and not some doppelgänger. *No more standing in for Robair McLean,* she swore. *The coward.* Once again, he'd made her the sacrificial offering to uncivilized newsies. Too bad they were, as a class, exempt from being challenged. *The cowards.* For a time, she wondered if challenging Robair for the lairdship would be worthwhile. He kept delegating more and more of the clan management to her while he played politics. She controlled the anger building in the back of her mind. *Not yet. No, not yet.* But the time was coming. *Do your job, Robair, or get out!*

She walked back into the house in search of her daughter and found her sharing a two-seat swing on the rear veranda with Emile Loche. They appeared to have been there for some time, from the scraps of a light meal sitting on the floor to one side of the swing.

"Hiding from the newsies?" she asked.

Molly started in surprise when her mother spoke. "Yes, we were."

"Molly was telling me of her adventures with Fabien," Emile said.

"I don't think Fabien would describe them as adventures. Adventures are when—"

"They happen to other people," Emile finished.

"Yes." Lena laughed.

"And about the dinner at McLean House, I wish I could have been there," Emile said.

"Fabien stood in for you very well. And surprised the busybodies."

"You, too, Mother," Molly added.

Emile tilted his head. "Surprised?"

Molly looked at her mother and then to Emile. "The busybodies, as Mother calls them, were plotting to marry me off to Fabien."

Emile blinked and, turning toward Lena, asked, "Really?"

"Until he mentioned his betrothment," Molly said.

"Exactly what did he say?" Emile asked with a notable change in his voice.

"That because of his betrothal to Reena," Molly said, "he couldn't be considered for marriage until a year had passed from the original marriage date. The betrothal didn't cease despite her death and the fact that they never got married."

268

Lena had been watching Emile Loche while Molly spoke, noticing something about his demeanor was… off. "You look as if there is more to be said, Emissary," Lena said when Molly was finished.

"I just remembered. Fabien admonished me to always be formally introduced in Inverness society. Have we been introduced? In all the confusion, I don't remember, and I most humbly apologize. I am Emile Loche, Member of House DuQuoin and Associate and Emissary of the Seat of Thirty Houses."

Lena blinked at the shift in the tone of the conversation. "I am Lena Harris, Clan McLean, Sept Harris, Chief of Sept Harris and Deputy Laird of Clan McLean. I am informally known as Lena."

Molly introduced herself too. "I am Mary Elizabeth Quinn, Clan McLean, Sept Harris. Please call me Molly."

"Thank you, both. Does that meet the *Proprieties*?"

"Uh, as Emissary and Sept Chief, yes," Lena answered.

"Good. Now that all that has been settled, I'll explain. What Fabien said about the betrothal was true—as far as it went. That is the protocol when two parties agree to break the proposal. That was about to happen— not due to any fault by Reena or Fabien. It was a family, a house matter. House Tyre added demands to the original betrothal agreement. They were getting greedy. House Tyre had fallen on hard times, harder than other houses, but it was not by their own doing. Their specialty was communications, and they were in direct competition with other SolSystem corporations. We refused to accept the changes. We were in negotiations when Reena was murdered."

"Murdered?" Molly asked.

"We believe so," Emile admitted. "We believe they were purposely targeted by the leaders of the mob. Reena's death broke the betrothal agreement—the formal contract had not been signed."

"So?" Lena asked.

"A delay, when a betrothal is broken, is to prevent the tactic being used for political or, in House Tyre's case, economic extortion. Since the betrothal was broken by Reena's death, no delay was—is required."

Lena's face whitened. Molly laughed.

Lena spun to face her daughter. "You think this is funny?" she demanded. "This insult to our clan and sept?"

"You've been caught in your own trap, Mother. For all your denials to me and Fabien, you are as much a matchmaker as Uncle Donal."

"Don't blame your uncle! Fabien Loche lied to me!"

"Did he?" Molly responded. "He described their customs, their proprieties. He didn't say there were other conditions."

"You say your sept is trying to unite with House DuQuoin by marrying Molly and Fabien?" Emile Loche asked, joining the discussion once again.

"Yes," Molly said.

"No," Lena insisted.

"Hmm," Emile replied. "Why not?"

The women's heads pivoted to look at Loche.

"Would you repeat that, please?" Lena asked.

"I just mean that a marriage between Fabien and Molly might be advantageous for both sides—if they both agree."

This time, Molly's face whitened. After a few moments, it turned red.

"I understand—maybe it is just an impression—that Molly and Fabien have spent considerable time together and have grown fond of one another," Loche continued. "Not so?"

Lena looked down at the floor of the veranda then back at the wall of the house. "How long has Marcus been here?" she asked.

"Three days, not that it means anything, Mother. As I told you before, Fabien and I have already been formally introduced. Twice."

"How old is Fabien?" Lena asked.

"I can't tell you exactly, with all the time contraction that occurs with interstellar travel. But he is physically twenty-six standard years old," Emile said.

"Molly is twenty-five." Lena nodded. "A good match. Let's talk about this later, Member Loche, house to sept, shall we? Now, I have to speak to Robair and admonish him about some recent events." With that, she walked back into the house.

"Do you object to this, Molly?" Emile Loche asked.

"I... I..." She didn't answer. Instead, she rose from the swing and followed her mother into the house.

Chapter 15. The Hybrid

Herrin's Falls, Hebridean Mountains, 9 Eightmonth, 3203

Donal Harris arrived at Herrin's Falls the day following Emile Loche's suggestion of the joining of Molly Quinn and Fabien Loche. Fabien had been deep in discussion with the three lairds while his father sat in the swing on the back of the house, talking with Molly Quinn.

Charles Demning was back on the job in Dundee Orbital, and with the director's return, Donal Harris submitted a leave request at his first opportunity. He didn't bother to wait for its approval and bought a seat on the next Dunnsport-bound shuttle. Four hours later, he arrived at Herrin's Falls.

He bounded up the steps to the house and rushed inside. "Where's Lena?" he bellowed.

She stuck her head out of the kitchen and looked down the hallway to see her brother standing inside the front door. "I'm here, Donal. Now, stop that yelling and come in here. I've just made some coffee and have some pastries fresh out of the oven."

"Where's Loche? Molly?" he asked, stomping toward the kitchen.

Emile Loche entered the hallway from the side conference room. "I'm here."

Harris stopped. He had not expected Fabien's father to be present. "Good. What's all this about marrying Molly off to Fabien?"

"Molly and Fabien are up at the falls. They need to talk without interruption. Come into the kitchen, Donal, and we'll all talk. No one is marrying off anyone. Not yet, anyway. Not without their agreement." Lena turned her back to her brother and walked back into the kitchen.

Emile Loche looked at Donal Harris, tilted his head toward the kitchen, and followed Donal's sister.

"Pack!" Donal Harris said softly and followed the other two.

†††

Fabien Loche rose early the next morning and dressed. He felt something was about to happen, and it wasn't the change in his relationship with Molly. He found Donal Harris and his sister in the kitchen. Lena was cooking a slab of bacon and also a dozen eggs in a second skillet. Donal was sitting at the table, drinking coffee. Her primitive kitchen continued to amaze him. A fully functional autochef sat in the corner, but there was Lena, cooking on a wood-fired stove. The smell of burning wood and frying bacon made his stomach growl.

"Molly up yet?" Donal asked Fabien.

"Haven't a clue," Fabien said.

"I thought—"

"He doesn't fully understand, Donal," Lena interrupted. "Leave it be. Molly will explain."

I guess Molly told her mother. I wonder what Molly hasn't told me yet.

A few moments later, Molly joined them. Donal opened his mouth then closed it when Molly glared at him.

"Need help, Mother?"

"No, it's about ready."

Fabien retrieved a mug from the cupboard and filled it with coffee. "Here," he said, handing it to Molly. "Sit. I'm sure Donal has questions. I assume you've talked with your mother." Fabien chuckled.

"What?" Molly asked.

"For a patriarchal society, women sure have a lot of power and influence here," Fabien stated.

"We—" All four links vibrated for attention.

<Unknown ship has appeared at the sixty-fathom line. It is asking for Emile Loche.> The message was from Caledonia System Operations, relayed through Dundee Orbital and McLean House.

"It's the hybrid," Fabien said as his father entered the kitchen. "They want to talk with you, Father."

"Is that possible?" Emile asked Molly.

"Yes, there is a secure communications room down the hallway," she replied.

"I've used it. You can use our house codes too," Fabien confirmed.

"I'll help you get set up and then leave you in privacy," Donal Harris added.

"Will you need me?" Fabien asked his father.

"No... Perhaps. Stay close. If I want you, I'll call," the elder Loche said before following Donal Harris down the hall to the communications room.

†††

Emile Loche waited until Donal Harris helped set up the secure link and left. Following Harris's instructions, he sealed the room. Returning to the link-console, built into a wooden desk, he asked, "Are you there?"

"Yes," said the other person. "Security code omega one nine seven."

Loche paused for a moment, sifting through passwords and counterpasswords, then replied, "Delta omicron epsilon three three." He activated the requested encryption via his link and slid it into a slot in the console. "This is Emile Loche, Member, House DuQuoin, Associate of the Seat."

Loche's link established a secure session with the other party, the captain of the hybrid ship, according to his coded introduction. "Emissary. Roger Blankenship, Member, House Nesterov, Associate of the Seat, Captain of the *Normandie*. We ask permission to land."

"How heavy is your ship? It was still under construction when I left."

"It masses one hundred sixty thousand tons, Emissary. However, we enlarged the landing pads to reduce ground pressure by half during its final construction."

"Good. That gives us options. I will bring my son into the room. He's been here longer than I and has more knowledge of planetary facilities."

The desk had a hardwired communication module specifically for situations like this. Loche flicked a switch and, when Donal Harris answered, asked him to send Fabien in.

"Stand by, Captain Blankenship. I'll get my son."

Fabien was standing outside the room when Emile opened the door.

"Come inside, Fabien." Emile secured the door and returned to the desk console. "My son, Fabien Loche, is here, Captain."

"Member Loche, we need a landing place. One on the surface of Inverness, visible from a wide area and able to support one hundred sixty thousand tons."

"A marketing ploy, Fabien," Emile whispered. "We want the ship to be seen by as many as possible."

"Just so," Blankenship confirmed with a chuckle.

"I would have said Port St. Regis, but it's no longer there. Dunnsport would be second, but it's built on landfill. That leaves the McLean Militia shuttleport on the top of the escarpment above Dunnsport or at Caernarvon Shuttleport in Williams territory. But since you want visibility, I'd suggest the McLean Militia port near Dunnsport. The plains around Caernarvon are pretty empty."

"Let's get Donal Harris up here and link in Robair McLean," Emile told his son.

McLean House Militia Shuttleport, 11 Eightmonth, 3203

The wind across the landing field was chilly. Summer was almost over in this hemisphere, and the wind coming down from the Hebridean Mountains carried a hint of autumn. Fabien, standing with Molly, shivered. Herrin's Falls weather was warmer than here on the coast. Molly was dressed more warmly. Fabien wasn't. He draped an arm across her shoulders and drew her closer. Warmth from any source was welcome.

<Thirty minutes.> The automated announcement carried across the field and was also heard inside the thick-walled observation bunker. McLean Militia shuttles that had been standing on the surface were gone, lowered into underground hangars within the granite massif.

"I still don't understand how this is possible," Jean-Paul Portee said to Herman Mieze. The two lairds were part of the Council of Clans' welcoming party. "An interstellar ship landing on the surface of a planet."

"It does seem incredulous, doesn't it?" Mieze responded. "Emile, Fabien, have either of you seen this new ship?"

Fabien shook his head. The question had interrupted his discussion with Molly. "Only when it was under construction at our Ceres yards. It was unpowered then."

"And it has two sets of engines?" Portee asked. "I'm having trouble believing it is possible. The power requirements are astounding."

"Four types of engines, actually," Emile Loche answered.

<Ten minutes.>

Donal and Lena Harris stood with Molly and Fabien.

"It should be in the atmosphere by now," Donal said, looking up and to the east. He squinted against the morning sun and saw a glowing object against the blue of the sky. "Is that it?" he asked a McLean aerospace traffic controller standing nearby.

The controller looked up, briefly checked his link, and looked up again. "Yes, that's it. It just dropped through mach seven and is at thirty thousand meters." He checked his link again. "And it's decelerating at four g's… no, five—six g's!" He looked back at Donal Harris. "I've never seen a shuttle pull that many g's coming down, not even a VTOL shuttle." He shook his head and continued to monitor the hybrid's descent.

"I think we should get inside," Fabien told the group. "I don't think we should be standing here, out in the open, when it lands."

<Five minutes.>

Boom! The hybrid had dropped below sonic level and was clearly visible. It dropped to three thousand meters and was hovering out over the sea.

No thundering reaction engines for this ship. Only a faint hiss, Fabien thought.

<Extending landing jacks,> said somebody else, someone within the hybrid, from the accent.

The ship was unlike any vertical or horizontal take-off design. Unlike the shape of a usual cylindrical shuttle or interstellar ship, the upper half of the hybrid was a hemisphere dotted with sensor arrays and weapons turrets. The lower half was a truncated three-sided pyramid. Each side of the shortened pyramid moved out from the hull, forming three landing jacks, each ending with a large triangular foot.

Down it came, slowly sliding inland to the designated landing pad marked with blinking lights. At one hundred meters, dust and grit swirled around the pad.

"That's from the contragravity engine," someone said.

"Ten meters… Five… Touchdown."

Fabien thought he felt a vibration through his feet as the hybrid's engine shut down, and the ship's 160,000 tons settled onto the granite surface.

"Is the ship armed?" someone nearby asked.

Fabien turned to see Robair McLean waiting for an answer. "Yes. It is a warship, as I told you. With dual FTL engines and a shunt drive, there

277

isn't much room for cargo, so we added particle-beam cannons and missiles."

"Is that economically feasible for a cargo ship?"

"I don't know. You'll have to ask the specialists on board. I know this ship is a loss leader—a sales demo—and it had to have some defensive capability, given the current situation in SolSystem and the System States."

A cargo ramp extended from the bottom of the hybrid, and several people were walking down it to the ground. *Oh!* Fabien looked over at his father and saw he also recognized the distant figures.

"Come, Fabien." Emile Loche led him, striding across the tarmac toward the ship with a string of other dignitaries following.

"I didn't know she was coming," Fabien told his father.

"I didn't either."

The party at the bottom of the ramp had grown to a dozen, men and women. Some women were elderly.

"Mother?" Emile asked.

"No. She'll be with the house when it arrives," answered a tall, elderly woman with long, flowing gray hair, standing in front of the others.

After Fabien and his father walked up to her and bowed, Emile said, "Grand Dam. Welcome."

She returned their bow with a small nod of her head. "It goes well?"

"I believe it has, Grand Dam. There have been developments. Fabien will explain when we have some privacy."

She looked at Fabien and beckoned him closer. After he did, she looked into his face, their eyes at the same level. *She was always taller than most in our house. She still is.*

"You look well, Fabien."

"I am, Grand Dam." He beckoned Molly Quinn to join him. "This is Mary Elizabeth Quinn, better known as Molly, of Clan McLean, Sept Harris. Molly, this is Elise Hémery, Grand Dam of House DuQuoin, Holder of the Seat of Thirty Houses, and my direct grandmother."

The elderly woman looked at Molly, examining her. Molly returned her gaze.

"Is this one of the subjects you will be speaking of?" his grandmother asked him.

"Yes, Grand Dam."

"Good. I look forward to your report. Please bring Mary Elizabeth with you."

Next, she turned to Emile Loche. "Introduce me to these others, if you will, Emile."

"With pleasure, Grand Dam," he said, tucking her arm into his and leading her to the waiting group of lairds and members of the Council of Clans.

"Brr! She could melt steel with that gaze," Molly whispered to Fabien as his grandmother was being introduced to the clan dignitaries.

"She is… impressive, isn't she?" Fabien Loche responded with a smile. "She likes you."

"How can you tell?"

"She invited you to my briefing," he said. "If she didn't like you, you would have been ignored."

They followed Emile Loche and the Grand Dam, joining the other members of her entourage in time to hear the last introduction.

"I've set aside several suites in McLean House for you, Holder," Robair McLean said.

Some other lairds grimaced. They would have preferred the initial meetings be held elsewhere. However, the ship was here, at a McLean militia base with McLean House below.

Lena Harris approached the ship's captain. "Do you need any maintenance, Captain Blankenship? Any resupply requirements?"

"Just the usual, Deputy Harris. Fresh water, fresh hydroponic biomass if possible, and some other minor consumables."

Lena keyed some instructions into her link. "Here's my link code and another for the militia support group. Please let me know if there is anything you need that they cannot provide."

"I will, ma'am. Thank you."

Lena rejoined the group in time to hear Robair McLean urge the party to move below, out of the weather.

"My deputy, Lena Harris, will ensure the Seat has all they need," he said.

Molly's mother muttered something.

"What, Mother?" Molly asked.

"He did it again, that son of a bitch. Dumped it all on me so he can play politics."

"I noticed he's put the Seat in the upper levels of McLean House. It'll be noisy if the militia resumes operations," Molly added.

"I doubt that came to Robair's mind," her mother replied. "I'm delegated to being an innkeeper… again."

✝✝✝

The Loches and their Grand Dam broke away from the group of clansmen and approached the two women. Grand Dam Hémery walked up to Molly and bowed. "My darling Mary Elizabeth, the Seat will be having a small soirée this evening, and I would be honored if you and your mother would attend."

Molly glanced quickly at her mother before replying, "We would be honored, Grand Dam."

"Excellent! Till then," the elderly lady said before she was swept away to join the Line Mothers being led to their quarters.

†††

Molly and Fabien Loche entered the suite reserved an hour before for the soirée. The Grand Dam had asked them to arrive an hour early. Emile Loche followed them through the door.

Robair McLean had thought to host a formal dinner in honor of the arrival of the hybrid ship and its passengers. However, he had been foiled when Grand Dam Hémery begged off, having planned this private dinner with Molly, Fabien, and Emile Loche. She and the Line Mothers from other houses of the Seat needed time together with their Emissaries. Fabien, his Grand Dam had informed him, had been uplifted to be equal to his father.

Grand Dam Hémery met them at the door. "Emile, Fabien, welcome."

Emile stepped forward and kissed the back of the Grand Dam's extended hand. Fabien did the same. Molly stepped forward but was halted by Fabien's arm. He shook his head and took Molly's hand in his own.

"I'll explain later," he said quietly.

The elder lady moved to Molly's side and took her hand from Fabien. "Let us retire with the Mothers and allow these two men to meet the hybrid's crew and engineers. We house women should introduce ourselves."

Molly, with a glance at Fabien, gave a small bow and allowed herself to be taken aside into a neighboring room. A woman, a Line Mother, Molly would soon learn, closed the door behind them. Inside the room, sitting in a circle of chairs, were the remaining Line Mothers, the Executive Board of the Seat. The woman who had closed the door returned to the circle and sat in one of three empty chairs. Two chairs remained for Molly and the Grand Dam.

"Mothers," Elise Hémery said, "this young woman is Mary Elizabeth Quinn of Clan McLean, Sept Harris, who will soon be, if I am correct, the betrothed of Fabien Loche of House DuQuoin."

"Is that correct, Clanswoman Quinn? You are to be betrothed to Fabien Loche?" one of the women in the circle asked.

"The speaker is Marian Lillian Frienze of House Tyre," Elise Hémery said.

Molly blinked. She hadn't expected a confrontation—if this was a confrontation. "That is under discussion between our families. Fabien and I have not had time to discuss more than the preliminaries… and after a suitable mourning time for Reena Elaine Chaim to have passed."

"Good," the other woman declared. "We can't undo the past, nor can we live in its shadow. Is this your freely given choice, Mary Elizabeth Quinn?"

"Yes. It is," Molly replied without hesitation.

"Now that that is clear, Mary Elizabeth," the Grand Dam said, "let me introduce you to these Mothers. Unfortunately, I am the only representative of House DuQuoin to protect you from these harpies, but I believe I will be sufficient."

The Line Mothers laughed.

†††

Fabien and his father found the crew of the *Normandie* in a side room. The staff of McLean House were flawless in providing support for the Grand Dam's entourage. Unlike those on Confederate ships, the crew of the *Normandie* were all male.

Roger Blankenship greeted the Loches and introduced his crew. When finished, he led them to a side buffet, where each filled a plate. Then Blankenship took them aside and quietly mentioned, "We're secure as far as we can determine. We've found no visual nor auditory spy devices."

"Thank you for checking, Captain, but it isn't necessary," Emile said. "The decision is to hold nothing back during our discussions with the Confederates."

"However," Fabien interjected, "the clans of Inverness are a subset of the Confederacy, a powerful subset whose agenda may not entirely mesh with the Confederacy's. Inverness has just suffered a civil war that was caused, largely, by our proposals and technology."

"Are we still committed to come to the Confederacy?" Blankenship asked.

"Yes," Emile answered. "With the elimination of the contrarian party, our position is much better than before. We have still to present our proposal to the Confederate Senate, but with the help of the Inverness clans, I am confident of success."

"Is clan support necessary?"

"I wish it were otherwise, but, yes, it is. Inverness is one of the most powerful planets in the Confederacy—if not the most powerful. The Caledonian system was chosen for the Confederacy's capital because it has three habitable planets. Inverness is the most powerful of the three," Emile explained.

"Then why is Cameron the capital planet instead of Inverness?" Blankenship asked.

"Stability. As evidenced by the recent civil war, Inverness is…" He looked at his son. "Help me, Fabien. I'm at a loss for a word."

"Hmm. 'Competitive' is the closest word I can think of. They're competitive in everything. Fortunately for the Confederacy, the competition is rarely violent. When violence does occur, as recently evidenced, the clans resolve the issue quickly—and in many cases, permanently."

"I see…"

Fabien knew Blankenship did not understand. This was another cultural issue. The houses were mutually supportive and cooperative. The clans were supportive too—among allies. Everyone else was a competitor.

"We have made some headway in that support. Four of the largest and most powerful clans, McLean, Portee, Mieze, and Williams, support us," Emile Loche said.

"You can't depend on McLean, Father. He has his own agenda."

"Then we must get him on our side, Fabien. That's your job. By the way, this is an excellent buffet. Have you tried the shrimp yet, Captain?"

†††

Another packing tour! Captain Roger Blankenship was tired. One group of clansmen after another wanted to see his ship. This group, with one exception, contained engineers from the McLean shipyard in the inner belt. The engineers all wore McLean Engineering patches on their jackets. One exception didn't. He wore the dark-blue uniform of the Confederate Navy with the three stripes of a commander on both sleeves and the hammer-and-atom engineering patch on his upper-left sleeve. He made Blankenship worry.

"Commander Isaac Thomas, Captain," he said when he first met Blankenship. "Tri-Cluster Navy Research and Engineering. Your ship astounds me!"

Blankenship wasn't fooled by Thomas's friendly manner. He knew what the naval officer was—a spy.

"Thank you, Commander. We hope your navy buys several when our production lines resume."

"Oh, I'm sure we will—with some modifications, of course. We are reviewing how best to use a ship with capabilities such as this one."

"Uh, what kind of modifications?"

"Well, this ship has three types of engines, correct?"

"Four types." Blankenship was concerned where the questions would lead.

"A new planetary drive? A contragravity drive, I believe?"

"Yes."

"And a normal sublight drive?"

"Yes, updated, of course—smaller and faster."

"And two! Two FTL drives?"

"Again, yes."

"How do you power all of this? Your power room is smaller than one in our smaller warships? What powers this vessel?"

That was a question he didn't want to answer... but he'd been ordered by the Emissary himself to answer fully and truthfully, the Seat's greatest asset in their quest for a new home. "A quantum power tap, Commander," Blankenship said reluctantly.

Thomas didn't immediately respond. His mouth hung half open. "My God, man! Truth?" he asked when he had regained his composure.

Blankenship nodded.

"That... that... One of those could theoretically meet the entire power requirement of Inverness."

"Not theoretically, Commander. Fact."

"With that much power, you could push a small planet into subspace..." Thomas's voice trailed off. "I... uh... just to make sure I understand, Captain—a ship this size with four... four different engines, room for a dozen missile launchers, and PB cannon turrets powered by a power tap scarcely larger than the power core in a frigate?"

Blankenship nodded again. "We have full specifications and engineering drawings with us. I'm sure they can be made available to you once we have an agreement with the Confederacy. My ship should be proof enough that our claims are real."

"Yes, I believe they are. If you will excuse me, Captain, I need to report. There will be further discussions, doubt you not."

"That's why we're here, Commander."

†††

"They've taken the bait, Fabien," Emile Loche said to his son. "The navy is now on our side."

"What's next?"

"I think a small junket to some nearby systems to demonstrate the other capabilities on the hybrid. Perhaps to Rajput..."

Fabien chuckled. "And allowing Amit Singh to add his views on the proposal?"

"Of course, my boy. Why exert yourself when there are others who can push our plans forward for us?"

"I expect the navy will provide some observers."

"So do I. More aid to us if they do. I'll meet with the Grand Dam and Captain Blankenship. If I recall correctly, the *Normandie* can carry twenty passengers. I'll let the Confederates decide who shall join us."

"Shall I come too?"

"No. You still have business here. Get McLean's support."

Chapter 16. Meeting of Minds

McLean House, Clan McLean Territory, 15 Eightmonth, 3203

Fabien's efforts to have House DuQuoin take over the former Monmouth territory was not progressing at all. Robair McLean was the stumbling block. Lairds Portee and Mieze, who held Clan Williams's proxy, lacked the votes to get the proposal through the Council of Clans. McLean, through political and economic pressure, controlled too many votes. The former Monmouth territory had a small common border with Clan McLean. Mieze and Portee suspected Robair's opposition was due to his desire to chew off a large chunk of Monmouth territory for Clan McLean—and for Robair McLean personally.

Emile Loche's discussions with representatives of the Confederation Senate moved forward. The *Normandie* lifted with him, Blankenship's crew, and a varied selection of naval and civilian engineers and shipbuilders for an "excursion," as Emile Loche described it.

With his father gone, Fabien suggested moving the negotiations back to Herrin's Falls. Many of the Confederate and non-McLean participants felt continued discussions in McLean House gave Robair an unfair advantage.

Grand Dam Hémery, with her entourage, joined them at the sept house. She said it had been too long since she had felt a breeze on her cheek. "I do so love it here," she confided to Fabien as they rocked on a swing on the evening of their arrival. "This… What do you call this?" she asked with a sweep of her arm.

"A *steading* is the common term, Grand Dam."

"Encompassing twenty-four thousand hectares?"

"A hundred square kilometers, yes, Grand Dam."

"So large. We, the entire house, have a quarter of that in Ceres Station."

"It took me some time to adjust to the scale. However, most of the land is unsuitable for agriculture or habitation. Except for the lurcats."

They rocked some more in the swing as dusk fell.

"I wouldn't be surprised if some 'cats come to visit," Fabien mentioned.

"They know we're here?" she asked.

Fabien laughed. "From the moment we put foot on the ground. Nothing happens here without their knowing."

"I would like to meet them," she said, for pets had long been banned from Ceres Station.

Fabien glimpsed movement in the shadows of the tree line. "You will, Grand Dam, when they're ready. Shall we go inside? It's getting cool."

"Yes. I'm getting chilled." She stood and paused. "It's a wonderful feeling here, Fabien. It's like… freedom! But before we retire, answer me truly. Are you well? So much has happened to you—how many assassination attempts?"

"I'm not sure. One at least, when I was injured in the Marines. The nannite-tagging incident wasn't an assassination attempt. It was inadvertent. The others were in the line of duty. Have there been any against you?"

"There have been some incidents when I was younger, but I wasn't the Holder nor the Grand Dam then. I think the incidents were just expressions of bigotry, nothing personal."

"That's my opinion, too, when I was in the Marines—nothing personal, just an opportunity to rid the Marines of another mutant."

Elise laid a hand on her grandson's arm. "Let's go inside."

††††

The *Normandie*'s bridge was small. Captain Blankenship's dais was in the center, raised above the others to provide him a view of all positions. To his left was the pilot's position. Navigation and engineering consoles were to his right. Behind the dais, on the far side of the engineering console, was a senior petty officer, the ship's gunner, sitting next to the communications and sensor consoles.

Emile Loche occupied a jump seat to the left of the captain, and Admiral Hector DeSota of the Confederate Navy's Bureau of Ships occupied the one on Blankenship's right.

"Sixty-fathom line in five minutes," the pilot announced.

"Prepare for tunnel," Blankenship ordered.

"Prepare for tunnel, aye," the pilot confirmed.

Status lights on his console flashed red and, one by one, changed to amber and then green.

"All compartments report ready for tunnel, Captain."

"Very well. Engage on my command."

"Engage on your command, aye."

"Sixty-fathom line in… three… two… one… now," the pilot reported.

"Engage tunnel."

On the monitor covering the front of the bridge, stars streaked into a starbow and blanked. In an instant, the ship arrived with a descending starbow and settled to a different visage of stars.

"Navigator?" Blankenship queried.

The navigator waited until he received a response from the *Normandie*'s initial ping to the system's beacon. "On the sixty-fathom line in the Oorda system, Captain."

Blankenship turned to Admiral Hector DeSota. "I think that is eleven and a half light-years in… elapsed time, Navigator?"

"Unmeasurable, Captain. Ship's clock shows less than one second, sir."

"Would you like to send a message, Admiral? Just to satisfy your curiosity?"

DeSota handed a data wafer to Blankenship. "If you'd send this, please?"

"Certainly. Will there be an answer?"

"Yes. Put it on the wafer, please."

The Oorda System, like the Caledonia System and most of the larger populated systems in the Confederacy, had a short-range subspace radio network.

"Message sent… and received, Captain," said the communications officer.

"Thank you, Comm," Blankenship said, retrieving the data wafer and returning it to DeSota. "Well, Admiral, another hop? Let's visit Rajput. How far, Navigator?"

"Ten point six light-years, Captain."

"Once we've used our second tunnel drive, we'll need a week to recharge before we can use them again—but we can use our shunt drive to get us back to Caledonia," Blankenship explained to DeSota.

"Ready whenever you are, Captain," DeSota replied.

"Navigator, course to Rajput."

"Sixty-fathom line?" the navigator asked.

"Excuse me," DeSota interrupted. "Rajput has a lot of rocks in its system. I would suggest we aim for a point on the hundred-fathom line and above the ecliptic."

"Make it so, Navigator," Blankenship agreed.

"Set course to Rajput, one-hundred-fathom line, fifteen degrees above the ecliptic, aye, Captain."

†††

Four days had passed since the departure of *Normandie*. Molly and Fabien returned to Herrin's Falls an hour before dusk from their refuge at the falls. The two spent every available hour away from the house and all the guests.

When Lena asked what they were doing, Molly smiled and said, "Assimilating."

Sergeant Nelson was concerned for their safety and asked to come with them. After introducing Nelson to some lurcats, Molly told him he needn't bother. He should, she pointed out, be guarding the Grand Dam of House DuQuoin as protecting her was more important than guarding Fabien. Nelson reluctantly agreed. His loyalty was to Fabien, and the house came second.

†††

Lena Harris was spending time with Fabien's grandmother. Lena had not mentioned that to Molly.

Today, Lena Harris and Elise Hémery were sitting in the veranda's shade with a pitcher of tea, a bucket of ice, a bottle of Irish whiskey, and frosted glasses on a small table between them. Grand Dam Hémery admitted to a fondness for "some Irish," as she called it. Alcoholic beverages were a rarity in the stations. The friendship between the two women had grown, and they were accustomed to using each other's given names.

"Do you think we are pushing them too hard, Lena?" Grand Dam Hémery asked. "I understand the need. However, Fabien is my favorite grandson, my only grandson. I don't want to force him into a situation solely for the sake of the house. His future happiness is important too. Others of my entourage are not so constrained, such as House Tyre."

"I don't know, Elise," Lena replied. "I know—not to be crude—that they're not up there sexing like a pair of bunnies in heat. Molly took some data wafers with her on the history of Inverness, the early centuries and the war years."

"*Assimilating*. Interesting word."

291

"Isn't it, though?"

The two women watched Fabien and Molly walking toward the house from the trail to the falls with two lurcats in tow. Elias Nelson waited for them. He refrained from following them to the falls but still hovered protectively at all other times.

"Have you met any of our lurcats, Elise?" Lena asked her companion.

"No. I've seen some from a distance but never up close."

"Well, you're about to have an opportunity. Those two 'cats with Fabien and Molly appear to be Lilith and Max, a mated pair and leaders of the local pride. Lilith is the black one. Max is the tan one."

"They look bigger than I thought."

"Some range two meters and more from nose to the tip of their tails and weigh around sixty kilograms."

"That much?"

Some are bigger. Some are smaller. It averages out."

Molly and Fabien walked up the steps, greeted the two ladies, and went inside. Max approached Elise and sat on his haunches before her.

<Hello. I am Max.>

Elise saw a small link attached to the harness Max wore. "Hello, Max. I'm Elise, Fabien's grandmother. I'm pleased to meet you."

<Welcome to Erroowe. The Pride greets you and those with you.>

"Erroowe?" she asked Lena.

"It's their word for Herrin's Falls. They have their own language but can't pronounce Standard, hence the link. They also use sign language. It's taught in all our schools."

The black lurcat came up past Max and butted Lena's shoulder.

"This is Lilith," Lena said. "She spends a lot of time here with Marcus and Ellen Louise."

Lilith turned her head and gave a nod to Elise.

"She's greeting you. She doesn't talk much unless she knows the person very well. Molly said she has just started talking with Fabien. Don't take it as an insult if she's a bit standoffish."

After another nod, the two lurcats walked into the house after Max stood to open the door, leaving the two women alone.

"We couldn't have pets in the houses," Elise reminisced, "although I suspect there may have been some. We didn't. I've often wished we had. Sometimes our life seems so… sterile."

"Molly has turned off her contraception," Lena mentioned, continuing their earlier conversation.

"I thought that may have happened. Fabien wasn't clear when he told me he and Molly were assimilating—understanding each other's culture, he said."

Lena, with a sip, emptied her frosted glass, then she refilled it with ice-melt from the bucket and a large shot of the Irish. She renewed the frosting on the glass by dipping it in a small icemaker.

"It's an old tradition, needful at one time," Lena explained. "Few follow the tradition these days," Lena said. "Molly surprised me when she said she was."

"Too young to be a grandmother?" Elise chuckled, chiding Lena. "We've a similar tradition from the plague years. We don't follow it now since our medical nannites can catch genetic anomalies. Usually."

"I cheated," Lena replied after a break in the conversation.

"Oh?" Elise responded. "How so?"

"I checked her medical log. As Sept Chief, I can do that."

"And what did you find?"

"Her last menstruation was last week. If they continue their assimilation, she'll be pregnant within a week."

"Ah. Perhaps we should begin wedding plans? Before or after?" Elise asked.

"Tradition says after."

"And Custom is?"

Lena laughed. "Oh, Elise, before, of course. You are assimilating."

"On some things, my dear. Only on some things." She extended her glass to Lena. "Refill, please?"

†††

Amit Singh met the party when the *Normandie* arrived. Boarding the station presented a problem. Mumbai Station's docking arms weren't large enough to grasp the hybrid ship's girth. It was too large. Nor could the ship get close enough to the station to use a boarding tube without damage. A transfer shuttle, while not the most appropriate vessel, as far as Singh was concerned, would do. *Needs must.*

The transfer shuttle was used to transport people between Mumbai Station and other stations and ships in orbit around Mandorva. The shuttle's hatch, now locked to the station, opened, and the passengers walked out.

"Emile, my friend, welcome back."

"Amit, I'm most pleased to be here, although we can't stay long."

"Is this the ship you mentioned in our last meeting?"

"Yes, the *Normandie.* This is Captain Blankenship, its master."

Blankenship, at Loche's insistence, was the next man out of the shuttle, following Loche.

"I believe the two of you need to discuss requirements for servicing ships like the *Normandie.*"

"The Senate has approved our proposal?"

"Not yet, Amit. But we're close. There are only a few holdouts."

Admiral Hector DeSota walked up to the two. "Why, may I ask, are we here?"

"A demonstration that we can do what we've said we can do—two immediate tunnel jumps. How long did it take to arrive here in Rajput from the time we left Caledonia?"

"Thirty minutes, not counting the time to move to and from the Caledonia and Rajput sixty-fathom lines. I get your point, Emissary."

"If you will excuse us, I have some business to discuss with Amit, here. I'm sure you have questions that Captain Blankenship can answer. I've instructed him to hold nothing back."

Amit Singh waited until DeSota left to join the others. "What is the problem, Emile?"

"One laird is blocking approval by the Council of Clans and placing our proposal for Rajput before the Senate."

"Who?"

"Robair McLean, and I don't understand why."

"What does he want?"

"That's it. He won't say. Some believe he wants the Monmouth territory for himself, hard as that is to believe, Amit. It won't gain him anything, and it would throw the clans into turmoil."

"What about the others?"

"Portee, Mieze, and Williams are on our side. They're adding other clans in favor of Fabien's proposal, one at a time—but it's taking too long."

Admiral DeSota was watching them from the group of civilians from the *Normandie*. Emile believed the admiral would support the Rajput proposal, but the navy wouldn't side with Fabien's plan. By Confederation law, they couldn't.

"I think you need to come back with us, Amit. Add your voice to the others."

"Gladly, Emile. Just give me a day to turn my office over to my deputy."

"Good." When Blankenship wrested himself from the other passengers, Emile waved him over and said, "One more passenger to join us on our return to Inverness, Captain. Do we have room?"

†††

Fabien and Molly were lying next to the pool at the bottom of the falls, sheltered from the cooling breeze flowing down the mountains by several boulders. The windbreak allowed Old Cal to keep them warm between sessions in the warm pool. Molly seemed to be getting chilled, based on the bumps that the occasional swirl of cool air triggered on her arms.

"Another session in the pool, Fabien?"

He had become chilled too. "Why—" A link message interrupted him.

<Nelson, sir. I'm coming up. The Grand Dam and Molly's mother want you both.>

"How close are you, Elias?"

<How far do you want me to be?> Nelson was nearly laughing. *<I could see you if I stretched and stood up on my toes.>*

"Give us five… ten minutes, Elias," Molly said loudly enough for Fabien's link to pick up her voice.

<Will do, ma'am.>

Fabien looked longingly at the pool then at Molly, who was already putting on her clothes. "I suppose the Grand Dam has something important if she sent Elias up here."

"Don't forget Mother sent him too."

Molly sat on the ground, leaning against a head-high rock for support, to put on her socks and shoes. Fabien, this visit, had worn his old house shipsuit and body sock. He discovered he could disrobe and clothe himself more easily with a shipsuit than with shorts and hiking gear.

Molly finished dressing except for her weapons belt, just as Elias Nelson approached.

He waved and asked, "Need any hel—"

Twack!

Nelson stumbled as his right arm flew away in a spray of blood and he fell to his knees.

Twack! A magrifle round impacted the boulder next to Fabien's head, sending rock shards flying, cutting his face and ear. Molly scooted backward farther behind the rocks on her hands and feet. Fabien ducked and rolled behind the rock to join her.

Elias, out in the open, fell forward, facedown and motionless.

"Alert! Sniper alert!" Molly screamed into her link. "Sniper at the falls, one down. Need immediate evac!"

Twack! Another round hit the rocks.

Fabien glimpsed its ionized trail. "On the ridgeline to the…" He checked the direction from their position. "Two six seven degrees from the pool," he added via his link. "Sergeant Nelson is down!" He looked longingly at their weapons, sitting in coiled belts out in the open with their backpacks.

<Coming.> The link message was from Lillith. Her pride had remained close by in the forest around the sept house since the battle with the Monmouth troops.

<On the way. Ten minutes,> Captain Barnabas reported. He and his alert team had farther to come from Benning's Bridge.

"Prisoners, Lilith," Molly said. "We need to know who sent him."

Lurcats had to be reminded to take prisoners.

<Prisoners,> Lilith reluctantly agreed.

297

"C'mon, Fabien. Let's get back into more cover. That last shot was from a different position."

"Two of them?"

"Or he's moving. Follow me."

Molly, keeping below line of sight from the sniper's last position, rolled over the edge into the pool. Fabien crawled forward.

Twock! The round impacted in the pool. Steaming water geysered into the air. Fabien reached the spot where Molly had entered the pool and followed her.

Molly waited with her head barely above the surface and next to the rocky edge of the pool. "Follow me. There's a safe room here," she said before diving into the depths of the pool.

†††

Fabien took two deep breaths and followed her. *Where is she?* Then he saw her swimming down to an underwater opening in the rocks beneath the waterfall. She grabbed the edge of the opening and disappeared inside. Fabien followed. The opening was larger than he'd thought.

Fabien, like Molly, grabbed the edge and pulled himself inside. The opening was a tunnel, two meters long and curved upward. Through the water, he could see Molly's legs disappear. The surface was not far.

He swam upward, pulling himself through the water until he broke the surface to find a chamber cut from the rock. Emergency lanterns came on, activated by Molly's link. By the time Fabien had climbed from the water, Molly was seated on a rock, removing her soaked boots followed by her wet socks.

"Strip, Fabien. This chamber isn't as warm as the pool. There are militia stores in back, dry clothes and blankets to keep us warm."

<Two snipers in sight. Proceeding,> Lilith reported.

<I'm landing our alert team on the backside of the ridge, Lilith,> Barnabas said. *<If you chase them our way, we'll roll them up.>*

<Acknowledged.>

<Molly, evac on the way. ETA two minutes.>

"Good," Molly replied. "Nelson is out in the open. I don't think the snipers fired at him after the first shot. His arm was blown off by a magrifle round."

<Pack. He's probably bled out by now.>

"Elias was a Dundee patroller and has Customs nannites. He may still be alive."

<Roger. Out.>

Molly was right. The chamber was cooler than outside—no, colder. Fabien was shivering when Molly returned with a handful of thermal blankets and two militia uniforms.

"Which do you want, Fabien? Blanket or uniform?"

"Blanket first to dry off, then the uniform."

In minutes, both were as dry as they could manage and in militia uniforms. "Now we wait for the all clear," she told him.

"What if they follow us?" Fabien asked, thinking of Elias and the snipers. He wanted to do something more than pacing the chamber and waiting.

"I've set booby traps. Nobody comes through that tunnel unless I want them to. Come over here and sit down. Pacing won't help Elias."

"I know." He sighed then walked back across the chamber and sat on the ground next to Molly.

A memory came to him, a question that Donal Harris had told him to ask Molly.

"I overheard your uncle and mother say there was something you should tell me after we started..." Fabien stopped—assimilation had started, but it wasn't complete. He didn't know the proper term for what they had been doing.

"Sexing like bunnies in heat? I think that's the term my mother would use," she said and laughed.

"Uhhh, yes."

"Do you know the difference between "Custom" and "Tradition," Fabien?"

"I'm not sure."

"Tradition is what we should do. Custom is what we actually do. In our case, tradition says we should confirm our ability to have children. Custom says we live together until I get pregnant." Molly shifted closer to Fabien. She had been sitting on a small rock.

"Oh. But we have been living together. Your bedroom is right across from mine."

"Together, Fabien. I had thought we might move into one of the guest houses at Herrin's Falls. Marcus and his family live in one. There are several others."

I'd like that. Why hadn't the thought occurred to me? Married stationers lived together. Because we aren't married, he realized.

"I'm not pregnant yet. A bed is softer than grass and rocks. We could get noisy and embarrass Marcus and Mother." Molly grinned at the thought. "Well, maybe not Mother. I've heard stories about her and Da."

"And after you're pregnant?"

"Why change a good thing? If we marry, it's for life, Fabien. I don't believe in divorce."

"We—I don't either. I like the idea. Could we get a bed that squeaks?"

"Fabien! Of course... and keep the little ones awake while we get them sibs."

<Evac here. We have Sergeant Nelson and are heading to Benning's Bridge. He's alive, barely. We're pumping him full of blood. His nannites closed all the major arteries, and we got to him before his system

300

collapsed. He will spend a long time in regen, though. His shoulder no longer exists.>

Fabien answered, "This is Fabien Loche. Nelson is a member of House DuQuoin. Please make sure my Grand Dam is notified. She'll oversee his recovery."

<Will do. The 'cats got the snipers. There were two of them. One resisted.>

"At least we got one," Molly said when their conversation with the evac ended. "Doesn't your Grand Dam have a link?"

"Well, yes, but she doesn't like it and rarely has it with her. Link addiction is very unfashionable in the houses."

"And here, too. I can't understand why anyone would want to spend their life in the link. Life is too much fun to waste time hiding from the real world."

"I didn't have one until I enlisted in the Marines. Then I was issued one and had to carry it, whether I wanted to or not."

Molly stood and brushed away some small pebbles on the floor with her damp blanket. "There are more dry blankets in the back. I mentioned I'm not pregnant yet. Want to change that?"

††††

Lena Harris sat across from the prisoner in an interrogation room four levels down in the Benning's Bridge militia base. With her were Captain Barnabas and Donal Harris. To one side of the three was a militia intelligence specialist.

"Name, clan, and sept?" Lena asked.

The prisoner remained mute.

Lena looked at the specialist. "Any suicide devices?"

"Three. We've removed them."

301

Lena noticed the prisoner's eyes widen. "Didn't know that, did you?" she asked him. "And you have implants for your link interface too. Bad idea, that."

A skilled interrogator—and her specialist was very skilled—could manipulate a prisoner's sensory input to anything they chose. Interrogators could create a reality of a prisoner's worst fears. Questions *would* be answered. Unfortunately for the interrogee, sanity did not always survive. Lena watched the prisoner, who squirmed a little in his chair. He knew. Yes, he knew what could—would happen if he didn't cooperate.

"I'll ask one more time, then if you don't answer, we'll go to more extreme measures. Understand? Understand?" she shouted.

The prisoner looked at all the faces watching him. He dropped his head for a moment then looked up at Lena Harris. "Kevin Lockmore, Clan McLean, Sept Culmore."

Lena sat back into her chair as Donal Harris entered data into his link.

"You're dead," Donal declared. "You died three years ago."

"I… I got into some trouble a few years ago. They purged me from the clan rolls."

"Who?" Lena asked, leaning forward to look Lockmore in the face.

"Neil Cooper."

"He's the Monmouth spy," Barnabas said. "I still have his wanted notice in my link."

"Was he? I examined Cooper's history and background data," Donal Harris said. "There was nothing linking him to Monmouth except for the discovery of his body in the forest with Monmouth's troops—that and a message from Monmouth himself to Cooper. Or so we believe." He entered another data request. "We found Monmouth's link when we recovered the rest of his body," Donal said.

"Whose body?" Lena asked.

"Monmouth's body. All we had linking Cooper to Monmouth was his disappearance after the attack on Fabien in McLean House—that and the message Cooper stupidly allowed to remain in his personal McLean House account. I didn't think much of it at the time. Now..."

"So?" Lena asked again.

"The timestamp of that damning message was after Cooper's disappearance. It had been altered to look as if it had arrived earlier. The archives say afterward."

Turning to the prisoner, Donal posed a new question. "How were you paid?"

"Credit tab. A Cameron credit tab."

"He had one on him when he was captured," Captain Barnabas added.

"Trace it," Lena ordered. She no longer believed this was a late Monmouth assassination attempt, and she feared what the truth could reveal.

†††

"How is he?" Fabien asked his grandmother. They were standing outside Elias Nelson's room at the Benning's Bridge med-center.

"They were concerned at first, the med-techs," she said, "but I think now he will live, but with his shoulder missing, he won't be able to do much for quite some time."

"I've discovered the Confederacy's medical technology is much better than ours, Grand Dam. They replaced the artificial nerves in my leg."

"I remember you said that. I hope it bodes well for the Sergeant," she said.

Elias has gained status, Fabien noted. *Grand Dam called him* Sergeant. Changing the subject, he asked, "How long do you plan on staying here at Herrin's Falls?"

"At least until your father returns. Lena and I have an understanding. She will be, after all, kin."

"Molly and I are moving into one of the guest houses at Herrin's Falls."

"Before marriage?"

"It's the custom, here, for Traditionalists."

"I see. Then Lena and I have things to discuss."

"What?" Fabien asked, suddenly wary. When senior women got together, no one knew what would happen.

"The marriage contract for one—"

"The clans don't do that," Fabien interrupted.

"Hush, boy. They will now."

Fabien sighed and remembered that assimilation worked both ways.

Chapter 17. Revelation and Retribution

McLean House, Clan McLean Territory, 22 Eightmonth, 3203

"Where is he?" Lena Harris shouted after she stomped into Robair McLean's empty office.

The two militiamen standing outside cringed. Lena Harris's temper was legendary.

She stopped before them and asked again, "Where?"

The senior guard answered, "We don't know. He didn't arrive this morning as he usually does, and the steward says he isn't in his rooms."

Lena Harris turned to one of the silent men who had accompanied her. "I want Robair Litton McLean found. I want him returned here. In shackles, if necessary."

"You can't do that!" said Lena Harris's deputy chief of intelligence, Robert Jilani.

"Article Nineteen, Robert. Do it."

"Charge?" he asked, visibly uncomfortable.

Lena knew he owed his position to Robair McLean. "Treason against the clan, among others. Now, go. Donal, with me." She turned and strode back into Robair's former office. "Sit down. I want you here. This may involve the Interdiction Office."

Inside the office, she walked around behind the former laird's desk and sat. "Sit," she told Donal Harris, pointing at a side chair. "Where are Molly and Fabien?"

"They should be here soon. You left before I could get another recon boat to the Falls," he admonished her.

"Who's with them?"

"Barnabas. He left a company on guard for the Seat."

"Marcus?"

"He's with Molly and Fabien."

She nodded. "There's just one more thing to do. Get the PR folks in here for a public announcement. However, I must tell our allies first."

"All or just Mieze, Portee, and Williams?"

"Hmm. Those three first, then the rest."

†††

Donal sent link messages to the head of the public-relations department and, as an afterthought, checked to see if the militia was on alert. PR acknowledged and said they would bring a crew to the laird's office for the public announcement. The militia was on alert, "Critical" status, up from "Priority."

Lena used her link code as deputy laird to establish secure connections to Clan McLean's three major allies. In moments, the holoimages of Herman Mieze, John-Paul Portee, and Alistair Davies hovered before her.

Herman Mieze took the lead, asking the question all three wanted to know. "Lena. What is this about?"

"Lairds, under Article Nineteen of our constitution, Robair Litton McLean has been removed from office. I am the acting Laird, pending confirmation from our sept council or the selection of another for the office. I expect them to act after some information has been shared with them."

"What are the grounds for removal, may I ask?" Alistair Davies was the quietest of the three lairds and often gave his proxy to Mieze and Portee rather than being swept into political intrigue.

"Treason against the clan, inciting civil warfare, and attempted assassination. Perhaps more egregious acts—a violation of the Ban. We're still investigating."

None of the three lairds made any comment. Mieze was stunned. Donal watched all three. He knew Mieze had been friends with Robair McLain all his adult life.

"Proof?" Mieze asked.

"Robair has been feeding data—false data—to Monmouth for several years, leading him by the nose. He acted, convincing Monmouth to believe that he, along with his clandestine organization, was from the System States. McLean, using a cut-out, had banned weapons smuggled to Monmouth. When the time was right, his plan was to reveal Monmouth's possession of those weapons—nuclear weapons."

"Why?" asked Alistair Davies, Laird Williams.

"Hatred. Pure, pathological hatred from their school days… and greed. He vowed to destroy Clan Monmouth, and he succeeded. But it wasn't enough. He wanted all of Monmouth territory or as much of it as he could get. Fabien Loche stood in the way. Robair sent two assassins to kill Loche—and my daughter too. He paid them with platinum credit tabs. We traced them back to Robair through several false accounts—and more illegal payments to other parties too." She paused to get her anger under control and to take a breath. She had been talking too long. "Does that answer your question, Alistair?"

Alistair Davies gave his head a quick shake then, looking Lena squarely in the eyes, said, "Yes."

"I have a data packet ready for each of you. You are the first to know. I'll have another session after this meeting with other McLean allies." She sat down in a chair next to Robair's desk and looked up at the three lairds. "I hope you will remain allies and my friends. Some clans won't believe us. Some will blame us. However, Clan McLean is innocent. It was Robair Litton McLean who fooled us all. And now that we know, we are taking steps to rectify the situation."

Donal Harris had been sitting at the edge of the holo's pickup. He stood and stepped next to his sister. "Herman, John-Paul, Alistair, I've been friends with Robair longer than any of you. I have trouble believing this too. However, it was others in the Interdiction Office that discovered and confirmed Robair's duplicity."

"My people are preparing a public announcement to our clan and the public as we speak," she said, sending instructions to transmit the data packets.

"Received," Alistair Davies confirmed as Mieze and Portee nodded.

"I will make time if you have further questions. But I would ask that you send them to Donal, my brother, who is now acting deputy laird."

Donal raised his eyebrows in surprise.

"I'll be busy," she concluded.

"Thank you, Lena," John-Paul Portee said. "We'll review your evidence. I know you. You wouldn't do this without solid proof. After we review your data, I believe you can count on our support."

"Thank you, John-Paul. Alistair. Herman. Until later, then."

"Until later," they echoed, and their holos disappeared.

"Deputy laird, am I?" Donal asked. "You could have asked first."

"I had to think fast. You were here. I can't be inundated with questions for the next few days."

"Pack. I've a job up at Dundee."

"It must wait, Donal."

"Pack."

†††

"I thought the vote would be closer," Donal Harris said as he walked with his sister, now his laird, from the council chamber.

The Council of McLean Septs confirmed Lena Harris as Laird. They also confirmed Donal Harris as acting Deputy Laird. Marcus Harris was appointed the new Chief of Sept Harris, pending the sept's confirmation. He took Lena's seat on the sept council.

"Truth be told, so did I. I hadn't realized how few supported Robair."

"His cronies, I noticed."

Lena Harris didn't answer as they approached the laird's office. The same two militiamen stood guard outside. The closest nudged the other when he saw them coming.

"Hut," he whispered, and the two came to attention.

Lena and Donal stopped before the two. "Anyone come looking for me?"

"No, Laird," the older militiaman answered. "Several stopped to ask us what was going on, however."

"And you said?"

"That an announcement would be made later today."

"Good. For your information, the holo has been made and should be on the link within the hour. In case anyone should ask. Tell them that."

Both militiamen nodded. The older one asked, "What happened, Laird?"

"For your information only until the announcement," she said, "Robair McLean betrayed the clan."

The two guards—her guards, now—appeared shocked.

"There are other charges, but that is the major one."

The guards stood aside.

"Come, Donal, there's work to do."

†††

The announcement was not long, only ten minutes. Clan McLean allowed half a dozen newsies to be present during the recording of the holo and afterward allowed each to ask one question. Donal suggested they pool their questions and each ask a different one rather than each newsie asking the same question, trying to find a discrepancy.

The newsies asked their questions after huddling together to pool their queries. As expected, one tried to ask an additional question but stopped when Donal Harris glared at him.

"Thank you, Laird Harris—"

"I'm Laird McLean. Lena McLean, Clan McLean, Sept McLean, now, in accordance with our clan constitution," she corrected the newsie.

"Thank you, Laird."

Several newsies muttered complaints as a militiaman escorted them out of the studio.

Donal Harris stepped forward. During the recording, he had remained in the gloom at the rear of the studio.

"Keeping out of sight, Donal?" Lena asked.

"As much as I can. Molly and Fabien are waiting in your office."

"Another item on my to-do list. Let's see them and then link in Mieze, Williams, and Portee. Let's get Fabien's proposal moving. I think we now have a majority in the Clan Council."

As the two approached her office, the older guard, a sergeant, knocked on the door to alert Molly and Fabien before opening it for his laird.

Why hadn't I noticed he was a sergeant before? Too wound up, I suppose, she thought.

Inside the office, Fabien and Molly stood. "Laird," both said.

They know this is an official meeting, not a family one. She wanted to get this business finished. They had family issues to resolve.

Lena settled herself into Robair's—*My chair now. Keep that in mind, Lena,* she told herself. Before business, she had one question to ask first. "Sergeant Nelson?"

"He should survive, Laird," Fabien answered. "Evac got to him in time, before he bled out. His patroller nannites saved him. Grandmother is with him. She's approved his adoption into House DuQuoin."

"Good." Lena noticed Fabien called Elise Hémery, Grand Dam of House DuQuoin and Holder of the Seat of the Thirty Houses, Grandmother. Nelson was now family.

"Please inform Holder Hémery that I have instructed Captain Barnabas that he and his company are under the Seat's orders until the Monmouth proposal is resolved. Since Robair won't be throwing obstacles in our way, I and Lairds Williams, Portee, and Mieze, plus our allies, will support your proposal in the Council of Clans and in the Confederation Senate."

"Thank you. When will the Council vote take place?" Fabien asked.

"I've asked John-Paul to handle that, but I would guess in about a week. We just need to make sure all the *i*'s are dotted and *t*'s crossed."

"That quick? Then I—we have work to do in Monmouth territory," Fabien replied.

"You have another task first," Lena countered. "A wedding," she said, looking at Molly.

"I'm not pregnant yet, Mother."

"Doesn't matter. You will be soon."

"Custom says—"

"Custom be damned, Molly. This isn't just an Inverness issue now. It's a House, Seat, and Confederation issue. Will there be a wedding? Yes or no?"

"Yes—"

"Then it will take place in two days at Herrin's Falls. Fabien, your Grand Dam and I have agreed. The Benning's Bridge Reconstituted Catholic vicar has waived the banns and will perform the wedding. The marriage contract will be signed and witnessed on the spot. Donal will sign for the sept. I will sign for the clan, and Fabien's father, assuming he's back by then, will sign for House DuQuoin. If he isn't, Elise will sign it."

Molly turned to Fabien. "Contract?"

"We haven't discussed that. I'd assumed we would follow Inverness Custom and Tradition. The houses don't have formal weddings. We have contract signings," he explained. "Covers rights, responsibilities, property, and inheritances."

"You want to keep Herrin's Falls, do you not?" Lena asked Molly.

"Yes. It's mine."

"No, it isn't, Molly," Lena said. "The land belongs to the sept and clan. You have the right, with your progeny, to live there and exploit it with clan and sept approval."

Molly's face turned red, and an angry glint appeared in her eyes. She had a temper to match Lena's own.

Lena knew the reminder of the true ownership of Herrin's Falls was a shock. Molly knew that—she just hadn't thought about it. All too many clansmen and clanswomen forgot that actual land ownership rested with the clan and sept. In some cases, like Clan Williams, ownership also lay with a family line.

"I made sure, Molly, that if Fabien's proposal was accepted and enacted, that Herrin's Falls would be transferred to Clan DuQuoin. Parts of it already border Monmouth territory."

Molly looked up at her mother.

"You'll keep Herrin's Falls, Molly. I promise you," her mother said.

Molly was still angry. However, it didn't last, and the redness faded. "Thank you, Mother."

†††

"What's the count?" John-Paul Portee asked Herman Mieze. They were seated outside the chambers of the Inverness Council of Clans with Alistair Davies.

"A good solid twelve for our side. Only seven for Monmouth's and Robair's old allies."

"Let's call for a vote and get it over with, for both proposals, Fabien's and Emile's. Is our senate rep outside?"

"Yes. Amit Singh will introduce the proposal to the Confederation senate, and our man will second and call for an immediate vote. Emile's proposal has already passed through the Senate's Commerce Committee. The vote is locked, and the Executor has agreed to sign it when it reaches his desk."

"Good. Let's get this moving." Once inside, John-Paul Portee was recognized and shouted, "Call to vote!" at Amat Diehl, who was presiding over this meeting of the Council of Clans. The discussion of the Monmouth-DuQuoin proposal stopped. A Call to Vote was always permitted, according to the council rules.

"Call to vote!" echoed Herman Mieze and Alistair Davies.

Their allies in the Council took up the call with them.

†††

"Bring him out," Donal Harris ordered.

Robair McLean had been found hiding in a container of perishables about to be lifted to Dundee Orbital. McLean stumbled as he stepped out of his cell, but he remained upright in the firm grip of a Dunnsport City patroller. One of his eyes was blacked, and his lip was split.

"Resisted arrest, he did, sir," the desk patroller said to Harris when McLean emerged from the cell. "Fired on our boys with a pistol. Nicked one. He needed to be encouraged to surrender."

"Get him cleaned up, have his eye and lip checked by a med tech, and then take him up to McLean House. Inform the laird when you leave here with him."

"Aye, sir."

†††

The laird's office was full when three militiamen, one in a powered combat suit, delivered Robair McLean to the laird's office. Donal Harris sat in a side chair alongside her desk. Fabien Loche and Molly Quinn sat

313

side by side on a small couch along one wall, while Marcus Harris and two other McLean sept chiefs stood along the wall next to Donal.

Two of the militiamen, each with one of McLean's arms gripped firmly, stopped before Lena McLean's desk. "Reporting as ordered, Laird, with one prisoner."

"Release him," she ordered.

The militiamen did so and stepped back, careful to remain within reach of Robair McLean.

Lena rose and walked around the desk to stand in front of the former laird. "Traitor!" she said and backhanded Robair across the face.

He rocked back from the blow. One militiaman, standing behind him, put a hand on McLean's back to prevent him from falling to the floor.

"I wish I could challenge you. I'd take you up top right now and put a bullet through your head. But I can't. So we'll try to hang you instead."

"With a short rope," Donal Harris added as she passed him to return to her seat behind the desk.

"I just want to know one thing, Robair. Why? Why did you start the war? All those people dead. Why did you try to have Molly and Fabien murdered?"

McLean straightened and shook his shoulders. "Why? I worked for fifty years to destroy Lionel Monmouth and the whole Monmouth clan. His father was a smart vulture, but Lionel wasn't. He was stupid. I led him around in circles. When I discovered he was trying to buy nuclear weapons, I saw my chance to put him and his clan under the Ban. They would be destroyed—eradicated like That Clan."

"Why Molly and Fabien? Fabien only arrived here a few months ago."

"Monmouth territory is mine. Mine! No damned Essie is taking it from me. I could make Portee and Mieze agree to give the territory to me. That weak-kneed Davies would roll over easily. He's their puppet. But

Loche would steal that territory from me. The clan will not suffer a thief nor her who's helping him."

"You're insane, Robair. You are not the clan. You were just the selected laird. I suspected you were delusional. Well, we have a cure for a laird who turns murderous," Lena said. "Is the Dunnsport Adjudicator here yet?" she asked Harris.

"No, but he's on the way. He should arrive at any time, and the sept council is empaneled in the council room as the jury. They're waiting at your pleasure."

Fabien Loche rose from the couch and walked over to stand in front of Robair McLean. "They, as laird and deputy laird, may not challenge you, but I can—"

"No, Fabien," Lena interrupted. "This is a Clan McLean affair. You may be one of the aggrieved, but you're not of the clan," she said from her desk.

Loche turned to look at Molly, who nodded.

A militiaman knocked on the door and stuck his head inside. "The Adjudicator's here, Laird."

Lena Harris stood. "All right, everyone. Let's get this done. Marcus, are you prepared to prosecute?"

"Yes, Lena, but I think a real prosecutor would be better."

"It has to stay within the clan. I compromised with the adjudicator, but he's a McLean clansman. It's the clan's and the sept's responsibility to keep our house in order."

†††

The wind on the edge of the escarpment was cold, flowing down from the Hebridean Mountains, causing Fabien and Molly to shiver. The trial had been recorded from beginning to end for the archives. Copies were sent to several newsie outlets. He and Molly testified about the attack on them at the falls. Lockmore testified under verification about his orders to kill Fabien and Molly. Wounding Sergeant Nelson fell under his orders to eliminate any witnesses. Sergeant Nelson's survival was the only reason Lockmore wouldn't meet his end alongside Robair McLean.

"I'm cold, Fabien," Molly whispered.

"It won't be much longer."

The small gallows, built by McLean militiamen, stood on the upper edge of the escarpment above McLean House and the sea. Robair McLean stood on the platform, noose around his neck, looking out eastward over the Gael Sea. He had refused a hood.

Someone out of sight flipped a switch, and McLean dropped... half a meter.

Donal Harris kept his promise to Robair McLean that he'd be hanged from a short rope. No one had been hanged in McLean Territory for a very long time. Whoever reviewed the execution protocol had missed binding McLean's legs, and Robair McLean jerked and kicked.

"We need not stay," Fabien told Molly. "It's done. Let's go back to Herrin's Falls. We've a wedding waiting for us."

"I see Mother leaving. We can go too."

The two followed the laird to the observation bunker and down into the massif to McLean House, leaving Robair Litton McLean alone, except for the three official witnesses, to dance at the end of his rope.

††††

Choosing the falls above Herrin's Falls for a wedding site might have been a mistake, Fabien thought. The day was sunny, but fog covered the falls, created by the geothermally heated water meeting the cool air flowing down from the upper mountains.

The local Catholic vicar stood at the edge of the pool with his back to the water. Fabien and Molly faced him, with Donal Harris standing next to Fabien and Line Mother Marian Frienze standing next to Molly. Grand Dam Hémery stood with Laird Lena McLean behind the couple. Other invited dignitaries, Lairds Mieze, Portee, and Davies, along with Customs

316

Director Demning and Amilie Schute stood inside the shelter, out of the chill air.

Fabien was dressed in his formal House DuQuoin black nouveau-silk tunic with the House crest on its upper-right shoulder, black nouveau-silk shirt, and matching trousers. Pinned to his tunic was a silver pin to show he was a Member of House DuQuoin. His final adornment on his black shirt, at the base of this throat on the short-banded collar, was a platinum emblem, encircled with diamonds, his badge attesting to his position as an Associate of the Seat. A silver five-pointed star draped around his throat on a ribbon ranked him, like his father, as an Emissary for the Seat of the Thirty Houses.

Molly was dressed simply. She wore her mother's wedding dress, altered to fit her greater height. On her head was her mother's veil, a family heirloom. A McLean tartan shawl encircled her shoulders with the added stripe of Sept Harris.

In a normal clan wedding, Molly would exchange her McLean-Harris shawl for one of her new clan as part of the ceremony. However, the new Clan DuQuoin had no tartan. Lena McLean had corrected that omission. Clan DuQuoin now had a tartan, a modification of the old Monmouth pattern with additional elements from McLean and Harris tartans.

"…husband and wife. You may kiss the bride," the vicar concluded.

Fabien leaned over and lifted the veil from Molly's face and kissed her.

"Ouch!" Her veil had become snagged on Fabien's Emissary star.

Lena and Grand Dam Hémery moved forward to untangle them. When that was done, Lena took the McLean-Harris shawl from Molly's shoulders. Fabien's grandmother walked forward and wrapped the new House DuQuoin tartan around her new granddaughter.

"Welcome to House DuQuoin, Molly," she whispered in her ear.

Boom! Boom… boom… The sound echoed across the falls and the valley below.

Fabien looked up to see the *Normandie* hovering above the falls. "I see Father has arrived. Late as usual."

The ship descended, drifting toward the landing pad at Herrin's Falls.

"Will your landing pad support that ship?" he asked his new bride.

"No, I don't think so, even with the bigger feet. I hope it doesn't tear up the pad. I just had it upgraded last year."

"It won't touch the ground," Grand Dam Hémery said behind them. "It'll just hover and drop a ramp to the ground. Emile can just walk down it. Let's get under the pavilion and sign the contract. There are four copies, so get ready."

"Four?" Molly asked.

"One for you, one for Clan McLean, one for House DuQuoin, and one for the Seat. The bureaucracy follows us all," the Grand Dam said and chuckled. "Come on. The wedding is only half done."

The final ceremony was completed under the watchful eyes of the Seat's Line Mothers and Lena McLean, with Marcus and his wife, Marion, witnessing for Sept Harris. Two Line Mothers made unalterable recordings of the signing. A Line Mother gave Lena McLean one data wafer for the Clan McLean's archives. Grand Dam Hémery received the other.

Molly and Fabien were greeting guests at a small reception inside the shelter when a silent craft appeared over the trees from Herrin's Falls.

"That's another demo," Grand Dam Hémery said. "A contragravity aircar. Ducted-fan aircraft are now obsolete."

The craft hovered over the pool. Emile Loche stepped out to stand on its rocky lip.

"Late as usual, Emile!" the Grand Dam shouted.

"But I made it!" he replied. He walked forward and greeted Molly with a hug. "Welcome to our family, Molly."

She hugged him back. "And you are welcome to Clan DuQuoin."

Emile looked at his son. "They approved your plan?"

Fabien nodded. "Yesterday. The public announcement will be made to those in the new DuQuoin territory with the recording of our wedding. Molly and I will be moving to Kilkenny tomorrow to begin the transition. That will be the Clan DuQuoin headquarters."

"And you will be laird?"

"Yes. We, Molly and I, are a compromise. The Council of Clans doesn't know you, nor the Grand Dam. No former Monmouth clansman would be acceptable, either. So, as part of the agreement, I'm Laird and Molly is Deputy Laird."

"Alone? Just you two?"

"No, there is a core of former Monmouth clansmen who will help us. We must reorganize the territory from end to end. It has been run as a dictatorship for several generations. That will change," he said.

Chapter 18. Reformation

Clan/House DuQuoin Meeting House, Kilkenny, 13 Twomonth, 3204

The exercise for the day was storming a warship. Loche's team was to enter via a personnel lock and move toward the engine room. Loche was in the middle.

Thurston, Reedy, you first, then me."

The two passed through the lock. They would lock the hatch for the rest of the team. It was his turn. He was half through when the hatch dropped. Loche had one leg through the opening, but something was blocking him. He couldn't move forward, and with the rest of his team behind, pushing, he couldn't move back either. He couldn't move back to get his leg from under the descending hatch.

The hatch continued down. He could hear the armor encasing his leg creak...

Fabien Loche awoke panting and to the sound of retching in the 'fresher attached to their bedroom. Molly hadn't been in bed during his nightmare. *Good.* He listened as she continued to retch. *She need not worry about me right now.* Their wedding had been three months before, and as her mother predicted, Molly was pregnant.

Molly's medical nannites noted conception occurring on the day of the sniper attack. Instead of following modern medical practice— removing the fetus to a gestation tank, Molly refused, insisting her pregnancy be as natural as possible—even to the extent of refusing hormonal adjustment to prevent *minor unpleasantness* such as morning sickness. He could hear her swirling mouthwash and spitting into the sink. Water ran for a moment then stopped.

Fabien rolled over and watched Molly's nude silhouette, backlit by a window looking out over Kilkenny, walk out of the 'fresher and return to bed. "Feel better?" he asked.

Molly didn't reply. She laid back on the bed, kicking the sheet and blanket down to the foot. "I checked the room's temp," she said, "and it's normal, but I still feel hot. I wonder if that is another part of pregnancy I didn't know about?"

"I wouldn't know." He noticed her abdomen was flat no longer but rounded. *Not much, but noticeable.* He checked his link for the day's schedule. His first meeting was an hour away. "Time to get up. Nelson is waiting for us."

"Urgh."

"You can't take off and go back to Dundee Orbital. You know Donal said you would go on maternity leave when you could no longer fit into your skinsuit."

"I know. Still… It seems to have been so much easier then. Shootouts, firefights, repelling invasions aside."

"The ceremony is at noon. Think you can be ready by then?"

"Your grandmother will make sure of that."

"Yes, she will," he said with a chuckle.

His Grand Dam was a stickler for protocol and saw it as her duty to ensure the integration of clan and house went smoothly. That day's ceremony was receiving fealty oaths from former Monmouth militia regiments. Sergeant Nelson, now Clan Counselor Nelson, had purged the law-enforcement units from the militia. No one trusted them. They'd been Lionel Monmouth's strong-arm bully boys, and the people no longer trusted the militia. The military side of the militia, however, was more respected in the eyes of people living in the new DuQuoin territory. They, once the situation was known, had refused to fight Monmonth's war.

Nelson guided the military and patroller side of the integration. He started it by identifying himself as "Elias Nelson, Clan DuQuoin, House DuQuoin, Sept DuQuoin." His shoulder was still in a regen mesh and would be for another year. He made sure everyone knew he had lost it in defense of his laird and wife.

"Is your mother coming?" Fabien asked Molly.

"Yes, along with all of the Council of Clans. I put Amat Diehl on the agenda to give a speech. He tried to remain neutral during the civil war but helped us surreptitiously."

"Before I forget, I received an application from Theodore Popelli to join Clan DuQuoin. I had the thought he might be a good deputy for Elias," Fabien added.

"Who is he, again? The name is familiar…"

"He was my bodyguard for a short period after I was attacked at McLean House. John-Paul assigned him to me. Truthfully, events moved so fast that he really didn't have a chance to do his duty."

"Could he be Portee spy?"

"Maybe. I don't think it matters. I wouldn't be surprised if every clan on Inverness has a spy here by now."

"Nelson will vet him," Molly muttered.

"Oh, yes. Without a doubt. Now, for me, I'm off to the 'fresher for a shower." He rose and looked down at her. "Want to join me?"

†††

"Here they come," someone said.

Fabien, Molly, his father, Grand Dam, Lena McLean, and the Council of Clans stood on the reviewing stand, waiting for the new DuQuoin militia regiments to pass before them. Elias Nelson was the organizer of the event, but he'd not bothered to update anyone before that morning. The agenda was simple:

First Infantry (Mountain) Regiment—The Borderers

Second Infantry (Mechanized) Regiment—Guards

Third Infantry (Mechanized) Regiment—The Third Herd

Fourth Logistics Regiment

Fifth Gendarmerie (Civil) Regiment

Sixth Guards Regiment (Security)*

Fabien struggled not to laugh as he read the informal name for the third regiment.

"There are other support units, but they aren't ready to be put on display," Elias whispered to Fabien and Molly. "I haven't started on the Aerospace regiment yet."

"The aerospace units can wait. There is a paradigm shift on ship design coming. No need to equip our regiment with obsolete ships," Fabien said. "But why a guards regiment, and why the asterisk?"

"There's still a possibility for a coup. I know the Sixth is loyal. Most of the 'orphans' are in it under our direct command. It has an asterisk because it is only three battalions instead of the usual four. When the territory stabilizes more, I plan to roll one battalion into the gendarmerie and the other two into the First and Second Regiments."

The first regiment entered the parade ground. Fabien watched them make the turn to march past the reviewing stand. The Kilkenny metropolitan skyline, with the curve of the *Normandie*'s upper hull visible from the city's shuttleport, framed the marching militiamen.

Note to self. Change the description of the shuttleport to spaceport. There will be more STS ships landing here, Fabien thought.

The skirl of bagpipes reached their ears. Molly nudged Fabien with her elbow. The First Regiment reached the stand. They were in their dress uniforms, black berets, kilts of the DuQuoin tartan, boots, knee socks with combat knives tucked in calf sheaths, and white shirts under dark-green ballistic armor. Ten-millimeter assault rifles hung over their right shoulders, and small packs rode on their backs. Fabien listened to the pipes. He could almost remember the name of the music.

"They look good, Elias."

"Thank you, Laird. I'll pass your praise along to them."

"Before I forget, Elias, you'll be getting some help. We've a volunteer for you."

"And who might that be, Laird?"

"Theodore Popelli. He comes from Clan Portee. Jean-Paul assigned him to me as a bodyguard when I first came down to Inverness. Unfortunately, the war started before he could get on the job. He has asked to shift his allegiance to us. Molly and I agreed."

"Hmm. Thank you, Fabien. I'll take him under my wing—when it's finished growing, that is."

"I wouldn't expect any less of you, Elias. Vet him first, of course."

"Of course, Laird."

†††

Molly was surprised to learn of two other applications to join the new clan. Amilie Schute was one.

"I figured you'd need some help—maybe a secretary or whatever and, when it's time, a babysitter," Amilie, outspoken as ever, told Molly.

"That will be months, yet."

"I'm sure I can be of use in the meantime."

"Did Herman Mieze send you as a spy?"

Amilie grinned. "He asked. I refused. Told him I wouldn't spy on kin, you bein' a cousin and all."

Molly laughed. That was so like Amilie—just blurting the truth out in front of everyone. "I'm glad you're here, Amilie, but what about Andreas and the girls?"

"Andreas has the *Kongrieve*, his ship. He's aboard it more than he's home with us."

"Has that become a problem?"

"Yes. Yonnie is old enough to make life choices. She wants to join her father and be a spacer."

"And Katje?" Molly was saddened to hear Amilie and Andreas were drifting apart, but that was not unusual for spacer families because the ship always came first.

"She'll come with me, at least at first. Andreas's mother, on Skye, has invited her to live with her. I told Katje she was free to choose, but I wanted her to stay with me. She'll join me... at least for now."

"Good. I'd like to have her here. She's sixteen now?"

"Yes."

"Just the right age to be a clan page, don't you think?"

Amilie smiled. "I think she would like that. But..."

"What?"

"She's not a clan member. She's always lived in Dundee, and Andreas wasn't a clansman. I told her she could join Clan Mieze— DuQuoin, now, when she was eighteen. Or not."

That may be a stumbling block, Molly thought. *Katje and I need to talk and see what she wants. She must join the Clan and House DuQuoin to be a page.* "Bring Katje in to see me. We'll have a little talk."

"When would be a good time, Molly?"

"Is she down here?"

"Yes."

"How does tomorrow morning sound? Not too early, unless she wants to see a pregnant woman heaving in the 'fresher."

"Looking for O'Rourke?"

Molly laughed at the old militia joke, though, given her circumstances, it was all too appropriate. When her laughter subsided, she said, "Getting back to you, I'll check with Elias Nelson and see what he has in mind. I'm wondering if you would fit in as an overseer for DuQuoin militia logistics. You've experience with that."

"I can do that. Now. Tell me. Boy or girl?"

Molly laughed. "Not even my mother knows. Everyone else can wait until the baby's born."

"What! Spoilsport."

Molly rose and headed for the 'fresher.

"I know that walk, Molly. Bladder or morning sickness?"

"I've already had my bout with morning sickness today," Molly said as the door to the 'fresher slid shut.

†††

Molly's link vibrated. "Yes?"

It was the front desk at the entrance of the DuQuoin Meeting House. "Visitor for you, ma'am. Katje Kappel."

"Get her an escort and send her up."

"Aye, ma'am."

Right on time. That's a good start. A few moments later, Katje was announced by a knock on her door.

The door opened, and Katje entered, followed by a militiawoman, who said, "Deputy Laird, Katje Kappel, by appointment."

"Thank you. You may leave now. Katje and I are old friends." The militiawoman saluted, pivoted, and walked out of the office, the door sliding shut behind her.

"Old friends, Molly? I'm not ancient?"

Molly laughed. "Sometimes, Katje, I feel like it. Let's sit over there," she said, pointing at a couch along the wall of her office. After they sat, she asked, "Did your mother say why I wanted this meeting?"

"She said it was a job interview."

"It is—and it isn't. The job is being a clan page. Basically, you would help different offices at different times, learning how a clan is organized and managed. However… there is an issue."

Katje waited for Molly to continue.

"All clan positions require being a clan member. I understand you are not—officially—a clan member. That was up in Dundee Orbital."

Katje looked puzzled. "I didn't have to. Dundee isn't Inverness."

"That's true. However, you are no longer at Dundee. You're here, and your mother has applied to join Clan DuQuoin. Clan Mieze agreed, and I approved your mother's request. I took her oath yesterday."

"I still don't understand, Molly."

"Ordinarily, if you were younger, your membership into Clan DuQuoin would be automatic. You'd join with your mother. But you're sixteen, Katje."

"Oh! I hadn't thought about that."

"Yes. I think you're beginning to understand. This clan, Clan DuQuoin, doesn't—won't—force anyone to join. It's voluntary, and you're old enough to make some life decisions. This is one of those decisions. Will you join Clan DuQuoin?"

"What are my options?"

"Only two, really. Join… or don't join."

"And," Katje asked, "if I don't join?"

"Nothing changes. You'll still have Confederate citizenship. You just can't be a page or take any clan position. There are some other conditions common to all who live on Inverness and who aren't clan members."

Katje squirmed. "Mother… She'd want me to join the clan. Yonnie…"

"Yonnie has the same choice. If and when. However, I doubt if she'll ever find a need, being an independent spacer like your father."

Katje nodded her head. "Yonnie always wanted to be a spacer. When do I have to decide?"

"Not today. Go home, talk with your mother, and then decide. I can't keep the page position closed for long. It must be filled, and I'd prefer to fill it with you."

"Mother's working today. She won't be home until this evening— evening! I never understood what that meant. And morning! Day and night." The girl started to sob.

Molly slid closer and wrapped her arms around Katje and rocked her.

"I don't want to leave!" Katje said.

"You'll never have to leave, Katje. You'll always have your mother and me. I don't abandon my friends."

"I'll join," the girl said.

"No decisions now. Talk with your mother. Decide when you're feeling better. If you still feel that way, come back tomorrow morning, and we'll schedule your training. You must also take some special training from Ted Popelli."

"What kind of training? Mother insisted I become competent with pistol and knife."

"Security training, how to fight dirty, hand-to-hand if need arises, and standard militia training." Molly laughed. "Usually, boys and girls your age go to summer boot camp for militia training and then receive specialized training with their home units. Yours will be one-on-one with Elias and Ted Popelli. You won't like it, but you'll be better trained than others."

Katje nodded. Her hand had slipped down from Molly's arm to rest on her growing stomach. "When," she asked, "is the baby due?"

"In about four months."

†††

Fabien had gotten out of the habit of being armed. With all his stints in medical and being surrounded by well-armed militiamen, he'd stopped wearing his pistol. Molly still wore hers, now in a shoulder holster. Her old pistol belt no longer reached around her waist.

"Wear it," Molly said forcefully, holding his pistol and pistol belt in one hand. Her order was not up for discussion.

"I didn't feel it was necessary here inside DuQuoin Meeting House."

"You need it more, here, than ever. There are still Monmouth partisans out there who would delight in shooting the usurper. And there are our clansmen. They expect their laird to be ready to defend himself as they expect him to be prepared to defend them. It's like you took the pin. No one would respect a laird who takes the pin. You'd be ousted in a month. Now, wear it, Fabien."

Fabien shed his outer tunic and wrapped his pistol belt and holster around his waist. "I think a shoulder holster, like yours, would be better," he said as he slipped his Moen pistol into its holster.

"That's better," Molly said as she walked up to him with his outer tunic in hand. She helped him slip it on and watched as her husband shifted his shoulders, making the tunic sit comfortably. She closed the top three closures on the tunic, leaving the bottom two open. "Now you can reach your pistol, and others can see you're wearing it."

"I can now move in political circles?"

"Yes. Don't harm the reputation of the clan, Fabien," she warned. "Now, give me a hug and go."

Fabien did so, awkwardly because of her growing stomach, and kissed her. Slipping back into old habits was easy since the Holder was there. The time had come to speak to Grand Dam.

†††

"Fabien, my boy, how good of you to visit. I know how busy you've been." Elise Hémery's quarters were next to those of Fabien and Molly's. She had been spending most of her time with various civil groups, helping with integrating Clan and House DuQuoin with the older Monmouth clan members.

"Busy, yes, but it's time to address some house issues."

"That sounds ominous, Fabien," she said, leading him to an alcove containing chairs around a small table. "Sit, boy."

"Thank you. It is, Grandmother. It's a House DuQuoin issue. When the Seat arrives, are you going with them or staying here?"

"Is that important?"

"Yes. If you stay here, you must assimilate with the clans and their culture. If you are to remain the Grand Dam, you must gain the respect of our clan members. Else, they'll just smile, agree, and then disregard everything you say as soon as they are out the door."

"Why?"

"Because, Grandmother, they don't see you as a member of the clan but as an interloper."

"Oh." She sank back into her chair, her expression troubled. "What should I do?"

"Talk with Molly. She's a born clanswoman. She has a friend who may help, Amilie Schute."

"Oh, Katje's mother?"

"Yes. And Molly's cousin. I expect she will hand you off to Amilie. She hasn't much free time at the moment."

Elise nodded. "I remember hearing Molly talk about getting the prototype autofac running."

"She's having a hard time selling it. Buyers don't believe the spec sheets about it, but that's her problem to handle. Yours is another, one you must address."

"Thank you, Fabien. For the record, I am planning on staying here. I've found that I enjoy living on a planet."

Fabien rose, gave his grandmother a quick kiss on her cheek, and left. Elise sighed as her quarter's door slid shut behind him. *He's grown so much.* That was not at all what she'd expected.

††††

Amilie Schute, as Fabien expected, was assigned to assist Elise Hémery assimilate into clan culture. The introduction was short: "This is Amilie Schute. This is Elise Hémery." Then Molly swept out the door.

Hesitantly, after Molly left, Amilie said, "Hello, Grand Dam." She wasn't sure how to address Fabien's grandmother. Better safe than sorry.

"Oh, don't call me that. I'm just Elise. The Grand Dam is a title, as the head of the house. I'm here, now, as a member of Clan DuQuoin. Fabien thinks I need some assimilation." The older woman laughed. "Please excuse me. I laugh every time I hear the word *assimilation*."

Amilie raised an eyebrow. "I assume there's a story behind that?"

"Oh, yes, but we haven't time for it. Fabien believes—and Molly concurs—that I need more assimilation into the clan culture. I've been trying to promote the integration of Clan and House DuQuoin, but people just won't listen."

"I think I know… I know what Fabien meant, but first, what about the others who came with you?"

"They aren't House DuQuoin. When the Seat arrives, they'll all go back to their respective houses."

"So it's just you?"

"For now. The rest of House DuQuoin will arrive with the Seat."

"That helps. I've an idea how to start. I'll get back to you later today. Are you prepared for an excursion around Kilkenny?"

"I will be by the time you return. May I bring someone?"

"Who?"

"Marian Frienze, House Tyre. She may be the next Holder and must be able to lead the houses, to understand the culture of the Confederacy. Fabien says there isn't much cultural difference across the Confederacy from Inverness."

"That's true. Two of you it is. I'll see you later," Amilie said.

†††

Amilie was accompanied by her daughter, Katje, when she arrived the next morning to find the two Mothers waiting. "Ladies, I am Amilie Schute, Clan and House DuQuoin, Sept DuQuoin—and Molly's cousin.

331

This is my daughter, Katje Kappel, Clan and House DuQuoin, Sept DuQuoin. She's a page for the Meeting House." She turned to the stranger standing next to Elise. "And you are?"

"I am Marian Lillian Frienze, House Tyre of the Thirty Houses."

"She is also a member of the Executive Board of the Seat," Elise added.

"Welcome. Please call me Amilie. There's no need for formality amongst us women."

"And I'm just Katje," Amilie's daughter added.

"We will, Amilie. Won't we, Marian?"

The other woman nodded. "As Elise explained to me, this meeting is to help us assimilate into the Inverness culture, correct?"

"It is for Elise. For you, I think your need is to better understand the Confederate culture. There are similarities, many similarities between the Confederate culture and that of the clans. You must learn the exceptions off-planet."

"Where are we going?" Elise Hémery asked.

"We will meet some ladies of Kilkenny's most prestigious social club, the Kilkenny Rifle and Pistol Club, for brunch."

"Tell me about it."

"It started around seven hundred years ago. It's grown over the years. The club sits atop a thousand hectares of rolling land just outside the city. On the grounds are numerous rifle and pistol ranges, two golf courses, polo grounds, and three small lakes, two for fishing. The clubhouse is enormous. However, the real draw is that every member is highly influential, socially and politically. Every Monmouth laird has been a member. So are Fabien and Molly, although I doubt either has had time to attend any of the festivities."

"I know of similar organizations," Elise admitted.

"Yes. Well, when I joined the clan, they offered me a membership. I suspect it was because I'm in charge of re-equipping the militia. I'm not in the habit of allowing a gift to escape my clutches. I accepted."

"Is that expensive? I don't know how much you're being paid, but—"

"Don't worry. I'm billing the clan as a business expense."

Their car pulled up in front of a pillared building behind a circular drive.

A doorman walked down the steps and opened the vehicle's passenger door. "Welcome to Burgess."

"Thank you," Amilie replied. "Amilie Schute, member, with guests, Elise Hémery, Marian Frienze, and Katje Kappel."

"Madam," he said to Amilie, "Madam," to Elise, Marian and Katje. "Your party waits inside in the second parlor."

Amilie walked up to the main entrance but stopped just outside the doors. "Here, put this on," she said, handing a small gold pin to Elise and Marian. "You'll be complying with one of the local customs."

"What is this?" Marian asked.

Elise looked at Amilie, waiting for the answer.

"It means you have no weapons, that you're defenseless."

"I don't understand," Marian said. "You're not wearing one, nor is Katje."

"We can't. We're armed." Amilie unbuttoned her jacket and swept it aside to reveal her pistol holstered under her left arm.

Katje, dressed as a Clan DuQuoin page, raised the hem of her kilt to expose a small pistol strapped to her thigh. "I keep my knife on my other leg."

"Then we need not be armed. You two will protect us," Marian declared.

Elise opened her mouth and then shut it.

"Why should we?" Amilie replied. "Why should we protect you if you're unwilling to protect us in return?"

"But… but—"

"Marian," Amilie interrupted, "you've just experienced a culture clash with one of the prime elements of our—Inverness—culture: being armed and being self-supporting. You feel that since I'm armed and your escort today, that I have some duty to protect you. I've said, in turn, that I don't, and you don't understand why. Correct?"

"Yes."

"Then I hope today's visit with the Kilkenny ladies will be a learning experience."

Elise and Marian attached the pins to their tunics. The doorman was waiting at the club's entrance and opened the door as they approached.

"Thank you," Amilie said as the three women and one teenage girl walked through the doorway.

A woman was waiting down the hallway, waving to them.

"Shall we go, ladies?" Amilie asked. "I think they would like to meet you."

†††

"Ladies, welcome to the Kilkenny Rifle and Pistol Club. I'm Donna McKown, the club hostess for this month. Would you please follow me?" the woman said.

Amilie had met her once before on her first visit to the club. Donna had greeted her and given her a tour of the clubhouse and grounds.

The hostess led the group down the hallway and through a side door into a generous room, empty except for a dozen women seated around a circular table. She touched her link, and the door behind her slid shut, providing privacy.

"Ladies," she said, "this is Amilie Schute and her daughter, Katje, of Clan and Sept DuQuoin."

"Excuse me," Amilie interrupted. "That's Clan, House," she emphasized," and Sept DuQuoin."

The Hostess blinked. She was not used to being interrupted. "Ah, yes, Clan, House, and Sept DuQuoin. The other two ladies are…"

Elise took the lead. "I am Elise Hémery, Grand Dam of House DuQuoin, Holder of the Seat of the Thirty Houses, and if I understand my grandson and new granddaughter correctly, of Clan and Sept DuQuoin."

"And you?" McKown asked Marian Frienze.

"I am Marian Lillian Frienze, House Tyre, Member of the Executive Board of the Seat of the Thirty Houses. I am not a member of Clan DuQuoin."

Donna McKown introduced the other women. Several claimed to be Sept DuQuoin.

"How is that?" Elise asked. "Until now, I had thought the only members of Sept DuQuoin were myself and those joining from other clans like Amilie and Katje."

The question appeared to embarrass the Sept DuQuoin women. Donna McKown hurried to answer the question. "These are… were former members of Sept Monmouth. Not the hierarchy, the rebels, but those left behind to be the target of the Vendetta's wrath. The laird graciously agreed to accept them into Sept DuQuoin, to protect them from those who didn't understand that these families and others were victims of Monmouth's duplicities, as was the rest of the clan."

"All is and has been forgiven," Amilie said, reinforcing McKown's explanation. "We're a new clan and sept. The current task at hand is for house and clan to understand one another and to merge—assimilate our two cultures."

"The last I heard, there are only twenty-five thousand Sept DuQuoin members. Will there be more?" one of the former Monmouth women asked.

"Around a hundred thousand," Elise answered. "The majority of House DuQuoin has yet to arrive. They will all be in Clan and Sept DuQuoin."

"That would make Sept DuQuoin the largest of the clan's septs," Donna McKown muttered.

"Just so," Elise confirmed.

"I expect some Sept DuQuoin members, those currently here in the territory, to shift to other septs," Amilie said. "Individuals and families too. Just remember: Assimilation will have to work both ways."

Chapter 19. Pursued

Clan/House DuQuoin Meeting House, Kilkenny, 23 Fourmonth, 3204

The courier broached from subspace on Caledonia's sixty-fathom line. Its commander found a nearby subspace repeater and sent an urgent message to the Holder of the Seat.

††††

Fabien found his grandmother lounging in the sunroom on the top floor of the Clan DuQuoin Meeting House. "Message for you, Grand Dam, in Seat encryption."

She appeared to have been drowsing as he walked up and blinked several times before answering. "Pah! Now I must find my link to decode it. Follow me, boy." She rose and walked out of the room without looking to see if he followed.

Grand Dam Hémery occupied a suite on the same floor as Fabien and Molly and Fabien's father. She found her link and, after Fabien transferred the message to it, began to read.

"Get your father, Fabien. Molly too. We need a conference with Portee, Mieze, Williams, McLean, Amat Diehl, Captain Blankenship, and… What's the name of that Confederate admiral up at the Fleetbase?"

"Honecker?"

"That's the one. Make sure he's present too."

"Why? What's going on?"

"The System States are coming. Apparently, they aren't happy we, the Houses and Seat, left SolSystem and took our people and technology with us."

††††

The clan's secure communications room was in the third sub-basement of the DuQuoin Meeting House. Elias Nelson set up the secure links to all the invitees then, at Fabien's order, secured the room and stood out of sight in a corner.

At the conference table, Elise Hémery was seated at the head as the one calling the conference and as the Holder of the Seat. Emile Loche sat to her right. Fabien was to her left with Molly, who could no longer cover her pregnancy. Roger Blankenship sat next to Emile Loche. The holoimages of the other conferees hung in midair before them.

"Admiral Honecker, I'm glad you could attend on such short notice," Elise Hémery said, opening the conference. "I have news for all of you, and it isn't good. The System States are disinclined to allow the Seat to leave SolSystem. They're coming after us—"

"They're chasing you?" Amat Diehl interrupted.

"No. We have the means to prevent them from detecting us and discovering our route."

"Then how—" Admiral Honecker interrupted this time.

"We left several ships as stay-behinds, Seat-built couriers, to watch and alert us to any action EarthGov and the System States might take. One of those ships arrived a few hours ago."

Molly suddenly looked uncomfortable. She rose and hurried to the small 'fresher attached to the communications room. Lena McLean's holoimage glanced at Elise Hémery and grinned. Both women knew Molly's bladder required immediate attention, a by-product of her pregnancy. The Holder of the Seat chose to ignore Molly's sudden departure.

"A fleet gathered in SolSystem for the purpose of forcing the houses to return to SolSystem. However, they could not determine what route we took. A spy or a leak said the Seat was going to the Confederacy—here, to Caledonia."

Admiral Honecker reached over and slapped an icon on his desk, and a red Alert icon appeared in a corner of his holoimage. "When are they expected to arrive?" he asked.

"Our courier left SolSystem fifty days ago. They made one short stop to drop off a message on the way here. Since passage here by fast packet is six months—and I don't believe any System States warship is any faster, I would estimate we have four months before they arrive."

"How many?"

"From the list provided by the courier, this is their order of battle: SolSystem Home Fleet. One hundred twenty ships, including a squadron of battleships and two squadrons of battlecruisers, and the rest comprising light cruisers and destroyers. Support ships, replenishment freighters—colliers, I believe they're called—and ammunition ships. The count also includes a division of marines and other assault forces."

She cleared her throat. "The Second System States Fleet is from Centauri Fleetbase. It contains seventy-five ships, the courier said. Fifty more ships are coming from the Tau Ceti Fleetbase… more colliers, but those ship types were unconfirmed."

"A three-hundred-ship capitation strike," the admiral said.

"I'll leave military matters to you, Admiral, and the Confederation Navy," Holder Elise Hémery said.

"When will the Seat arrive?" Amat Diehl asked.

"By my estimate, at the same time as the System States fleet or a little before."

"Then they aren't any faster than the System States fleet."

"No, the Seat is much faster. We could make the passage in four months if we could do so in one subspace flight. Unfortunately, we can't, the Seat will have to broach at regular intervals along the way for navigational reasons. Our ships are big—they have to be, to bring all the houses and the outer stationers—and we can't take the same route, the more direct route packet ships follow."

"But if you arrive first, I assume you have your own forces to assist us?"

"Oh, yes, but we don't have enough to stand against the System States by ourselves."

Honecker turned to someone out of sight of his holoimage and gave several orders. While he did so, Molly returned and sat next to Fabien.

"Feeling better?" Fabien asked and grinned.

She sighed. "Yes. Mother never told me about this part of pregnancy. Makes me wonder what else she hasn't told me."

When the admiral finished his off-line discussion, he turned back to the conference. "You're not the only ones with fast ships. Ours are faster than those from the System States—not as fast as yours, though. I've just issued orders for a recall of all navy assets that can get here before the Essies. From our intelligence, our ships are better than theirs. I hope so. We can't match their numbers in the time available to us. Most of our fleet is out guarding the Coterni and the DeeCee border."

"The *Normandie* will join you. It is better armed than many would believe. And it brought designs for some weapon systems that you may get into production before the... Essies"—she used the Confederate term for the System States—"arrive."

"Such as?" Lena McLean asked.

"Such as a missile—we call it a skip missile—that can bypass, skip through, defensive shields, and subspace mines that can sync with a ship."

"We already have subspace mines. The McLean yards already build those for the navy," Lena McLean said.

"Ours have a successful sync rate of eighty-five percent. I believe the best yours can do is forty-five percent."

"That would help," the admiral admitted.

The other clan lairds in the conference remained silent. Elise watched them. She knew what they were thinking. Each one was concerned how the assault strike would affect them and Inverness. By their nature, clans were self-serving. They had no deep-space forces. Many, but not all, had near-space militia ships for planetary defense.

When the DeeCees had attacked decades earlier, she was told, the clans rallied to defend their low-orbital infrastructure, Dundee Orbital and Weyland Fleetbase. The clans also remembered how heavy the Confederate toll had been.

"Our inner-belt shipyard can build your mines, Elise. What else do you have?" Lena McLean asked.

"We have a design for a deep-space system-defense fighter. That might be a better choice than making mines and the new missile."

"We have several shipyards, Elise. Clan McLean has four shipyards if you include the 'yard at Dundee Orbital."

"Would you please see how soon you can build the fighters, Laird McLean," Admiral Honecker asked, "and your projected construction rate?"

"I will, Admiral. Later today if I can. We must review the design first and see how many standard components we have on hand." She paused a moment before continuing. "There is one area where you can help, Admiral. I must improve the defenses at the 'yards—expand our current defense systems. Could you assist us getting the permits from Caledonia System Control?"

"Certainly, Lena. Just let me know when."

Alistair Davies, Laird Williams, spoke. "Williams Freight Lines will assist you, Admiral. Our ships may not be up to naval standards, but all are armed and our crews trained. We can also haul any stores if it comes to that."

Portee and Mieze had been conferring on the side.

John-Paul said, "Herman and I will add our militia fighters and will provide companies of our Marine-trained militiamen for the defense of Dundee Orbital."

Fabien's father, who was standing next to the Grand Dam, glanced toward Fabien and Elias in the background. He had just completed a deal between Clans Portee, Mieze, and Williams to license the contragravity engines from the Seat. Clan DuQuoin, as broker, received a nice commission from the three clans. Clan McLean had declined the offer to join the three. Lena McLean had her sights on the STS ships and was retooling a shipyard in the outer belt in anticipation of a license from the Seat. Emile Loche and Lena McLean had signed the memo of understanding earlier that morning.

Fabien leaned over to him. "Too bad your plans have been interrupted. When had Lena expected to finish her first STS ship?"

"She bought the complete plans for a medium freighter-version STS ship. Her engineers estimated they could tool up and finish the first one in six months. Later ones could be built faster." He sighed. "That plan just got flushed down the disposer."

"Dundee is a tougher nut to crack than many think," Honecker was saying to Mieze and Portee. "I believe the navy can provide some surprises to help them—some items we have on hand just for such a contingency."

"Harrumph. Please excuse me," said Roger Blankenship. "I wasn't finished describing what we can contribute."

"Oh, I'm sorry, Captain. Please continue."

"Thank you, Admiral. In the *Normandie*'s hold are six new power sources. You may have already received a report about them from Admiral DeSota."

"No, I haven't. He's BuShips, and I ordinarily would not be informed about BuShips affairs."

"Admiral DeSota discovered the *Normandie*'s power source. The ship is powered by a quantum power tap. The units are small. I suggest you install them at your more important installations—like Dundee Orbital, Cameron Upper, Skye Harbor, and some of your other major installations, Weyland Fleetbase, for instance."

"What are you suggesting, Captain?" asked Honecker.

"The primary limitation for shields and particle-beam cannons is power. Because of their size, large installations are vulnerable. Most lack power to support stronger shields and particle-beam point defenses. Given sufficient power, the survival of those stations can be improved."

"And the drawbacks?"

"Integrating the power taps into the existing power distribution infrastructure. With four months, I would expect there's sufficient time for integration and improvement of defenses."

"I think we all have work to do. I've issued a system-defense alert, and I've a call to the Confederation Executor and his executive board in a few minutes." He looked at Emile Loche. "Do the Essies know about Rajput and Mumbai?"

"No. And neither does the Seat, yet."

Honecker frowned and, looking at Elise Hémery, said, "I thought the Seat was in the loop."

"I'm the Holder of the Seat—the equivalent to your Confederation Executor. The Seat, like your Senate, has yet to arrive."

Honecker nodded. "If you would excuse me, my meeting with the executor is about to begin." His holoimage winked out.

Clan/House DuQuoin Meeting House, Kilkenny, 13 Fivemonth, 3204

Katje Kappel loved her job. As a clan page, she was introduced to and worked with the growing clan administration in the Meeting House. Today, she was escorting a guest to Molly, as Lady DuQuoin. The guest had asked for the laird, but he wasn't available.

"From your accent, you aren't from Inverness, no?" she asked. The number of off-worlders who wanted to meet the laird or the Mothers of the Seat was growing—dealers and dealmakers.

The man looked down at her and smiled. "No, I'm not from Caledonia. I'm an old friend of Loche's."

"The laird," Katje corrected him.

"Yes, the laird. I understand Lady DuQuoin is pregnant, not so?"

"Yes, six months."

"Wonder of wonders," the visitor muttered.

They arrived at Lady DuQuoin's office door. "How shall I introduce you?"

The man looked down at her. "As Imar Kolskov. I'm a former customs inspector now living on Cameron."

Katje palmed the annunciator at the side of the door. "Lady, Page Kappel, a visitor for you, one Imar Kolskov from Cameron."

<Enter.>

Katje opened the door and stepped inside.

Kolskov followed her. "Hello, Molly. I'd hoped to meet with Fabien."

"Imar! He's not here," Molly said.

"When will he return? My business is with him."

"He's off planet. I don't expect him back for a few more days."

Kolskov's face fell. "Forgive me, please."

Molly's left hand slid along the edge of her desk. Katje frowned, turning to speak to Kolskov, but he roughly pushed her aside.

Molly's hand pressed a hidden icon on her desk.

Falling, Katje twisted to land on her left side. As she hit the floor, she drew her pistol from under her kilt.

Molly slid off her chair to take cover behind the desk, her right hand on the butt of her pistol in its shoulder holster as she disappeared behind her desk.

Choog! Choog! Kolskov fired twice with his suppressed pistol. Each bullet splattered against the armor built into Molly's desk.

Bam! Bam! Bam! Katje fired from the floor into the man standing above her.

Kolskov looked down at her with surprise in his eyes. "I didn't expect you to be armed, little girl."

He turned back to Molly, swayed, and said, "I'm sorry. I didn't want to do this."

Katje, on the floor, kicked Kolskov's knee. *Get him down. He'll be less of a danger on the floor.* His leg buckled, and he fell on her. She used her other leg to push Kolskov off, her clothes covered with his blood.

Molly stood from behind her desk, pistol in hand, and retrieved a medical aid kit. "Resuscitation team to my office. Now!" she shouted into her link.

The office door slammed open, and a militiaman entered, followed by Elise Hémery. "Are you hurt, Lady?" the militiaman asked.

Elise, seeing blood on Katje's clothes, rushed to her, kneeling at her side. "Katje, where are you hurt?"

"I'm find, Grand Dam. It's all his—please excuse me!" She stood and looked down at the former customs inspector.

He raised his head, returned her gaze, and nodded twice before his head fell back to the floor. Kolskov's eyes glazed, and he relaxed with a sigh.

Katje blinked and ran for the office 'fresher.

"What?" Elise didn't understand.

Molly stood over her and extended a hand to help her stand. "I think Katje's throwing up. She's just shot a man… an assassin."

Elise looked toward the 'fresher. "So young, only sixteen," she murmured. "She'll need help." She started to follow the girl into the 'fresher.

Molly caught her arm. "A moment. Now you see why everyone is armed—expected to be armed. No place is safe this side of Heaven. We all have a responsibility for each other. In the Confederacy, 'To Protect and Serve' is not just a slogan. It's part of our life. Katje shot him to protect me. I would have done the same for her. Any clansman in Inverness and most Confederates would do the same. It's important you understand."

Elise put her hand on top of Molly's. "I believe I do. I wish the lesson wasn't so... brutal."

Molly tilted her head toward the 'fresher, where the girl was retching inside. "Go. Katje will need some comforting."

†††

"Amilie's proud of her," Molly said. "Nelson gave her a combat pin. Ted Popelli wrote the citation. For service to the clan."

<How is she doing? Any nightmares?> Fabien was still off planet with some engineers from the *Normandie*. The house engineers were helping the McLean shipyards retool to build small fighters using the Seat's design. He and Blankenship would visit Skye Harbor, above the large military reservation on Skye, Caledonia's fifth planet, to check the status of the power-tap installation.

"Amilie hasn't reported any yet. Andreas and Yonnie will come down in a few days when their ship docks at Dundee." Molly was sitting behind her desk in the her, the deputy laird's office.

<That's good. Did Amilie say whether he and Yonnie are thinking about joining the clan? I hate to see families break up.>

"No, not yet," Molly replied.

<How are you doing? I should have asked first, but I was worried about Katje.>

I should be asking him. Fabien's face in the holomonitor was drawn, with dark smudges under his eyes.

"I'm fine," she said. "Elise checks me every day, but you're not looking good, Fabien. You need to rest."

<We've only three more months—>

"Hush, Fabien. Get home. I'll take care of you."

Fabien's face lost some of its fatigue in the holomonitor. *<Perhaps a day at Herrin's Falls for some more assimilation lessons?>*

"I'm close to time, but we can find some alternate lessons."

<We'll have to experiment.>

Molly laughed. "On a serious note, I think your—our Grand Dam understands, now, why we go everywhere armed."

<What about Kolskov?>

"The resuscitation team got to him in time. The physicians are concerned about brain damage. Fortunately, we have his scans from Dundee for comparison. He'll remain in a coma for a while."

<Keep him guarded. We want nothing to happen to him.>

"Nelson has taken charge. I think Imar's safe."

<Good.>

A barely audible voice sounded outside Fabien's link pickup.

<What?>

Molly could only hear his side of the conversation.

Fabien nodded to whoever was out of sight and turned back to Molly. *<Have to go. See you in a couple of days.>* He turned aside, said, *<Clear,>* and blinked out as the transmission ended.

†††

"I kept two power taps back, Fabien," Roger Blankenship reported.

All the Confederate orbital installations were being upgraded. Now that the power taps had been integrated into the orbitals' power infrastructure, boosting the shields and particle-beam weaponry was next.

"What shall we do with these last two?" Blankenship asked.

"Install one right here in Kilkenny and the other in the PDC site at Killarney. We'll increase coverage of the shield walls. We don't have time to add more missile sites." Fabien looked at Blankenship where they sat in his office in the Meeting House. "What kind of laird would I be who didn't protect his own people when he could?" he said. "Killarney is our second largest spaceport after Kilkenny and will be a major militia base—once we have a space arm."

"What about particle-beam splash? Killarney is away from any major population centers, but the Kilkenny spaceport is right across the city."

"Add secondary shields all around the city. The power tap can support them, the regional militia center, and the spaceport. I'll have engineers get with you on the upgrade."

"Will do. I don't think the Seat has any more work for us until we join the Confederate fleet. We'll need to train with them and learn their methods."

When Blankenship left, Molly, who had been watching the holo from outside its pickup range, walked to Fabien's desk and slid into his side chair. "I'm getting too big to fit into this. You must get a bigger one just for me."

Fabien laughed. "Why not? You've told me we're having another as soon as—"

"Don't say it! We don't know who's listening."

"The baby is born."

"That's true, but I'll use a gestation tank the next time. Mother was a Traditionalist, too, but she didn't tell me how… uncomfortable being pregnant would be. I can't walk! Just waddle around."

"Don't blame me. It was your decision."

Molly squirmed in the side chair. "That's true." She sighed. "Do you think we can be ready before the Essies arrive?"

"It will be close, but I think so. The navy is spreading mines and skip-missile pods throughout the navigable corridors into the inner system and has changed the transponder codes for all Confederate ships, military and civilian. Caledonia's outer shipyards are producing the new fighters and missile pods at an astonishing rate—hundreds of missile pods and forty fighters a day, with the promise of more when the new production lines are active."

"What about bigger ships?"

"Dundee Orbital is producing two frigates and a destroyer a week. The inner shipyards are concentrating on battlecruisers. The navy decided battlecruisers would be more effective against the Essie battle line than trying to build battleships or smaller cruisers." He shrugged. "I'm no naval strategist. I just hope they know what's best."

"Oh, before I go home and soak in the tub, how's Kolskov?" Molly didn't have any ill will toward the former Essie customs inspector. He clearly didn't want to follow his orders.

"He's cooperating. When the Essies canceled the treaty, he and the others received orders to stay behind. He was ordered to eliminate me if I became involved in Confederate politics. The security service on Cameron has taken Jacob Swensen and Clifford Tanaki into custody. They admitted they received orders, too, but ignored them. Swensen's orders were for him to eliminate selected Confederate senators. Tanaki's orders were to kill any Confederate flag officer he found off a military installation. Honecker was a prime target."

"Why?"

"All three said that a state of war existed. The declaration just hadn't reached the Confederacy yet."

"But their orders did."

"Yes. Curious, that."

Molly stood, put her hands on her back and stretched. She was round now. She glanced at Fabien and saw him admiring the view.

"Scared?" he asked.

349

"Of birthing the baby? Some," she admitted. "Elise and mother will be here when it's time."

"I wish Mother could be here, but..." Fabien didn't say more since no one knew when the Seat and the houses would arrive, just an estimated date two months in the future. "Did you know Grand Dam is our house's leading midwife?"

"Yes, she told me when she first learned I was pregnant." Molly checked the time. "I need to go. Remember Elise, Amilie, and Katje are coming for dinner. I don't want you to be late... again."

"Yes, Molly."

Chapter 20. Refuge

Weyland Naval Fleetbase, 8 Sevenmonth, 3204

Captain Benson Witek, the senior watch officer on duty in the navy's system operations and control for Caledonia, had allowed his mind to wander. He checked his link—almost time to send someone for sandwiches and coffee for his watch crew.

"Sir! The Deep Space Array has detected... something. I don't know what it is—it matches nothing in our database," Lieutenant Inez De Gracia called from her console.

"Essies?" he asked, focusing again. The System States fleet was expected at any time.

Caledonia's Deep Space Array had been expanded during recent months. Its detection range now reached two light-years.

"I don't think so... I'm picking up IFF codes... not Confederate... The IFF matches—it's the Seat, sir!"

Witek sighed and allowed his heartbeat to slow. "Send the alert—inbound unknowns, possibly friendly."

"Aye, sir. Coded and sent."

"What's the ship count?"

"Uh, I can't say. The data doesn't make sense. I'm seeing six major objects and a number of smaller ones."

Witek stood and walked over to Lieutenant De Gracia's console and checked the scale of the objects. "Unbelievable," he muttered. After a second check to confirm his initial finding, Witek shook his head, returned to his own console, and entered a message to Admiral Honecker and the Holder on the planet below, copying the Confederate Executor and Navy headquarters on Skye. The message was a single sentence. *<Ships of the Seat of the Thirty Houses have been detected by the Deep Space Array and are estimated to arrive in six hours.>*

†††

The duty runner awakened Fabien Loche a few minutes after midnight and handed him a message. He dismissed the runner. The message was printed on one-time-use material. Fabien placed his thumb on the upper-right corner. The text appeared. *<They're here!>*

He nudged Molly. "Wake up. They're here!"

"Huh?" Molly was slow to wake.

"I have to tell Grandmother."

"What?" she asked, still not understanding what Fabien had said.

"The Seat is here!" Fabien rummaged in their bedroom's closet, found a robe, and almost running, left their suite and hurried down the hall to the one occupied by the Grand Dam and Line Mothers of the Seat.

When he arrived at her door, Fabien slapped the annunciator. "Grandmother, they're here!" he shouted into the panel on the door sill. In a moment, the door slid aside. He entered and found her sitting on the side of her bed.

Elise Hémery blinked, rubbed her eyes, and asked, "How many?"

"The navy says the count is uncertain—six major objects and a dozen or so smaller ones. I think they are all there, Grand Dam—Ceres, Vesta, Pallas, Hygiea, Interamnia, and Europa. The smaller ones could be the outer stations."

"Nothing bigger?"

"Not yet… It would be slower than the others."

"You think…?"

"It's too big? I don't know. We'll just have to wait."

The Grand Dam stood and stretched. "Call Captain Blankenship. I want to meet them in the *Normandie*."

Fabien nodded. "The aircar is on the roof. It can get you to the spaceport in minutes. But it will take Roger at least a half hour to get clearance to leave Weyland Fleetbase and come down to pick you up."

"Do it. Now, go. I have to roust the others and get dressed."

"The message said they would arrive in six hours. Roger should be able to get you there in time to meet them."

"They won't broach on the sixty-fathom line—too dangerous. They'll be at Caledonia's outer marker."

†††

Emile Loche was off planet in Rajput. Fabien asked the navy to send a courier to retrieve his father. Both of them would be reporting to the Seat to brief them on the situation and the political agreements negotiated in the Seat's name.

Fabien and Molly stood to the side as the Grand Dam and the House Mothers departed from the roof of the Meeting House. The navy had been prepared. The *Normandie* arrived at the Kilkenny Spaceport an hour after the DSA detected the Seat. Blankenship was heading toward the planet before Fabien could call. Admiral Honecker notified him after receiving the alert.

The *Normandie* landed. Elise Hémery and her entourage boarded, and the ship lifted off—the total time on the spaceport's tarmac was six minutes.

Boom! Boom... boom. The *Normandie* was transonic before reaching a thousand meters altitude, and its sonic boom echoed across the city. One of the capabilities of the pseudograv drive was the ability to land and take off directly to space with no need to achieve orbit or follow a ballistic route off the planet.

"Remind me to institute a noise ordinance for the spaceport, Molly. Our clansmen and women would not care to be shaken up every time an STS ship arrived or took off."

"I'll make a note of that," Molly replied, the *Normandie* already out of sight. "What's next on the agenda?"

"Hmm, let's see," Fabien mused. "System alert out?"

"Check."

"Courier sent for Father?"

"Check," Molly confirmed. "We can tell Mother we won't need one from Clan McLean. The navy sent one."

"The Clan Council notified—we did tell our allies first?"

Molly shivered. Springtime had arrived at Kilkenny, but the wind across the rooftop was still chill. "Yes, we did. Amat Diehl notified the other clans—oh!"

"What?"

She held her stomach with both hands. "The baby's rowdy. Let's get back inside."

"Yes, let's. It's time to kick the staff awake. Breakfast?"

"Not for me. Not yet," she said as they approached the elevator that would take them down to the residence level.

"Morning sickness? I thought you were over that," Fabien said as they entered.

As the elevator dropped, Molly's face whitened. "Usually."

†††

Admiral Honecker entered the Navy's Caledonia system operations and control room, nodded to Captain Witek and asked, "How far out?"

"We're estimating two hours, Admiral. Lieutenant De Gracia has just had another anomaly detected by the DSA," Witek answered.

"What is it, Lieutenant?"

"I can't really tell, sir. It's just a large mass about five hours behind the Seat."

"The Essies?"

"No, sir. They will have conventional ships. I can tell the difference. The house courier copied the Essies' IFF codes. Unless they were changed in flight, we'll know if they're Essies as soon as they get in DSA range and we can pull IFF."

"Then what's this new… blob?"

"If the data from the DSA is correct, it's the size of a small planet," said De Gracia, pointing to a shaded area in her holomonitor.

"Pack! I hope it's part of the Seat, whatever it is."

Captain Witek shrugged his shoulders. "Me too, Admiral. Me too."

††††

The *Normandie* reached the sixty-fathom line.

"The Confederates say the Seat is a light-year out and rising from the deeps. We can take a short tunnel hop and wait for them at the system's edge," Roger Blankenship told Elise Hémery.

"Do that and then dive into subspace on shunt drive. We'll greet them and lead them around the system to the planned broach site, where they won't bother anybody."

"Aye, aye, Holder." Blankenship nodded to his executive officer. "Prepare for tunnel. Comm, make the announcement."

"Prepare for tunnel, aye," the helmsman responded, following the exec's orders.

The Normandie's interlink carried the announcement. *<All hands, prepare for tunnel. All hands, prepare for tunnel. Close all air-tight hatches… We're going home.>*

"Execute, Helm."

The *Normandie* activated its tunnel drive and disappeared from the navy's monitors.

††††

"Mother, I think it's time you came. I just had a contraction." Molly was leaning against the cool wall of the 'fresher off their bedroom.

<How long did it last?>

"I'm not sure… It's stopped now." She placed her forehead against the cool tiled wall, one arm held across her stomach. "It's been a half hour."

<I'm on my way. Send a message to Elise. She'll be disappointed she can't be with you.>

"Fabien sent one. The *Normandie* tunneled. It may take some time for the message to arrive. It'll be waiting for her whenever they link to a subspace repeater."

<Good. I'll be there in an hour—less if we have a shuttle ready for takeoff.>

"I'm not going anywhere, Mother. I called the med-center here in the Meeting House. They're on their way too. Just in case."

<Good.>

The link dropped. Molly turned and leaned back against the wall. Questions filled her mind. *Where is Fabien? He said he'd be right back. Has my water broken?* She couldn't tell. She'd felt no gush of fluids, which the Mothers had mentioned. She was scared too. *Why didn't I choose a gestation tank? Why did I have to go Traditionalist?*

Fabien!

†††

"We should be picking them up at any moment, Holder," said Captain Blankenship as the *Normandie* sat in subspace at the edge of the Caledonian system. "They're slowing… rising—"

The ship's comm officer interrupted Blankenship. "Contact, Captain. I have a positive IFF on Ceres and Hygiea."

"Tell them to close on me," Blankenship ordered. "We'll all broach together when the others get here."

"Aye. 'Close on me' sent."

"Ask them about the Essies."

The comm officer sent the message and received a reply from the Seat. "They passed them three days ago. They estimate they'll arrive in ten to twelve days, sir."

Blankenship sighed. "Connect to a subspace repeater and pass the info to the navy."

"Aye, Captain." A moment later, the comm officer said, "Message sent, and we received one for you, Holder."

Elise Hémery searched for her link. "Where'd I put that thing?" she muttered.

Marian Frienze touched her arm. "Here, Holder. You left it in the mess… again."

"Thank you, Marian." She opened the message and skimmed it. "Pack!" she said softly.

"What is it?" Marian Frienze asked. The Holder might have spoken softly, but it was loud enough.

"Molly has started labor. I promised her I'd be her midwife."

"Elise, you shouldn't make promises you may not be able to keep."

"You'll learn, Marian, when you become the Holder, the unexpected happens. Sometimes you have to make a decision and it's the wrong move, but sometimes it's the right move. Molly will understand, and Lena will be there."

Marian Frienze nodded.

"A month, Marian, now that the Seat is here. A month, and it's all yours."

Elise had told Marian a month before that she was resigning as Holder. Marian Frienze was next in line to be the new Holder, provided the other Line Mothers agreed.

†††

357

"God. Look at them," Lieutenant De Gracia murmured when the Seat broached. Their surface point was near Barrington Light, and the beacon was providing full visuals of the Seat ships.

Admiral Honecker watched the large holomonitor in the center of operations as six minor-planet-sized ships and fifteen smaller ones appeared with data tags identifying each station. "I didn't know, when the Holder said the Seat was coming, that they were bringing the asteroids too."

"The big ships are Ceres Station, Pallas Station, Vesta Station, Hygiea Station, Interamnia Station, and Europa Station, according to their IFF."

"The asteroids are the stations. What of the others?"

"They are conventional stations, sir. Maxwell-16—I know about that one. My great-grandfather came from there. It used to orbit Oberon, a moon of Uranus."

Other officers were finding excuses to visit the operations room. When Honecker noticed the growing crowd, he ran everyone out except for those on duty.

"Inbound link from the Holder, Admiral," The comm officer reported.

"Put it on my console holo."

"Aye, sir."

Elise Hémery appeared in Honecker's holomonitor. She gazed over his shoulder at the Combat Information Center before returning her gaze to Honecker. "The Seat is here, Admiral. We've one laggard, but it should arrive shortly. Where do you want us?"

"Our previous choice is still good, Holder—ninety degrees above the ecliptic outside the outer marker but in line with your arrival course."

"Very well, Admiral. I've attached data on our line of battle—our strengths and weaknesses too. Two hundred twenty-five subspace capable ships, mostly in the frigate and destroyer classes. However, we do have six battlecruisers, twelve cruisers, and three carriers in that count. Oh, thank you, Roger," she said to the side, "and a hundred fighters."

†††

A tall, willowy, and elegantly dressed woman walked down the *Normandie*'s boarding ramp, accompanied by Elise Hémery. Fabien trotted toward them, slowing to a walk as he neared the two. He nodded to the Grand Dam, but his attention was on the other woman.

"Mother, I'm so very glad to see you."

She stopped short of him, a hint of tears appearing in her eyes. "Oh, Fabien, how I have missed you. I had thought I would never see you again." She stepped forward and wrapped her arms around him—a very unusual greeting for a Line Mother of the house. She held him tight, sobbing into his shoulder.

"Come, Katherine, we're blocking the others," the Grand Dam whispered.

Katherine Hémery allowed herself to be dragged across the spaceport's tarmac to a house-built aircar. For a moment, she swayed.

"Are you all right?" the Grand Dam asked.

"Just a momentary attack of agoraphobia—all this open space…"

Fabien led her to the aircar and opened its doors.

"Where's Emile?" his mother asked before leaning over to enter the car.

"Father is off planet. He's expected back at any time. We sent a courier to fetch him."

"He was successful?" she asked.

"Yes. And more."

She entered, and Elise Hémery followed.

"What about Molly?" his grandmother asked.

359

"She had, according to our resident midwife, false labor. She's in bed, resting. Here, I've had my link on."

<Hello, Elise. I'm fine. Mother's here. I just got scared. I thought it had started, and no one I knew was here.>

"I promised you I'd be your midwife, Molly."

<I know. I also know sometimes promises can't be kept.>

"Katherine, say hello to your daughter-in-law," Elise said.

"Hello, Molly. Please call me Katherine. I see I've a lot to learn. I never expected to find Fabien married when I arrived."

<I don't think he expected to be, either, when he arrived here.>

Another voice was audible in the background.

"Who is that, Molly?" Elise asked.

<Katje. She's been hovering over me all day. I'll introduce her to you, Katherine, when you arrive.>

"Bye, Molly. We're taking off now." The aircar rose silently from the tarmac, pivoted, and gaining altitude, headed toward the DuQuoin Meeting House.

"Who is Katje?" Katherine asked.

"A Clan DuQuoin page. A nice girl. She shot an assassin who tried to kill Molly," Elise said.

"Assassin!"

"It's a long story, Katherine. Lean back and enjoy the view. You're about to meet your daughter-in-law and, soon, a new grandchild."

"Yes. Fabien, what is this clan business Elise has been telling me about?"

The aircar skimmed over and around Kilkenny's taller buildings.

"House DuQuoin is no longer spacebound, Mother. It is still a member of the Seat—if the Seat allows—"

"We will. Marian will see to it," Elise interrupted.

"But the house is also, now, a clan of Inverness. We're still House DuQuoin, but we're also Clan DuQuoin, a new clan with more than ten million members and eight million square kilometers of land. Our people and our land—territory.

"I made a deal. Grand Dam, as head of House DuQuoin, approved it, and the Council of Clans voted to accept us as a clan. A civil war started it all… No, that's not right. A fifty-year-old grudge and conspiracy started it all."

The aircar approached the landing pad on the roof of the DuQuoin Meeting House; hovered, aligning the aircar's door with the enclosed rooftop entrance of the Meeting House; and settled onto the pad.

"The wind is brisk up here. Let's get inside. Mother, you have a room on the same floor as us and Grand Dam."

The aircar's doors opened, and the occupants exited and quickly walked to the elevator.

†††

Katherine Hémery fought a moment of panic. The drop of the elevator—no pseudograv here—gave her a flash of nausea. Elise's recitation of events was coming too fast. *Emile, I need you now!* They reached the residence level. *Is this whole building part of House DuQuoin?*

"That is Father's suite—yours, too, Mother," Fabien said, pointing at a doorway just off the elevator. Ours, Molly's and mine, is over there, across from yours. Grandmother's is down the hall, next to ours."

Katherine followed the group. When they approached Fabien's suite, the door ahead slid open, and Fabien walked in. Elise followed and, with her arm tucked into Katherine's, pulled her inside.

Katje Kappel waited inside the doorway. "Molly's in the bedroom. She wanted to freshen up before seeing visitors."

361

Elise rolled her eyes and, with Katherine's arm still in hers, continued across the room and into the bedroom. "Molly, don't bother 'freshening up!" Elise shouted as she approached the door. "We're going to see you in a more unkempt state soon."

The two women, with Katje following, disappeared into the bedroom, leaving Fabien standing alone. He looked at the closed door for a moment, shrugged, and left.

†††

Ted Popelli's report on the state of Clan DuQuoin's civil defenses was not good. Monmouth had funded defenses for him and his sept. The remaining septs of the former clan were ignored.

"Recommendations?" Fabien asked.

"Flee to the hills. It's the only thing I can think of. Pack!" Popelli said. "Monmouth should be dug up and hanged... leaving his people defenseless like this."

"Can we do that? Flee to the hills, I mean. I know McLean and other clans have food and arms caches scattered across their territory. Do we?"

"To a much smaller extent, yes," Elias Nelson replied.

"I have a map of all the known caches and their door codes," said Edgar Dail, the newly confirmed gendarmerie and Fifth Militia regimental commander. "Unfortunately, Sept Monmouth didn't share their data."

"Field rations?"

"There, we're good. I've asked our neighboring clans, Mieze, McLean, and Williams, if they have any surpluses. With your permission, Laird, I'll see if they will share with us. It will require a clan obligation." Clan DuQuoin lacked the funds to buy the rations outright.

"If you think it's necessary, I'll negotiate with the lairds for terms," Fabien said.

"I hope it won't be necessary, Laird."

"I do too. Next?"

"Evacuation drills," Elias Nelson said. "We can't allow a last-minute panic. I... we—Ted, Edgar, and I—propose..."

†††

Admiral Honecker, newly commissioned commander in chief of the Caledonia Home Defense Force, sat in his office in the Weyland Fleetbase. On a wall was a real-time holo of Inverness piped through the miles of nickel-iron to the admiral's office. The navy had carved the Fleetbase from the center of a thirty-two-kilometer nickel-iron asteroid from Caledonia's outer belt and towed it into synchronous orbit above Inverness.

Will we be ready? he thought as he read the production reports on the new fighters, skip missiles, and ships nearing completion. He had stopped the construction of any ship that could not be completed a month before the projected arrival of the Essies. Instead, he had the yards concentrating on building fighters, mines, missiles, and PBC and point-defense pods.

Confederate fleets had been recalled to Caledonia, those that could be reached and return in time to greet the invading fleet. The Essies were bringing three hundred ships. Honecker's best estimate would be two hundred defending Confederate ships... plus those of the Seat. The combined count, Seat and Confederate forces, outnumbered the Essies by a small margin. However, most of the Confederate and Seat units were smaller: cruisers, destroyers, and frigates. The Confederation's capital ships were all elsewhere, out of reach.

Honecker's aide knocked on the door.

"Enter," the Admiral called.

Captain Benson Witek, Honecker's newly acquired senior aide and flag captain, stepped into the admiral's office. "An update on the Seat ships, sir. Their fleet is more powerful than we thought. Look at their shield strength. It's twice that of ours, and their PBCs outrange ours by as much."

That is good news! I wonder... If the Essies follow doctrine and keep their colliers and transports back, out of battle... There may be an opportunity here.

"Thank you. Please forward that report to all unit and ship commanders. Info copy to the Seat as well."

"Aye, aye, Admiral."

†††

Wham! The *Normandie* shook, and the ship's pseudograv flickered, dropped, and returned. Audible and link alarms screamed. *<Hull rupture at frame 71. Frames 72 through 80 exposed to vacuum. Missile tubes B and D inoperable. PBC mounts 12 and 14 damaged and open to space—>* A litany of damage reports flooded Roger Blankenship's link.

"*Lima* has dropped out of data-net, Captain, and she's streaming air. Her power level has dropped to thirty-five percent," the electronic warfare and communications officer reported.

"Very well, Reconfigure the data-net with *Wilhelm Deeds* to cover her. Order *Lima* to tunnel to the rendezvous site."

The tactical situation was not good. The house ships were tasked to attack the Essie fleet train. Standard System States doctrine said only light ships would guard the colliers and transports.

The Essies had *not* followed doctrine. A squadron of Essie capital ships guarded the ships, not frigates, destroyers, and light cruisers. House losses were heavy and growing.

In the central holomonitor, a House ship flashed and disappeared. "That was the *Toulon*," someone said.

<End Simulation.>

Lights and gravity steadied in the *Normandie*'s bridge.

"Well. That did not go well," Blankenship told his bridge crew. The *Normandie*, with *Caen* and *Wilhelm Deeds*, formed a House flotilla of three Normandie-Class battlecruiser-rated hybrid ships, along with three smaller destroyer-equivalent hybrids. Roger Blankenship, as senior captain, was more familiar with Confederate tactics and commanded the flotilla. "Captain's conference and tactical review in one hour. Invite first and tactical officers too."

"Aye, aye, Captain."

†††

"What have we learned, Captain Hennings?" Blankenship asked.

John Hennings, captain of the House hybrid frigate, *Carmi*, was the junior ship commander. "We don't have the missile capacity of the Essies. After we exhausted ours, the Essies stood off and shot at us with missiles beyond our PBC range."

"Your recommendation?" Blankenship asked.

"Our skip missiles have a longer range than the Essies' and are passing through their shields. Close with them until we are just outside their missile range before firing. We fired too soon—gave 'em too much time to counter our missiles."

Blankenship had noted that. The *Normandie*'s PCBs outranged the Essies', too, but the House ships were picked off by Essie missile swarms before the House ships could get close enough to use their primary PCBs.

The remaining captains spoke in turn, with observations and suggestions.

At the end, Henning made a proposal.

"It's a risk, but what if we tunnel into their midst and salvo a spread of missiles and fire our PBCs before they can react? Target the capital ships first, then we can knock off the smaller ones."

Captain James Orloff of the *Wilhelm Deeds* concurred. It was the first time he'd spoken. He, like Blankenship, was one of the few House captains who was a graduate of the System States' Naval Academy. "An insertion into the middle of their formation followed by a missile volley? Tricky."

Blankenship agreed. "Would you, James, and Henning work this up, make some trial simulation runs, and get back to me by… tomorrow?"

365

"Aye, we can do that. Before or after our tussle with the Confederates tomorrow?"

"Before. Maybe we can test it against them."

Orloff smiled at the idea of embarrassing the Confederates. "We'll see what we can do. We'll send copies of our tactical runs to everyone here."

†††

Vice Admiral Henry Smith, Tri-Cluster Navy, stood at attention in Admiral Honecker's holomonitor. "I demand a repeat, sir! They... they—"

"Beat the pants off you. I was watching, Admiral. Be glad this was only a simulation. A repeat wouldn't be fair since you would be prepared for the tactic. How many ships did you lose?"

Smith remained silent, but his shaking frame could not hide his anger. "Four battleships, eight battlecruisers, six heavy cruisers, plus fifteen smaller ships."

Honecker checked his laughter. So many in the navy discounted the Seat's capabilities. The parochial elements in the Confederation Navy just been given a very hard lesson.

"Thirty-three ships, if I count correctly, Admiral. Almost an entire fleet. Against how many House ships?"

Smith didn't answer.

"Eighteen ships, I believe, Admiral. And how many did they lose? Hmm?"

"Three."

"Three? Really? I seem to remember that one disappearing—as if it had tunneled away from the battle..." Honecker delighted in embarrassing Smith, whose arrogance went back as far as their academy days. They were not friends. "And all three were smaller ships, not of the Normandie class."

"Very well," Smith said through gritted teeth. "Two frigates destroyed and one destroyer damaged, unable to continue the fight."

"And the length of battle?"

"Four minutes, fifty-two seconds... sir."

In the simulation, the House ships tunneled into the middle of Smith's formation, salvoed all their missiles—their new skip missiles that were designed to penetrate shields, and used their stronger, improved particle-beam cannons to lay waste upon Smith's capital ships. Then the Seat ships tunneled away to sanctuary, to fight again.

"What are the lessons learned from this encounter?"

"I'll need to consult with my staff."

"Oh, yes, your flagship was one of the early casualties. You missed the rest of the battle. Confer, then, with your staff and send me your recommendations to counter a similar attack. You never know—the Essies may have weaseled the design of tunnel drives from the Seat and have hybrids of their own."

Smith turned whiter. Honecker doubted that possibility, but preparedness was the word for this game.

"Carry on, Admiral. I await your report."

†††

"That could be the Seat's laggard, sir," said Captain Benson Witek, Honecker's flag captain, pointing to an amorphous globule in the monitor.

"How big is it? That's planet sized. Can they haul an entire planet through subspace?"

"With a quantum power tap? Who knows, Admiral?"

Witek had called Honecker to Weyland's new Combat Information Center. Caledonia's Deep Space Array found the late-arriving Seat station. CIC, when the data arrived, had called Witek who, in turn, called Admiral Honecker.

"No IFF yet," said Witek.

"Is there any doubt that it's a Seat station?"

"Not really, sir."

"IFF received," reported the center's sensor-and-communications officer. "Seat Station Titan."

"Notify the Seat. Their wayward child has arrived. When we're in communications range, instruct Station Titan to not approach closer than one hundred AUs. It's big enough to affect the orbits of our planetary bodies and stations."

"Aye, aye, Admiral."

†††

"They can't stay here," Emile Loche repeated. "They're too big and are nigh-on defenseless."

"I know, Emile, but we need their autofacs. They could double our production capacity," Roger Blankenship argued.

Elise Hémery listened to the debate. She let the two argue point and counterpoint. Admiral Honecker had given his argument an hour earlier. Titan's course, before Honecker had issued instructions to direct Titan to the Seat stations, would have altered the orbit of the Barrington Light beacon. *Enough. Emile's right. Sorry, Roger.*

"Emile has made his point, Roger. I agree. Titan Station will proceed to Rajput and begin operations there. Their first priority is to start building the system's defenses."

Roger Blankenship had been leaning forward into his holo's pickup. Now, he leaned back, accepting her decision. "Very well, Holder. Emile, do you have any questions for me? How may I assist you?"

"Nothing that I can think of at the moment, Roger. Elise, I would like to take Katherine with me. We've been separated for almost a year."

"I'll leave that up to the two of you. She may want to stay with Molly."

368

Emile nodded. "I'll ask. Regardless, we should have Titan leave as soon as possible."

"Make it so, Emile. I leave you in charge. Rajput should see what we're contributing to our amalgamation."

"A possible second inhabitable planet with an established industrial base? I think the Rajputs will approve."

Chapter 21. Battleline

Clan/House DuQuoin Meeting House, Kilkenny, 20 Sevenmonth, 3204

Fabien's link vibrated, waking Molly and Fabien from a sound sleep. His planning for the defense of the populous areas of the territory took twenty of Inverness's twenty-five-hour days. He slapped his link, shutting off the alarm.

"What is it?" she asked while Fabien read the message.

"Condition Delta—the Essies." How casually he could use the term now. It used to irritate him—not anymore. He was no longer an Essie. "Honecker says they're a day out. A tunnel picket ship just detected them."

"Okay, I'll send the alert, start the evacuation. At least we'll have a day," Molly said. She crawled to the side of the bed, her swollen abdomen making movement difficult.

While she sat on the edge of the bed sending messages, Fabien, as commander in chief of the DuQuoin Militia, dressed in a DuQuoin Militia field uniform and added body armor and a weapons harness. He kissed her and left the bedroom.

Molly would have preferred, if she could, to wear a militia field uniform too. That, however, was out of the question at her stage of pregnancy. She rummaged through her closet but found nothing appropriate. *Pack.* She settled upon a knee-length pullover dress. "At least I'll be more comfortable," she muttered.

By agreement, Fabien and Molly would spend the coming days apart. He would be with Nelson and Dail, the gendarmerie commander, to ensure the DuQuoin militia was ready to repel any Essie invasion. She would be with the sept council, Elise Hémery, and clan administrators in an underground facility to continue civilian administration of the territory. Part of Molly's duties would be to manage the dispersal of city clansmen into the countryside—unless the Council of Clans determined the planet would not be invaded or bombarded.

Far to the south of Kilkenny, in the grasslands below Herrin's Falls, Max and Lilith trotted into a large cleared meadow, a burn-off from a past forest fire, and looked east.

Weyland Fleetbase was the Confederation Navy's headquarters for the Caledonian system. It lay below the western horizon in the same orbit as Dundee Orbital, trailing the military station by one hundred twenty degrees. Dundee Orbital was visible above the eastern horizon.

Flickers of fire ascended in the east. The Inverness clans' space arm would defend the stations, planet, and low-orbital infrastructure. More specks followed from other clans—Mieze, Portee, and McLean, Max guessed from the direction of the climbing fighters. The two lurcats lost count of the rising militia ships.

A constellation of larger ships rose over the western horizon from the naval base and headed outward. *The Weyland task group is heading out to rendezvous with the rest of the Confederates,* Max assumed. The militia had briefed him and other lurcat pride leaders on the plans to defend Inverness. However, the prides would not take part in the fight unless the Essies landed.

When no more militia ships rose, the two lurcats turned and loped toward the local militia command bunker at Benning's Bridge. They would join Captain Barnabas while watching the coming battle.

†††

The dispersal order was an hour old. Fabien, with Elias Nelson, landed outside the entrance of the DuQuoin Militia Regional Command Center. A crowd of newsies waited.

"Laird, why did you bring the Essies here?" someone asked.

"Pack," Elias said under his breath. "Look at the ghouls."

"Laird, is it true you're a spy for the Essies?" A different person this time.

"Look at the coward taking shelter while he leaves the people exposed to attack!"

Fabien stopped.

He ran his gaze across the line of newsies, his eyes cold with suppressed rage. "Who said that?"

No one answered.

Fabien walked toward the line of newsies. "Was that you?" he asked one.

The newsie shook his head.

"Look, over there," Elias whispered. "The one with no pin."

Newsies on Inverness were immune from being challenged. However, for that immunity to be operative, the newsie had to wear the gold pin of a noncombatant.

Fabien stopped before the pinless newsie. "Are you the one who called me a coward?"

"So what if I did?" Arrogance oozed from the newsie.

"Where's your pin?"

"Pin?"

"You're not from around here, are you?" Fabien turned and addressed the other newsies, who had fallen silent. "This man claims to be a newsie but wears no pin. Do any of you recognize him?"

None of the newsies spoke, but several shook their heads. None admitted to knowing the pinless newsie. He was not a local, Fabien assumed.

Turning back, Fabien asked once more. "Did you call me a coward?"

"Yes, damn you. So what?"

"So this." Fabien punched him fully in the mouth. When the man hit the ground, Fabien reached down, grabbed the newsie's collar and punched him in the face three more times before letting the man drop. Rubbing his knuckles, he joined Elias, walking toward the command center's entrance.

"Pack."

"What?" Nelson asked.

"I think I jammed a knuckle." Loche extended his hand with its bruised and swelling middle knuckle.

Nelson laughed. "I'll get you some ice when we're inside, Laird. Now you know why I carry these." He reached into a side pocket and pulled out a pair of padded gloves. "I'll get you a pair."

Elias glanced back. The newsies were heading for their aircars. They knew the command center would likely be a target and decided that discretion would be better than valor. They ignored the pinless newsie, who was struggling to sit up.

"Think he'll challenge me?" Fabien asked.

"Him?" Elias snorted. "No. He's the coward. I ran a scan on him. He's a staffer from the DeeCee Resident's office in Culhane. Don't know why he's here."

"Find out later. See if he has diplomatic credentials. If he does, we'll have Amit Singh *non grata* him. If he doesn't, I'll challenge him myself. There will be no precedence that allows anyone to call the laird a coward."

"Aye, Laird."

A militiaman greeted them inside the main entrance. With the laird inside and descending to the Operations Center, steel shutters slid down, sealing the upper portion of the command center. Three hundred meters below, Fabien and Elias walked into the ops center.

"Shield up," someone ordered.

"Local shield up," another confirmed. "Kilkenny shield's up too."

"Glad we finished getting the last power tap and shield upgrades installed for Kilkenny," Elias whispered.

"If we get through this, I promise every city in the territory will be shielded. The Kilkenny shield is stronger than this one. Molly should be safe… I wish Father and Mother were here with her."

"Your grandmother's there. But pardon me for saying so, your father is no military man. He's a diplomat—your mother too. Best they're still at Rajput."

Fabien and Nelson sat before consoles above the central holomonitor.

"Militia command centers are online, secure link-networks confirmed and locked," someone announced, and more status icons appeared in the corner of the holomonitor.

Fabien drummed his fingers on the arm of his chair. Most of the territory's space defenses had been destroyed during Monmouth's attack on Weyland Fleetbase.

Fabien leaned over to Elias. "How many defense sites have we rebuilt?"

"Half, Laird. Only half."

Pack.

†††

Admiral Archer Honecker wished he could have been aboard a ship heading for the rendezvous point. Admiral Garrett's Third Task Group, from Weyland Fleetbase, was about to join Admiral Clemmon's First Task Group from Skye Harbor. Admiral Kirchoff's Second Task Group would join them later from Cameron Upper. Cameron was on the far side of the system. However, his battle station was here, in Weyland's Combat Information Center, buried in the center of the nickel-iron asteroid that was the Fleetbase.

Honecker turned to his aide. "Status of Blankenship's Task Group Sigma?"

"In position, Admiral. Blankenship has sixty cruisers and smaller ships plus three carriers, all sitting above the ecliptic. The Seat's planetoid and conventional stations are ECM stealthed, hidden from the Essies. His 'Force Normandie,' with eighteen tunnel ships, sits inward of the sixty-fathom line where intelligence expects the Essies to broach."

"Anything from the outer picket?"

"No, sir."

Honecker sighed. He hated waiting.

†††

Roger Blankenship hated waiting too. He glanced at the data feed from the Deep Space Array node at Barrington Light. No ships had been detected yet.

His executive officer followed Blankenship's gaze. "Nothing from *Pickle*, either," he said.

Pickle was a small House-built courier that had been modified to accept a one-shot tunnel drive. *Pickle's* conventional shunt drive had been removed to provide room for the new drive and subspace search array.

After the conversion, *Pickle* was towed a light-year out from Caledonia and placed into position as an early warning picket ship. When the Essies arrived, it would snoop their formation and ship distribution before tunneling to Caledonia with the intelligence.

"Everyone in battlesuits?" Blankenship asked.

"Yes, Captain."

"Good, good," Blankenship said without listening to his exec's answer. He knew everyone would be suited. "Make your rounds. Let the crew see you. Tell them we'll have a thirty-minute break in an hour if *Pickle* doesn't show up."

"Yes, sir." The exec walked over to his console, picked up his helmet, and walked through the bridge's hatch.

Blankenship wished the *Normandie* had a Combat Information Center. But she didn't. *Normandie* and her sisters weren't designed to be warships. They were limited-production design concepts with weapon

375

suites added as afterthoughts, a lure for military buyers. The bridge would just have to make do.

He reached inside a pocket of his battlesuit and pulled forth a deck of cards. After shuffling the deck twice, he laid down the cards one by one. Solitaire was a stress reliever.

†††

Molly, with Amilie, Katje, Elise Hémery, and Ted Popelli, gathered in the underground command center half a kilometer below the DuQuoin Meeting House. The DuQuoin Sept Council joined them. The command center was similar to a warship's bridge Molly had once seen on a tour of the Dundee Shipyard. A large holomonitor provided status updates from the local militia headquarters, the Kilkenny Gendarmerie, and various city-service departments: comm, power, water, and sewage. A red icon on the militia feed indicated the defensive shields covering the city and regional militia headquarters were operative. Below the shield icon were three rows of green icons, missile and PBC defense sites for the city.

A placard before Amilie's position said Communication and Transport. Another, before Popelli's, read Military Liaison. Elise Hémery's placard said House DuQuoin, while Molly's read, simply, DuQuoin. This left no doubt, for the former Monmouth clansmen, that Clan and House DuQuoin was in charge.

"Status?" Molly asked.

"All communications lines are open. Outbound traffic has stopped at the shield's edge. The occupants are being herded into nearby underground shelters. I have sent home anyone not yet evacuated. It's too late for them to leave," Amilie reported.

"Confederation sources say the Essies have not yet reached the outer pickets. The fleets are in position, wherever that is, and ready. Nothing else to report." Ted Popelli's report was, as always, short and to the point.

"And the galley is open," Katje said. "A buffet is available if you, like me, missed breakfast."

"Girl has a growth spurt, I'm thinking," Amilie told Molly.

The thought of food made Molly's stomach clinch. *Clinch?*

Amilie saw her expression change. "You okay?"

Molly checked her nannite status. Elise said there would be a hormone change just before labor… and there it was. Her hormone levels were climbing.

"Just a cramp, Amilie… I think."

"Elise!"

The older lady was in the buffet line but turned at Amilie's call.

"Check Molly! It may be time."

Other heads turned toward the deputy laird. The chain of command in the bunker went from laird to, in the laird's absence, the deputy laird to the House DuQuoin Grand Dam, followed by the local militia leader in the command center, Ted Popelli.

"Clansman Popelli, take over until we return," Elise Hémery said.

"Aye, ma'am."

†††

"Katje, help Elise. Do whatever she says," Amilie ordered her daughter.

"Yes, Mother." Katje moved to Molly's side and helped her stand while Elise fought her way through the gathering DuQuoin clansmen.

The older woman and the girl helped Molly walk to the doorway into the command center's infirmary. Amilie noticed a stream of fluid running down Molly's leg. She checked the time. "Pack," she muttered. Her choice in the clan's baby pool wouldn't be winning.

Time to send Fabien a message. <Molly's water just broke. Elise and Katje are with her. Labor hasn't started yet but should soon.>

†††

Fabien read the message and nudged Nelson. "Do we have time to get back to Kilkenny?"

"No. The shield is up. We can't get out. Why?"

"Molly's started labor." He showed the message to Nelson.

"Sorry, Laird, we're sealed in. You know we can't get out until it's all over."

"Yeah." *Pack! Pack! Pack!*

✝✝✝

The two-man crew of the *Pickle* were patient. When they arrived on station, they deployed a wide-area sensor array to sweep sub- and normal space. So far, the crew had detected nothing. The two switched places every two hours, and the time for another change-off was near.

Ping! The array detected a ship, an Essie scout.

"Let's wait until we see the rest," the operator said to his partner. He glanced at the courier's control panel. All they had to do, when it was time to leave, was hit a single, shrouded button to trigger the preprogrammed tunnel drive.

"There's more," the operator added. "One… two… three… four formations—that last one is smaller."

"Think it's the colliers and transports?"

"Checking…"

"The first three groups are rising in subspace, out of the depths. That last one has made a course change and is rising too."

"Got it. New course plotted. It's rising above the ecliptic."

"Toward the Seat?"

"No. The course is twenty degrees off the line for the Seat."

"What about the others?

"The scout is past us. Didn't see a thing. The other three formations are making minor course changes."

"Give me the data, and I'll run a plot."

"Here it is."

"I'm getting a ship count. Now… ship types," the operator announced.

"Got them. Data encoded. Time to go?"

"Just about… Now." The operator slid his chair across the compartment, flipped open the covering shroud, and hit the tunnel-drive button.

††††

"Picket's back." The soldier was stating the obvious.

Data from the *Pickle* flowed into Honecker's command center.

"Close battlesuits. Send the general order." Honecker picked up his helmet, put it over his head, and with a twist, locked it in place. Sealed in his battlesuit, Honecker looked like everyone else in the CIC, with a dark, navy-blue shipsuit—armored coveralls over a skinsuit. The only difference was Honecker's one broad and four smaller gold stripes on his cuffs.

††††

"*Pickle*'s back," the *Normandie*'s exec informed Roger Blankenship.

††††

Honecker watched the Essie fleet data flow into his holomonitor. "Look at that," he told his aide. "They're following doctrine right down to the last paragraph. Colliers and transports held back and above the ecliptic, one task group to each of our inhabited planets. See"—he pointed at one icon—"the divergence there. It's heading for Skye Harbor. These two… one for Inverness and the other to Cameron. A decapitation strike, like we expected."

"Incoming identification," one of the tactical officers reported. "Task Group A is the Tau Ceti Twenty-first Fleet. Task Group B is the Eighth Fleet out of Proxima. Task Group C is the Solsystem Second Fleet and elements of the Home Fleet. Nothing on the fourth group."

"The colliers are whatever the Essies could sweep up, not a numbered fleet," Honecker said to himself.

"Orders, Admiral?" his aide asked.

"Get me a link to the task group commanders and Blankenship. It'll be Op Plan Beta."

†††

"Orders from Admiral Honecker, Captain. Plan Beta," Blankenship's exec said.

"I thought so, from the data dump we got. He say which one?"

"Not yet. They're waiting to see where the big boys are."

†††

"Op Plan Beta sent, sir. The three planetary stations are deploying pods. Minefields are on standby. Shields are up. The clans are covering Dundee Orbital and are deploying for missile intercept against the station and planet."

"Very well," Honecker said absently while examining the data from the picket. *Where are the capital ships?* Confederate doctrine would put them together for best effectiveness. *Where are the buggers?*

Honecker was glad the stations had stronger and improved shields, courtesy of the Seat's power taps. The system's stations had regularly upgraded their defenses since the DeeCee raid decades before. *The stations will be a tough nut to crack—if the Essies can.*

More data flowed in, ship counts and types. *There they are.* "Send to the task group commanders, Op Plan Beta Four—repeat, Beta Four."

"Aye, aye—"

"And to Blankenship, Beta Four C-for-Charlie. Got it?"

"Aye, sir, C-for-Charlie."

"Well don't just stand there—send it!"

†††

"There it is," Roger Blankenship said to his gunnery officer. "Honecker has found where the Essie battleships are. All in one spot too."

"Barrington Light has shut down, but its passive data from the DSA is still coming in," the comm officer said. "We're getting a clear view of their command fleet's disposition. Spherical formation, escort ships to the front, battleships shielding the command ship in the middle, and the battlecruisers forward, deployed behind the escorts."

"Good. When Honecker says go, we'll tunnel into the middle of them. There's a gap between the battleships and the command ship. Primary targets are the command ship, the battleships, and battlecruisers in that order. We'll shoot until we're down to forty percent remaining in our magazines then tunnel to Waypoint Forty-five to meet the rest of the fleet and take out the colliers and transports."

"Order seal suits, Mister Exec."

"Aye, aye, Captain."

†††

Three System States battle fleets reached Caledonia's sixty-fathom line and prepared to broach into normal space. The Essies knew they had been detected. Any sensor would detect them this close to the inner system, but the Confederates should have been unprepared. Nothing could arrive faster than a packet ship—or a warship—and the Essies had allowed no packet ship to depart SolSystem, nor any Essie system, before the fleets were on their way.

Admiral Jonas Pleed, commanding the System States fleet, was watching from his flagship's CIC. "Broach," he ordered. All his ships would appear in normal space as one.

The task forces—named Alpha, Beta, and Charlie by the Confederates—broached.

†††

"To Blankenship," the *Normandie*'s comm officer reported, "from Admiral Honecker. Engage the enemy."

"All ships in data-sync. Tunnel," Blankenship ordered.

††††

"Sir! Ships in our formation!"

Pleed barely had time to understand the alert before those strange ships opened fire. His ship shook and rang.

"Shields up!" he shouted. In his CIC monitor, three battleships flared and died. Damage-control alarms streamed down one side of the central monitor.

Crash! The command ship shuddered. Internal gravity flickered and died.

"Engines off-line!" someone shouted through the din.

"Dive! Dive! Dive!" Pleed's flag captain shouted.

But it was too late. The command ship blossomed into a ball of plasma and faded away.

††††

Bam! The *Normandie* shook from the detonation of a nearby Essie missile. Blankenship's strapped-down battlesuit suddenly became rigid, cushioning him from the shock. So far, the *Normandie* had taken only minor damage.

"Magazine level?" he asked through the ship's linknet.

"Sixty percent, sir," one of the gunnery POs replied.

The *Normandie*'s executive officer was fighting the ship, allowing Blankenship to tend to the Seat's fleet.

"Begin targeting battlecruisers. I don't think there are any Essie battleships still fighting."

"Orders sent," the comm officer confirmed. "Essie losses are now one command ship, eight battleships, ten battlecruisers, and a number of escorts that got in the way."

"Ours?" Blankenship knew they had lost several.

"The *Wilhelm Deeds*, sir, plus *Appomattox, Trieste,* and *Lima.*"

That hurts. One Seat pocket battlecruiser, a destroyer, and two frigates. A sixth of my force. James Orloff was a good friend. I'll mourn later.

"The last battleship is gone, plus three more BCs. Magazines at fifty percent."

Boom! The *Normandie* shuddered. Another Essie missile had breached her shields. Blankenship's skinsuit tightened. *Normandie*'s bridge was in vacuum.

"Very well, let's get out of here. Send to all ships. Tunnel."

†††

When Blankenship sprang his surprise on the Essies, Honecker activated the preplanted mine fields in the path of the three Essie fleets. The mines were nothing more than ECM-stealthed missile and PBC pods with small station-keeping engines. Each missile pod held a dozen skip missiles. Weyland Fleetbase would send targeting data to the mines through Caledonia's subspace communication systems.

"Send targeting. Priority is ship size for missiles, the inverse for the PBCs."

"Targeting, aye. Sent."

"Activate fields thirty-two, seventy-four, seventy-six, and one oh one."

The two unscathed Essie fleets ran into a faceful of missiles. A two-meter-bore particle-beam cannon fired and speared a destroyer that broke apart, lifepods streaming. A light cruiser disappeared in a fireball when hit by three PBCs. The attrition of the Essie fleets had started.

"Missile pods have exhausted their magazines, Admiral," reported Captain Benson Witek, Honecker's flag captain. "Our PBC pods are picking off the lighter ships at a regular pace. It seems our PBCs outrange the Essies."

"Good. The fewer Essie ships that survive, the better the lesson. Very well, Ben. Orders to the fleet: 'Advance and engage the enemy.' They have their assignments."

†††

Max and Lilith didn't fully understand the symbols of the space battles moving on militia Captain Barnabas's monitor. Dots moved, and dots vanished. The Essie task group on course to attack Inverness was approaching. However, Admiral Garrett's Third Task Group was on an intercept course. The Essies would have to go through them to reach Inverness and Dundee Orbital.

The two 'cats sat on their haunches in a corner of Barnabas's underground bunker. Lilith stood to reposition her battle harness. The 5mm magrifle clipped to her harness was poking her in the ribs.

Let's go upside. There's nothing for us here, Max signed to Lilith.

Neither 'cat liked being underground.

Above ground, the militia base was dark. Local residents were in shelters, and all outside lighting was off. They didn't need to advertise their location. The Essies had detailed maps of Inverness, but the darkness helped impress the seriousness of the situation on the local clansmen.

Dundee Orbital's external lights were off. Captain Barnabas said the station's stealth ECM and shields were up. Normally, the station was visible at night, by its lights. It wasn't currently.

Max found a small rise that gave them a good view of the horizon. He and Lilith curled up next to each other and waited for the battle to reach Inverness.

Why do people come out at night and look at the stars? Lilith signed.

Lurcats didn't do that. Stars were just points of light in the night sky.

Molly and Fabien often came out here at night.

I think that is part of their mating rituals, Max signed. *They always mated when they came out here.*

384

†††

"The fleets are engaging, Admiral. Essie Groups A and C have merged and are heading our way. Third Task Group is moving to intercept. Clemmon's First and Kirchoff's Second Task Groups are engaging Essie Task Group B near Skye. Task Group Sigma, the Seat ships, are about to engage the Essie fleet train. They destroyed the core of Group C and all of its capital ships except for a handful of battlecruisers."

"Very well. Send to Dundee Orbital and the clans, 'Condition Delta.' Activate all the minefields along and before the Essies' path. Let's attrite them a bit before we bite."

"Orders ready… and sent," Captain Benson confirmed.

Essie Fleet Charlie should make a course change about now if he's really heading here. "Flag, watch for a course change."

"Sir, the Essies are targeting our subspace repeaters. We've lost ten percent, and the count is rising," the comm officer reported.

"They've made a course change, Admiral."

"When?"

"Now, sir."

"Communication lag?"

"Five minutes, sir. They're destroying more of our subspace repeaters. They know exactly where they are."

Wondered when they'd start that. "Activate Canary. Tell me when the backup repeater network is online."

"Aye, aye, sir."

The Admiral watched the holodisplay. It flickered, and the Essie ships jumped forward. "Canary network online. Partridge network on standby."

"Suggest to the Council of Clans to set planetary defense to Condition Delta. That will allow the clans' fighters to dock at Weyland Fleetbase to rearm and refuel."

Honecker turned back to watch the fleets in the central holomonitor. *What am I forgetting? I should have made a list.* "Benson, what am I forgetting?"

Captain Benson Witek pulled a small notepad from his battlesuit's pocket. He removed its attached stylus and checked off several line items. "The clans' PDCs and the research stations on the moons."

God, I'm glad Witek has a list. "Alert the clans' Planetary Defense Centers and the research stations on Dagda and Morrígan. The moons will have to be on their own. The militias will be too busy to help them." As he considered the research stations on Inverness's two natural satellites, all Honecker could think was, *Hunker down, boys. Just hunker down.*

†††

"The Council has issued Condition Delta, Laird. Not that it affects us much, with no space arm and only one PDC." Elias Nelson sat at Fabien's left. His right arm was still in the regeneration mesh.

My right-hand man… when it's regrown. I'm getting to sound almost feudal. In retrospect, the clans of Inverness are almost feudal. Oaths of fidelity given and received. At the moment, I'm glad that it is.

"Anything about Molly?"

"Just Katje's update a few minutes ago. The contractions have slowed. Molly's resting right now. Lena left when the alert came in. She's gone back to McLean House."

The state of Molly's labor did not calm Fabien. He didn't know what it meant. He'd been too busy to attend the birthing class with her. "Anything for us—me—to do right now?"

"Just wait, Laird. Just wait."

†††

Max and Lilith slowed from a jog to a fast walk. They were heading eastward, following the edge of the hardwood forest, into the coming dawn. A ripple of bright streaks rose from the eastern horizon and climbed into space.

386

More militia ships, Max signed. He checked his link. *Condition Delta. The battle is coming, Lilith. I wish them well and good hunting.*

†††

"Very well. Set Battle Condition One. Update Dundee Orbital and the moons. Send 'seal battlesuits' and close all vacuum-tight hatches."

"Aye, aye, sir." The tactical officer relayed the order and closed his helmet. With the others in the CIC busy with their incoming flow of data, the tactical officer checked Weyland Fleetbase's interior status. Across the base, hatches and firewalls were closed and secured.

"Done, sir." The tactical officer received another report via his link. "Garrett's Third Task Group has engaged the Essies," he added.

†††

The *Normandie* shivered as a shipkiller missile detonated against its shields. The thermal bloom from the warhead scorched its hull. *<Minor air leak in Compartment 73-2a. Pressure holding.>*

Their tunnel drives were of no use now. They couldn't be recharged until long after the battle was over. However, the Essies had not completely followed their doctrine. Their escorting force protecting the fleet train included two battlecruisers. The remaining escorts were one heavy and half a dozen light cruisers with destroyers and frigates as escorts.

Blankenship ordered the *Caen* and the *Normandie* to attack the two battlecruisers. The remaining Seat ships would attack the fleet train with the troopships as their priority.

"Make it expensive for the Essies," the Admiral had ordered. "We'll not have to fight them again; the ones lost here."

"Just as long as we don't make it expensive for ourselves," Blankenship muttered.

<Missile strikes on targets one and two. Both are streaming air.> Target one seemed to be the task-group commander.

"Range?"

387

"One million klicks. PBC range in five minutes," Blankenship's gunnery officer reported.

Whang! Audible and link alarms sounded. The *Normandie* jumped and bounced.

<Missile strike on PBC mount twelve. Mount inoperative.>

"The whole packin' mount's gone!" someone on the bridge yelled.

"Quiet on the bridge," the *Normandie*'s exec said. "Do your jobs. No need to get excited."

"*Caen*'s hit again, sir. She's streaming air," Blankenship's tactical officer reported.

"I wouldn't be surprised if we are too," Blankenship replied. "Magazine status?"

"Forty percent, sir. We've enough to take these two out, I'd wager."

An Essie cruiser slid in front of the enemy battlecruiser.

"In PBC range!"

"Fire!" Blankenship's exec ordered. He wasn't going to waste a missile on a cruiser that he could reach with PBCs. He would save the missiles for the battlecruisers.

Four of *Normandie*'s two-meter particle-beam cannons pivoted to bear on the cruiser. All fired, and the cruiser became a ball of plasma. The battlecruiser, the ship the cruiser had tried to protect, received two more skip missiles and broke in half. The rear half flared into a fireball.

"Battle status?" Blankenship asked.

"Our frigates have destroyed seven of the eleven troopships and half of the colliers. There's one more—strike that, the last battlecruiser is gone. Only six more escort ships remain."

"IFF zero-zero-zero, Captain. They're surrendering."

"Any fire coming from any Essie?"

"One heavy cruiser. Redirecting all missiles in flight to it—it's gone. No offensive fire from any other Essie ship."

"Send 'Cease fire' to all ships. Open a call to the senior surviving Essie commander."

"Aye, aye."

Thank you, God. This part is over was Blankenship's silent prayer.

†††

"Targeting data downloaded to the pods, Admiral. Priority, as you ordered, is on the battlecruisers and cruisers. The militia has reached Dundee Orbital and is moving into defensive positions," the tactical officer said. "Weyland Fleetbase is at battle stations," he added.

Honecker nodded. *Nothing unexpected so far.* "Fire when in range. Activate local defense stations."

The tactical officer received another report via his link. "Garrett's task group has engaged the Essies. IFF is stable and confirmed. We won't target any of our ships."

If they don't move in front of our missiles, that is. Honecker was ever a pessimist.

Weyland Fleetbase was armed with embedded missile tubes, particle-beam cannons and point-defense emplacements. Docks, hangars, and repair yards lay inside the asteroid with their entrances protected by heavy armor and shields. Weyland, the entire asteroid, was enveloped within an upgraded shield powered by a power tap. The upgrades doubled the Fleetbase's defense capability. Most of its PBCs were now up to Seat standards.

"Missiles inbound, Admiral. ETA is five minutes. Ours will hit the Essies at the same time."

Honecker nodded. "Are you sure Garrett knows our missiles are coming?"

"Yes, sir. I called him myself."

Good. Witek covered my ass again. The battle was becoming automatic, a dance between offense and defense. He checked the monitor.

Garrett had broken off his attack when the Fleetbase missiles entered engagement range. He checked the ship columns at the edge of the monitor. The Essies' Task Group A was down to forty-six ships from seventy-one. The Confederation had lost eight battlecruisers and six lighter cruisers plus a dozen destroyers and frigates. *Our battlecruisers are doing better than I expected.*

He glanced again at the central monitor. Sixty militia fighters protected Dundee Orbital. Another thirty were staying in low planetary orbit to protect the lower-orbit infrastructure and planet. Fifteen more fighters were rising from the far side of Inverness. *Clan Collins finally got its act together.* Forty navy fighters from Weyland were outbound to attack the Essie ships.

†††

Admiral Harmon Garrett, commanding Caledonia's Third Fleet, was fighting for his life. The Essie fleet opposing him was stronger than expected—more state-of-the-art ships.

Whang! Garrett jerked and bounced in his command chair. His battlesuit tightened. The missile had breached the hull, exposing the CIC to space. A line of damage reports climbed on a monitor.

"Fighters from Weyland should join us in four minutes," his aide said.

"I hope so. These Essies are beating the shit out of us."

"We're doing better statistically, sir."

"Yes, but they've more mass and can survive our fire more than we can take theirs."

Another stream of missiles left the fleet, skipping in and out of subspace toward the Essie ships. Flares erupted across the enemy fleet.

"The fighters are engaging. IFF is up," the aide reported. "We're within the Essie PBC—"

The aide's comment was cut short. An Essie PBC beam penetrated the ship's hull, and the aide was in its path. Molten vapor from the strike sprayed across the CIC, splashing across consoles and those who sat before them.

Something snatched Garrett's arm. He glanced down. It was missing below his elbow. His medical and suit nannites began to close the wound and seal the stump. Someone called for medics as his consciousness slipped away.

†††

The local battle commenced. Max and Lilith watched from the hilltop while signing with each other. Flares appeared here and there as missiles were intercepted. Dundee Orbital sparkled, its point-defense blisters in action. A large flash appeared near the station.

That was a shipkiller, Lilith, a high-megaton nuke or an antimatter warhead. Didn't get through to Dundee Orbital, though.

From beyond the western horizon, a bright flash bounced off the atmosphere, lighting the dust floating in the air. *That one must've hit Weyland*, Max commented. *It's in the right region of the sky.*

†††

Weyland Fleetbase rang like a bell. Honecker was strapped in his command chair, watching the progress of the battle. At that point, he had little to do, for the battlestaff knew their jobs. The shock from the shipkiller shook him in his command chair. Fortunately, like all his CIC crew, he was strapped in. Else, the shock would have thrown him to the deck.

"Status?" he asked more loudly than he had intended. His mouth tasted of blood as he'd bitten the inside of his cheek.

"Hit near the repair-yard entrance. No critical damage. All systems report still in service. We've lost ten percent of our point defenses. It was a one-hundred-megaton nuke."

"Be thankful for small favors," Honecker muttered.

If the hit had been from an antimatter warhead, the damage could have been worse—not fatal but still worse than that of a fusion warhead.

"Targeting priority?"

"The battlecruisers first, as before," the tactical officer said. "Heavy and light cruisers next—the Essies just lost another battlecruiser and a cruiser. Our missile penetration aids appear to be better than we anticipated, sir."

"Dundee?"

"Holding their own. They intercepted one shipkiller. It was close, but Dundee didn't receive any critical damage—penetration of one torus, the long-term storage docks. The station's self-defense militia reports ready to repel borders. They will augment the Marine company onboard."

"Good."

Witek continued his stream of updates. "More missile impacts on the Essie task group. Dundee's pods are in action. The Essies are down to thirty-eight ships—wait… Twelve ships have split off from the Essie task group… They're flanking Dundee—my opinion, Admiral."

And you're probably right. "Notify the militia and Dundee. Visitors coming in the back door."

†††

Weyland Fleetbase shuddered again. Another missile made it through the base's defense network.

The Essie task group was down another two battlecruisers, a heavy cruiser, and eight destroyers, not counting the group that had split off to flank the Inverness forces. The Essies were finding Dundee Orbital, the clans, and Weyland Fleetbase more difficult than they had estimated.

"How's Dundee doing?" the admiral asked his flag captain.

"Holding their own," Witek answered. "Their point defense is greater, proportionally, than our own. There was one missile hit near the docks, but Dundee's shield limited the damage to just that torus. The clan fighters are very effective. Between them and the station's defenses, there's only been one missile hit—that splinter group just fired a shotgun salvo. Target: Dundee and Inverness!"

†††

"Uunnng!"

Aboveground, in Kilkenny city, sirens were winding up, and the alert for the inbound missiles flashed across the linknet. Molly, however, wasn't listening.

"Push, Molly, on the wave... Wait for it..." Elise was watching the medical sensors. Timing was critical, and Molly's baby was about to crown.

Katje leaned forward and wiped Molly's face.

"Breathe, in... out... push!" Elise said.

"Uunnng!" *I will not scream. I will not scream. I will—*"Uunnng!"

††††

<Weyland reports inbound missiles. Targets: Dundee Orbital, Inverness. All point-defense stations online. Weapons free.>

"It's a shotgun spread, Laird." Elias Nelson's report went unheard by the militia operations crew.

"Kinetic-energy warheads. They're going after targets on planet," Fabien added.

"Bastards."

"Better than nukes, Elias."

"Targeting data confirmed, Laird. Two inbound for Kilkenny, one for us," the operations officer announced.

"Guess we'll see how good our shields are, Elias." Fabien hoped he sounded calm.

Whang! The militia command center bounced on its shock absorbers.

"Direct impact, fifty-kiloton kinetic strike."

"Damage reports?" Fabien shouted over the din as everyone seemed to be talking at the same time. *They're glad to still be alive. So am I.*

"Kilkenny?"

"Two fifty-kiloton strikes, Laird. No reported damage."

Molly's safe. He sighed. "Elias, call Ted. See how they're doing."

†††

"Incoming, Grand Dam." The messenger from Popelli used the title that had become common among the Meeting House staff. "Kinetic warheads, supposedly."

Elise acknowledged the report with a nod.

Katje wiped sweat from her forehead.

"Thank you. Now get on back to your station."

Molly had reached the critical point. *Better to strap her down until the attack is over.*

"Katje, let's secure Molly's bed and strap her down for now. I don't want her knocked out of bed when we're—"

Whang—whang! The room shook as the lights blinked but remained lit. A glass of water toppled, spilling its contents across the table and down onto the floor.

"Never mind. Back to work, girl."

†††

A Mieze militia ship died in a flash, and Jean Gabriel found himself in command of the remaining Mieze fighters defending Dundee Orbital. Five flights of four Mieze militia fighters had lifted from Inverness. Twelve fighters remained. The fighter that just disappeared had contained the ranking pilot of the clan's fighters, leaving Jean Gabriel next in command.

"Mieze Leader, Dundee Control."

Militia ships were under the operational control of Dundee Orbital, according to the Condition Delta op plan.

"Leader, go."

"That splinter Essie group has launched fighters. We're reducing them with our point defenses and the other militia ships. Can you attack the heavy cruiser?"

394

"Affirmative," Gabriel said. "Mieze flights, Code Theta, repeat Theta."

The other militia fighters, except those from Clan Mieze, swept over the station to intercept the inbound Essie fighters. Code Theta was the plan for a direct attack on a warship, the Essie heavy cruiser.

The fighters from the other clans were armed with particle-beam cannon and missiles. Mieze fighters had few missiles but did have a large 40cm spindle-mounted railgun. The non-nuclear missiles of the clan militias would barely scratch the surface of the cruiser's armor. However, the large caliber railguns on the Mieze fighters could penetrate the armor. At close range, the railguns could turn the cruiser into Swiss cheese—if the fighters survived long enough to get that close.

"D Flight, merge with B—B Leader in command. A, E Flights merge with C—C Leader in command. Prepare to execute Code Theta," Jean Gabriel ordered. He was now in overall command.

"Execute!"

†††

<Observe and report any debris landing in your respective areas. Observers elsewhere have reported landings of Essie lifepods and landers.>

Lilith looked over at Max, who was lying on his back at the peak of the hill. *Do you expect any falling here?* she signed.

I don't know, Lilith.

The battle over Inverness moved closer. Until then, most of the fighting had been out beyond Dundee Orbital and Weyland Fleetbase. Missiles and ships, fighters most likely, Max thought, were being destroyed in the flashes of light in the heavens.

Lilith could not comfortably lie on her back while wearing her weapons harness. However, she was doing so to view the sky. Max watched the eastern hemisphere while Lilith watched the west.

Look at that, Max signed. High overhead, a large flash appeared. *That was at Dundee Orbital.* A second, larger flash followed the first. *Another hit.*

†††

"B Flight, attack the rear—go for the engines. C Flight, we will attack head-on. Go for their shunt nodes."

Jean Gabriel turned to his gunner. "Peter, pick one spot on the bow and focus on it. I want our rounds to spit that ship. Put a hole through it, front to back."

The gunner acknowledged. The cruiser had twenty feet of armor at its bow. The fighter's railgun could empty its ready magazine in a minute, enough to pierce the nose armor. Then all Jean needed to do was keep his fighter surviving for another minute while the magazine reloaded from its reserve. His job was to give his three-man crew that time.

"Engage," he said over the flight's intercom.

†††

"Report from Task Group Sigma, Admiral," reported Captain Witek. "The Essie survivors of the fleet train have surrendered."

"Blankenship's force?"

"Heavy damage among Blankenship's fighters and smaller ships… sixty percent of the House ships, mainly their lighter ones. Seventy percent of his fighters."

"The Essies?" Honecker asked.

"Seven of the eleven troopships, half of the colliers. Five escorts survive."

"What did the Seat lose?"

"*Caen* and *Normandie* are damaged but repairable. They lost *Wilhelm Deeds*, plus *Appomattox, Trieste,* and *Lima* in the first strike against the Essie Task Group. Sigma is heading for Ceres Station to rearm and make any critical repairs they can't perform on board."

396

"Pass the word to the task-group commanders. The Essies are weakening."

"Aye, aye, Admiral. It'd better be quick. We're losing too many ships for this to last much longer."

Honecker cocked an eye at Witek, thinking that comment was best unsaid. Privately, he agreed with his aide. Losing Admiral Garrett was an irreparable blow.

The CIC comm officer sent a message to Honecker's link. *<Essie Task Group A is surrendering.>*

I see the word about their colliers has reached the main Essie fleet. I sense a lack of confidence among their leadership. Honecker thought the Confederacy was winning the battle of attrition. *It's a close win, however. Keep your mind on track,* he reminded himself. *We can still lose this fight.*

<Task Group B is heading for the sixty-fathom line. Beta and Gamma will intercept before they reach it,> the CIC comm officer continued. *<Essie Task Group C has been effectively destroyed. Their remaining ships are surrendering.>*

"Will any Essies escape?" Honecker asked.

Witek reviewed the continuing reports. "I don't have a complete count. I think sixty will escape, maybe more. We can't account for four cruiser squadrons and some smaller ships."

"What about Dundee?"

"Minor damage to Dundee. No reported casualties yet. Mieze fighters riddled the last cruiser. Two fighters survived. Fighter casualties have been heavy. The clans will mourn, Admiral."

According to the plot in the holomonitor, the wreck of the cruiser that had attacked Dundee Orbital would skim Inverness's atmosphere.

"Will that cruiser hit the planet?" he asked Witek.

"The plot says, no, sir. From the strike reports, it should break up if it did. Some clans are concerned it may make a planetary strike as it passes. I doubt it. It appears to be a hulk."

"Pass the plot to the PDCs. They're free to fire on it if they believe it could be a danger."

"Aye, aye, Admiral. By the way, I've made notes about the effectiveness of the railguns Mieze mounted on their fighters. They turned that cruiser into a sieve."

Honecker grunted. Many people would be taking notes on this battle.

The admiral closed his eyes and took a deep breath and tried to relax. "Benson, issue a system-wide order: 'Cease fire unless fired upon.' Begin search and rescue. We've a lot of people out there who need help."

"Aye, aye, sir."

Confederation losses continued to climb on the holoscreen as badly damaged ships were abandoned. *Thirty percent of our fleet.* Honecker didn't look forward to briefing the Confederation's executive board on the battle. The fleet would have to rebuild, which meant taxes. He sighed. *Not my battle. Not yet.*

†††

Here it comes, Lilith.

The two 'cats had been warned via their links that an Essie cruiser was about to enter Inverness's atmosphere. The report said the ship should hit and skip off the atmosphere before moving into an elliptical orbit. However, in case it entered the atmosphere, observers around the planet would watch and report.

Lilith sat on her haunches next to Max, her long tail splayed out behind her, its tip twitching. Both faced the east, where the ship was expected.

A speck appeared high in the eastern sky.

There it is, Lilith, Max signed.

The speck grew, its fiery tail expanding, trailing behind the falling ship. Pieces separated from the ship to glow and burn in the slipstream.

"Lifepods, I think." Max spoke in the 'cats native language. He couldn't sign while sending a report to Captain Barnabas's militia post.

An azure bar flashed up and speared the ship. One of the clans' planetary defense centers was in action with a particle-beam strike.

More pods erupted. These later ones, upon exiting the ship, flared and winked out. No one in them would survive. Another PBC strike hit the ship, centered in a fireball of atmospheric friction. After the second PBC strike, the ship tumbled. Larger pieces separated from it. The ship was breaking up.

Max updated his earlier report. The ship was not skipping out of the atmosphere—it was coming down.

The fireball was passing over them, moving toward the southwest in three diverging pieces. *Ka-boom-boom-boom.* The shockwave of its passage rolled across the countryside.

Thought it'd be louder, Max signed to Lilith. *I think it will come down in the Dragonback Mountains or the Orkney Ocean.*

They could now see the grasslands around their perch on top of the hill. Dawn was coming. Old Cal was not above the eastern horizon yet, but he soon would be.

Let's head out, Lilith. I'd like to be in place when those pods land. We'll see if they need help—or are enemies.

Chapter 22. Epilogue

St. Brigid's Church, Kilkenny, Clan DuQuoin Territory, 17 Eightmonth, 3204

Father James Robert Hoobey, SJ, stood before the church's baptistery, accompanied by the parents, Mary Elizabeth Quinn and Fabien Loche, and the godparents, Elias Nelson and Amilie Schute. Emily Sarah Quinn had just been baptized into the Reconstituted Catholic Church. Accompanying the parents and godparents were numerous other relatives—three grandparents, a great-grandmother, great-uncles, and cousins beyond counting.

That neither parent was Catholic didn't matter. The children of the former lairds of Clan Monmouth were, by tradition, baptized in the Reconstituted Catholic Church. Given that most of the members of Clan DuQuoin were former Monmouth clansmen, Fabien and Molly decided to follow their custom—a new entry into Clan DuQuoin's Customs and Traditions.

In nomine Patris, Filii, et Spiritus Sancti, amen, Father James "Jim-Bob" Hoobey pronounced.

While the attendees filed out, members of St. Brigid's Methodist Christian Church scurried to restore the sanctuary to its former setting. No RC churches existed in Kilkenny. The only RC church in the territory was now at the bottom of a sea-filled crater where Port St. Regis once was.

Father Jim-Bob had been imported from the Huston diocese in Mieze territory. Initially, he was reluctant to perform the service, especially in a former Monmouth city that had no RC church of its own. Fabien, aided behind the scenes by Herman Mieze, successfully argued his case.

"We lairds have to help one another, eh, Fabien?" Mieze replied when asked to provide a Catholic priest for the baptism.

400

Before the last guest was out of the church, Father Jim-Bob was on his way to Kilkenny's spaceport for a shuttle back to Huston. The C$100 platinum credit tab from Donal Harris sat comfortably in his pocket.

†††

"I thought you were going to follow clan conventions," Lena McLean told her son-in-law.

"We were, Lena, but Elise reminded me that on this issue, clan should give way to house."

The issue was of naming conventions. On Inverness and across most of the Confederacy, children assumed the father's family name. The Houses differed. In the Thirty Houses, male children received their father's surname—female children, their mother's.

"Besides, I like the name Quinn," he said with a grin. "DuQuoin may be a clan now, but it is also still one of the Thirty—Thirty-two—Houses. Clan DuQuoin must build Customs and Traditions of its own."

Lena paused before continuing. "Very well. I know I've lost this argument, and truly, I don't mind. When will your parents be back? I thought they'd be here for the baptism."

"I'm not sure. Father is up to his ears, integrating the Houses with the Rajputs. Titan Station is a game-changer. Rajput could have two inhabitable planets instead of just one. The question of the moment is whether to continue terraforming Mandorva or to stop and begin terraforming Titan. Mother is overseeing timelines and cost analysis. It's what she does best, but she'll be back here soon, if only for a few days now that the tunnel-drive couriers are in service."

†††

"That's my girl," cooed Katherine Hémery. "She has your eyes, Molly."

"So everyone says," Molly replied.

Emily Quinn began to squirm and cry.

"I remember that wail. I think she's hungry, Molly."

"Yes, I think so too. Give her to me."

Emily was passed from grandmother to mother. In a moment, she was quietly nursing.

"I'm amazed you've stuck to all the old customs, Molly," Katherine said.

"I was foolish and had some idea about restoring some of the older ones."

"Was it worth it?"

"Yes, I think so. I've started a fad among DuQuoin clanswomen. The numbers who say they will adhere to the tradition are growing. I had the thought of establishing some traditions of our own, not just copying those of McLean or other clans."

Elise Hémery stuck her head in the door, saw her two kinswomen, and said, "The first House DuQuoin contingent is coming down. Are you two ready to meet them?"

"I will in a moment, as soon as Emily finishes. You two go, and I'll follow."

"Mustn't disappoint our people. Come, Katherine, we needn't wait for Molly."

"How many this trip?" Katherine asked as she stood up. House DuQuoin members had been shifting from Ceres Station to Kilkenny for a month, almost as soon as the Battle of Caledonia was over.

"A thousand. I've worked a deal with Lena McLean to charter a large passenger ship to shuttle our people from Ceres Station in Rajput to Dundee Orbital. I think we can get everyone and everything of ours moved in two, maybe three more months."

"Faster than I thought." Katherine looked down to see Emily had stopped nursing and appeared ready to nap. "Elise, wait. I think Emily is about finished."

"Yes, she is," Molly said, handing Emily to Elise and tucking her blouse back into the waistband of her kilt. She still hadn't slimmed into her former clothes, but a kilt would fit a wide variance of waists.

†††

Fabien Loche and Roger Blankenship were passed into Admiral Honecker's office in Weyland Fleetbase.

"Please be seated," the Admiral said. "I understand you have some information for me, Captain?"

"Yes, Admiral. Another of our stay-behinds has arrived. From their reports, it appears that a rump Essie government is forming at Clairinton, in Tau Ceti. They're still calling the new organization the System States. However, some of the outlying systems are breaking off, declaring their independence."

"May I bring in Admiral Witek? He's now in intelligence."

"Benson's been promoted?" Blankenship asked. He had become friends with Honecker's former flag captain and senior aide during the workup before the Essie invasion.

"Yes, last week, to rear admiral."

"Bring him in, by all means."

Honecker buzzed Witek. A moment later, the new admiral walked through the door.

"News from SolSystem, Benson. Take a seat," Honecker said.

Blankenship took a sip from the coffee cup the admiral's secretary had given him. "We left several stay-behind ships in SolSystem and other important Essie systems. Periodically, one of the stay-behinds will leave to find and update us on what is going on."

"This is how we discovered the Essies were chasing us. We now know they had learned of our tunnel drive and quantum power tap. They wanted them. The growing bigotry of the isolationists notwithstanding, they wanted our technology, our shipyards, and our research stations—but not us."

The admiral's CPO secretary passed a cup to Witek, refilled the cups of the others, and placed a plate of sandwiches on the admiral's desk before leaving Honecker and his guests alone.

Blankenship took another sip from his cup and went on. "This last ship brought news that EarthGov and SolSystem have collapsed. EarthGov destroyed Diemos and nuked Hellasport. The Mars rebels, in turn, nuked EllFive, Luna Upper, and El Siad stations above Luna. After reprisal and counter-reprisal, most of Mars is wrecked. Only two lunar cities survive, and much of Asia and Europe has been scorched." He paused to check his link to refresh his memory. Accuracy, as ever, was important.

"That brought about the collapse of EarthGov," he continued. "Following the collapse, numerous civil wars broke out across the planet. The remaining lunar city-states and outlying unaligned stations are starving. The lunar agricultural cities were the ones destroyed. SolSystem no longer has a unified government. The rot that had spread throughout the System States over the centuries has erupted. While a rump System States government exists, more regions of the System States alliance are breaking off. Some have formally seceded. In our opinion, civil war is inevitable."

Witek raised his hand to interrupt Blankenship. "Our merchant ships that have returned—those not sequestered by the System States—report Hiver ships are raiding along the old Essie border."

Fabien sat, listening to the reports. *The System States is gone. They just don't realize it yet. Oh, the rump will retain the title, but the unity, the alliance once known as the System States, no longer exists.*

"That will be a problem for the Confederacy, Admiral. The Essies have always been a buffer between the Confederacy and the Hivers," Fabien stated. "Our war with the Essies still exists. We can't ignore it."

"Yes, it does. However, that will be addressed another day. Your report, Roger, confirms others we've received through our own agents."

Honecker changed the subject. "Would you be willing to take a proposal from the Confederacy to the Holder about integrating your

404

remaining warships into the navy? It is illegal for Confederate members to possess warships capable of interstellar flight and to possess nukes. So far, we've turned a blind eye to the House fleet. That can't continue if the Thirty Houses want to join the Confederacy."

"I will, Admiral. We knew of the, uh, constraints upon us. Holder Lillian Frienze has said she's willing to deal."

When Roger Blankenship and Fabien Loche were gone, Honecker turned to his former flag captain. "What do you think, Benson, for Blankenship—a captaincy or a rear admiral?"

"He's proven he can handle a fleet, sir."

"That's what I thought. When this integration is over, we'll make the offer, Rear Admiral Roger Blankenship. We'll need experienced officers when we take the war to the Essies."

"And the Hivers," Witek added.

†††

Molly Quinn and Fabien Loche sat in lounge chairs on the roof of DuQuoin Meeting House, looking at stars and Dundee Orbital far overhead. Emily Quinn was below, being cared for by her great-grandmother.

"What do you say," Fabien said, "maybe next week, we go to Herrin's Falls? Just for a few days."

"What brought that up?" Molly asked.

"Things seem to be rushing by. Donal asked if I wanted to keep my Customs commission, not that I, as laird, could be recalled to duty."

"He told me he's now the customs director since Charles Demning has moved to Rajput," Molly replied. "He asked me the same."

A rumble reached them from the Kilkenny spaceport. Another scheduled shuttle was heading up to orbit. "And what did you say, Molly?"

"The same as you. I said yes."

405

They both laughed.

"Yes," Molly said.

"To Herrin's Falls?"

"Yes. I miss the land—"

"Your land."

"And Marcus, Marion, and Ellen Louise."

"And the falls?"

"That too," Molly said and laughed again. "Perhaps we should continue our assimilation lessons."

"A boy next time?"

"You knew!"

"I overheard Amilie talking to Katje about choices and responsibilities. Apparently, Katje has a crush on another clan page. That aside, I knew you could choose the sex of the baby. It just never came to mind until the other day." Fabien shifted in his recliner to see Molly better. "Marcus Emile Loche is a good name. Your father should be remembered."

Released

The Beacon at Barrington Light. A novella of the Tri-Cluster Confederation. Available at Amazon.com. Please leave a review.

Coming soon...

Dundee Orbital: A Collection of stories based in Dundee Orbital (3Q2020)

Come visit me at https://m-watson.com and subscribe to my email list. If you liked my novel, please leave a review here.